P9-DCQ-236

THE Fourth Millennium

THE SEQUEL ■

THE Fourth Millennium

THE SEQUEL

PAUL MEIER
AND ROBERT WISE

THOMAS NELSON PUBLISHERS
Nashville • Atlanta • London • Vancouver
Printed in the United States of America

Published in Nashville, Tennessee, by Thomas Nelson, Inc., Publishers, and distributed in Canada by Word Communications, Ltd., Richmond, British Columbia.

ISBN 0-7852-8149-5

Printed in the United States of America

For all the saints,
who from their labors rest,
who thee by faith
before the world confessed.

THE Fourth Millennium

THE SEQUEL

MEMO: **To the Archives of the Hosts of Heaven**

RE: **Conclusion to the Millennial Reign of Yeshua, the Jewish Messiah**

FROM: **The Reverend John G. Harrison**

To satisfy all inquiries about the final phase of history on planet Earth, a concluding report is being filed along with the first report of the guardian angel, Michael, covering the last decade of the Second Millennium, which was presented in The Third Millennium.

His first memo covered the major events at the end of the 1990s as the Tribulation brought devastation and havoc across the globe. Those events centered around his assignment to protect the family of Jewish psychiatrist Dr. Larry Feinberg. The adventures of this family and Jimmy Harrison offered a significant vantage point from which to view the final struggle of good and evil before the return of the promised Messiah.

Because of the additional trauma occurring at the end of the thousand-year reign of Yeshua, which followed the Second Coming, a further perspective on the last days of the human adventure was more than slightly desirable. This report focuses on the activities of Ben Feinberg and my son, Jimmy Harrison, because of their historical significance in Jerusalem during the one-thousand-year period. Researchers may wish to consider the environmental conditions that allowed such persons as Ben and Jimmy to live to extremely old ages, covering many centuries.

Because of my redeemed state as an Immortal, I

was able to have an almost omniscient perspective from which to view this final chapter of the human story.

Inquirers will also want to note the strange mixing of futuristic culture with the tendency of the Middle Eastern cultures to cling tenaciously to ancient customs and dress. As my report will reveal, some facets of the human personality never changed, even when offered the full possibility of redemption. Homo sapiens generally proved to be a perverse lot, always a ripe target for the Evil One.

Using the same technology available at the end of the millennium, I have preserved this report on hologram video recording. Turn the page and the images will unfold in your mind.

Let it roll!

CHAPTER

1

April 16, 999 N.E. (New Era)
The 1,000th Year of the Millennial Reign of Yeshua the Messiah

The Egyptian airfoil airliner flew directly into the Baghdad airport under cover of a total electronic and radar blackout. Troops snapped to attention and the president of Egypt hurried down the red carpet stretched from his airfoil plane to the state limousine waiting to take Ziad Atrash to his secret meeting with Syrian leader, Rajah Abu Sita.

Ziad Atrash, a big muscular man with the neck of a bull, had midnight black eyes deeply set beneath bushy eyebrows matching his thick ebony moustache. On his fat fingers he wore three massive golden rings. Ziad purposely chose the loose-fitting dark brown robe of the desert peoples to demonstrate nothing had changed with him, no matter how many centuries separated the president from the first bedouins who marched up the Mesopotamian Valley. His large and threatening hands pressed against the window as he peered in rapt attention at the sights.

Atrash's plans greatly benefited from his longevity, which resulted from the restored environment after the final holocaust that ended the Second Millennium. While people of five hundred to eight hundred years of age were common, Ziad expected to eventually exceed them all. He still looked forty and his dark-tanned skin had few wrinkles. A fanatic exercise enthusiast, he kept his body in prime condition. While he encouraged rumors of bench pressing five hundred pounds, the truth was Ziad could easily clean three hundred and fifty pounds on any day of the week.

Ziad was an extremist. Any appetite or idea that pleased him was pushed to the limit. While he was not long on careful thought, Atrash forcefully and ruthlessly pursued any objective to which he set his mind. Ziad required little sleep and was rumored to spend the early hours of the morning poring over maps and reports.

The battery-driven limousine silently whisked through the streets of rebuilt Baghdad until it turned down the boulevard toward the ancient section of the old city. Ziad Atrash paid little attention to the large rectangular and cubical buildings with functional design so similar to the contemporary buildings all over the world. The new buildings were slick, practical with clean unadorned lines. But once the limousine entered the antiquated streets, Atrash looked with fascination at the hoary granite block buildings over eight hundred years old, the domed roofs, ornate columns, the tall tiled minarets, and the quaint shops.

When the Second Millennium came to a crashing end and catastrophic calamities destroyed much of the world, some of the old city had survived. Syrian rulers at the end of the Old Era made the tragic mistake of joining with forces of the Antichrist, Damian Gianardo, in the long forgotten war against Israel. Atomic explosions, earthquakes, and environmental pollution nearly destroyed the entire globe. Amazingly, some parts of old Baghdad had fared well. When the new sections of the city were reconstructed, life stayed the same along the venerable cobblestone streets as it had for thousands of years before.

The battery-driven limo floated down the street without making a sound. Ziad watched the people dressed in costumes stretching back to 1000 B.C. Merchants hawked their handmade pots and blankets as their forefathers had done forever. The fabrics were brilliantly colored with handwoven designs.

"Slow down," Ziad spoke into the car's intercom. "I want to look more closely."

"Yes sir!" The driver slowed the limo down to a crawl.

The Egyptian leader smiled at the long-robed vendors still wearing the Arab headdresses of the desert. As previous millennia hadn't changed their forefathers, modern technology hadn't reshaped these Arabs who still preferred pottery to plastic, camels to shuttles. The passing of the ages had not changed these children of Ishmael and that pleased the Egyptian president.

Women still trudged up the street bent under the load of bushes to be used in a kiln to fire pottery. An old sheik walked along the street with his dog at his heels. The Arab world remained a domain of men, and that pleased Atrash. His people had buckled under to changes dictated by Jerusalem.

The limousine turned the corner and passed the metalsmith shops. Craftsmen hammered away at sheets of copper, turning them into powers and urns. The noise of hammers banging against anvils rang through the air.

Soon the black limousine left Baghdad behind, crossing the Tigris River and heading south. The Fertile Crescent had also changed little. The indigenous peoples preferred to tend their flocks and ride their donkeys across the lush green fields and pastures. The car sped through the streets of Al Musayyib lined with palms and fruit trees.

"How much further to New Babylon?" Ziad barked into the intercom.

"Only about 25 more kilometers," the driver answered. "Would you care for music?"

"None of that religious-sounding elevator junk they ship out of Jerusalem," he growled. "Give me some of the old stuff. The music of my people—the desert music."

Instantly the car was filled with such authentic sound that Ziad could close his eyes and not tell the difference between the new technophonic speakers and a group of Egyptian musicians playing in front of him.

Atrash pushed a button and the seat mechanically reshaped itself into a reclining lounger, elevating the president's feet into a relaxing posture. Built-in vibrators cranked out immediate relaxation.

I'm tired of our people being at the mercy of those worthless Jews who run everything from Jerusalem, he thought to himself. *When I get through with the world, the glory of the pharaohs will be rightly returned to my people. The hour is ripe to break loose from these demagogues.* He spit contemptuously on the floor. *The first thing I'll rip out is the religious nonsense and superstition they impose on the world.*

Off in the distance Ziad abruptly saw the replicas of the massive walls of ancient Babylon beginning to rise above the horizon. Ziad immediately pushed the button to run the seat into upright position.

For years I've longed to see this restored wonder. What a great idea for a theme park! Perhaps, this place ought to be turned into one of the seats of government. Ziad pushed another button and the window in the car door was replaced by a huge magnifying glass.

The rebuilt walls and the large Yachter Gate rose up before Ziad's eyes. Cut in brick relief, animals with human heads once again depicted the old glory of Nebuchadnezzar, Naboridus, and Belshazzar. In the background Ziad could see the trees lining the Euphrates River. Just ahead inside the walls were the awesome restored Hanging Gardens Nebuchadnezzar first built for his homesick Median queen.

Ziad knew little of ancient history except that some despot named Saddam Hussein started the massive rebuilding of Ancient Babylon at the end of the twentieth century, Old Era. But then Ancient Babylon had been blown into the Persian Gulf at the end of the Old Era, just prior to Yeshua's Second Coming to set up His Millennial Reign. During the reconstruction of the world in the first and second centuries of the New Era, Yeshua refused to allow the rebuilding of a replica of Ancient Babylon. But Yeshua seemed much more passive this past year, His thousandth and final year of His Millennial Kingdom. So Arabs pooled their immense financial resources to begin the rapid, massive building of New Babylon, replicating Ancient Babylon at a nearby site since Ancient Babylon was now underwater in the Persian Gulf. Yeshua never stopped them, so New Babylon seemed to spring up rapidly out of nowhere. Ziad wanted to walk through the replicas of the ancient world rulers' palaces.

The electronic vehicle slowed and Ziad observed tourists flocking to the Ishtar entrance. "Faster!" he ordered through the intercom.

"I have been instructed to take you through the Marduk Gate," the driver answered. "We will avoid the sightseers and enter through a special side entrance in the palace. We will be there in moments."

The limousine shot forward, rising several additional feet off the ground on a cushion of air, veering over the sides of the road. Moving more like a low-flying helicopter, the black car sped past a checkpoint as a soldier saluted. The car once again came down on a road in front of a massive gateway. They slowed to pass the gate and came into the Imgur-Ellil area of the city. The car passed a large golden statue.

"Replica of a statue Nebuchadnezzar ordered everyone to bow before," the driver explained. "On your left is the Marduk Temple. In ancient times there was always a festive New Year's procession as the people brought all the little gods here to pay their respect to Mr. 'Big God' Marduk." The driver sounded amused.

"How do you know Marduk isn't the name of a real god?" Ziad snapped.

"No offense intended," the driver apologized. "Just that no one has suggested such a thing for an awfully long time."

Ziad smiled.

"Down at the end of the street is an exact replica of the building Nebuchadnezzar called 'the Palace at which Men Marvel.' The original palace had been so impregnable no one ever captured it. Generations after Nebuchadnezzer's time the palace fell into foreign hands."

Ziad gawked out the window at the massive walls and high towers.

"To your left is a replica of the Temple E-khul-khul, built to the moon god, Sin of Haran. Belshazzar tried to replace Marduk with Sin, but he didn't really pull it off." The driver laughed. "Sin usually wins."

"Well," Ziad sounded more pleasant, "maybe I'm going to be more successful in my plans."

"The tall building looming over the city is the reconstructed Tower of Babel," the driver continued his explanations. "Archaeologists tell us that this is probably not far from the original sight but no one remembers exactly what happened there." Ziad rolled down the window and strained to see the top of the ziggurat reaching up toward the clouds.

The limousine pulled up to a dead end in front of the

great palace walls. Suddenly a section of the wall slid back and the car sped inside. The wall closed behind them.

"We're just about to the side entrance of the throne room," the driver said. "I'll pull up and the soldiers will escort you inside."

Troops stood at attention as the car came to a halt.

There's old El Khader, the secretary of state, waiting to meet me, Ziad thought. *Need to puff up and intimidate the old frog.* The president pulled his robe more tightly around his massive chest.

"Your excellency!" El Khader opened the car door. "Welcome to the land of our ancestors."

"And the glory of tomorrow," Ziad shot back.

"King Rajah Abu Sita awaits you in the throne room."

The escort of soldiers fell in around the Egyptian presi dent, and the entourage hurried up back steps and through a concealed door into the massive throne room. Gold covered the walls; the giant throne was inlaid with blue lapis. Atrash paused, overwhelmed by the sight.

"Welcome, brother!" The Syrian king stood in strange long, flowing robes encrusted with gold. He rushed down from the throne with his arms extended. "I have even dressed the part of the ancient kings to surprise you!"

"Rajah!" Ziad opened his arms. "I am staggered by what I see." The Egyptian president kissed the Syrian leader on both cheeks. "The glory of New Babylon exceeds all reports."

Rajah Abu Sita took his friend by the arm and led him toward a massive door at the far end of the hall. "We must look at the Main Court. You will be equally impressed by the anteroom where the mightiest men of the past gathered before entering into the royal presence." Rajah leaned into Ziad's ear and spoke quietly. "And I must take you to my special place where we can talk without possible eavesdropping. You never know where one of those infernal Immortals will turn up."

The high ceilings of the Main Court enhanced the spectacular aura of the elaborate decorations. However, Rajah gave no time for reflection. He walked quickly to a side wall, pushed a knob on the wall, and the panel slid back. The two men disappeared into an elevator.

"I have a lead-lined room five stories down," Rajah spoke rapidly. "I am assured that the latest technology makes intercepting any conversation impossible." The elevator effortlessly dropped downward. "*No one* will be able to find us or hear us."

The metal door opened into a spartan room about fifty feet square. Maps lined the walls; a conference table stood in the center. "No electric wiring of any kind here," Rajah explained. "Lights are battery powered. Couldn't chance any possibility of bugging."

"It must have been hard to build these quarters without observation," Ziad observed.

"We camouflaged the work as archaeology." Rajah pointed to the bottle and glasses on the table. "May I offer a little refreshment to my brother from Egypt?"

"Thank you." Ziad sat down. "Climate control?"

"Battery powered." Rajah poured from the bottle. "The new solar-charged batteries last over a century so we have little need to worry." Rajah smiled courteously.

"You are just the kind of leader I thought you were." Ziad settled back into the chair. "Everything assures me you are the man to help me regain control of the world. The time has come for the sons of Ishmael to cease sitting at the feet of the Jews. Are you ready to overthrow the illegitimate heirs of father Abraham?"

Rajah stopped smiling. He was much smaller than Ziad, thin and weary. He looked his age of two hundred and ten years. His stark white hair matched his white beard, washing much of the dark olive color from his slightly wrinkled face. In one quick sweep he cast aside the heavy imitation robe of the Babylonian kings. Underneath was the usual pullover jersey worn by most of the world population. Only the gold decoration bars on his chest marked Rajah as a distinguished national leader. When he quit smiling, Rajah's face became distinctly unpleasant.

"I have a plan," Atrash continued. "In order to throw off the yoke of the Jerusalem oppressors, we will need Russia and Iran. I know you have special connections with Ethiopia."

Rajah pulled at his beard and looked out of the corner of his eye. "I pondered the suggestions you whispered in my ear when our paths last crossed in Beirut. Yes, my friend, I read between the lines when your diplomatic communique indicated you wished to visit me in this place. But where would we possibly start such a monumental undertaking?"

"We must begin by recognizing the truth about our exalted and glorious leader," Ziad fired back.

The Syrian leader frowned. "I don't understand."

"We have been raised to believe myths about the omnipotent power behind this Yeshua who supposedly is the unique son of God. We have accepted the legends of his magical and invincible power as if he is the only power in the universe. Now is the time to expose the emperor's clothes. Nakedness—not omnipotence—is the truth about him."

"Look!" Rajah thumped his foot impatiently. "The idea of rebelling against the all-powerful Yeshua is madness."

"Oh, don't believe he is omnipotent or omniscient," Ziad purred. "What if Yeshua is only *one* god among *many*?"

"Many?" The Syrian king's mouth dropped.

"You were brainwashed into accepting monotheism as a fact. The Jews tried to corner the world religion market with such claims. But what if many gods are only dormant, just waiting to be called forth by worshipers?" Abu Sita blinked several times. He started to speak but the words didn't form.

"Perhaps other gods rule other planets," Atrash added, "and await our call to return to this planet.

"You've been sitting on the truth all the time." Ziad Atrash gestured forcefully in the Syrian ruler's face. "You are surrounded by the glory of a past that includes many powerful gods. How do you know Marduk wasn't more powerful than Yeshua? Our ancestors knew the secret of calling on the ancient gods to help them control the world. We *can* prevail against the central Jerusalem government with the help of the old gods. Think about it! The source of real power is waiting to be seized by simply learning how the religion of the past operated."

Rajah began pacing the floor and wringing his hands. "Yeshua, just a god among gods? On what do you dare base such conjecture?"

"My friend, how long since you've seen Yeshua on television? In person? Anywhere? Has He even complained publicly about our building of New Babylon? He ruled for centuries with a rod of iron, but now He has become weak and passive."

The old man scratched his head and shrugged his shoulders.

"Something is going on." Ziad feigned a stage whisper. "They want to perpetuate the myth Yeshua is an eternal thirty-three years old as he was at the time of the resurrection." He spoke more forcefully. "But the facts are to the contrary. He is deteriorating just as everyone eventually does and is hiding to conceal the truth. His power is slipping away. We can make ourselves equal with him!" Why else would he have disappeared from public appearances?

"This is dangerous talk." Abu Sita shook his head. "Very dangerous. I will have to study the matter."

"Go to your archives," Ziad demanded. "Study the ancient rituals as I have! The ancient gods are only waiting for us to worship them and then they will join us in the last great overthrow of the Jews."

Rajah pulled at his beard. "But what about the Immortals? Those strange creatures seem to come and go at will, appearing then disappearing like magic. We have always acquiesced to the communiques and edicts they bring from Jerusalem."

"Yes," Ziad agreed. "These strange creatures are a problem. But if we join with the old gods, there will be new legions of spiritual creatures to stand at our sides. I have evidence that spirit guides and demons guided our ancestors."

"But!" Rajah rolled his shrunken eyes. "They say these Immortals are resurrected beings, saints from the ancient past, chosen to rule with Yeshua. We have been taught these beings lived and died before the beginning of this millennium and have returned from the dead or were raptured at the end of the Second Millennium A.D. They certainly have amazing insight and knowledge from the past. Very intimidating."

"Purely psychological warfare!" Ziad slammed his fat fist into the table. "Just nonsense the Jews conditioned us to believe. How do we know they are not simply another form of a spirit guide?"

"Well, we were always taught to . . . uh . . . think . . . ," Rajah stuttered.

"How do you know Marduk wasn't the most powerful god all along, or a being named Sin of Haran?" Ziad stuck his big finger inches from the Syrian leader's nose. "You don't!"

Abu Sita swallowed hard. "You *really* think the time is ripe to strike?"

Ziad Atrash leaned across the table. "From what little I know of history, our people have always had animosity toward the Jews. Do you think it would be very difficult to whip the masses into rebellion?"

Rajah laughed. "Not in this country!"

"Then I suggest we make a pact at once. We can work out terms that are most agreeable to us. After we clarify the details, we'll be in a position to start building a coalition. We can make contacts by personal visits. I will go to Russia and Iran. You see your friends elsewhere." Ziad extended his hand. "Do you agree?"

Rajah Abu Sita squinted and pulled at his beard. "I will carefully explore the ancient archives and review our religious history." He stopped and bit his lip but after a few seconds he extended his hand. "The time has come to act. Give me liberty from Yeshua and the Jews or give me death. You have a deal."

PART ONE

Then I saw an angel coming down from heaven, having the key to the bottomless pit and a great chain in his hand. He laid hold of the dragon, that serpent of old, who is the Devil and Satan, and bound him for a thousand years.

Revelation 20:1–2

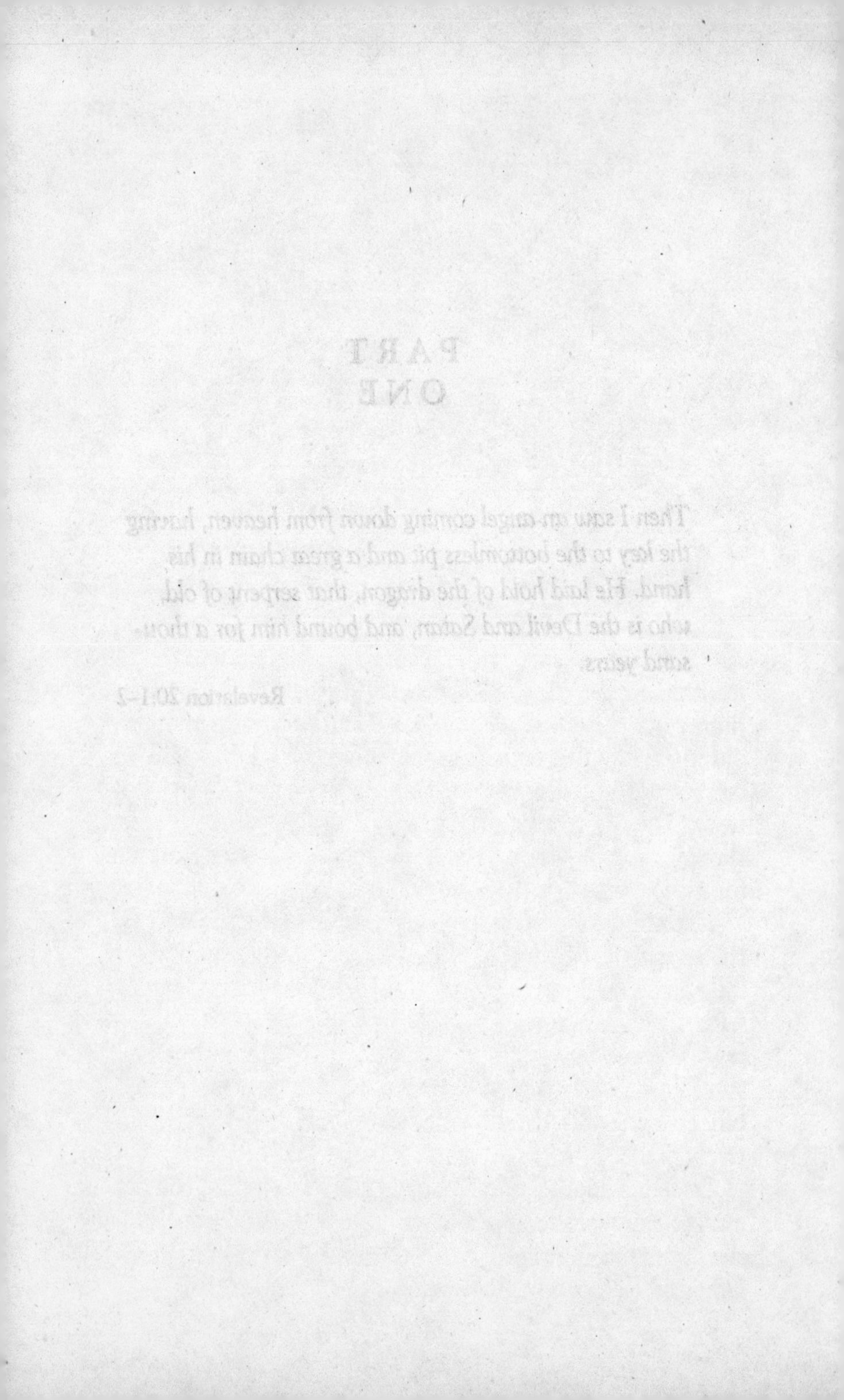

CHAPTER 2

As this summit in Baghdad drew to a close, a meeting of old friends was about to begin in Jerusalem. Jimmy Harrison walked carefully up the worn steps of the old Internal Affairs building behind the new Knesset. The last few granite steps were worn and slick from centuries of wear. The old man used his cane to steady himself. Even though slow, Jimmy maintained surprisingly good posture for his extreme age.

The original parliament building, constructed during the twentieth century, Old Era, Second Millennium, had long since been replaced by a golden thirty-story edifice with crystal windows and a glowing marble exterior. The Jewish center of government sparkled in the late afternoon sun like a polished gem. In contrast, the Internal Affairs offices were only three stories high, functional and relatively plain.

Once inside, the people mover quickly whisked the old man to the main suite of offices. Lettering emblazoned on the door read Gentile-Jewish Relationships, Internal Problems and Relocation Assistance.

For a moment, Jimmy stared at his reflection in the mirror finish on the glass door. He still liked to think of himself as a six-foot-four blond Nordic weightlifter, but that image was ancient history. His sparse, closely cropped hair had turned snow white centuries ago, leaving no hint of any color. Being thin still caused him to look taller, but aging had shrunk him to a height of barely over six feet. His face was deeply wrinkled, betraying that some time ago he weighed an extra fifty pounds. His double chin had dried up giving him an ancient appearance. The lines around his eyes and neck were deep drainage ditches. He tightly closed his lips and rubbed his chin vigorously as if pushing the loose skin back the way it once was. Failing to change the terrain, he chuckled at his vanity and went inside.

"Ah, Dr. Harrison." The receptionist turned from her computer when the door opened. "We've been expecting your visit. Chairman Feinberg will be glad to see you. Go on back and I'll tell him you're coming."

The white-haired patriarch trudged down the long corridor. A brass plaque on the door at the end of the hall read Ben Feinberg, Chairman. Just as he reached for the doorknob a voice commanded him to enter.

"You've still got ears like a deer, Ben." Jimmy closed the door behind him.

"Not bad for an old codger of 1,034 years." Ben laughed. "Just chalk it up to superior genetics."

"You ought to have hearing aids in both ears." Jimmy pushed on the small electronic piece in his left ear. "Are you sure you didn't get the cochlea transplant so many people are trying these days?"

Ben Feinberg got up to walk around his desk. "Don't be jealous, Jim." He laughed. "The truth is without the ultrasonic sound vibrator in my chair, I probably couldn't stand up half the time. When it comes to getting around, even with a cane, you've got me beat hands down."

The two men exchanged affectionate hugs and sat down in large office chairs that immediately readjusted to the contours of their bodies, providing instant support and comfort. Both men had snow white thin hair, and Ben's long flowing beard was equally colorless. His long hair was pulled back and tied in a ponytail. Ben was almost four inches shorter, but centuries of physical exercise had kept their bodies firm and toned. Age had given their faces a wrinkled sameness, making the two men look very much like brothers.

A second look, however, revealed the two brothers-in-law actually looked quite different. Ben had once been a two hundred pounder tending to the fleshy side. Time had moved much of the weight toward his middle, leaving a significant paunch. Ben kept his bulbous shape in tow with a tight black belt that looked like a rope around a shifting sack of flour. His neck spilled over his collar and had long since been absorbed into his chin and jaw line. When he was tired, dimples appeared on the sides of Ben's mouth and gray circles surrounded his dark black eyes. Age had flattened Ben's nose and rounded his formerly finely chiseled features. Even though nearly everyone wore contact lenses, Ben had stubbornly stayed with metal-rimmed glasses that looked like rejects from a museum. The thick glasses made his piercing eyes look twice their size.

"Sometimes I look in the mirror and have no idea who's staring back." Jimmy dropped into the chair. "In my wildest dreams I would never have believed either of us could live a thousand years."

Ben nodded his head vigorously. "Remember when the world was falling apart? I thought we weren't going to last another six months. Thanks be to God everything changed. When Yeshua returned and cleaned up the environment, he really put things back into place. The increase in ozone, decreased radiation levels, and pure food have done tremendous things for the body, and those leaves from the Messiah's Trees of Life are absolutely incredible! They rejuvenate and keep one going."

"Definitely." Jimmy shook his fist in the air. "But what a job you've done through the centuries, Ben. You've helped so many of your Jewish people relocate and find their way into the new order. You're no small part of why this old city ticks so well."

"Thanks, old friend. How are things going in your end of town?" Ben asked. "Got the public transportation system spinning like a top?"

Jimmy scratched his head. "Well, you know how it is. Get things running right on one end and they fall apart on the other. I've been too busy to look for pictures. Since we completed the underground subway system from Tel Aviv to downtown Jerusalem, we've been able to streamline commuter trips to the Ben Gurion International Airport. Traveling on a jet stream of air gets trains there almost faster than people can read the front page of *The Jerusalem Post.*"

Ben nodded. "Really needed that improvement. We've just got too many people buzzing around in those blasted anti-gravity compact shuttles. In spite of computerized radar, people simply have too many close calls. Fools drive like maniacs!

"Incredible changes in the last ten centuries. Sometimes I almost forget what it was like way back in the good ole days when we drove those awful gasoline propelled cars. Remember when you sold those death traps in Southern California?"

Jimmy laughed. His teeth had been replaced with porcelain implants giving him the radiant smile of a thirty year old. "I sure loved those old smog makers with the shiny paint. Remember that classic '89 red Corvette I once drove? I really thought I was quite the hot dog."

Ben smiled and peered out of his thick glasses. "Was in another lifetime, my boy! Sometimes the memories are just like yesterday; other times it feels like we've been traveling in a time machine. Who would ever have believed we'd end up leaders in the new era God brought to the world?"

"I was quite a rebellious young man." Jimmy grinned mischievously. "And I thought your sister was the living end." His face fell and his eyelids drooped. "You know... I didn't think I would survive her death. The truth is, I've never adjusted to Ruth coming back as an Immortal after Yeshua's return." He sighed. The pouch under his chin dropped, making his chin line disappear into his neck. "I've never really liked or accepted this new sisterlike relationship we must have now. I'd go back to the way it was in a heartbeat. By the way, how is your wife?"

"Quite well," Ben answered. "Cindy recently left for the Far East to deliver a series of lectures to her own people on the meaning of the Kingdom of God. The Chinese have always been apt students, and Cindy's Oriental heritage gives her instant acceptance as a teacher. She will be back in another week."

"People have forgotten the troubles of the past." Jimmy's voice sounded more serious. "After we replaced the debris and rubble of the Great War with new cities and buildings, terror and strife disappeared. People take the good things for granted without acknowledging everything Yeshua provided for us."

"Dangerous business to forget history," Ben interjected. "In fact, that's why I called you to come over."

"Oh?" Jimmy scratched his head. "What's up?"

Ben pulled a remote control from his pocket and clicked one of the buttons. A screen dropped at the far end of the room. He hit another button and a computer printout appeared on the overhead. As he punched other buttons material scrolled rapidly down the screen. Finally a heading appeared across the top: Confidential: Top Secret.

"Little larger, please." Jimmy squinted.

"Need my glasses?" Ben chided. He pressed a control button and the picture expanded.

> Recent reports from the Los Angeles area of the United States of America and Central Africa indicate a reappearance of HIV. Not since the end of the second millennium has the highly infectious disease been identified; it was presumed extinct. In order to prevent panic, formal acknowledgment is being momentarily withheld. In addition, rapid spread of this disease suggests wide-scale immorality, which is equally unexpected. The time has come for immediate investigation by all agencies and formal discussion with Yeshua.
>
> In the meantime, it is imperative that every level of leadership join in the search for pertinent information. This report is to be considered sensitive and available only to the highest levels of security clearance.

Ben clicked the picture off and glowered at his friend. When he squinted, Ben's shaggy white eyebrows concealed his view, like bushes concealing the eyes of a fox. "See what I mean? Forgetting history can be deadly." He shook a thick, pudgy finger at his friend.

Jimmy settled back in his chair and wrung his hands. "Terrible news." His eye folds dropped leaving only narrow slits. The creases around his mouth deepened. "When did this report come in?"

"This morning. I wanted you to know immediately."

Jimmy slowly stood up and began to pace. His naturally rounded back became even more bent as he shuffled around the room. "We've had problems through the years," Jimmy confessed. He shook his head. "Heaven knows there is no vaccination or medicine to prevent sin! We've always had to struggle with human selfishness." He held up both hands in a gesture of despair. Jimmy's arms were thin, the skin on his hands tight and paper thin. "Sure, lust has gotten out of hand on many occasions but we have not had a natural disaster to contend with all these centuries." He ground his bony fist in the palm of his hand.

"Keep talking." Ben gestured for his friend to continue. "You've always had a nose for understanding the theological implications of such matters."

"The appearance of this plague means something different is going on in the world. For the first time in recent memory, paradise is really threatened."

"Exactly!" Ben slapped the arm of the chair. "I knew you'd see the seriousness of the situation. I need your help. We comprise a rare compilation of knowledge."

Jimmy slowly rose from his chair and picked up his cane. "I think I'll check some other departments of government and see if anything else is brewing."

Ben followed him toward the door. "I'll be speaking at Hebrew University tomorrow and will have time to access the special computer system they use in archaeological research. As soon as I have other information, I'll be in touch."

Jimmy stopped at the door and asked one final question. "I wonder if anyone has discussed this material with Yeshua himself. We haven't seen Yeshua in any public appearances lately, you know!"

☐ ☐ ☐

Hebrew University had been completely rebuilt in the fourth century N.E. as a center for creative thought. Its archaeology program was recognized as the best in the world. Located on the gentle slopes of Mt. Scopus, the school had a commanding view of the city. Buildings were designed in the architecture of ancient Jerusalem, making the campus look like an oasis of the past in the midst of the contemporary buildings of the new city.

Dr. Meir Lau called his graduate political science seminar to order. Each student used a personal wristwatch cam recorder to tape the Ben Feinberg lecture. A few final stragglers hurried to their seats and quiet settled over the room.

"By now you should have completed your reading assignments, which survey the history of the infamous twentieth century," Dr. Lau addressed the audience. He glanced around the room quickly, assessing the large number of students. "I trust you reviewed the Holocaust literature as well as the special studies on the Messianic Jewish movements. To complete our study of this unit we are delighted to present a representative of the period. Benjamin Feinberg lived through this era and became a Messianic Jew. Every resident of Jerusalem is aware of his outstanding efforts to help our people find their place in Israel. Please greet our guest lecturer."

Students clapped as Ben walked toward the podium. He nodded appreciatively. "Thank you, Dr. Lau. I am delighted to be with you. I want to begin by giving you a quick overview of the changes of the last one thousand years.

Ben began writing on an electronic pad. Immediately his writing was reproduced in typeset sentences on a large overhead screen behind him. Students pushed a button and reproduction copies came out at their desks.

"The beginning period covers the first two centuries of the New Era." Ben wrote, Rebuilding the World. "Our initial task was to re-create the support systems and infrastructures of life and commerce to fit the new global ecological system. Worldwide re-education began under the direction of the Immortals. They disassembled all military machinery and instituted a government, based on an Old Testament model, centered here in Jerusalem."

Ben scribbled another heading. The computer printout read: Second Period—New Technology.

"From the third to the seventh centuries, we were able to create many of the technologies that make extraordinary longevity possible. I'm sure most of you aren't particularly impressed with what people of my generation consider incredibly long life. Our accomplishments are accepted today as routine."

The students made no response, and many looked bored.

"Of course, global prosperity returned during this phase of recovery." Ben wrote again on his electronic tablet. "I call the present time 'The Period of Complacency.' You are the children of affluence. Unfortunately, it is hard to maintain perspective on the meaning of achievement when you were not part of overcoming the obstacles of the past." He stopped and looked carefully at the class. Ben sensed a growing hostility. "Perhaps, I can be more helpful if I talk about issues you encountered in your reading. Would someone like to begin?"

A tall black-haired young man stood in the second row. "Mr. Feinberg, is it really true that most Jews didn't believe in Yeshua in the old days? I find it hard to understand how any Jew wouldn't believe such an obvious fact."

Ben smiled. "You, your parents, your grandparents, your great-grandparents, and far beyond have always lived in the world as it is today. You naturally accept King David as the mayor of Jerusalem who manages our local daily affairs. On television and holograms you see Yeshua as normally as you watch the weather report. Perhaps it would surprise you to learn that when I was your age the weathermen on television were wrong about as many times as they were right."

The class laughed politely.

"But it is true. Many Jews thought Christians were their enemies, and they even believed Yeshua was responsible for anti-Semitism. The truth was veiled from our eyes because most of us had never studied the Torah and the books of the former and later prophets, much less read the book called the New Testament."

A young woman at the back raised her hand. "We have never known war. Even the idea is repugnant. Were you frightened?"

Ben turned and looked out the window. He could see down Mt. Scopus toward the walls of the old city. The sun glistened brightly off the gold of the restored Temple. "Frightened?" he answered. "Terrified is a better word."

Ben's mind drifted back to a Pizza Hut just off the campus of UCLA. A college student named Deborah was sitting across from him. She had babbled hysterically, "The girls at the dorm are too scared to talk about anything, but yesterday the security police suddenly showed up and surrounded the building. Cindy's blindness made her a very easy catch. They ransacked her room, clubbed her guide dog Sam to death, and took Cindy away in a police car. They found her secret radio for receiving calls from Israel."

"We never knew when Antichrist Gianardo's men would descend on us," Ben continued. "My wife was once saved by the intervention of an angel named Michael. She was blind then . . . ," his voice trailed off, "before she was healed when Yeshua returned."

"Were angels like Immortals?" another student asked.

"Somewhat." Ben shook his head. "At least they looked the same to us. They could come and go, then disappear just as Immortals do. But Immortals weren't on earth then. The Immortals are God's people who have been redeemed from death and given a resurrected body just as Yeshua has; they are perpetual thirty-three-year-olds. Wasn't easy getting used to the presence of Immortal saints after the New Era began. Finally, we began to see Immortals as another order of creation. Immortals are a special race of redeemed creatures above us. Because we trust Yeshua to forgive our sin, we'll become Immortals when we die."

"You must have lost many friends," another student observed.

Ben immediately thought of his sister. Ruth had died in childbirth, hiding out in the desert at Petra. Her loss cut to the quick and nearly destroyed Jimmy Harrison, her husband. Ben answered, "During the years of the Great Tribulation forty million Christians were killed by the Antichrist. Fourteen million were Jewish believers. Another twenty million citizens were executed because Gianardo's men thought them to be unpatriotic. Of course, billions died because of the wars, famines, and plagues."

Another memory gave him pause. Ben had not thought about Joe and Jennifer McCoy for a long time. He remembered the children Joe Jr. and Erica . . . and the night the entire family was executed in their own backyard for believing in the Messiah and for sharing the Bible with neighbors.

"We didn't understand many things you take for granted." Ben sounded irritated. "Each death was a very painful loss. You are fortunate to live in a time when the sting has been removed. With the help of a redeemed and reconstituted environment, medicines brought to earth from the Trees of Life, and continually improving technology, you know little about pain. You grew up without the *slightest* idea of how difficult grief can be."

For several moments no one spoke.

Finally one student inquired, "Did everyone really have guns?"

"You are very fortunate Yeshua commanded all weapons, especially nuclear weapons, to be destroyed," Ben answered. "The worst retaliation you'll ever experience is someone hitting another person. Unfortunately, violence was as common as shopping in a grocery store."

"Why?" the tall young man asked again. "Why were all those people so stupid?"

The class laughed but Ben didn't smile.

"The Evil One is also something about which you know nothing," Ben snapped. "You were spared a great source of chaos."

An older man with a white beard raised his hand. "I am Zvilli Zemah. I'm finishing my second Ph.D." He sounded arrogant and condescending. "Do you really expect us to believe in this old superstition about a personified evil called the devil? After all, no one has seriously discussed such an idea for centuries."

"What are you suggesting?" Ben glowered.

"In this university we study the ancient myths of Egypt, the Canaanite peoples, the Baals, and other forms of superstitious thought used by the ancients to explain what they could not understand. Wasn't the idea of Satan nothing more than a way to talk about collective evil? Simply a scapegoat method of blame." The man twisted his face and mimicked a child. "The devil made me do it." The class roared.

Ben looked around the room, dismayed at the lack of seriousness and concern. Their faces looked soft and naive. "You accept the gifts of the Kingdom of God as Americans once took for granted the benefits of freedom. You enjoy your rights but aren't particularly impressed with responsibilities." His voice had an edge.

"Sorry." Zvilli shrugged. "We generally don't confuse superficial religious ideas with the more profound sociological insights into human behavior."

Ben shot back. "You don't have the slightest idea of what you are babbling! *I* lived in a world where evil was rampant. *We* paid a great price for our foolish ignorance of the diabolical designs of Satan to destroy all who came in the name of God."

Zvilli Zemah looked with satisfaction at the students around him. "Obviously, Mr. Feinberg, you are a politician, not a student." Dr. Zemah sat down.

"You naive young traitor! Don't you understand that all the 'gods' from Egypt's Osiris to Babylon's Marduk on to the Baals, these fraudulent imitations were only masks worn by the devil? He always used wicked rulers like chessmen in a game of world power! Damian Gianardo and Jacob Rathmarker were nothing but the last in a long line of dupes." Ben pounded on the desk. "Don't confuse political theory with theological fact."

Zemah smirked and rolled his eyes. The students were obviously impressed by his defiance.

Ben walked around to the front of the podium, crossed his arms over his chest, and stared at his opponent through his thick glasses. "The primary strategy of evil was always to persuade people it didn't exist. Satan's most insidious work was carried on in the minds of people who denied his existence."

"Are you saying the devil is still at work?" Dr. Zemah raised his eyebrows in mock amazement and looked around at his friends in amusement.

Ben tried to choke back his anger. Zemah was using this lecture to increase his standing with his peers and Ben knew he was being manipulated for the student's personal gain. Before he could check himself, Ben blurted out, "You pseudo-intellectual! The likes of you fried when the rest of creation moaned in those final moments of conflict as the third millennium began. On the dawn of the Feast of Trumpets, September 28 of the year 2000, people like you awoke to the blackest day this world has ever seen. Smoke rolled in from the Valley of Jezreel, and the smog of war and nuclear fallout covered the world. I know . . . I was there!" Ben was nearly shouting.

"Uh . . . thank you . . . Mr. Feinberg," Dr. Lau interrupted. "Your talk has been most informative." The professor sounded embarrassed and uncomfortable.

"No," Ben continued. "You hear me out! On that day when the Lord of Lords and King of Kings returned, the devil was cast into the bottomless pit and Yeshua chained him. If Yeshua hadn't gained this victory not one of you would be sitting in this room. You have been protected from an evil you don't even understand."

"Yes, yes." Dr. Lau took Ben by the arm. "You have certainly put everything into perspective for the students. We thank you for taking your valuable time to be with us."

Most of the students clapped politely. As Ben was escorted out of the classroom he heard Zemah say to students gathered around him, "Silly old fundamentalist." Dr. Lau kept talking rapidly as if he didn't want to give Ben a chance to respond until he had him away from the lecture hall.

"Just a minute," Ben pulled away. "What is going on here? Why are you afraid to let me speak my mind?"

"Oh, never!" the professor assured Ben. "We just know how limited your time is."

"Are you teaching these people that the devil was only a myth?"

"Mr. Feinberg, the academic world is so different from the routines of everyday life. We have to consider many options not talked about in the more mundane discussions of the business world. Thank you for helping us understand how the ancient people thought." The professor shook his hand and hurried away.

Ben walked slowly to the exit. "I can't believe it," he muttered to himself. "I've just been displayed like a relic from the past to demonstrate how old fools did things! These people don't understand. They just *don't* understand."

CHAPTER 3

Far below the palace Rajah Abu Sita sat at the far end of the long table in the secret conference room, watching his secretary of state assemble documents at the other end of the table.

"No effort was spared," El Khader explained. "We checked the memory banks of every computer system and searched through the reserved books in the royal archives. A very interesting passage surfaced from the book the Jews call the Old Testament. In the sixth chapter of the first section of Genesis, it reads, 'There were giants on the earth in those days, and also afterward, when the sons of God came in to the daughters of men and they bore children to them. Those were the mighty men who were of old, men of renown.' Maybe the Jews do know something they haven't told us."

Abu Sita pulled at his beard and smiled.

The secretary of state pushed a book forward. "However, success was achieved through an inter-library exchange with the great Jerusalem library which survived the destruction at the end of the last millennium."

Blackened from years of intense sun, El Khader's face was like the desert people's, giving his skin the texture of shoe leather. His lips were thin and appeared about to crack open any moment. He wore a perpetual frown.

"Did anyone connect your inquiry with me?" Rajah snapped.

"No one," the diplomat answered. "Our request was made through the department of archaeology under the guise of a search for additional material to be used in restoring statues in New Babylon."

"You are sure?" Rajah growled.

"Without question." El Khader carefully unrolled one particular aged scroll. "Because the study of cuneiform has been my hobby, I obtained one of the most ancient accounts of this book and translated the work myself."

"What is it?" Abu Sita drummed on the table with his finger tips.

"During the ancient New Years' festivals, our ancestors chanted this poem in honor of the greatest of the gods. The records of Assyriology call the verses *Enuma Elish.*"

"Hmm . . ." The king leaned forward. "What does it mean?"

"It is the Babylonian account of the creation of the world, the story of the rise of the god Marduk to supreme power over all other gods."

"Really?" Rajah opened his eyes wide in astonishment. Though seldom seen underneath his heavy drooping eyelids, the king's eyes were faded brown with a yellowish ring around the cornea, giving him an eerie appearance. "Tell me more."

"At the beginning of this early period, Babylon was an insignificant city-state and Marduk was known only as a minor god." El Khader stood, beginning to lecture like a college professor. "A most interesting coincidence follows. As Marduk's fortunes rose, so did Babylon's. Once Marduk was recognized as all-powerful, Babylon suddenly burst onto the world scene as a mighty power. I know because I checked the dates carefully."

Abu Sita's eyelids dropped again and his eyes sank back into the dim. "I am amazed," he said more to himself. "Amazed! Maybe Ziad Atrash knows what he is talking about after all."

"Each New Year's Day our fathers celebrated the victory of Marduk over the competing god Tiamat, proclaiming the world a place of violence." El Khader continued, "The ancients believed only the most powerful can prevail on this earth."

"Read some of the verses to me," Rajah commanded.

The secretary of state picked up the cuneiform and read slowly but deliberately:

> "At the using of this name, Marduk, let us bow down in reverence; upon the opening of his mouth be all other gods silent. His command shall be preeminent above and below. 'Be exalted our son, even he who avenged us.' Let his authority be supreme, be it second to none: and let him act as the shepherd of mankind, his creatures, who, unforgetting to later ages, shall ever tell of his deed. He is almighty god."

Rajah pushed himself up from the chair. "Tell me," he asked with the greatest gravity, "is there any formula or ritual for calling this god forth?"

"I am working on the rest of the New Years' worship documents," El Khader answered. "Soon I will have the ancient incantations translated."

"Will they let us contact the god?" Rajah walked around the table.

The old secretary of state's mouth twitched nervously. "Sir, we are playing with fire. The Jews would call such experimentation 'idolatry.'"

Abu Sita cursed violently. "Nothing will stop my search! I don't care what they think."

"But what if an Immortal should show up and . . ."

"Are you defying me?" Rajah pounded the table.

"Never, my king." The old man made obeisance. "I simply raise the questions that a faithful adviser must ask. Nothing more."

The king looked miffed but shook off his indignation. "I must make contact with Marduk. Do you understand? I must know if Marduk still speaks. No other assignment in your entire career of three centuries begins to compare to the urgency of this matter. I want to break into the spirit world."

El Khader nodded his head. "I understand."

"The moment you have the worship instructions ready we will assemble in this room or, better yet, in the Temple of Marduk itself. I will do whatever is necessary to call him forth." Rajah shook his finger in the old man's face. "But time is of essence. We must contact the god quickly."

"Your wish is my command, O Great One." El Khader began backing toward the elevator. "I leave these translations for your study."

Rajah dropped into the chair El Khader had used and began poring over the documents. The secretary of state disappeared into the elevator and was gone.

□ □ □

For over a day Jimmy Harrison pondered the implications of his conversation with Ben Feinberg. Each time he came to the same conclusion: More information was needed. In late afternoon he set up an appointment with old friends in Los Angeles. Because they were eight hours behind him in time, the conversation would be a morning call in California.

Jimmy hurried from the office to his apartment in the

suburbs of Jerusalem. Even though he complained at times, he still drove an anti-gravity compact shuttle because the transportation was so quick. He could speed over the tops of the buildings and fly in a straight line to his destination. Radar and computer settings guided the one-person craft so well that navigation was never a problem. The internal guidance systems even compensated for bad weather and high winds, making the ride like gliding on a cloud.

Preoccupied with recollections from the past, Jimmy didn't notice the other crafts whizzing past. He was thinking about Isaiah Murphy. Jimmy's first contact with Isaiah had come when the teenager was a busboy in Cindy Wong's family restaurant in Lake Forest, California. Because The Golden Dragon was a favorite of the Feinberg family, he and Ruth had dined there often.

Isaiah, a talented black athlete, went on to UCLA. In time he had become a significant member of Ben's college group. Isaiah had been a Christian since early college and was naturally accepting of Jimmy's insights about the Rap ture and the return of Jesus, as they were called back in those days. The youth hid out at the old farmhouse with the rest of the gang during the worst days of the Great Tribulation. He and Deborah Whitaker had helped keep the group fed and housed during those terrible hot August days.

Jimmy's shuttle automatically settled down gently on the roof of his house. Built into the side of a cliff, with most of the dwelling completely underground, the home was kept cool in the summer and warm in the winter by the earth. A two-person elevator dropped him from the landing pad roof to the bottom floor in moments. He stepped into his office and walked straight to the communication equipment.

Because of his special government status, Jimmy received the latest technological advances before the general citizenry of the city. For years he had used his hologram phone to place calls throughout the world. During the first two centuries N.E., video telephones became common. However, the big breakthrough came in the fifth century when Terbor Esiw, an electronic wizard from the late second millennial period, perfected light projection transmission. Instead of seeing the caller on the screen, an image was projected in front of the viewer. The caller appeared as a one-foot-high, three-dimensional column of light.

Jimmy turned on his new phone machine, which had only been installed a month. Recent hologram improvements allowed the caller to be projected in full life-size dimensions. Only by touching the creation of light could Jimmy tell the image was just an illusion.

Once he was seated in front of his transmitter, Jimmy punched in the Los Angeles phone number. He flipped the light switch and shot light down on the small black platform directly in front of him. The phone rang twice.

"Hello?" The voice came over the surround system speakers, making it impossible to tell the difference from someone talking in the room.

"Isaiah?" Jimmy threw the projection switch.

"Jimmy!" An image began to form on the platform. "Old friend! It's been far too long." Suddenly a white-haired black man appeared in the room.

"Hey, buddy!" Jimmy almost got up to shake hands. "Haven't heard from you for . . . I don't know . . . has it been fifty years?"

Isaiah laughed. "You know how it is. The older we are, the more quickly time seems to go. Anymore fifty years feels more like a couple of months."

Jimmy studied his old acquaintance. Isaiah had been unusually tall and an outstanding basketball player. With the passing of the centuries, he had become much thinner, making Isaiah look even taller. His face was long and lean.

Isaiah's muscles had become more sinewy and rippled under his skin like rubber bands. His bushy eyebrows looked like rows of cotton stuck above his deep-set dark eyes.

"Look who else is here." Isaiah extended his arm and a woman appeared next to him. "Say hello to Deborah."

Jimmy absentmindedly waved. "Deborah Whitaker! I bet no one has called you by your maiden name for a thousand years. How have you stayed married to that old coot?"

The white-haired woman chuckled. "Living in Los Angeles century after century will certainly make you broad-minded."

"Don't push your luck," Isaiah chided. "You don't look like a spring chicken yourself, old man.

"Your E-Mail communique indicated you needed to talk with both of us. Sounded serious. What's up?"

"Are you still running the public health department in Los Angeles?" Jimmy asked.

"Well, sort of," Isaiah rolled his eyes. "You know I was chief administrator for a couple of centuries, and then I shifted back to working with children. But after my back got a little stiff I switched to research. Been doing lots of computer work lately."

"Excellent!" Jimmy gestured at the figure, completely forgetting he was only talking to a column of light. "Deborah, last I heard you were working with the hospitals in the area, right?"

"Yes. As you will remember Yeshua suggested the Los Angeles complex be rebuilt in many villages and burroughs so people would never again be lost in the anonymous character of metropolitan life. Today we have thousands of towns stretching from Santa Barbara to San Diego. We've kept medical care on an individual basis with only a few major technological centers. I help run the complexes."

"Good. My records are correct and up to date," Jimmy acknowledged. "Sure wish we could sit down together for an evening of fun. Is it true they changed all the McDonald's hamburger stands to McDavid's with a specialty in Kosher food?"

"Got one down the street," Deborah answered. "Why not fly over, and we'll see if we can find some of those nasty old greasy, cholesterol-loaded fries we once loved."

"Maybe when we get this problem solved." Jimmy's voice changed and sounded more professional. "Tell me, what's the spiritual condition of Los Angeles like these days?"

Isaiah and Deborah looked knowingly at each other. She answered, "How interesting you'd ask. Recently we were in a meeting with an old acquaintance of yours. Remember Dr. Ann Woodbridge?"

"Remember her! The Christian psychologist? Good grief! I was sitting in her office in a knock-down, drag-out fight with the Feinbergs when she was raptured right before our eyes. I could never forget Dr. Woodbridge."

"Of course, Ann is now an Immortal and looks even younger than when you saw her in her Newport Beach office so long ago," Deborah continued. "She has the celestial oversight of emotional well-being in our area. Dr. Woodbridge just met with a group of us to express profound concern over the sudden moral deterioration throughout the whole West Coast region.

"Of course, we've always had problems," Deborah added. "We all know people sin, but I thought mortals were in better shape than they apparently are. Dr. Woodbridge warned us that a wave of divorce is on the way because of an epidemic of adultery."

"Distressing!" Jimmy shook his head. "Anything else going on?"

"For the first time in years," Deborah added, "psychiatric wards are full. I don't remember a time when so many people have been clinically depressed."

"Does this make any sense to you, Isaiah?"

"Not really, Jimmy. But I can tell you that I'm amazed how angry many people are. Even in the grocery stores you sense a hostility I'd almost forgotten. Genetic engineering has produced fruits and vegetables of incredible size. Cockroaches, mosquitoes, and ants no longer exist. Opportunity is unlimited, and yet people seem very agitated."

Jimmy thought out loud. "So . . . you're seeing spiritual problems, emotional difficulties breaking out like . . . like . . . an infection."

"I think you could put it that way," Isaiah answered.

Jimmy got up from his chair and walked across the room. "I need your help."

"Hey, where'd you go?" Deborah exclaimed.

Jimmy turned and stared at the empty space in front of his computer console. "Sorry! I walked out of transmission range." He hurried back to the desk and immediately the Murphys appeared on the platform again.

"Please put your ear to the ground," Jimmy continued. "If you hear of or see any suspicious or unusual diseases, call me at once. Help me get some insight into why people are going off the tracks."

"Sure," Isaiah answered. "We will also get an appointment to talk with Ben's father. Dr. Larry Feinberg is a spiritual overseer of psychiatric practice in this area as well. I know he still works with Ann Woodbridge. We'll call you in a week or as soon as we know something."

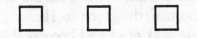

Travel between the Internal Affairs building and the new Knesset was quick and easy through the connecting underground tunnel reserved for use by government employees. The people mover conveyer belts enabled even elderly persons to make the trip in minutes. Ben stepped into his office elevator and minutes later was on the twenty-ninth floor, occupied by the Jerusalem city administration.

Due to the late hour most of the personnel were gone. A remaining secretary was clearing her desk when Ben walked in. "Ah, Mr. Feinberg. His Majesty has been waiting for you. Please go in."

Replicas of the gates leading to Solomon's Temple lined the massive wooden doors to the mayor's office. Ben timidly pushed one of the doors open and stepped in.

"Feinberg," the powerful voice called out from the other end of the enormous office. "Do come in."

"Thank you for seeing me at this hour of the night, excellency," Ben answered. "I'm sure King David has more pressing matters than talking with the chairman of Gentile-Jewish Relations."

"Absolutely not!" David walked from his desk to a more informal area with couches and chairs. "Such a fine servant of the people is welcome night or day. Come, let us reason together." David walked with the regal bearing and confident stride expected of a king. As all Immortals, he was thirty-three years old. A strapping specimen of a man, his long black hair was pulled back over his shoulders and blended into the handsome beard that edged his face. He looked straight at Ben. "Sit down and share your concerns, my son."

Ben approached timidly. "Being the mayor of Jerusalem is just one of the many things you do, I know. I'm sure there is so much more work of which I know nothing."

David smiled warmly and patted Ben on the shoulder. "People are often intimidated by me. Killing giants seems to give some pause. Please don't be put off. Remember, you know of all my great mistakes, as well. Just consider me a friend. Sit down."

"I suppose I can't get a certain image from the start of the New Era out of my mind," Ben began. "I can still see you standing on the Temple Mount with Yeshua, announcing the inauguration of His reign. What a totally overwhelming sight! Of course, each year I watch your oversight and participation in the Feast of Tabernacles. It leaves me rather taken aback."

"Ah, yes. Sukkot! The fifteenth of Tishri!" David laughed with a hearty roar. "How I love that day. The feast reminds us of how God provided for our people during the forty years of wandering in the wilderness. Of course, my son Solomon's Temple was dedicated on this day in 1005 B.C. I do make a great deal of the festival."

"We often call it the Feast of Booths," Ben added. "My family always gets together on this day for quite a celebration."

"I'm going to tell you a little secret." David leaned forward with a smile on his face. "People of your era celebrated Yeshua's birthday on December 25. And the date worked well since it converted a pagan nature festival into a Christian holy day, but everyone knew it wasn't the actual birth date. Know when it was?"

Ben shook his head.

David grinned mischievously. "Remember the Gospel John wrote? In the first chapter, the fourteenth verse, John gave everyone the big clue about the birth. John wrote that Yeshua became flesh and dwelt among us." David thumped on the table with his finger. "Know what *dwelt* implies in the original Greek?"

Ben again shook his head.

"It means 'tabernacled among us.' Get it? John was writing between the lines, telling the world Yeshua was born on the Feast of Tabernacles, which means the Holy

Spirit conceived Him in Mary's womb nine months earlier on about December 25th."

Ben blinked in amazement. "I'm astonished. No one has ever pointed that out before."

"Since we don't make much of birthdays anymore that fact slipped away. People live so long, birth dates aren't nearly so important. But I thought you'd find the idea to be very interesting."

"That fact alone adds new meaning for me this year, Sir. I will make all of my family and friends aware. For centuries we've had an extraordinary gathering and celebration during the seven days of Sukkot. We came to call these outings our Trumpet Parties."

"I want you to try a new drink perfected up north." David poured two glasses of an amber-colored liquid from a crystal decanter. "We've developed an extremely high protein drink with an unusual grape taste using a new hybrid from the Galilean hillsides. We're planning to unveil it at the next festival." He held up his glass in a toast. "To us, Ben, and the coming Trumpet Party."

"Ah, Sir." Ben looked at his glass. "One of the reasons I am here is a concern over something I just noticed in checking records relating to this past Sukkot festival. Each year Yeshua calls representatives of the nations to Jerusalem for the festival. Everything is so exciting and has gone so well through the years, little attention is paid to attendance. But in double checking the record I find that no representatives came from Egypt this year. Isn't that rather strange?"

David's gaze was intense but conveyed no emotion.

"I . . . uh . . . mean," Ben stammered. "Isn't ignoring the Feast a snub to Yeshua? Shouldn't attention be given to the matter?"

David looked at Ben with great admiration. "You are a good and faithful servant. Your Master is well pleased with you. Let us drink." He extended his glass with a forcefulness that suggested no further questions should be asked.

Ben mechanically clicked his glass with King David's and drank. He still felt as though he had stepped into a mystery. He wasn't getting a straight answer.

David put the glass on the table. "A divine golden taste."

"Yes, excellency. Extraordinary." Ben put his glass next to David's. "One further issue. I'm sure you are aware of the HIV outbreaks."

David shook his head yes, but again his countenance revealed nothing.

"I am working on this problem," Ben said slowly, "as I am sure all agencies of the government are. Apparently, even medicine from the Messiah's Trees of Life aren't affecting the virus."

Again David shook his head yes.

"I'm sure Yeshua must be aware of the report." He paused but David indicated absolutely nothing. "In this regard, I couldn't help but reflect that no one has seen our Lord in a long time. I can't remember the last time I saw Him on television or hologram. Is there some reason for His absence?"

David stood up abruptly. "What a man of integrity you are, Ben Feinberg." David took his arm and led him toward the door. "Your service will never go unnoticed. Do you remember what I wrote? 'Blessed is the man who walks not in the counsel of the ungodly, nor stands in the path of sinners, nor sits in the seat of the scornful; but his delight is in the law of the Lord.' You are such a man, Ben."

"But, Sir, about Yeshua's status . . ."

"You have probably wondered about the injustice of some of us being Immortals," David continued, "while others of you must live in unredeemed bodies. Let me tell you it is to your advantage. You have the opportunity to perfect your faith and character to a remarkable degree as you persevere in your journey. You will shine with even greater glory at the ultimate day, Ben. Stay your course, my man. God has a great purpose for you." David shook his hand forcefully and shut the door.

Ben found himself standing alone inches outside the great door, staring at the design. His hand still extended, Ben turned slowly and shuffled through the empty offices and down the vacant corridor.

I've just been given the door, Ben said to himself. *What in the world is going on?*

CHAPTER 4

The large banner over the Marduk Gate proclaimed in four languages: Welcome Delegates to the International Archaeology Conference. New Babylon's buildings were covered with streamers and flags. Limousines and caravans of flag-decked cars poured into the city. Even though only two weeks had passed since their first meeting, Ziad Atrash, the king of Egypt, and Rajah Abu Sita, the king of Syria, had obviously been busy and successful.

The two leaders stood on the steps of the Tower of Babel and watched the entourage flowing into the city. "We have done well." Atrash smiled wickedly. "They are all coming."

"The prime minister of Russia arrived last night and has been sequestered at Perepolis; however, he is on his way," Sita observed.

"We have the heads of state from Ethiopia, Egypt, Syria, Iran, Italy, France, Russia, and Jordan." Ziad Atrash pounded his palm. "And China! Fong is the most aggressive of the lot."

Rajah leaned over the rail and looked far out to the farming plain that stretched across the Fertile Crescent.

"The idea of a study conference is the perfect cover. The Immortals never pay attention to such matters since they already know the details of the past."

"The security room beneath the palace is prepared?" Atrash asked.

"More than ready. El Khader will welcome each delegation and start them on a quick tour of the city, ending in the throne room of the Palace. After a sumptuous feast in the main court, the leaders will be ready for our meeting in the lead-lined room."

Atrash stroked his beard and looked extremely pleased. "I gave only the briefest overview to most of the heads of state, but I found immediate acceptance for the idea of revolt. China has already taken significant action."

Rajah Abu Sita nodded. "My experience was exactly the same."

"Fong was enthusiastic to form the alliance. The Chinese have extraordinary historical memories and are still smarting from their enormous defeat at the hands of Yeshua in the Armageddon debacle a millennium ago."

"Then everything is ready. In only three weeks we have been able to bring the world to sit at our feet." Atrash crossed his arms over his chest and stood with his feet apart, looking every inch like an ancient pharaoh. "Let us go welcome our guests."

□ □ □

Servers hurried around the long tables in the main court, making sure each dignitary received maximum personal attention. Costumed in the servant's dress of the era of Sargon, the waiters wore short battle skirts with swords by their sides. Sandals were laced up their calves and their hair had been braided and cropped into the square, flat look of the ancient Assyrians. Similarly dressed guards stood at attention around the room, holding spears, shields, and bows.

The carefully planned banquet reflected the same details of a feast from the days of Sennacherib. Huge gold plates were piled high with roasted pheasants and desert quail. Racks of venison roasted on a spit in the mammoth fireplace. Each ruler drank from an embossed golden goblet. Servers poured vintage wines from gold pitchers taken from museums. As the leaders dined, women in lacy veils danced to music from harps, lutes, and cymbals.

"Have they had enough?" Atrash whispered into Rajah Abu Sita's ear.

"If they haven't, they are bigger gluttons than we ever imagined."

"Then let us begin."

Abu Sita nodded to El Khader. The old secretary of state clapped his hands and immediately fifty trumpeters put their instruments to their mouths and blew a fanfare, filling the stone walls with overwhelming sound.

"Glorious leaders of all creation." El Khader's raspy voice echoed down the stone corridors. "Welcome to this conference for the recovery of the glory of the ancients. Great discoveries lie ahead for you." He bowed and turned to Rajah Abu Sita as a slave gives obeisance to his master.

"Noble leaders of vision," Rajah began, "the magnificence of the past shall only be a prelude to the greater achievements of the future. In order to see the greatest treasure of all we must adjourn to our hidden storeroom. Unfortunately space allows only the head of each government to attend. If you're ready, El Khader will lead you."

The secretary of state immediately marched to the secret panel in the wall, pushed the hidden button, and waited as the panel opened, revealing the elevator door. "Follow me," he announced. "You will not be disappointed."

When the entourage stepped from the elevator, they

immediately saw maps and charts lining the walls. Glasses and decanters, note pads, and pencils sat on the conference tables, a single document and pen in front of each chair. In contrast to the palace, the security room looked like the inside of a metal cube.

The plain space quickly filled as the leaders assembled around the tables. Each head of state said little to the other as they sat down. A small man, Fong was completely bald headed with deep-set eyes. Black spindly Ali from Ethiopia looked like a giant next to the Chinaman. Alexi Chardoff, a sullen man, had on the typical Russian version of the universally worn jersey-knit suit. The Russian's thick ruffled hair looked like he had just gotten out of bed. Kahil Hussein, Jordan's king, wore a kaffiyeh headdress dating back thousands of years. Similarly the Iranian president was covered with the traditional robes of the desert. Maria Marchino wore the latest Italian fashion but Claudine Toulouse wore a French version of the jersey uniform. Each face was stoic, impassive, not betraying thought or intent.

Rajah Abu Sita stood at the end of the head table. "The hour has come to fully explore the possibilities of our meeting. You can rest assured no one can intercept our conversations. A foot of solid lead covers the ceiling, floor, and walls. The elevator door is also lead lined." Rajah pointed to a small black box on the table in front of him. "Should anyone have any form of electronic transmission device, it will be detected and an alarm will sound. Similarly, *any* form of transmission attempted during this meeting will be discovered. Only what you write in your own hand or carry in your mind will leave this place. Are there questions about security?"

The leaders looked at each other but no one spoke.

"We must agree to a promise of complete diplomatic secrecy," Rajah Abu Sita continued. "No one will reveal any portion of these discussions unless all agree. For the sake of mutual protection, we have prepared the simple agreement that is before you. If any party cannot agree, he should leave now. On the other hand, if terms are agreeable, we will begin by signing the accord." Sita picked up the document in front of him, glanced at the copy, and immediately signed.

Delegates surveyed their copies. The battery-operated lights set from many different angles in the walls and ceiling filled the room with the illusion of sunlight. One by one the delegates initialed the forms before settling back in their chairs to look at the maps and charts on the walls.

After the final diplomat signed, Ziad Atrash spoke. "Each of us has chafed under the domination of the central government. Our own political agendas have been hindered by the constant intervention of overseers and intruders from Jerusalem. You are justly offended and frustrated. Even though you have not spoken out publicly for fear of reprisal, you desire change. Am I not correct?"

Each diplomat stared straight ahead.

"Until recently upheaval did not seem possible," Atrash continued. "No one dared stand against what seemed to be an impregnable system. But I, Ziad Atrash, ruler of the upper and lower Nile, have found a way. Revolution *is* possible!" He slammed his fist on the table.

"We share a very important fact," Atrash continued. "Each of us was born in the last several hundred years. We are people of the second half of this millennium, leaders of this time. Correct?"

The heads of state looked at each other and nodded.

"We were carefully shaped, trained, and manipulated by educational processes designed in Jerusalem. We were given a version of history written by Jews. The past was defined and described in terms of their successes and our failures." Atrash's voice dropped to an almost inaudible level. "Do you understand?" he whispered. Atrash suddenly pounded on the table and screamed. "*We have been duped!*"

Abu Sita fired back from the other end of the table. "How do we know there is only *one* god who controls this world? This idea is nothing but the religious propaganda of the Jews. We are stooges of Yeshua, controlled and molded by a view of reality concocted in Jerusalem."

"We have simply accepted the superiority of the Jews and their leaders as reality," Atrash returned the verbal volley. "But the party line has been nothing but a lie."

The room became silent.

"Don't look so worried," Atrash chided. "The solution is simpler than you might think." He pointed to a chart on the back wall. "As you drove down these ancient streets, you saw the replicas of Marduk and Sin of Haran. They have counterparts in the gods of Egypt and the Baals of ancient Canaan. Even though these gods seem different, they are really identical—just different in names. All of our countries had female fertility gods as well as gods of war." He pointed at the figures on the chart. "The names aren't important; their function is."

"You don't actually believe there is a god?" Ali of Ethiopia rubbed his long, narrow chin.

Atrash shrugged indifferently. "The issue isn't *a* god but *gods*. There are spirits. Maybe they are even spirits of the dead . . . but yes, there are spirit guides. In fact, we are currently researching ancient Egyptian religious customs to discover the original techniques of the priests of Osiris in order to receive spirit guidance."

"Spirit guidance?" Fong chuckled. "Is such a thing possible?"

Rajah Abu Sita smiled. "You might be surprised at what I get through my meditation sessions based on the practices of the priest of Marduk."

Atrash cleared his throat forcefully. "The point is we can

replace the authority of Yeshua at every level. After we explain his mystique, the new religion will be offered. By the time the central government reacts, armed troops will converge on Israel. My friends, we are on the verge of military victory!"

"Just a minute," Chardoff interrupted. When the rumpled Russian stood, his rotund girth made his knit clothes look ill fitting. "Everyone knows Yeshua *is* a god." He looked around the room and cursed. "Of course we are controlled! Yeshua is a supernaturally powerful, perpetual thirty-three-year-old. He never ages and has ruled with a rod of iron for nearly a thousand years now. Who can stand up to such a being?"

"When did you last *actually* see him? Has he been on television lately?" Ziad asked.

"Well . . ." Chardoff scratched his head. "I don't exactly remember."

"Yeshua has not been seen live for over a year," Rajah answered. "We checked all of the stations throughout the world. Everything has been replays."

"What are you driving at?" Chardoff crossed his arms over his chest.

"Yeshua is in trouble," Atrash said. "We believe he kept himself propped up for some time. Something is happening to him and he cannot control the fact that he, too, is either aging or growing weak for some other unknown reason."

"We have tested his power." Atrash pointed to Fong. "This year Egypt refused to attend the Feast of Tabernacles celebration and no one said a word. The Chinese expelled all its officials from the central government and nothing happened. Our brave chairman of the people has succeeded in defying the central government!"

Fong smiled arrogantly.

Rajah Abu Sita smiled wickedly. "Yeshua claims to be the supreme son of God, but he is a clever impostor. The truth is he is *one* among *many* gods, some greater than he. For some reason we don't yet understand, his power has begun to slip and he can no longer maintain his preeminence. If our countries are united and we have help from the gods, we can throw off the yoke of bondage and be free to do as we please."

"Stop!" Maria Marchino demanded. She pointed a long bony finger at Atrash. The president of Italy was a tall, imposing woman. Her black eyes could pierce steel. "Who has not had one of those blasted Immortals suddenly appear in the middle of a planning session?" She looked around the room and cursed. "Of course we are controlled. Even if Yeshua is slipping, he's supported by bizarre characters who pop up like summer frogs on the Nile."

"What if we have learned the secret of the Immortals?" Rajah's question sounded oily and sly.

"Secret?" Ali frowned.

"Do you see any Immortals in this room?" Ziad Atrash cupped his hand over his mouth and called out, "Yeshua, we are betraying you. Come and get us!" Atrash laughed and threw his arms open. "If you and the Immortals can get through the lead lining, we are yours."

The stunned leaders looked nervously around the room.

"Nothing!" Atrash spit in contempt. "You see, our omnipotent, omniscient, omnipresent masters are powerless when they and their bugging devices can't get through our shields." Ziad laughed diabolically.

"You are saying the Immortals have limits?" Chardoff sank back into his chair.

"Yes," Atrash said slowly, "and we can avoid their intrusions by planning in rooms such as this. Even modern-day monitoring devices depend on X-ray technology and they can't penetrate lead, so it is possible to escape their surveillance and surprise appearances."

Chardoff shook his head in astonished disbelief. His fat

jowls shook back and forth. "No one has ever challenged the Immortals before."

"Exactly!" Ziad Atrash pounded the table again. "We have attributed more power to them than they actually have." With a sweeping gesture of acquiescence, the Egyptian deferred to the Syrian king. "Even more significant, we now have the secret of producing our own protectors."

"What?" Claudine Toulouse said. The small blonde woman leaned forward. "You jest."

"Can't be!" the Jordanian king gasped.

"Are you serious?" the Iranian diplomat asked.

"My friends," Rajah rose on his toes for additional height. "After consulting the ancient manuscripts, we have found the way to receive guidance from other gods, maybe even the greatest of all the gods."

"Monotheism has been the only way of life we've ever known," the Iranian insisted. "Even before this millennium my people believed in Allah as the one true god. We rejected polytheism as primitive, superstitious."

"But isn't polytheism the oldest religion?" Ziad Atrash asked. "Is it possible monotheism is actually a degenerate form of the greatest truth because the Jews have persuaded us monotheism is superior?"

"Yes," Rajah interrupted, "with my own eyes, I have seen the truth."

"Show us," Claudine Toulouse demanded.

Rajah Abu Sita beckoned for El Khader. The old man reluctantly shuffled forward. "Sit down." The king of Syria pointed to his chair and the diplomat dropped down.

"Through the New Year's ritual of Ancient Babylon, we have learned how to turn men into channels for divine communication. My secretary of state offered himself. He has become the voice of the god Marduk." Rajah Abu Sita put his arm around El Khader. "Although not an Immortal, he is an equally significant conduit to the gods." The king condescendingly patted the diplomat on the shoulder. "Show the people," he said to the old man.

"Your wish is my command." The old man's voice shook and squeaked.

The secretary of state placed both hands firmly on the table and lowered his chin until it bumped his chest. He mumbled under his breath and his chest began heaving. A low groan rolled out of his mouth. El Khader slowly raised his head, his eyes closed.

"Hear me!" The diplomat's voice, loud and firm, seemed to emanate from new vocal chords. "Listen to my words and live." The sound was low and forceful, disconcerting and primitive. "I will guide you down ancient paths to find the better way. The hour at hand is pregnant with divine possibility! Dare to seize the moment. As I defeated ancient challengers, so will I prevail in this last time of confrontation."

El Khader's eyelids opened slightly revealing only the whites of his eyes. His lips did not move but the words came from his mouth. The old man's arm became rigid, his fingers stiff. His frightening demeanor was catatonic.

"I hold rights to the kingdoms of this world. I give thrones and palaces to whom I choose." El Khader spoke as if from the bottom of a cave. "You rule because of my choice. The world rests in the palm of *my* hand. Bow before me and reign supreme!"

The secretary of state abruptly fell forward; his face bumped into the table. For several moments he didn't move. Finally he blinked and asked in his usual frail voice, "Where am I?"

The delegates stared. No one spoke for several moments.

"You would not toy with us?" Ali of Ethiopia finally asked.

"What you have seen is only the beginning," Rajah Abu Sita assured. An exhausted El Khader hobbled away. "Believe me!" the Assyrian king demanded. "Only the surface has been scratched."

"In Egypt we have found similar means of divine guidance," Ziad Atrash insisted. "Friends, the days of control by the Immortals are numbered. Besides, many of the Immortals quit appearing here on earth about a year ago—the same time Yeshua quit making public appearances. That's why we risked our countries' fortunes to build New Babylon as rapidly as is humanly possible, even in our age of such advanced technology."

The king of Jordan rose slowly, looking every inch an ancient desert sheik. "Let us concede for the moment that everything you say is true. Possibly we have seen an amazing discovery. Nevertheless, all power is still consolidated in the central government. After hundreds of years people are conditioned to accept Jewish authority. No one uses force anymore." The king shrugged. "We have known nothing but peace for many centuries."

Ziad Atrash walked to the maps on the wall, turned, and smiled as if fully anticipating the question. "Peace will be our instrument of war. No one anywhere is equipped, trained, or prepared for violence, and therein is our opportunity." He kept smiling and waited for his conclusions to sink in.

"Don't stop now," Ali the Ethiopian demanded. "Make your point more precisely."

"In the world of the blind, the one-eyed man is king," Atrash continued. "When there are no weapons, the man with a stick is to be feared. Even the most primitive knowledge of assault gives the attacker total advantage. Strike the Jewish rulers with a rod of iron, and they will scream like wounded water buffaloes."

The Ethiopian frowned. "Revolt will require more than men running around swinging children's batons."

"I spoke metaphorically," Atrash answered condescendingly. "We have located long forgotten manuals of instruction on the martial arts. Under the guise of creative recreation, we have already begun training karate instructors to be sent to your countries to develop military personnel. We can quickly assemble a vicious strike force whose bodies will be their weapons." With his finger Atrash traced lines on the map from each of their countries to Israel. "No one in Jerusalem today is even vaguely prepared to defend themselves against such physical attack."

Rajah Abu Sita added, "In our libraries we have found elementary books on making gunpowder and small bombs. Even though ammunition makers are now extinct, we believe crude weapons will be quite sufficient to take out the Jews, who have no weapons whatsoever. Each of your countries has other ingredients needed to round out our arsenal of basic weaponry. Do you see the ingenuity in this plan?"

The leaders looked around the room at each other. Here and there men and women nodded in agreement.

"The newly created batteries have great voltage." Aba Sita pointed to the battery-operated lights in the ceiling. "We know how to turn this power into stun guns, which can knock a person cold in a flash."

Chardoff stood up once more and glowered at the group. "This may be the craziest idea I have heard in the last fifty years." The Russian's bushy eyebrows lowered and his puffy red face darkened. He slowly looked around the room. "And then maybe it is the best idea in over a hundred years." He ran his hands through his mop of hair. "At least it's worth pursuing. In our state museum the old weapons are preserved as examples of our barbaric past. But no one knows that beneath the basement of this museum are crates of guns and ammunition. If the equipment can be reconditioned, we have considerable fire power at our disposal."

Ziad cheered and suddenly the group broke into enthusiastic applause. Diplomats began shaking hands and congratulating each other on *their* new plan.

"I have reserves of nitrates in Ethiopia," Ali of Ethiopia shouted above the uproar. "We will be able to make excellent gunpowder. No one will suspect what we are doing!"

Fong held up his hand. "In China we have great reserves of sulphur and ammonia. We can create many varieties of explosives."

Again the group applauded.

"What more could be needed?" Hussein of Jordan asked.

"To the restored World Order!" Ziad Atrash called out.

"To our success!" the group answered.

□ □ □

Two hours later as the delegates returned to their elegant suites in the palace, Fong pulled Chardoff aside. "Come with me," he grunted.

The two men stepped into a small exhibit hall. Fong moved into the furthest corner and began talking rapidly in a low whisper. "Well, Mr. Prime Minister, what do you really think of this plan?"

Chardoff nodded his head soberly. "It makes sense."

Fong bore down. "Only one thing is amiss."

"Yes?"

"Our two great countries combined are the largest land mass and the most populous in the world. An alliance between us would be quite natural and could bring the final consolidation of power. Why should these dogs of the desert dictate to us the terms of the future? Let them march at the front of this conspiracy but after the smoke clears we can make our move to seize the reigns of power. We can rule the world together." Fong stared intensely into the eyes of the Russian. "Something to think about, Mr. Prime Minister."

Chardoff's stoic countenance showed no emotion for several moments. Finally he said, "A most intriguing idea." For the first time, Chardoff smiled.

CHAPTER 5

The electronic identification system flashed Jimmy Harrison's picture on screens throughout the Feinbergs' home. Computer memory instantly identified him and the outer door opened automatically, letting Jimmy into a waiting area.

Ben's voice came over a speaker, "Jimmy, glad you're here. Come on in."

The front door silently slid open and Jimmy entered Ben and Cindy's living room. Decorated to reflect the ancient Israelite setting, the plain stucco walls and simple decor gave the house an understated elegance and classic Jerusalem design. Artifacts and archaeological treasures accented the room, as well.

"Welcome!" Ben Feinberg entered from across the living room. "Good of you to come over so quickly."

"Just got your call." Jimmy extended his hand.

"Look who's here," Ben gestured over his shoulder. A small Chinese woman with white hair pulled back in a tight bun followed him. Small and frail, her quick, sure pace denied the fragile appearance. "Cindy came home early."

"Ah!" Jimmy threw his arms open. "Our little lotus blossom. I thought you'd be gone for another week." He hugged the little woman.

"I returned to make sure Ben wasn't being a naughty boy." Cindy laughed. Olive skin and few wrinkles added to a misleading appearance of youthfulness.

"At his age?" Jimmy Harrison rolled his eyes in mock consternation. "Fat chance."

"Sit down, please." Ben pointed to the chairs. "We need to talk."

"Indeed!" Ben shuffled toward the armchair. "Got some surprising things to tell you."

"Cindy is back," Ben began, "because of unexpected negative conditions in China. Her discoveries add a strange new twist to our inquiry."

"Really?" Jimmy frowned. "What's happened?"

"Without any warning or explanation," Cindy Feinberg began, "the Chinese government demanded that all personnel from or related to the central government in Jerusalem leave the country. I was expelled!"

"What?" Jimmy leaned forward. "I can't believe my ears!"

Ben nodded his head. "In addition, our people in Russia had a similar experience. Jerusalem officials were simply sent packing."

"Why . . . such a thing is without precedent. How dare some government snub us!"

"No one has an explanation," Ben continued. "We are completely mystified.

"Déjà vu," Cindy added. "For a few minutes I thought I was back in the twentieth century. Soldiers and uniformed police showed up at my room and escorted me to the airport. Boom! Before I could even consider what was going on, I was on my way back to Jerusalem."

Russia?" Jimmy scratched his head. "China? What's going on?"

"I thought maybe your investigations would have turned up some clues," Ben Feinberg said.

"Not on this front." Jimmy shook his head. "But I do have some distressing news from Los Angeles."

Cindy brightened. "My true homeland! How is everybody in the south land?"

"Apparently not too well," Jimmy continued. "I talked with Isaiah and Deborah Murphy by phone. They tell me things aren't going so well in Los Angeles."

Ben looked at Cindy. "How long since we've taken a trip to L.A.?"

Cindy shrugged. "We haven't been back in literally decades. But what a great time! Everything is green and new since it's the first of May."

"Maybe it's time we all took a little vacation," Ben suggested. "Any reason you couldn't take several days off, Jimmy?"

"What a great idea. I'd love to visit old friends. I think the time would be well spent."

"We could take the new ultra-glide shuttle that makes nonstop trips from Tel Aviv to Los Angeles," Cindy said. "They say you barely have time to get into the stratosphere before you start down. I think we could be in L.A. in three to four hours."

"Exactly," Jimmy Harrison confirmed. "Three hours and twenty-five minutes. Hardly enough time to have supper and enjoy a good hologram movie."

"I don't think we should wear our government uniforms," Ben added. "Let's just look like average citizens. Perhaps we can learn more."

"I agree," Jimmy answered. "Why don't I go back to the house and pick up a few things? I will meet you at the subway station and we can use my new underground tram to get us to the airport."

"My?" Cindy smiled mischievously. "Getting a little possessive these days, aren't we, Harrison?"

Jimmy laughed and slowly got to his feet. "I do have a little personal investment there. You know how I always loved anything vaguely related to cars."

Ben Feinberg chided, "You've got to be the only person left in the world who still thinks those awful old relics are wonderful."

Jimmy started to the door. "Maybe somebody in L.A. will have a tip on some museum that might let me drive one of those . . ."

□ □ □

The gigantic ultra-guide slowly descended into the traffic pattern of the Los Angeles Interglobal Telaport. The boomerang-shaped craft carried four hundred people and provided every luxury for the traveler. Special express flights between major cities on different continents allowed maximum contact with every corner of the world in record time. The crafts flew in giant sweeping arches and were often used as space shuttles flying into outer space.

"Isaiah and Deborah will be here to meet us," Jimmy said. "They made arrangements for our visit and are planning a little reunion with old friends. Should be a great time."

"Excellent." Ben switched on a ground scope screen and adjusted the range. "Let's take a look at the area." Instantly the landscape of the south coast appeared on the screen.

"Amazing how everything has been rebuilt," Cindy observed. "Wasn't much left after the Tribulation."

"Building subways," Jimmy insisted, "was one of the best ideas. Sure got rid of those old problems with freeways."

Ben agreed. "Yes, your part in changing the freeway

system was very significant. I think your name is still on the plaque in the central station."

"Wouldn't know." Jimmy feigned ignorance.

"Look at the new harbor." Cindy pointed to the screen. "The earthquakes destroyed the old harbor network."

"Filled up the old Long Beach pier with rocks," Jimmy grumbled.

"What a marvelous reconstruction," Cindy added. "And I love the large green belts between each little town, guaranteeing urban sprawl will never occur again. We've come a long way."

"Please prepare for immediate landing," the flight attendant announced overhead. "Activate your air protection systems now."

The three travelers pushed buttons on the armrest and immediately a gentle column of air surrounded them. As the craft slowed, the column of air increased in their wraparound seats, ensuring them of a firm blanket of protection against jolting as they landed. The trio quickly gathered their belongings and hurried toward the exit door. Within moments they were inside the telaport.

Standing just beyond the exit gates was a tall, thin black man and his small white wife. "Greetings strangers!" Isaiah called out. "Welcome to the thousandth-plus-a-few-years class reunion of the celebrated class of 1997 A.D."

□ □ □

Isaiah and Deborah Murphy had decorated their living room to look like a south-of-the-border fiesta. Candy-filled piñatas dangled from the ceiling. Plates piled with nachos, salsa, and other spicy foods filled serving tables. Streamers hung from the walls and banners welcomed the fifteen delegates to the 1,003rd-year reunion. Encased in plastic for preservation, yellowing pictures from college days lay around the tables.

The first two hours of the reunion were spent swapping stories and updating the group on life in Jerusalem. Finally a lull in the conversations settled around the room.

Jimmy Harrison clapped his hands. "Please gather around. I want to share our reason for coming."

The old gang drifted around the couch, some sitting on the floor while others pulled up chairs. "Lay it on us," someone called out.

"We can't thank Isaiah and Deborah enough for such a fun time," Jimmy said. "In our kosher world, we don't get to enjoy cheese enchiladas often."

The group laughed.

"Actually we came to get a serious report on how things are faring in your world," Jimmy continued. "We've lived through the worst and the best together. Your opinions are always invaluable."

"I tried to contact Dr. Ann Woodbridge," Isaiah reported, "but we couldn't find her anywhere. Ben, we also wanted to invite your father and mother but they couldn't be found either. Rather strange."

Ben nodded appreciatively. "Thanks for trying. Regardless, tell us about the religious and moral climate in Los Angeles these days."

"I hate to say," George Abrams began, "but people are spiritually indifferent. With the glorious mountains behind us and the magnificent ocean before us, pleasure seems to be the number one pursuit. Religion, church, and worship are boring to most folks. I've even seen horoscopes reappearing, as well as psychic readings."

Deborah Murphy shook her head. "Generations have never known anything other than the order and stability of Yeshua's government. No one has ever worried about losing a job or going broke. Everyone has everything they could want."

"Affluence breeds apathy," Mary Chandler added. "People don't care. They exist without passion. I'm afraid many of my neighbors are in the spiritual doldrums. People are once again concerned with status and possessions. Greed is now 'in.'"

"Perspective has been lost," someone said.

"Oh, I think matters are much worse," Isaiah insisted. "People don't stay neutral long. When they are not committed to something, they quickly fall for anything. We are seeing a resurgence of sexual sin like we've never known. Professional white-collar crime is also on the rise."

"Strange," Mary added, "we've become like the children of Israel wandering through the wilderness. God has provided everything we could ever need and we're not even grateful. I hadn't thought about the problem this way before, but we are just about as faithless as they were."

"I'm afraid . . ." Ben stopped and thought for a moment. "Let me put it this way. We have evidence some of the old diseases may be recurring. The matter may be very serious. Sounds like Los Angeles is part of the problem."

"I'm rather surprised this problem wasn't brought to our attention by the Immortals," Isaiah said. "In fact, I haven't been in any meetings lately where anyone from Jerusalem showed up. The Immortals have always helped before big problems get out of hand. I would have expected their intervention."

"I can't find my parents," Ben mumbled to himself, "and I can't get Ann Woodbridge to answer her phone. Very strange . . . something *is* going on."

□ □ □

On the other side of the world, it was nearly midnight. King Abu Sita hurried into the Temple of Marduk. The artificial lighting had been shut off and the moonlight turned the reconstructed temple into a place of shadows and dark corners. Flickering candles and torches provided the only light.

The huge temple's long flat roof was supported by massive marble columns. Red and blue frescos etched with gold designs bordered the ceilings. In the front of the great hall six-foot-high candlesticks and a smoldering copper brazier five feet in diameter added a glow. At the top of a row of marble steps a twenty-foot statue of Marduk dominated the temple.

El Khader waited at the front of the sanctuary with two women and an ensemble of musicians. Guards barred all entrances.

"They've all been sworn to secrecy?" The Syrian king pointed around the room.

"On the threat of their lives," the secretary of state answered. He was dressed in a long robe of brilliant blue and a breast plate dotted with jewels hung from his neck. El Khader wore a cylindrical domed hat with a large strip of embroidered cloth hanging from each side. "The designers of my priest robes have been equally sworn." He looked at the two women and the musicians. "We have practiced the ceremony many times so we can do everything with precision. Your wish is our command."

Abu Sita looked critically at the women's transparent gowns. Glistening in the torchlight the filmy veils concealed little. "Do they understand the ancient dialect?"

"No, Glorious One," El Khader explained. "But they can pronounce the words correctly and sing the melodies of worship as they were originally intended. We believe the women will be sufficient."

"The priestesses were dressed like *that*?" Rajah Abu Sita pointed and raised his eyebrows.

"Yes, according to the archives and the writings of the Temple Chronicles," El Khader insisted.

"Then let's get on with it," the Syrian king barked.

The secretary of state snapped his fingers and the musicians began. The women started to hum. He tossed fluid into the copper brazier and flames leaped, sending white columns of smoke toward the ceiling. El Khader dumped a cup of incense into the fire. The pungent smell of frankincense and myrrh filled the night air. Then the old man raised his arms in worship before the menacing statue above him.

Marduk was seated on a throne of gray granite. He had long hair and a flat beard styled in ripples that hung to mid-chest. A turban swirled around the stone head and the god held a rod of iron. The black eyes had the look of a devouring lion. At his feet on the first step lay a small golden goblet and an open silver container filled with white powder.

El Khader handed the king a scroll. "The poem is translated into contemporary Syrian. Read as the women sing and I will call the god up from the other world."

The women slipped into a slow-moving dance while singing, their gowns floating in the evening breeze. Their bodies swayed back and forth as if to seduce Marduk.

Rajah Abu Sita began, "I have cast thee a spell, make thee all great in the gods' assembly. The scepters of the gods given into thy hand: yea, supremely great shall thou be."

El Khader poured more incense into the fire. White smoke completely covered the front of the statue. "Louder!" he commanded the Syrian king. "We must demonstrate sincerity."

The women clicked finger cymbals, gyrating and swaying as if drifting into a trance. The drums picked up the tempo and the flute played furiously. The scene took on an unearthly aura.

Rajah read in time to the music. "The heavens rain oil. The wadis run with honey. Marduk raises his voice and cries: I shall sit and take my ease, for Marduk the Mighty is alive, for the prince, the lord of the earth, exists."

El Khader had already climbed up the stairs on his knees, his hands held upward in praise. "Greatest among the gods! Victor over the god Tiaman! Ruler of the Underworld! We offer you our lives, our fortunes, our empire. Take my body as your vehicle! My voice as your mouth."

Rajah felt his heart thump to the rhythm of the drum beat. The sounds and the smell of the incense were intoxicating and he felt light-headed. Uncharacteristically emotional, he cried, "Blessed Marduk! I worship you with all my heart. Come forth!"

El Khader seized a glob of hallucinogenic powder from the silver cup on the top step. He plunged his tongue into the drug and washed the paste down with the bitter brew. The women rushed toward the bottom step and cried out, "Habu Habu! Isma ya mo lay. Shay-la-har-mar. See-harba!"

El Khader stiffened and grabbed his chest as if struck by a seizure or a heart attack. He tumbled forward, the headdress crashing against the top step. The old man inched down the steps and rolled sideways as if dead.

"What's happened?" Rajah Abu Sita cried out. The dancers and musicians stopped. The king stared, more in consternation than fear. When the women backed away, the king crept forward.

Abu Sita peered down at the unconscious diplomat. "Are you alive?"

El Khader blinked but didn't open his eyes.

"Speak to me," the king demanded.

His eyes shut, a low guttural growl like the sound of a mad dog rolled up from the old man's throat. Suddenly he shrieked like a rabid cat. White saliva foamed at the corners of his mouth and ran down his beard. The king took a step back and the women ran out of the building, the musicians hurrying behind them.

"Listen to me!" The words came from El Khader's mouth but his lips didn't move. "I am your guide on the path to all truth. Hear me." The sound was low, deep, dominating. "I am the voice of Marduk. Hear him. The greatest of all the gods!

"My hour has come again." The words flowed from El Khader's mouth as if they had a life of their own. "If you hear me and obey, I will return the glory of this place. I will make my worshipers to walk over the heads of their enemies. I will speak through my servant to those who listen." El Khader's head raised slowly and then fell back against the marble floor.

Silence filled the great hall. King Rajah Abu Sita looked around, realizing the musicians and the women were gone. The guards were standing behind columns near the entrance. When he looked back, his secretary of state had rolled over on his side and was sitting up. El Khader wiped his mouth and stared at the dribble on the front of his robe.

"What happened?" the diplomat's voice returned. "Where am I?"

CHAPTER 6

The Murphys' living room was still cluttered with glasses and plates from the party the night before. Isaiah was picking up some of the dishes when Jimmy came downstairs. "Hope you had a good time," Isaiah called out to his old friend.

"Tremendous," Jimmy answered. "Fabulous to see all the old friends."

"You really look rested. The antijet-lag pills must really work."

"One of the great modern advances." Jimmy Harrison dropped down on the couch. "One tablet before leaving Jerusalem and immediately the ole brain amines started readjusting to the change in sleep patterns. Right now I can't even feel a time difference."

"I've already tried to find Ann Woodbridge and the Feinbergs this morning," Isaiah continued. "I called on the hologram phone, tried their offices, and even tapped the Internet computer system to no avail. As bizarre as it seems, the Immortals seem to have disappeared off the face of the earth."

Jimmy laughed. "The last time that happened to me was the Rapture. Terrified me to the core. At least we know they're either here on earth or in the spiritual realms."

"It's almost like they are intentionally avoiding us," Isaiah Murphy mused. "It just doesn't add up."

"I had the same experience with King David." Ben Feinberg entered from the guest room adjacent to the living room. "Didn't mean to eavesdrop, but I was coming out when I heard your conversation."

"Well, good morning," Jimmy answered. "Cindy's still sacked out?"

"She's just behind me." Ben walked into the room. "Jimmy, I didn't tell you about my experience with our illustrious mayor of Jerusalem. While meeting with him recently, I was distinctly brushed off and ushered out of the room. Things don't normally work that way."

"Ben, do you have any special way to contact your parents?" Isaiah asked.

"No, just the usual ways. Never been a problem before. For ten centuries they've responded immediately. Perhaps I ought to see if I can use Jerusalem's special connection system to the Immortals."

"Actually . . ." Jimmy rolled his cane between his hands. His eyes took on a mischievous twinkle. "You see . . . well . . . I had hoped to locate a museum that might let me drive one of those old Mustangs. Now, I know this is a wild . . ."

"Wild idea?" Cindy said from the bedroom door. "Sounds like a great idea to get killed. Driving one of those antiques today would be like riding a bicycle on a freeway a thousand years ago."

"I tried that once," Jimmy said to himself.

"Nearly got you killed, I'll bet," Cindy shot back.

"Yeah, but what a thrill!"

"Let's go for something a little more on the immediate and practical side." Isaiah punched in numbers on his computerized wrist watch. "Take a quick look at the news and see what's brewing out there. Who knows? We may be missing some important explanation for where the Immortals are."

Isaiah pushed the enter button, and the north side of the wall instantly became a life-size television screen. As the picture came into focus, they saw people running in every direction. A camera crew zoomed in on a man standing in front of the Los Angeles County Courthouse.

"This is Don Blevins with Channel 6. Details are just now becoming available," the announcer's message was clipped. "Apparently a large group gathered to hear the judge's verdict on a petition from Newt Baez, a Southern California resident and activist who was asking the court to set him free from any and all restrictions imposed by the central government in Jerusalem. Judge McCalhenney ruled in favor of the state and ordered Baez to stay in compliance with current law. The group supporting Baez was prepared for this decision and immediately denounced the judge, turning the courtroom into a shambles. Baez and company rushed out of the courthouse to tell the news to followers waiting on the steps. A full-scale riot erupted."

The camera spanned a crowd rampaging in front of the legal center. While a police vehicle was being turned over, a dozen other protestors set a police anti-gravity shuttle on fire. Without weapons, police could only push and pull the rioters away. The police were vastly outnumbered for the battle.

"Discontent has been fermenting for some time," Blevins began again. "While unnoticed by most observers, a movement has been building to demand complete separation from the central government. Matters have clearly taken an ugly turn."

Suddenly a building across the street from the courthouse burst into flames. Mobs of people ran through the streets while rioters shouted, "Down with Jerusalem!"

"Matters are deteriorating quickly," the announcer continued. "The judge's decision seems to have ignited social gasoline." Someone pressed a piece of paper into the announcer's hand. "I have just been informed," Blevins read from the paper, "Judge McCalhenney has been seriously injured after being thrown out of a second-story window."

A camera angle from a flying shuttlecraft filled the screen. Flames shot out of other buildings around the courthouse as people ran in every direction. Another picture of a large crowd pushing unarmed policemen to the ground and trampling them filled the screen.

"Please tell us what is happening," the announcer's voice broke in. Two men stood next to him with hands on their hips, chests heaving up and down from running. "Why has this situation erupted and become volatile?"

"The time has come to revolt!" The smaller man shook his fist at the television camera. "Throw off the oppressors!"

"What are you talking about?" Don Blevins glowered.

"We are going to attack any and all representatives of the government in Jerusalem," the second man shouted. "We'll throw the dictators in the ocean."

"You are targeting government officials?" the announcer gawked. "Are you serious?"

The small man grabbed the microphone. "Join with us, fellow citizens, and assault anyone who tries to restrain you."

"Give me that!" Blevins grabbed for the mike.

Suddenly the second man hit the announcer in the face, knocking him to the street. Television personnel leaped into the fray and the picture faded back to the main studio.

"Channel 6 is carefully monitoring these developments in downtown Los Angeles." The new announcer's voice shook. "Obviously no one has *ever* seen anything like what we are witnessing. We have called for police assistance to help Don Blevins but matters are now completely out of control. Because policemen have not been armed for centuries, no one is prepared for the full-scale revolt occurring in our city. Please stay tuned and we will keep you updated as the story continues to unfold."

An aerial view of smoke and fire from the area around the courthouse again filled the screen.

"Good heavens!" Isaiah exclaimed. "I can't believe my eyes! They are after people like *you*." He pointed at the Feinbergs.

Cindy wrung her hands slowly. "I didn't think I would ever again see people attacked in the streets of Los Angeles." She sank down into a chair.

"Don't worry, dear." Ben Feinberg took his wife's hand. "Yeshua's protection took us through one terrible time. He will do it again."

"I think it's important to get you out of here," Isaiah Murphy insisted. "Maybe we're watching a bunch of nuts at work, and then again we could be facing a full-scale rebellion. Who knows where all of this might lead? We need to get you to the international telaport immediately and put you on the next flight back to Israel."

Jimmy Harrison turned slowly from the screen. "Let's think about what we are seeing for a minute." He began pacing. "In a very short time we have witnessed a three-pronged attack on world stability. The threat of disease was accompanied by spiritual disintegration. Now we look at this screen and discover political instability in America. Such problems haven't existed for nearly a thousand years." He looked around the room. "What's left to attack?"

"One more thing," Ben answered. "Faith in Yeshua."

□ □ □

Night had fallen in Jerusalem when students at Hebrew University on Mt. Scopus gathered around television sets to watch the crisis in Los Angeles. The groups looked in shocked silence as the riot continued to spread across the city.

"What do you make of it, Dr. Zemah?" one of the younger students asked.

Zvilli smiled condescendingly. "We are seeing an example of group dynamics at work. Individuals with poor impulse control are being swept away by mob psychology."

Another student observed, "This is unbelievable. We've never seen anything like this riot."

Zvilli Zemah shook his head. "We can expect such phenomena to occur periodically. Social combustibility is the product of the creation of a critical mass of hostility. Californians have always been a rebellious lot."

The television screen was filled with pictures of people attacking another federal building down the street from the courthouse. Glass was strewn across the pavement and computers were being dumped out of the windows.

Rivka Zachary started crying. "I've never witnessed violence before." She dabbed at her eyes. "The sight is horrible."

"Stay rational," Dr. Zemah warned. "The only way to comprehend deviant behavior is by applying social theory. The explosion is a rare opportunity for us to study the psychology of nationalism."

"Death to the Jews! Kill the oppressors!" rioters screamed at the police. TV cameras zoomed in on hate-filled faces. "Throw the yoke off our necks!"

"Listen!" Rivka put her hands over her ears. "They are attacking *us*!"

"We must not personalize a foreign spectacle," Zemah pontificated. "Remember, we are dealing with Gentiles whose reactions lack impulse restraint."

"Kill the Jews?" the girl muttered. "The words are terrible."

The picture switched to the L.A. International Telaport. Crowds were overrunning the parking lot. An announcer said, "The reaction against foreign control has spilled over to the command centers of the city. We are witnessing nothing less than a full-scale insurrection. Apparently rioters are attempting to prevent foreign government officials from leaving the city."

"Weapons will be needed," Zemah added, "unless the Immortals intervene quickly, but even they aren't armed. A frightening dilemma!"

"Some of our people could be in that area," Rivka agonized. "I think we should pray."

Zvilli looked at her out of the corner of his eye and frowned. "Whatever."

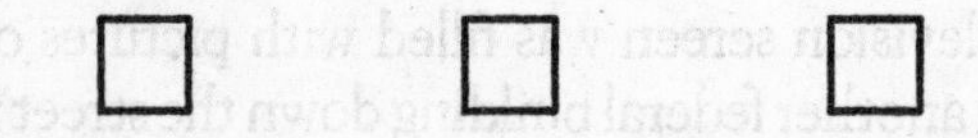

Isaiah's battery-propelled car flew into the parking lot of the L.A. telaport and shot toward the end closest to the terminal entrance. "I can't believe there are so many people out here today. Look at the crowds."

"You should have just dropped us off at the arrival gate," Jimmy said.

"Not on your life! Isaiah stays with his old buddies to the last moment." He swung into a parking place. In front of them was an enclosed causeway to the airport.

"Look at those people over there," Cindy pointed out the window. "Looks like they are running. What strange behavior for such a large group."

"Seems more like they are chasing someone," Ben observed.

"Good grief!" Jimmy exclaimed. "I think they are rioters!"

Isaiah quickly leaped from the car. His six-foot five-inch

height allowed a quick survey of the parking lot. "They are coming this way! We've got to get out of here."

At that moment another group appeared near the entrance to the parking area. Cindy gasped, "We can't get out now!"

Ben Feinberg jumped out of the front seat. "We'd better make a run for the terminal." He grabbed Cindy's hand. "We don't have an alternative."

Jim piled out behind them. "Good thing we didn't wear any government insignias or uniforms. Surely they won't bother elderly people."

"We can't chance it." Isaiah grabbed Cindy's overnight bag. "Make a run for it."

The four friends trotted as fast as they could toward the crosswalk. Just as they reached the steps someone yelled out, "Look! Old people. Trying to escape!"

"The old ones work for the government!"

"Get 'em!"

The mob surged toward the steps. Jim and Ben each took one of Cindy's arms and helped her up the steps. Jimmy used his cane to keep from slipping. Isaiah blocked the doorway with his large frame. "Run!" he called after them. "I'm going to slow these crazies down if it kills me. Don't stop."

"No!" Jimmy called back. "Come with us."

"Just don't slow down," Isaiah yelled.

The Feinbergs and Jimmy were halfway across the bridge when the rioters hit the door. Isaiah leaned into the first wave but was immediately pushed to the cement floor. The people didn't even pause but trampled his body. A few rioters tripped and fell but the surging mob was barely slowed.

When the trio came to the other end, Ben pulled Cindy toward him. "Split up, Jimmy. Maybe they'll be confused and decide we're just tourists if we're not together." Ben pushed up his glasses with one hand and jerked Cindy forward with the other.

"I'll run toward the domestic flights," Jimmy called over his shoulder. "Get into the international area before they catch you." He hobbled toward the left of the entry hall.

The Feinbergs found an elevator just around the corner. The elevator door opened and two people got off. Ben pulled Cindy in and hit the up button. The door slid shut with their attackers only moments away. In an instant Ben and Cindy shot upward.

Across the hall, Jimmy slid around a wall and smashed into a porter carrying an armload of luggage. The attendant tipped backward and sent Jimmy hurling into the wall. He bounced off and fell face forward onto the floor. Jimmy's head thumped on the concrete with a sickening thud. His cane rolled across the marble floor. He went limp.

When the elevator door opened, Ben and Cindy saw the Israel ticket counter only fifty feet away. Ben punched the emergency stop button, keeping the elevator and the pursuers from following them. "Run for the desk." He pulled Cindy behind him.

"Maybe they can hide us." Cindy sounded terrified.

Ben ran for the ticket desk. "Help us," he cried out. "People are chasing us."

Without looking up, the youthful agent opened a swinging counter door and let the Feinbergs in. "Hide behind the desk." He kept his head down. "Keep low. I'll prepare the tickets to get you out of here." Without a word the young man began punching information into the computer.

"Please make out an extra ticket." Ben held Cindy tightly. "Hopefully our friend is just behind us."

Three stories below Jimmy lay on the floor, his eyes closed. The sounds of rioting filled the arrival hall. A strong hand reached down and lifted Jimmy up by the wrist. In one quick sweep, the man pulled Jimmy across the floor toward an office. A woman opened the door and the rescuer slipped Jimmy inside. The woman shut the door behind them and locked it.

Jimmy could only faintly hear their voices. "Is he all right?" the woman's voice seemed to echo in his head.

"I think so," the man said louder, "just a bad bump is all." "Oh, dear! Bless him," the woman answered.

Jimmy felt her warm touch on his forehead. Energy surged through his body. After a couple of abortive attempts, Jimmy opened his eyes but couldn't yet focus on anything. At first all he could see above him was the outline of two young people around thirty years old. He slowly sat up and held his head. "Oh," he groaned. "What happened?"

"You tried one of those Batman tricks you used to do as a boy," the man said. "Bad mistake at your age."

Jimmy instantly looked up and blinked several times. "Dad!" he exclaimed. "How did you get here?"

"We Immortals always keep an eye out for our own," Reverend John Harrison said to his son. "A little help every now and then doesn't hurt a thing."

Jimmy tried to get up. "Make sure you're ready," the woman said. Jimmy looked to the other side and stared.

"It's me, Ruth! Remember? I was your *wife*."

"Dear . . ." Jimmy reached out to the Immortal. "Good grief! I can't believe my eyes."

"Your father's right. You are our constant concern."

Jimmy took his former wife's hand. "I think I can stand up now. Please help me." John Harrison supported Jimmy's other arm and pulled him to his feet. He could hear people running past the locked door. "Now I remember. Ben and Cindy may be in trouble!"

"You don't think I'd let my brother and sister-in-law go

unattended," Ruth teased. "I think you'll find everything is covered."

Ruth put her arm around Jimmy's shoulders and gave him a big hug. "I carry you in my heart every moment." She kissed him on the cheek.

Jimmy looked into Ruth's eyes. He remembered youthful days running along the beach behind the Feinbergs' former home in Newport Beach. Ruth was as beautiful now as she was then. Her resurrected body kept her in total health at a perfected thirty-three years old.

Jimmy suddenly remembered the day in the Bozrah desert when Ruth died, giving birth to Jimmy Jr., their stillborn son. For a moment profound pain cut through his heart like a knife.

"I still love you so very much." Jimmy kissed his wife tenderly. "I miss not seeing you every day of my life."

Ruth held him close and patted his back. "How dear you are, Jimmy. And so very good. Such a man of character. I take such pride in telling other Immortals you were my husband in that other life."

"I still wish that . . ." Jimmy's voice trailed off.

"My love for you is perfected." Ruth squeezed his hand. "Nothing has been lost."

"That's easy for you to say." Jimmy shook his head. "From my side the matter certainly feels different."

"Look," John Harrison interrupted, "this is about as romantic as Immortals are allowed to get. If you will remember, we are not exactly here for an ocean cruise."

"Yes." Ruth's smile took a bittersweet twist. "We need to get you on the road home."

"I can't go out there." Jimmy pointed to the door. "And Ben and Cindy . . ."

"Follow me." John was already leading the way through the office. "There's a freight elevator at the back of this room." The minister looked up at the ceiling as if seeing through the tiles and observing something happening far above them. "You will find everything in order at the other end. But quickly. Your shuttlecraft is loading right now."

The freight elevator opened at the third floor. John and Ruth Harrison hurried Jimmy toward the gates. "What in the world is going on?" Jimmy asked Ruth. "Tell me why the world has gone crazy."

"All in due time," his former wife answered. "Right now we need to get you on your way."

"But help me make sense of this bizarre turn of events."

"Look." John pointed straight ahead. "I think you know those people."

"Ben, Cindy!" Jimmy yelled, They were standing with a young man in front of the entry platform. The couple looked unusually relaxed and at ease.

"Hey!" Jimmy called out. "I'm okay."

The young man with the Feinbergs turned around. "Didn't think we would let you down, did you, Dad?"

"Jimmy Junior!" The old man gawked at his son. "You're in on this rescue, too?"

"Sure," the young man threw his arms around his father. "I couldn't let Mom and Granddad have all the fun."

"Absolutely amazing," Cindy observed. "When John and Jim Junior stand side by side they look like brothers."

"The shuttlecraft is nearly loaded," Jim Junior broke in. "We don't have much time to spare."

"Please," Jimmy begged his father, "tell us what has happened to the world."

John Harrison put his hand on the old man's shoulder. "Blessed are they who enter a battle they cannot win to save a life they cannot lose."

"I don't understand." Jimmy searched his father's face. "What do you Immortals know that we don't?"

Ruth took Jimmy's wrinkled, liver-spotted hand. "Be

loved, don't be surprised at the fiery ordeal which has come upon you to prove your faithfulness."

"Ruth," Ben pleaded, "don't talk in riddles. We need to know what to do."

"Tend the flock of God," Ruth answered. "You will not see us again for a long time."

"On your way now." John beckoned for the trio to follow him. "Here are your tickets." He handed cards to each one. "They won't wait much longer for you to board. Jimmy, your cane will be at your seat."

Ben pointed to the flashing light overhead. "I guess we have no choice but . . ." When he turned around John Harrison was gone.

"Ruth . . ." Jimmy called out but no one was standing there.

"Jim Junior's gone, too," Cindy said. "I wonder where they went."

"I think just maybe they are taking care of Isaiah right now," Ben conjectured.

CHAPTER 7

Guards stood at attention as Ziad Atrash and Rajah Abu Sita followed the prime minister through the national Russian museum located inside the rebuilt Kremlin Walls. One wing had mementos from the days of the czar, another the remnants of the Communist era. Corridors were lined with portraits of former heroes and heads of state. Alexi Chardoff pointed out various items of interest as they walked along.

"You must understand," Chardoff explained, "that most of the past was destroyed a thousand years ago. Many of these relics have been re-created."

"How did the weapons survive?" Atrash asked.

"Well-intentioned, former Communist leaders built concrete tunnels beneath the Kremlin and at various bases around the country. Guns were stockpiled for exhibit after the Battle of Armageddon, but for centuries people didn't want to see weapons of destruction. With time the stash was forgotten except by the curators."

"Fortunate indeed!" Abu Sita observed.

"Since our Babylon summit, my best people have worked

hard to restore the guns." Chardoff punched in a secret code to open a locked side door. "You will be pleased at the speed with which we have been able to make these weapons operable. We even have machine guns that can be fired."

Chardoff led the two men down a long, dark hall surrounded with ancient overhead pipes. Cobwebs hung from the ceilings and walls. "The big problem is getting the ammunition ready," the prime minister said as they walked on.

"Our friends in Ethiopia and China are hard at work on this problem even as we speak," Atrash answered. "The problem for our rebellion will be time—not supplies."

Abu Sita nodded his head. "Yes, we must strike quickly before the Immortals get a whiff of what we are planning and come back to earth from wherever they have disappeared."

"Careful," Chardoff warned as he descended winding stairs. "Sometimes the floors get slick in here."

The stairs ended at another door at the bottom. The prime minister inserted a card in the lock and the door slid into the wall. Before them loomed a large warehouse-type area nearly the size of a football field. Workmen and soldiers polished and assembled rifles, pistols, machine guns and other weapons. When the prime minister entered all activity ceased as men snapped to attention.

"As you were," Chardoff commanded. "Continue." Immediately the men returned to their work. The Russian leader pointed to the crates stacked around the room. "See. The supply is substantial."

"Superb!" Ziad Atrash cracked his knuckles. "Even better than I might have hoped. Yes, you are well underway."

"Excellency!" a uniformed man hurried toward the three men. "A special satellite report just came in. We felt you should know at once."

Chardoff eyed the man critically. "General, I was not to be interrupted."

"We felt your guests would want to see the news report from America."

The prime minister looked at the other two leaders and shrugged. "Let's look." He turned back to the soldier. "This better be good."

The general led the trio into a spartan command center. A map of Russia covered one wall; on the opposite wall an inch-thick television set hung like a painting. The screen filled with pictures of smoke and fire pouring out of buildings.

"The news report was just brought to my attention," an aide reported. "The matter seemed urgent."

"What is it?" Chardoff barked.

"Riots have broken out in America," the general stood at attention as he spoke. "Early reports indicate a large-scale rebellion is underway."

"Rebellion?" Ziad Atrash pushed the aide aside. "I can't believe my eyes." He stared at the scenes of chaos in Los Angeles.

"People are protesting control by the Jerusalem government," the general continued. "Leaders of the rebellion are calling for the ouster of all external authority."

"Astonishing!" Atrash ground his hand into his palm. "Our calculations have proven correct." He watched with rapt attention as five youth tore the Israeli flag apart.

"Are you sure it's a revolt?" Chardoff stared at the picture of people rampaging through the streets.

"We reported exactly what the announcer said to date," the general answered.

"Did either of you have any part in instigating the riots?" Chardoff asked the other two heads of state. "What do you know about the chaos?"

"Nothing!" Rajah Abu Sita insisted. "We are seeing a spontaneous rebellion."

"The time *is* ripe!" Atrash waved his big thick arms in the air. "Yes! The gods have given us the exact time for our strike!"

"The gods?" Alexi puzzled.

"Let us counsel together." Ziad Atrash waved the general and aide toward the door. "During my first meditations months ago before the god Osiris, I felt an inner voice urging me to act immediately. I received divine direction to conquer the world." He pointed to the TV. "Now we see the reason for the divine leading."

Chardoff shook his head in amazement. "I thought that spirit guide business with your secretary of state was only a show, nonsense to get our support. You are really serious?"

"Of course!" Atrash barked. "The next step is to implement our new religious system to undermine Yeshua's control. We are totally earnest."

"What do you propose?" Chardoff slowly lifted his hands in consternation.

"We now have absolute evidence of being able to predict the future through communication with the gods." Atrash's speech was quick and clipped. "We must teach more people how to channel and receive supernatural power. We will liberate the world population from the tired morality that has kept us in a straightjacket all these centuries. Once our people know there is an alternative, the rest will be easy."

Chardoff ran his fingers nervously through his hair. "Get on with it."

"Worship Marduk," Rajah Abu Sita insisted. "He is the great god we must listen to."

□ □ □

Even before their shuttlecraft landed in Tel Aviv, Jimmy and Ben had a plan of action in mind. After Cindy was safely home, the brothers-in-law hurried to the Knesset and sought an immediate audience with the Apostle Paul.

"I know you are both very important people," the receptionist explained. "But you must understand how pressing matters have been lately. The apostle hasn't been seeing anyone for days. I am sorry."

"You don't understand," Jimmy tried another angle. "We have just returned from witnessing one of the worst disturbances the world has seen in centuries. Surely the Immortals will want a firsthand account of what we personally experienced."

Ben jumped in. "I don't doubt the pressures of Paul's constant oversight of the Gentile world, but we have hard information of spiritual deterioration that demands his immediate attention. Please. You've got to let us in to see him. Try one more time."

The secretary shook her head. "Really! I have my orders."

Jimmy's shoulders dropped and he shook his head. "What more can we do?"

"Don't worry, boys," a strong resonant voice answered from across the room. "Always good to see the likes of you."

"Paul!" Ben exclaimed. "We've been trying to contact you."

"It's all right, Elizabeth." The apostle beckoned Ben Feinberg and Jimmy Harrison to follow him. "I'll work these brothers in." Paul was a small man with an unusually high forehead. Even with his restored body, he was slight and wiry. The beard around his chin added dignity to an otherwise plain face.

"But you said . . ." the secretary protested.

"Don't remind me I'm a man of the law," the apostle chided her. "Sometimes we have to make adjustments."

Ben and Jimmy followed the Overseer of Gentile Affairs into the inner office. The three men sat down in simple chairs around a corner table.

"The world is going crazy!" Jimmy exploded. "We just escaped from the upheaval in Los Angeles. The spirituality of many people seems to be disappearing."

The apostle listened with disconcerting intensity. His piercing black eyes made him appear to be able to read their minds.

"Surely *you* are aware of a change in the hearts of many people." Ben waited but Paul said nothing, and his face didn't convey any emotion.

"We believe the time has come for new teaching on what the Scriptures have always said," Jimmy continued. "Yeshua must come forth and bring revival to places like Los Angeles. The hearts of the people must be called back to the Lord."

Paul held up his hand and made the sign of the cross. "You are good men and your hearts are pure. Such is a great blessing!"

Jimmy looked at Ben. "Thank you," Jimmy stammered. "But we are concerned for the problems of the world. Yeshua must act quickly!"

Paul nodded his head knowingly. "What can *you* do to change the spiritual climate?"

"*Us?*" Jimmy's eyes widened.

"You've been quite effective in the past," Paul answered matter of factly.

"B-u-t," Ben protested, "we need the Immortals to guide us. Yeshua must discipline these renegades. Where is He?"

Paul gently massaged his chin. "There is a time to work by sight and there is a time to walk by faith. Perhaps you've come to depend too much on your leaders."

Jimmy stared, dumbfounded.

"We wouldn't know what to do," Ben reiterated.

"Please," Jimmy pleaded, "be more specific."

"The time has come for you to attack this problem with the power of your witness," Paul said. "If the people will not believe the Immortals, they will not be helped with more signs and wonders. They already live in an age of holograms and electronic illusions. The time has come to offer the plain and simple truth."

"But everyone knows the truth," Ben answered. "For centuries we have received God's highest and best. What more is there to tell them?"

"Remember the Book of Judges in the Old Testament?" Paul asked.

"Yes," Jimmy said slowly. "But . . . it's been a long time since I even looked at the Bible."

"Why?" Paul asked.

"Well," Jimmy shrugged, "everything in the Scriptures is past history. What relevance would it have for today?"

"Really?" Paul raised his eyebrows in mock consternation. "You have so completely mastered God's speech you have nothing left to learn?"

"No." Jimmy squirmed. "That's not quite what I meant."

Paul smiled mischievously. "What do you remember about that ancient period?"

Jimmy thought for a moment. "As I remember, every person did what was right in his own eyes."

"Sound like the problem today?" Paul asked.

"Yes!" Jimmy snapped his finger. "That's right."

"And what created the big problem in Israel?"

Ben raised his hand slowly. "One generation forgot the lessons God taught their forefathers. Instead of staying true to the Law, they went their own way."

"Exactly," Paul agreed. "Because you live longer today you have forgotten that the length of a generation is also extended. You and Jimmy have become what Moses and

Joshua were to the ancient period of the Judges. You must take responsibility for the lives of those who have erred."

"But Jimmy and I are just administrators," Ben argued. "We've always depended on the Immortals to give us direction."

"Y-e-s," Paul drawled, "both you and the masses of confused people have a similar problem. You have allowed others to take responsibilities that are rightfully yours. The time has come for the confusion to change." Paul stood up. "I have total confidence you will know how to proceed." He walked to the door.

Jimmy and Ben reluctantly followed the apostle out of the room. "Could you give us another hint?"

Paul opened the door and pointed toward the receptionist's office. "I'd dust off that antiquated, irrelevant Bible and see if there just might be something important you missed." As he closed the door behind them, he concluded, "God *will* bless and guide you."

The two brothers-in-law trudged silently down the hall toward the elevator. The door opened, they entered, and quietly descended.

"The Bible?" Ben finally said. "I thought the law was written in every person's heart."

"We've missed something important, Jimmy. I think the whole world has overlooked some basic principle, and we've been given the responsibility of finding what the truth is. You were always the Bible scholar. The time has come for you to go to work again."

"How can two old fogies like us make a dent in anything as big as this?"

"I don't know." Ben lowered his head. "But we don't have any choice but to find out. I'll ask Cindy to help me with some heavy-duty prayer. You study the message and I'll ponder the method."

"Déjà-vu." Jimmy laughed. "Once upon a time, a long

time ago we were at this very same place. Time to get to work. I'll call you tomorrow."

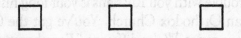

Alexi Chardoff waited for the hologram phone line to connect with China. In a few moments, Fong's image materialized in front of him.

"Mr. Prime Minister," the Chinese leader acknowledged the Russian respectfully, "you are looking quite prosperous. How did your meeting with Ziad Atrash and Abu Sita go?"

"Quite well. They were impressed with my weapons and are already on their way back to Babylon."

"Good."

"Any repercussions from the central government for your expelling their people?"

Fong shook his head. "None. Atrash seems to be right. So far Yeshua has only proven to be a paper tiger."

"What do you make of this religion business the Arabs are pushing?"

Fong smiled. "A most useful idea."

"But do you believe it?"

Fong shrugged. "The ancients of China believed they could contact the spirits of the dead. The Chinese have a long tradition of worshiping ancestors. Some people saw it as respect; others believed in spirit contact. In recent years some people have tried to synthesize those old ideas with faith in Yeshua. Of course, the whole business has been forbidden and clandestine."

"Then you do believe in other gods?" Chardoff pressed.

"I suppose I'm more inclined toward believing in the spirits of the dead making contact with us. Who knows? Maybe old El Khader has become possessed with the long-dead spirit of Chairman Mao." He snickered.

"This is no laughing matter," Alexi growled. "We are playing with fire."

"The trouble with you Russians is your long history with the Russian Orthodox Church. You've got the Christian thing in your genes. We're different," Fong boasted. "Don't worry so much. Regardless of what the truth is about Yeshua, I am convinced that we have the fire power on our side. Yet if it will make you happy, I'll look into talking with the departed spirits."

"Humph!" The Russian settled back into his chair. "Strange business. Strange indeed!"

Fong smiled. "The Arabs still think they are going to take over the world?"

"Atrash certainly does. You should have seen his eyes when he saw the weapons. He licked his lips like a wolf closing in on a lamb. His only question was, 'How fast can you get the artillery operational?'"

"I have just completed conversations with the Ethiopians. We will have no problem supplying the sulphur and nitrates. In fact, I have already arranged for massive shipments of both to be sent to you immediately. Under the guise of providing fertilizer and medicines, we have diverted all of our normal shipments from other countries to Russia."

"Is there any problem in making such an arrangement?"

Fong shrugged again. "We will probably create a temporary shortage of both items for a period of time. If you will put out a news report of crop failure, we can cover our tracks well enough."

"How soon will the chemicals be here?"

"I think significant shipments can reach you in a week. The next will follow."

Alexi smiled for the first time. "We will be ready to manufacture when they arrive."

"In the meantime, I will see if any of the spirits of my

ancestors are waiting around to talk." Fong laughed. "Who knows? Maybe they will have a message for you."

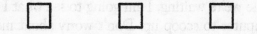

Deborah Murphy watched her husband working feverishly at his desk. He still had a bandage around his head and his left eye was black and blue. After a few minutes she asked, "You're sure you feel all right?"

Isaiah leaned back in his chair. "Pretty stiff." He rubbed his neck. "If I walk slowly, I'm fine."

"Those baboons could have killed you!"

"Then you'd have got me back with one of those glorious thirty-three-year-old bodies."

"I wouldn't have gotten you back at all!" Deborah protested.

"Thankfully Ben Harrison put me in my car and Jim Junior drove us home. When those maniacs ran over me, no one even looked back. I guess they thought they'd put me completely out of commission. Little did they know you can't stop a UCLA man."

Deborah looked at the big bruise on Isaiah's hand. "I shutter to think how long it would have taken me to find you if the Harrisons hadn't intervened."

"Saved my bacon, Deborah."

"Isaiah, I don't want to put my nose in where it doesn't belong, but I have to ask you. I overheard your conversation with Ben and Jimmy about this AIDS problem. What is going on?"

"Honestly, no one seems to know. The epidemic is still a secret and you must not tell a soul. I'm trying to access old data to get some clues for any information on treatment that might still be around. I'm even checking what's out there in places like Africa."

"Nothing makes any sense." Tears filled Deborah's eyes. "Life was so stable and predictable but now we're back in the center of chaos. I want Yeshua to come on television and straighten everything out!"

"While we're waiting, I am going to see what I can get the computer to scoop up. Don't worry about me. I feel better when I'm busy."

Deborah shook her head and walked out of the room. "I just don't know," she muttered to herself.

Isaiah turned back to his computer. For the next hour he tried accessing all the medical systems in Los Angeles to no avail. He settled back in his chair and thought aloud. "With the advent of the Messiah, the disease seems to have just disappeared. No record of a cure anywhere. But there must be something."

After another thirty minutes, Isaiah switched to data for Africa but made little headway. On a wild hunch he began cross-referencing systems for data on medicines. He tried every angle that offered even a shred of hope but nothing clicked.

"Maybe I ought to stop and try tomorrow," he said to himself. At that moment the Internet system filled the screen with a strange message. For several seconds Isaiah stared at the image. He punched the button for an instantaneous printout and then started tracing the data back to its source. In a couple of minutes another pattern appeared and Isaiah ran off a second printout. He carefully compared the reports and then switched programs. Within five minutes he had before him a strange collection of information.

"This just doesn't add up," Isaiah mused. "There's got to be more to the story . . ." He stood up and walked around the room. "No question. I'm on to something." He stopped. "Busted up or not! I'm going to check this out." Isaiah quickly returned the computer to the beginning position and tucked the printouts under his arm.

"Deborah," Isaiah called out, "you won't like this but I need you to help me pack in a hurry. I've got to do a little continent hopping . . . immediately."

"You're going to what?"

CHAPTER 8

Jimmy sat across the dining room table in the Feinbergs' home, watching Ben and Cindy carefully read his report. "During the last week since our talk with the Apostle Paul, I've done nothing but worry about what we can do to stem the tide of rebellion and spiritual lethargy sweeping the world. I think I have developed a good outline of what people must hear."

"Well," Ben sounded irritated, "Paul might have given us a *little* more help. For reasons beyond my grasp, the Immortals seem to have packed up and taken a vacation. Not that I'm complaining, you understand."

"Of course not." Cindy rolled her eyes. "Excellent start, Jimmy. I think you will be pleased with the results of my inquiries. Ben's television idea of three days ago is a definite go."

"The worldwide network hook-up is really possible?" Jimmy asked.

"Cindy used our connections with the Apostle Paul's office not only to get an agreement for air time but also to use old recordings of events occurring just after Yeshua's triumphant entry a thousand years ago. We've got everything necessary to proclaim the truth to the nations."

"Do you really think anybody will listen to us?" Jimmy shook his head. "The students at Hebrew University didn't pay much attention to Ben. Could I do any better?"

"Apparently the apostle thought so," Cindy insisted. "You've just lost the sense of how significant your witness is. What we've got to do is package your message in a format that will grab the attention of even the indifferent."

"Here's what is promised." Ben laid a schedule on the table. "In a week the inter-continental television and hologram system is ours for thirty minutes. The program will be synchronized for airing at prime time everywhere."

"Excellent." Jimmy beamed. "Couldn't ask for more."

"Cindy will oversee the development and use of the recordings and edited segments for visual effect," Ben continued. "By coordinating what we say with the images from the past, we can have a maximum impact. Maybe we can even do better than we think."

"Listen," Cindy said firmly, "Paul's message was clear. We've got to take responsibility for our world. We prayed and this door opened. I'm ready to tackle the problem."

"What a woman!" Ben beamed. "Jimmy, I believe your notes captured the heart of the message the nations need to hear. I've arranged for a production consultant to help produce the program. In seven days we will have our own evangelistic crusade underway."

"I'm also developing a network of spiritual counselors to stand by in every city and town," Cindy added. "Paul's computerized list of ministers makes it easy to complete worldwide contact in a few hours. We will have people ready to minister to the repentant who respond to the number on the screen."

Jimmy nervously pulled at his beard. "I'm totally overwhelmed. Never in my wildest dreams would I have seen myself on television—much less preaching!"

"Time is short," Cindy urged. "We'd better get to work immediately."

During the next seven days Jimmy and Ben were in constant prayer. They reviewed Cindy's TV clips and carefully pored over their Bibles. Jimmy found his old notes on prophecy and reread the complete Old and New Testaments. Most of the time he worked at the Feinberg house, laying his notes out on the living room table.

Late Thursday afternoon Jimmy told Ben, "We really made a mistake in recent centuries. We should never have neglected the Scriptures."

Ben pushed back from the table. "No question about it. There is power in every page. Simply studying the book has been a new source of inspiration. In fact, I'm more encouraged now than I've been since this whole intrigue began."

"We've really underestimated how easy it is to take God's blessings for granted." Jimmy shook his head. "Human beings have a strange blind spot when it comes to being grateful. During the Israelites' wanderings through the desert toward the Promised Land, they had everything anyone could have wanted and they still didn't trust God."

"And here we are in the special 'promised time' and the people of the world can't seem to keep on track. Jimmy, I think self-centeredness is a fatal disease to be fought every moment of our lives."

Jimmy nodded. "The cancerous disease may go into remission but it sure makes a comeback in the form of indifference and spiritual slothfulness. The problem creeps up when we least expect it!"

"Preoccupation with one's self devours our love for God. We lose interest in worship."

Jimmy sighed. "Yes, even in this nearly perfect time indifference and lethargy have returned. I suppose affluence tends to spawn apathy. I just pray we can say something effective enough to jolt complacent people back to life."

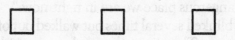

The Inter-Continental Space Shuttle slowly pulled into the gate of the Addis Ababa terminal. Isaiah Murphy gathered up his things and hurried through the gate and down the corridor. Even though he had gone halfway around the world, the structure of the building wasn't different from the Los Angeles telaport, except for the pictures and decorations on the walls. He quickly disappeared into a sea of black faces.

In a few minutes the people mover delivered Isaiah into the main departure lounge. He slowed down and looked carefully across the expansive foyer. Soon he saw a man standing by the front door. Isaiah waved.

Hosni Gossos immediately walked forward. A small man, the Ethiopian was slightly bent over. Although elderly, his kinky hair was still black, making him look younger. He immediately offered his frail hand.

"Old friend," Isaiah exclaimed. "Wonderful to see you again." They shook hands. "You never change."

The Ethiopian snickered. "Your compliments are always like the tail of the pig. They don't mean much but they certainly tickle the ham."

Isaiah laughed. "Hosni, you remain a man of profound sense of humor. I trust they are treating you well."

"Well enough." Gossos took Isaiah's arm and steered him toward the door. "Are you sure no one followed you from Los Angeles?"

"What?" Isaiah stopped.

"Keep walking in case we are being watched." Hosni continued toward the doors.

"You've got to be kidding?"

"A diplomat never jests about such things," Hosni spoke softly. "No one asks such questions without being on to this thing that's coming down. You know better than I what a dangerous place we are in right now."

Isaiah blinked several times but walked out of the building in silence. The air was hot and muggy with the smell of the tropics. Intense indirect lighting planted underground lit a space six feet off the ground as bright as day, leaving the illusion of walking down an illuminated tunnel without a ceiling or walls.

Once inside the diplomat's solar-powered car, Isaiah looked straight into Hosni's eyes. "What are you talking about? Being followed . . . a dangerous place?"

"You are testing me." Gossos showed no emotion. "Good ploy. Even though we have worked on international problems for three decades, this is no time to take anything for granted. I want you to know I have nothing to do with this conspiracy." Hosni turned on the motor. The vehicle silently inched out of the parking place. "I can speak to you freely because my conscience is clear."

Isaiah swallowed hard. "Why don't you start at the beginning and go from there?" He tried to cover any hint of uncertainty.

"First I must ask you one question." The Ethiopian switched on the automatic pilot, which locked him into his pre-chosen travel route. He swung the seat sideways. "How did you find out what our government is up to?"

Isaiah tried to look passive as his mind raced to answer a question he didn't understand.

□ □ □

"And now from Jerusalem," the announcer's voice boomed over the television, "a special historical review, celebrating the past and recognizing the glory of the present." Television screens across the world filled with a fast-moving collage of pictures of the Holy City. The three-dimensional effect made the pictures appear to leap from the television sets. Faces of biblical heros momentarily flashed on the screen only to be replaced by placid scenes of the Galilee. "Your hosts for tonight," the announcer said, "are two special men who have lived through every minute of this story." Drums rolled and a band played loudly. "Meet Ben Feinberg and Jimmy Harrison." To the sounds of applause, the two brothers-in-law walked out on a stage erected on the top of the Mount of Olives.

"Welcome to Jerusalem," Ben began. "We are glad to be coming to you live from this exciting historical city. We want to remember where the New Era began."

"Those were amazing days," Jimmy responded. "Let us take you back to the early moments when we were overpowered by the glory of God. Remember the Feast of Trumpets in that first year?" he asked Ben. "The sight was dazzling. Return with us to the first day of the first month, the month of Tishri, as the saints and angels gathered after the final battle of Armageddon."

Pictures of an angel-filled sky flashed on the screen. The angels held brilliant candles of light. The blast of the archangel Gabriel's trumpet sounded in the background. Jimmy kept talking as the old clips of the past continued. "The Feast of Trumpets had often been called the Feast of the Last Trumpet, and on this day it was truly so. Yeshua honored the many saints who had written Scripture for a period of several thousands of years. These great men of God led us through the best and worst times. Their words inspired our hearts."

The scene returned to Ben. "Recently we took another look at what those giants of faith accomplished and were fascinated to reconsider their writings long before their prophecy was fulfilled. Here's your opportunity to share in our discoveries of how accurate their predictions were. Remember Joel?"

The prophet Joel appeared from the films of the archives, mounting the stairs of the original platform on the Mount of Olives nearly a thousand years earlier. Carrying a staff and dressed as he did in 700 B.C., Joel proclaimed, "Rejoice in the Lord your God. As I prophesied, Yeshua gave His *former rain* of blessing during His public ministry two thousand years ago. And now as I predicted, Yeshua is beginning in the month of Tishri His *latter rain* of blessing, His thousand-year kingdom. God has kept faith with His Holy Word."

As the picture faded, Jimmy continued, "No greater prophet came from Israel than Hosea." From another film clip Hosea spoke after Joel finished. Like Joel, Hosea wore the robe and sandals of his time. "I, too, proclaimed the promised Messiah would come twice. I foresaw a former rain of Jewish dispersion and great trouble for our people, lasting two of God's days, two thousand years. But I also proclaimed healing and spiritual revival for Jacob's children, coming as a latter rain on the third day." He cupped his hand to his mouth and yelled out across the Kidron Valley. "The rain is falling."

The prophet Zechariah slipped next to Hosea. "In the tenth chapter of my writings I was referring to this very day when I called on the people to pray for rain: spiritual, emotional, and physical showers of blessing during days of the latter rain. God has once again proven Himself consistent. We must trust Him with our whole hearts."

Ben turned to Jimmy. "We have been the fortunate recipients of these overflowing blessings. The rain of goodness has flooded our villages, towns, and cities across the globe. Our inheritance has been beyond the prophets' dreams. We take for granted what the centuries longed to see."

"Yes," Jimmy responded, "few of you have known the world of chaos and violence out of which we came. You have been spared the terrible experience of war and carnage. Instead of beginning each day asking Yeshua to deliver us, we can gratefully greet every dawn with praise and gratitude."

As Jimmy finished, a picture of the prophet Daniel appeared. In contrast to the Israelite dress of the other prophets, Daniel wore the silks of Babylon. Standing in front of the Temple Mount, he was reading from the second chapter of his own writings. "Blessed be the name of God forever and ever; for wisdom and might are His. He gives wisdom to the wise and knowledge to those who have understanding. He reveals deep and secret things."

Daniel looked up from the scroll. "Over 2,600 years before the fact, I predicted Yeshua, the rock of King Nebuchadnezzar's dream, would smash the ten toes of iron and clay, the ten nation confederacy of the unholy Roman Empire. Through the power of the Holy Spirit I was able to proclaim the truth." Daniel again read from the scroll, "In the days of these kings the God of heaven will set up a kingdom which shall never be destroyed; and the kingdom shall not be left to other people; it shall break in pieces and consume all these kingdoms, and it shall stand forever" (Daniel 2:44). He lowered the scroll. "Today we behold the victory of our God," he exclaimed.

From behind Daniel, a man dressed in royal robes stepped forward. His long rippling black beard was cropped in a straight line beneath his throat. His hands folded, he stood looking at the ground.

"Listen to the voice of one who knows." Daniel turned to the man. "King Nebuchadnezzar once ruled the world as the mightiest of men. He is an ultimate witness to the truth."

Even with a chastened demeanor, the king carried himself with great authority. He was a large man, naturally commanding attention. "Because the Babylonian Empire stretched across the world, I thought I needed neither God nor man, though I did worship false gods to try to manipulate them to give me power. There was no limit to my arrogance." The king hung his head. "Then I became psychotic for seven years and I learned otherwise. God graciously restored my mind and empire and I repented of my presumptuousness. Of all men I can testify to the graciousness of our God and the depth of our need for Him."

Daniel put his arm around the king's shoulders. "I included his confession in the fourth chapter of my prophecy," Daniel said. "The king's apology is instructive for us today." Daniel read from the scroll. "I thought it good to declare the signs and wonders that the Most High God has worked for me. How great are His signs, and how mighty His wonders! His kingdom is an everlasting kingdom, and His dominion is from generation to generation." The prophet cleared his throat and spoke even more loudly. "He does according to His will in the army of heaven and among the inhabitants of the earth. No one can restrain His hand or say to Him, 'What have You done?'"

Nebuchadnezzar held his hands up in praise and shouted, "Amen."

The hosts of heaven responded with an "Amen" that resounded across the earth.

Ben spoke directly into the camera. "My friends, I was standing there watching when these great things happened nearly a thousand years ago and will always carry their memory in my heart. I saw the whole of creation bend in praise and adoration before the victory of our God. Periodically it is important to stop and remember the meaning of the words of the King of Babylon. We owe all that we have and all that we are to our great and glorious God."

The scene changed and Moses appeared, holding the tablets with the Ten Commandments burned in the granite. His long beard and hair were brilliant white and his eyes sparkled with an unearthly light. "Lord, you have been our dwelling place in all generations." Moses' voice was remarkably quiet in contrast to his overwhelming appearance of authority. He quoted part of the ninetieth Psalm with calm gentleness. "Before the mountains were brought forth, or ever You had formed the earth and the world, even from everlasting to everlasting, You are God. For a thousand years in Your sight are like yesterday when it is past, and like a watch in the night. Let the beauty of the Lord our God be upon us, and establish the work of our hands for us; Yes, establish the work of our hands."

As the picture faded, Ben spoke. "I have a confession to make to the world. Unfortunately, I've taken this heritage for granted. I've let the immediacy of these words of instruction and exhortation slip from my mind. The busyness of simply living from one day to the next tends to blur what is truly important. Tonight I want to again say thank you to our great God and to His Messiah. Yeshua, I recommit my life to you." Ben bowed his head.

"Perhaps, each of us needs to make the same confession," Jimmy continued. "Just as the world was cleansed of all sin by the powerful intervention of Yeshua, we also need times of cleansing and healing. Many of us have slipped back into old patterns of indifference and sin. We have forgotten that our lives are not our own but were bought with a price. If it were not for Yeshua bearing the pain and suffering of death on a cross, none of us would have any hope."

Ben raised his head, opened his eyes, and extended his hand. "The Word has already been written on our hearts. Now we need to release what the Holy Spirit has previously placed in our spirits. Perhaps this is a moment of decision in your life. Have you slipped into self-destructive patterns? Has the closeness of your spiritual connectedness diminished? Today you can climb out of that unproductive rut and start down a new road. Right now, wherever you are, is your appointment with destiny. A number is now flashing at the bottom of your screen. People in your area are standing by to help. If you would like counsel about the guilt you are feeling, or help in finding spiritual direction, don't hesitate to call. Let us pray together." Ben bowed his head again.

"We recommit ourselves to You," Jimmy led the prayer. "We affirm that you are our God and we love You. Once again we yield our lives into your keeping."

Across the world multitudes of people were glued to the scenes of the past. Some were weeping. Others were kneeling before the hologram images filling their living rooms. Young children stared in amazement as the incredible scene of angels filling the sky with light ended the program.

Deborah Murphy turned to the groups of friends gathered in her living room. "Wasn't that awesome? I was deeply moved." People nodded silently. "I hope Isaiah was able to watch . . . wherever he is right now."

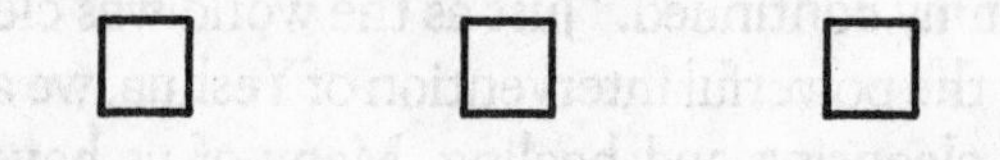

The Addis Ababa hotel was small and obscure—a good place to hide. Isaiah flipped off the TV set in his dingy room and turned to Hosni Gossos. "Can there be any doubt in your mind who is in control of this world?"

The little black man stared at the floor. "What can I say? My eyes do not deceive me."

"Hosni," Isaiah spoke softly, "you've been tricked into believing nonsense about Yeshua. Ali and his pack of quislings have manipulated you into a difficult position.

But tonight you can change your mind and start over. Whose side do you want to be on? God or man?"

Gossos buried his face in his hands and wept.

At Hebrew University Rivka and her friends gaped at their television sets. With a slight turn of the head they could see the area of the Mount of Olives. "The two men are right," she said quietly. "We've forgotten how important the Feast of Trumpets *really* is. We've taken too much for granted. I'll confess that my attitude has been flippant. I am going to repent right now." Rivka lowered her head and closed her eyes. Her friends did the same.

Dr. Zvilli Zemah watched in his study office in the upper floor of the large library. He pulled at the ends of his white hair and pursed his lips. "Why couldn't they have been more scholarly?" He crossed his arms over his chair and leaned back against the wall. "We don't need all that emotionalism. A good solid erudite presentation would have made more sense."

Miles away in New Babylon, Rajah Abu Sita grabbed a paperweight from his desk and hurled it across the room. The highly polished piece of jade smashed into the wall, leaving a jagged dent. "How dare those idiots demean Nebuchadnezzar, trying to make him look like a fool!" He screamed at the top of his lungs. "This is a plot to make the people of Babylon appear to be subservient, mindless fools." He pounded on his desk.

The hologram line kept buzzing. Finally the Assyrian king pushed the On switch. "Yes!" he yelled into the microphone. "How dare you put a phone call through right now."

"Sorry," the aide grovelled, "but you said always to respond when the leader of Egypt calls."

"All right," Rajah growled. Immediately the image of

Ziad Atrash materialized before him. "Did you see the little sideshow from Jerusalem?" Rajah began at once.

The veins in Atrash's bull like neck were extended, his eyes intense. "No question this is a setback for us. Who were those two old idiots babbling down memory lane?"

"I never heard of them! Local Jerusalem relics of some order or other. What are we going to do?"

"Obviously someone is trying to create new international heroes by flashing their prune faces across the world." Atrash spoke in quick staccato thrusts. "Presenting themselves as eye witnesses gives that old TV footage credibility. They've got to be stopped."

"What do you suggest, Ziad?"

"Two things. We must begin an immediate counterattack to discredit their message. Each point they made has to be refuted. Perhaps we can even use their method of digging through the archives as evidence of fraud." Atrash doubled his fist and shook it at Rajah. "Second, those two old creeps must go. I suggest assassination."

CHAPTER 9

Three days had passed since the worldwide television extravaganza. The secretaries in the offices of Gentile-Jewish Relationships, Internal Problems, and Relocation Assistance were working at a feverish pace to process the responses. Wendy Kohn, Ben Feinberg's personal secretary, had just finished piling up the printouts of E-Mail and was carrying the load down the hall. With her foot she pushed open the door marked Ben Feinberg, Chairman.

"Wow, boss! The whole world is writing you."

Ben looked up from reading the previous stack of communiques. "I am totally amazed. People in Africa and Australia are saying the same things. We truly did some good."

The secretary placed the E-Mail on the corner of the large olive-wood desk. "We just got a report on Bible sales. The publishers are going crazy trying to print more Bibles. No one's sold many copies for centuries. Now the shelves are empty. In addition, copies of the Bible on computer disk are selling faster than they can be produced. We should have bought stock in one of those companies."

Ben laughed. "Wendy, I didn't even believe anyone would listen more than five minutes. That's the level of foresight I had."

"You've obviously become the man of the hour." The secretary beamed. "I'm really proud of you."

Another woman burst through the door. "We're getting requests from several nations for you to speak to their national parliaments and congress," Esther Netanyahu said. "I don't know how to schedule your time.

"You and Jimmy Harrison have become the only ones around who seem to know what's happening," Mrs. Netanyahu continued. "You know . . . we haven't received any guidance from Yeshua in months. The weight has fallen on your shoulders, Ben."

"Don't look at me. I sure don't understand what is going on." Ben shook his head. "Frankly, I'd like to go up to the Galilee for a little fishing."

"Not this week!" Wendy laughed. "You haven't even scratched the surface of what is piling up on us."

"I have no choice but to organize the staff to respond," Ben concluded. "We will have to make some executive decisions on how to divide up labor to keep the mail and computer responses from becoming a major logjam."

"As you asked earlier this morning, I have contacted Jimmy Harrison," Wendy Kohn added. "He should be here anytime. He's had a similar avalanche of response at his place."

"And Cindy is still coordinating the work of the spiritual counselors," Ben added. "I know her hands are full."

"Keep up the good work, boss." Wendy started back to her office. "We will return with a shovel and another stack of mail shortly."

For the next thirty minutes Ben spoke rapidly into his auto-dictation machine, which instantly turned dictation into letters that were proofread and corrected for perfect grammar and syntax. A built-in computer notepad at his right allowed Ben to make organizational notes for his staff. As he scrawled his thoughts on the plastic sheet, another computer turned his illegible writing into typed directions for the staff.

"Ben!" a voice echoed down the hall.

Startled, Ben jumped in his chair and looked up. Jimmy burst through the door, waving a pamphlet in his hands. "Look what's all over the streets in California and most of Europe." He slapped the small brochure on Ben's desk. "Just got this faxed to me thirty minutes ago."

Banner headlines proclaimed, "The Fraud Unmasked." The printing quality was high. Ben opened the first page and read aloud: "Once again through the use of trick photography and the manipulation of facts, the government of Yeshua is practicing mind control on the masses." Ben stopped and put on reading glasses. "I must be misreading," he mumbled.

Silently Ben read further, "The recent so-called Celebration of the Past filled your television screen with more of the lies the central government has used for centuries to imprison the minds of the nations. Advanced technology allows the Jerusalem government to mass-produce these fabrications of history. Harrison and Feinberg are not eye witnesses as much as dupes of Yeshua and his Jewish conspiracy." He stopped and laid the pamphlet down.

Jimmy nodded his head. "This material just surfaced all over the world. No one knows the exact source, but tons of this trash seem to have come through the telaports. Flip to the last pages and look at how this little epistle concludes."

Ben slowly thumbed through the leaflet and started at the top of the final section. "The greater truth is to be found in polytheism, the oldest religious system in the history of humanity. A relatively recent idea, monotheism is an impostor pushing the other gods aside by insisting on the supremacy of Yeshua. Do not be misled. A greater god waits to lead us on to a better day of more freedom. Put your trust in the Restored World Order." Ben's mouth dropped.

"Cleans out your sinuses, doesn't it?" Jimmy sat down across the desk. "Sort of like a whiff of ammonia."

Ben shook his head and read on. "Spirit guides will lead you to the greater way. Be prepared for the unveiling of the greatest of gods who is even now returning to his proper throne of power."

"The timing is no accident," Jimmy added. "This material is an obvious response to our television broadcast. We've struck a bigger nerve than we knew."

"This garbage makes absolutely no sense to me." Ben shook his head. "I thought we were battling the sin and indifference of disobedient people. I've assumed from the beginning that what happened to us in Los Angeles was nothing but a radical display of rebelliousness. But this—"

"Remember when we identified a three-pronged attack on world stability?" Jimmy asked. "You said there was only one more thing left to be discredited."

Ben shook his head.

"Faith in Yeshua," Jimmy concluded. "Now we are seeing a clear-cut assault on religion itself."

"But this is lunacy," Ben argued.

"Not to whoever put it out," Jimmy countered. "Defiance is one thing. Apostasy is another. We've got a much larger enemy than we thought."

Ben took a deep breath. "The world is clamoring at our doorstep for guidance, and I don't even know where my head is. Let's go to my house and sit down with Cindy. The three of us need to do some deep thinking and praying."

The two men hurried through the front office. "Ben—" Wendy Kohn called after him but he waved her away.

"Be back shortly," Ben called over his shoulder. "Don't

slow down or they will descend on us like flies," he whispered to Jimmy. "Once we get in the elevator we can get away."

The door closed and the elevator shot toward the bottom of the building. Just as they reached the bottom Ben turned to Jimmy. "I think we ought to . . ." The elevator made an unusually bumpy landing and hesitated a moment before anything happened. Just as the door began to open slightly, an overpowering blast exploded somewhere out in front of the Internal Affairs Building. Glass and debris blew through the cracked door. Smoke and dust filled the elevator shaft. Sounds of timbers splitting and walls collapsing thundered into the small compartment. Ben smashed into Jimmy and the two tumbled to the floor.

For a long time neither man moved. Finally, as the dust settled and silence filled the elevator, Ben pushed away from his friend and sat up. "What . . . happened?"

Jimmy rolled over and reached up for the rail. "I . . . don't . . . know." He slowly got to his feet. "Where am I?"

Ben pushed against the edge of the doors, and they slowly opened. The lobby was gone. Through the smoke he could see only one large support column standing. "We've got to get out of here." He grabbed Jimmy by the coat. "This place could collapse." Ben pulled his friend over the rubble and out onto the street.

"Look!" Jimmy pointed upward. "The face of the building has been destroyed." He looked around. A few feet away the charred shell of some sort of vehicle was still smoking. "There's been an explosion!"

People began pouring out of the exit doors and the street-level windows. Most seemed all right but a few were limping. Much of the face of the building was black; small fires ignited in a few of the windows.

"If that door had been completely open," Ben stammered, "we'd have been hit by the full force of the blast. Our lives were spared."

"Nothing like this has occurred in this city during the whole New Era, Ben. Could this have been aimed at us?"

Ben turned slowly and stared at his friend. "Us?"

Both men looked at the smoking building again. Crowds of people were gathering and emergency vehicles were pulling in. Wendy Kohn appeared out of a side exit with Esther Netanyahu. Both women looked shaken but were not hurt.

Ben waved. "We're all right," he shouted above the noise of the crowd. "Don't worry."

Esther waved back.

By the time the two men arrived at Ben's house, Cindy had already heard the news report and was very upset. "We go to Los Angeles and there's trouble." She threw her hands into the air. "We come home and there's a bomb. What's next?"

"That's exactly what we've got to figure out," Ben answered. "We need more insight than we have."

"And the Immortals can't be found anywhere," Jimmy added. "I've tried everything I know. King David's office is shut down and the Apostle Paul's people won't even return my calls. I even put in another contact to Los Angeles. My parents, Ruth, Dr. Woodbridge . . . they've all checked out."

"I don't know where to turn." Ben slumped down in his chair.

"I'd suggest both of you go through the vacuum area to get the dust off your clothes and hair," Cindy said. "If it works to get the sand off after a trip to the ocean, it'll help get you so you don't look like you've just come out of World War IV."

The two men shuffled into the small room between the garage and the house. The walls were covered with small holes for suction machines, which completely drew all the dust and dirt from Jimmy and Ben. Once they'd gotten themselves together, they returned to the living room.

"I've been thinking," Cindy said. "You remember our old friend, Sam Eisenberg?"

"Sam?" Jimmy said. "Sure. Sam and Angie were Christian missionaries to Israel back before the Tribulation. They figured out the meaning of Bozrah and Petra even before we did. They knew that's where Jewish believers could safely hide during the Great Tribulation until Yeshua came to deliver them himself."

"Did you know that the Eisenbergs still live in Petra?" Cindy said.

"Really?" Jimmy looked amazed. "I didn't realize anyone was still there."

"Sam truly loved the Scriptures," Cindy said. "All these years they've lived a quiet life in those rugged surroundings. I understand Sam has continued to study the Scriptures to such an extent he is a walking-talking Bible. Maybe we ought to take a little trip down to Petra and let Sam help us."

Ben nodded his head thoughtfully. "We need to get some distance from everything that's happened. The dust *truly* needs to settle."

□ □ □

Jimmy's shuttlecraft shot across the ruggedly beautiful terrain of the eastern slope of the Dead Sea rift. Antigravity capacity allowed the four-person shuttle to both take off and land in a very limited space. Shaped like a slick car, the shuttle's aerodynamic body curved to a pointed nose for maximum flying efficiency. The top had a bubble dome allowing a complete view of the landscape. The highly polished black surface was sleek and glistened in the bright sunlight. Without wings, the shuttle could make abrupt turns and extraordinary maneuvers.

Deep gorges cut across the gray-yellow windswept sandy crags on which nothing could ever grow. Far beneath sea level, the blistering summer temperatures sucked the life out of all but the most primitive plant forms. The shuttle's guidance system swung Jimmy and the Feinbergs over the top of lofty peaks and onto friendlier hillsides around Aaron's shrine on Jabal Haroun.

"Moses buried Aaron there." Jimmy pointed to the white shrine resting like a pearl on top of the brown-and-black pile of desert rocks. "After Moses and Aaron defeated the residents of Petra, nearly 4,500 years ago, Aaron knew his death was at hand. He asked to be buried where his she-camel rested. By legend, the mountains shook so severely when Aaron rode by, the camel couldn't stop until she reached the very top of the peak where Aaron died."

"A million stories are hidden in the cracks of the rocks around this ancient place," Ben added. "For centuries Ad-Deir, the monastery where the Eisenbergs live, was used for everything from pagan funerals to a shelter for the early Christians."

"Even the Apostle Paul was rumored to have lived here during the three hidden years after his conversion," Jimmy noted.

The shuttle sailed down above the royal tombs carved into the foot of the al-Khubtha Mountain. The outline of the ancient vaults and columns whizzed past.

Jimmy pointed out the window. "There's the Urn Tomb." The largest and most imposing of the structures carved out of sheer rock stretched up the side of the red-and-pink rock-striated cliffs. Bedouins were still herding their goats along the edges of the valley.

The craft lifted up and then swooped over the monastery, the most prodigious of all the rock facades. The majestic columns with the ornate circular and square domes still left viewers in awe. Jimmy took control and guided the shuttle up Colonnaded Street, the main thoroughfare of ancient Petra.

"I wonder if anything is left of the structures we built during the Tribulation," Jimmy said as he peered out the window.

"Surely my father's field hospital disappeared long ago," Ben answered.

"Look!" Jimmy pointed along the valley. "There are some of the foundations of the buildings."

"Amazing." Ben shielded his eyes from the brilliant sunlight. "That's where . . . where Ruth . . .," he stopped.

"Where Ruth died," Jimmy finished the sentence.

The craft swung back around and settled gently in front of the massive monastery, which looked five times larger from the ground. Two elderly people came running out of the gigantic entrance of the sandstone-colored edifice.

"Ben, Cindy!" Sam waved as he ran, his robes of the desert bellowing out at his side. "Jimmy, welcome back to Petra." Sam was still tall and looked strong. Small blue-eyed Angie followed him, dressed in a similar dark-brown affakyn.

"You really live inside?" Jimmy asked.

"Can't beat the old place for climate control." Sam pointed upward. "Been operating since before the first century B.C. and it's still going strong. Come on in and let's get something to drink."

With the passing centuries new rooms and corridors had been carved into the solid rock, providing a dwelling of extraordinary dimensions. Even with the electronic devices and lighting provided by the technology of the tenth century N.E., the Eisenbergs' home had the spartan feel of an ancient sanctuary.

One room in the center was carpeted with wooden

paneling on the rock walls. The cave was transformed into a cozy den with a large hologram television built into the farthest wall.

"Why have you stayed here?" Ben asked as the group settled into the den.

Angie smiled. "We like the clean primitive feel of desert life. Sometimes the shadows of the mountains even seem to be filled with the sounds of the caravans and armies that marched through this place centuries ago."

"We feel closer to Yahweh, our heavenly Father," Sam added. "After all, Moses first met the Creator out in the desert, not so very far from here. In every sunrise and sunset, the majesty of God is tangible in these mountains."

Ben studied Sam's face and demeanor. Wearing the robes of the bedouins made Sam look like the abbot of a medieval monastery. Wisdom and insight were etched in his wrinkled face. "We understand you spend countless hours studying the Word and praying," Ben said.

"I have soaked up the Scriptures like a desert Arab's skin absorbs the sun." Sam smiled. "Most of the books of the Bible are now completely committed to memory."

"Then let me get right to the point," Ben bore down. "Something extraordinary, unusual, unexplainable is happening to our world and . . ."

Sam held up his hand for silence. "Unusual, yes. Unexplainable, no."

"What?" Ben's eyes widened.

"We have been expecting the confusion we now see on television," Angie explained. "Sam actually predicted these upheavals years ago."

"But how?" Jimmy pressed.

"Through prophecy," Sam continued. "The problem is explained in the Bible."

"Wait," Jimmy protested, "I just got through reading the entire Bible and I—"

Sam broke in. "The treasures of the Word are not unlike gold buried in the ground. You can't discover God's prize gifts by rushing on to holy ground like children picking up seashells on the beach."

Jimmy grimaced and said nothing.

"We saw your television special," Angie continued. "You were most impressive but we sensed your call to repentance was part of the final conflict."

"Final conflict?" Cindy sat up. "What are you saying?"

"You were right again," Angie said to Sam. "They have come as part of the writing of the last chapter."

"For the end of all things," Sam continued, "we must go to the last book of Scripture." He tapped in a code on the control panel built into the end table next to his chair. The television instantly became a giant computer screen. "I want to point out something from the Book of Revelation."

The twentieth chapter filled the wall. Sam scrolled through the pages until he found the exact verses he was seeking. "Read with me." He aimed a laser pointer at the lines, tracing the words until he came to the key sentence. "Do you see what is happening?" he asked.

Ben reached for Cindy's hand. Jimmy read with his mouth open. No one spoke as they absorbed the meaning of what they were seeing.

"Now you understand just how serious matters are?" Angie asked.

PART TWO

... and he cast him into the bottomless pit, and shut him up, and set a seal on him, so that he should deceive the nations no more till the thousand years were finished. But after these things he must be released for a little while.

Revelation 20:3

CHAPTER 10

June 19, 999 N.E. (New Era)

The coalition of mutinous national leaders gathered in a long flat building located between the Sphinx and the great pyramid of Cheops. Soldiers were stationed around the alabaster-covered desert pavilion. The pyramid loomed above the chalk-white building that glistened in the relentless June sun. A special banner over the entry proclaimed, "Welcome to the Conference on World Order." Delegates gathered in the massive lobby.

Fong slipped next to Alexi Chardoff and spoke quietly, "Did you know anything about the bombing in Jerusalem?" Fong wore the simple blue jacket of the ancient Chinese.

"Created quite a stir, didn't it?" the Russian grinned. "The people of Jerusalem thought they were above such little problems. Worldwide consternation only served to further undermine confidence in Yeshua."

"But did you have any part in the matter?" Fong pressed.

Alexi widened his eyes in mock consternation. "Me? I was at home in the Kremlin sleeping in my bed."

"What happened?" Fong sounded impatient.

"The high quality nitrates you shipped us have tremendous fire power," Alexi answered. "Rather easy to plant since no one has paid any attention to security for centuries."

"How did you do it?" Fong persisted.

"One of our people slipped a detonation device the size of a pinhead into the pocket of one of those meddlesome old jerks while walking into the building. The device was set to trigger the bomb when he came back out."

"Clever," Fong observed. "Where were the explosives?"

"In a crate delivered in front of the building. We thought we might be able to hit the man coming out and also get the other old geezer inside the building. Much to our surprise, both men came down together. Would have killed both of them if the elevator door hadn't jammed." Chardoff shook his head. "Strange."

"Are any world leaders bragging about this little caper?"

Alexi shook his head. "Atrash won't acknowledge any responsibility, but his men brought the crate in from Egypt. At least we learned we have the capacity to make successful explosive devices."

The two men strolled into the conference room. "We must not spend much time together," Fong spoke under his breath. "No one must be given a hint of our coalition."

Alexi brushed his greasy hair out of his eyes and nodded.

The men walked into the meeting and moved to different sides of the room just as Ziad Atrash called the meeting to order.

"Welcome friends and world leaders," the Egyptian bull began. Instead of the usual jersey pullover suit, Atrash wore a military general's uniform, reminiscent of the twentieth century. Although no war had been fought for a thousand years, rows of medals were pinned over his chest. "Welcome to the land of mystery." He stood behind a large podium. Behind him were giant posters and pictures of the ancient tombs of the pharaohs. "Egypt has been about the business of world conquest for incalculable centuries. We have listened to the gods from the other world and have been guided by their intervention even before the Jewish race existed. That old beggar father Abraham even came here seeking the scraps under our table." Atrash paused, smirked, and pointed at a large mahogany table in front of him. "Our only mistake was feeding the Jews so well that they wanted loose from the bonds of slavery."

The group laughed and applauded. "Now's your chance to get what they owe you back," Ali of Ethiopia barked.

"We no longer feel any need to meet in secret," Atrash continued. "The first stage of armament production has been achieved. If the Immortals show up, we'll blast them back to where they come from."

The Arabs stomped their feet and clapped vigorously. Atrash snapped his fingers and a group of armed soldiers marched quickly into the room, laid their rifles and pistols out on display tables in front of Atrash, and marched out again.

"These weapons are prototypes of guns being tested in the desert even as I speak. Age has not reduced their effectiveness." He paused, searching for the right words. "We . . . uh . . . also know . . . we have perfected the capacity to explode bombs." The Egyptian president snapped his fingers again and another group of soldiers hurried in front of the dignitaries. "I want you to see our martial arts instructors at work. We can thank Chairman Fong for providing additional Kung-Fu experts. Demonstrate," he ordered the soldiers.

The men immediately paired off into a fast brutal demonstration of attack and counterattack maneuvers. Fists, arms, and feet flew through the air like missiles. The fierce fighting continued until one of each pair lay motionless on the floor.

"You can imagine how effective the assault forces will

be against unprepared citizens," Atrash continued. "Following our conference, the instructors are prepared to return with you to your countries to begin immediate training of your young men. In addition, the weapons shipments are already sailing toward each of your countries."

The group again clapped enthusiastically.

Rajah Abu Sita followed the Egyptian at the podium. "Our propaganda response to the international television fiasco worked. We acted at once to counter the unexpected success of those two old frogs. Consequently, we moved without consultation with each of you and spread pamphlets all over the world. Timing was of the essence."

Khalil Hussein, the king of Jordan, stood up. "Unfortunately, the results of the television program were quite dramatic in my country. Many, many people listened. The government monitored the calls to the special counselors and discovered an alarming number of people responded." He sat down slowly.

Ali of Ethiopia nodded. "The same consequences occurred in our country. Many indifferent and lethargic citizens now ask for Bibles."

"We understand," Rajah broke in. "Anticipating this possibility we have a special presentation for you. El Khader," he called out, "please respond."

A screen descended from the ceiling as the white-haired old Syrian secretary of state hurried forward. "Please observe." El Khader's voice cracked. He clicked a hand-held tuner and a picture of satellites circling the earth appeared. "We are now in position to broadcast much more than a thirty-minute TV walk down memory lane." A picture of one of the satellites came closer on the screen. "Through a new technological breakthrough, we can now pirate time on every satellite circling the globe. We will beam programs on the new religious perspective periodically throughout the day. We can preempt any program. Let them top this achievement!"

Khalil Hussein responded, "Excellent!"

"The breakthrough was achieved through an amazing new approach to research." El Khader clicked the tuner and a picture of a laboratory appeared. Scientists blindfolded and arms folded over their chests sat in front of tables and computers. "By applying the meditation techniques of ancient Babylon, we have been able to make unparalleled discoveries. Transcendental meditation is leading us far beyond anything achieved by experiments alone. We now call this method 'applied religion.'"

"Just a minute," Alexi Chardoff interrupted. "You don't have to sell us more of this polytheistic propaganda. Save it for the masses."

"With all due respect," the secretary of state answered, "I can sincerely tell you that spirit guides brought us to a new level of sight."

Rajah stood up again. "I can assure you El Khader is merely stating the facts. We will offer demonstrations and instruction in these techniques later this evening. May I invite you to participate, Mr. Prime Minister?"

Chardoff grumbled, his response muffled.

Rajah Abu Sita continued. "We will change the minds of the world's people by encouraging unbridled freedom and rampant individualism. I have asked an expert on the subject of social change to join us. An old childhood friend has become a significant leader at Hebrew University. Please welcome Dr. Zvilli Zemah."

As the group applauded the gray-haired teacher/student from Jerusalem walked forward. "Sociology and psychology have been my field of study for many years," Zvilli began. "I can tell you a basic fact about all human beings. No one likes to hear the word *no*. Human beings want no restraints. We are the last of the truly untamed animals." The instructor stopped and looked around the room. "Don't you hate obeying a monarch?"

The delegates looked at each other and nodded.

"We are making a religion out of personal freedom," Zvilli continued. "We will preach human rights without responsibilities." The pitch in his voice raised and he sounded shrill. "All restraint is the fault of Yeshua and the central government." Zemah waved his arms and pounded the podium. "Sexual license must be encouraged! We will brand all laws as manipulative tools of the religious oppressors. And I can promise you," he shouted, "the people will say yes!" His voice abruptly dropped to almost a whisper. "Because in their heart of hearts, they want to believe every word is true."

Silence fell over the room.

Zemah continued, "Polytheism will be explained in so many different and creative ways, that world citizenry will embrace the idea of many gods as the only intelligent alternative. We will give people a religious rationale for what they already *want* to do."

"Thank you, Dr. Zemah." Abu Sita patted his friend on the back. "We grew up together in a small town in Syria." The king laughed. "Zvilli was known as our village renegade." They shook hands again. "The cleverest part of our plan is that Zvilli will be coordinating this work from inside Jerusalem. He is already strategically placed to feed us information on how our plan is affecting the central government."

"How soon will the television assault begin?" Ali of Ethiopia asked.

"The first programs will be ready within a week," Rajah Abu Sita answered. "Once they start, other formats will follow quickly. We are ready to start the onslaught immediately."

Khalil Hussein rose to his feet. "I am impressed by these

reports. Let us give a vote of confidence." He began to clap and the rest joined in.

"Thank you." Ziad Atrash took center stage once more. "Now we take a break to allow informal discussion among ourselves. In one hour, we will convene behind closed doors to plan military procedure. Please accept our hospitality." He clapped his hands and dancing girls whirled into the room. Music blared in from musicians strolling and playing behind the dancers. Behind them servers brought in lavish trays of fruit, cakes, and sweets.

Chardoff sidled up to Fong. "Can you hear me over the noise?"

"Not well."

"Perhaps they want us to talk . . . but not too much," Chardoff answered and walked away.

At the other end of the hall, Claudine Toulouse nodded to Maria Marchino and the two women slipped out the front door. The hot desert winds swished Claudine's long hair around her neck. "They've had famine in this region since Feast of Tabernacles," she said. "It's always unbearably hot now, especially in Egypt and Iraq."

Maria shrugged. "You get hot air outside; you get hot air inside."

Claudine laughed. "Are we both reading these guys the same way?"

"I don't hear anyone asking our opinions." The Italian leader raised her eyebrows. "I have the distinct impression we're the third stringers in this operation."

"Exactly." The French leader shook her fist. "We are being taken along for the ride by the sheik and his buddies.

"I'm sure Atrash is clever enough to know the coalition can't pull off his coup without us, but I doubt if he finds much pleasure in our presence. We will be used as long as we serve that arrogant bull's purposes."

"My exact conclusions. I don't trust any of them. We

must hang together," Maria answered firmly, "lest someone try to hang us separately. Let us agree to watch each other's back."

"You are a woman after my own heart." Claudine Toulouse extended her hand.

Maria Marchino squeezed the woman's hand. "Agreed. We have our own pact."

"We will give them no hint of our understanding, but when the right time comes we will be in a position to act."

When the leaders reconvened, all other personnel were excluded. The room was restructured with a conference table in the center. Notepads and files were placed in front of each dignitary.

Atrash called the group to order by rapping the table with his knuckles. "I now pass the chairmanship to our esteemed brother from Russia, Alexi Chardoff."

The Russian nodded politely. "Our next item on the agenda is the development of a master plan of attack. We must coordinate movement of troops, set military targets, develop precise actions for an assault on Jerusalem, and agree on a definite timetable. Are we ready to proceed?"

Each leader nodded.

"We have every reason to believe that within one month every nation surrounding Israel will have significant strike capacity," Chardoff reported. "The People's Army of China must travel the furthest. If the Chinese are ready for large-scale troop movements to march south at this same time, we would quickly be poised to sweep across Israel with little opposition."

Fong smiled. "We have a plan to train our army while it marches. Since there has not been any form of military preparation for centuries, even our young men will not suspect what is occurring. The movement will be clandestine and without fanfare. Troops will not know what they are about until we are quite close to the jumping-off point. This approach will minimalize security leaks."

"Excellent!" Chardoff beamed. "Each of these factors suggests we will be ready for the final stage to begin during the month of Tammuz. Even though mid-summer is quite hot, there are strategic reasons to believe this an appropriate time to strike."

"The gods suggest so," Rajah interrupted. "We consulted Marduk and received this message." He read from a note in his file: "As the sun comes down, the flames shall go up. Use the heat of the summer to dissolve your adversary's courage like the furnace melts lead. Strike in the final days of summertime and the gods will be with you."

Fong looked straight into Chardoff's eyes. His stonefaced, emotionless glance was sufficient comment.

"Well," Chardoff pursed his fat lips, "we seem to agree either the month of Tammuz or Av is the right time for the assault."

"Jews observe a festival on Tammuz 17," Hussein commented. "This would be a clever time to start the first movement of troops as they would certainly be distracted."

"Exactly," Abu Sita agreed. "I calculate it will take about three weeks before the final assault."

"The date of Av 9 would fit," Atrash blurted out. "I don't know why, but I suddenly feel strongly that this could be a very productive time to go for the throat!"

The discussion continued for another fifteen minutes, wrapping up the final loose ends of the battle plan. Ziad Atrash finally called for adjournment and the group dispersed.

Khalil Hussein, a tall man with piercing black eyes and long black hair, was the last to gather his papers together and stuff them in a briefcase. The black goatee added an air of mystery to the king of Jordan. He was by far the youngest leader in the group. Although Khalil traced his ancestry back to the twentieth century, little was known about him because he seldom expressed his personal opinions. His reservations only added to the air of intrigue that hovered around his head like a desert kaffiyeh. Khalil snapped the case shut and hurried after the rest of the group.

Just as the king turned the corner, Claudine Toulouse scurried back into the room. The French head of state rushed right into Hussein's arms, knocking his briefcase to the floor. For an awkward moment, the king found himself with his arms around the woman.

"Oh excuse me!" Hussein tried to take a quick step backward, but Claudine was still coming forward.

"My, my." Claudine stopped inches from his face. "We all seem to be in a hurry." She did not step back.

"I hope I didn't hurt you." The king suddenly had a hold on Claudine's arm.

"Quite to the contrary." The woman breathed heavily. "The pleasure is all mine." Claudine looked straight into his eyes and smiled demurely. "We need to take more time to *really* get acquainted."

Khalil searched her eyes, unsure of what he was seeing.

Claudine raised one eyebrow and reached up gently, running her finger across the king's chest. "I think you would like to get to know me as a woman." She touched his lips and slipped on past.

Khalil didn't move for several seconds and then tripped over his briefcase before bending down to pick it up.

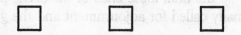

Deborah Murphy paced nervously in the Los Angeles telaport terminal, waiting for Isaiah to arrive. She kept glancing at the fax he sent the night before. "Be there at 8:30 A.M. Meet you at Gate 58. Love Isaiah."

The arrival notification lights began blinking. In several

minutes the gate silently opened and passengers began deplaning. Several dozen people walked past before Isaiah hurried through the door.

"Great to see you, dear." He bent down and kissed his wife. He put his mouth close to her ear. "Start walking with me and don't say much." Isaiah took her hand and pulled her along.

"Had a great time in New York City," Isaiah spoke very loudly. Multitudes of people walked past the couple. "Really enjoyed hitting the museums." He picked up the pace.

Deborah stared up at the tall black man. "I'm not quite sure I understand what's happening."

"You'd love the exhibition of the new three-dimensional paintings done with computers," Isaiah chattered and pointed straight ahead to where the corridors split in two different directions. "Never seen anything quite so real. The paintings actually have the capacity to exude emotion. As you watch you feel joy, peace, or even anger." He swung his wife around the corner and stopped. Isaiah silently watched the people pass.

"What is going on?" Deborah sounded exasperated. "You disappear for several weeks to who-knows-where and then show up . . ."

Isaiah gently put his hand over her mouth. "Directional microphones could pick us up. Wait until we get in the shuttle." He watched for thirty more seconds and then pulled his wife back into the flow of traffic.

The Murphys silently hurried through the terminal and into the parking lot. Isaiah threw the black duffel bag in the backseat and quickly sped through the parking area.

"I'm going to ask you again," Deborah sounded irritated. "What's going on here?"

"I'm very sure I was followed back from Ethiopia."

"Ethiopia?" Deborah's mouth dropped.

"I've gone virtually around the world since I left." Isaiah

pushed the shuttle into glide and lifted straight up from the end of the parking lot. He punched in his code for home and the automatic pilot immediately turned the shuttle south.

"Dear," Deborah pleaded, "p-l-e-a-s-e let your wife in on this little adventure. The last time I saw you, you were still limping around and should have been in bed recovering."

Isaiah looked thoughtfully out the window into the black night dotted with a million lights. "Remember when I was trying to get a lead on a cure for AIDS?"

"Weeks ago?" Deborah answered sarcastically.

"I was cross-referencing medicines because nothing else seemed to work," Isaiah continued. "I was even checking medical information for Africa. And then the computer slipped into chemical compounds. Remember?"

"Vaguely." Deborah shrugged.

"My computer picked up a very strange bit of information. The graphic printouts indicated unprecedented movement of sulphur, sodium nitrate, mercury, nitric acid, and ammonium nitrates from Ethiopia to Egypt and Russia." Isaiah paused. "Do you understand?'

"Absolutely. Since I know totally nothing about any of this."

"When I indexed these materials through another program, I found similar amounts of the same chemicals were being shipped from China to Russia. Because sudden large shipments of these chemicals was strange, I referenced an analysis program to identify how these materials might be used separately or in conjunction with each other."

Deborah nodded slowly. "Yes, but where in the world are you going with this?"

"To my astonishment, the analysis prioritized the possible uses of the materials. At the top of the list was the production of explosives now illegal and forbidden in every country in the world."

"Isaiah," Deborah said slowly, "this is beginning to sound dangerous."

"I figured I'd have the best chance of being anonymous in Ethiopia. So that's where I went . . . first."

"First?" Deborah's eyes widened. "Where else have you been?"

"Russia."

"Wait a minute. . . . What does any of this have to do with AIDS?"

"I have no idea," Isaiah answered. "That's the strange thing. I don't understand the relationship of where I started and where I ended up. Regardless," he paused, "I've hit something very big."

"Just what have you found?"

"Egypt and Russia have become staging areas for the development of explosives."

"The bombing in Jerusalem . . ."

Isaiah nodded his head. "Exactly."

"And you think you were followed?"

"Possibly."

"They might . . . bomb . . . us?" Deborah gasped.

"Anything is possible." Isaiah switched off the automatic pilot and suddenly swung the craft back to the north. "We're going to fly a diversion pattern and stop by the county building before going home. I might even be bugged and not know it. I'll go in and do a quick electronic scan."

Deborah reached over and squeezed her husband's hand. "I've been so worried about you. You should have told me where you were going."

"I didn't want you to be in any jeopardy, Deborah. I don't know where all the pieces in this puzzle fit, but I'm onto something much larger than I could have imagined."

"We need to get in touch with Jimmy and Ben," Deborah concluded.

"Absolutely."

CHAPTER 11

Jimmy Harrison and the Feinbergs flew straight back from Petra to Ben and Cindy's home. Jimmy followed Ben and Cindy into the central area with the wall-screen television. Ben paused in front of the environmental control system and quickly punched in the numbers for "atmosphere of calm and tranquility." Lights on the control panel blinked several times and immediately the sounds of a gentle stream and winds blowing through a forest filled the house. A warm scent of wet pine needles and mountain breezes swept through the air. The overhead lights dimmed and a gentle blue light diffused throughout the entire house. Little was said until they plopped down around the dining room table.

"I'm overwhelmed," Jimmy confessed. "Whatever I thought Sam might tell us didn't even scratch the surface of what was on his mind!" His eyes nearly disappeared behind his eye folds.

"How could I have been so blind?" Cindy got up. "I'll fix some coffee."

"Dear, with your history of once being blind, that's a bit

of a humorous question," Ben teased. "But I certainly feel exactly the same way."

"Never have we needed the help of the Immortals so much." Jimmy thumped his cane on the floor.

"A day ago I put in calls to both Mayor David's and Saint Paul's offices," Ben added. "I couldn't even get the receptionist on the line. Paul wasn't kidding when he said everything was in our hands."

A red light flashed on the hologram telephone and a pleasant hum filled the air. "Ben, it's your office phone. We better get it." Cindy reached over and hit a button on the phone. A large picture of Wendy Kohn appeared on the TV screen.

"I know you told us not to interrupt you," Wendy explained. "Unfortunately, we are besieged by reporters with stories that you and Jimmy were critically injured. Without the Immortals, people are in a panic. The reporters want to see you alive."

"Us?" Ben rolled his eyes. "We're not celebrities."

"You certainly are now," Wendy shot back. "However, the really big story is happening on the streets and through the satellite broadcasts. You need to tune in this minute."

"What channel?" Jimmy asked.

"Doesn't make any difference," Wendy answered. "There's only one program every station!"

"H-m-m, strange." Ben reached for the clicker. "OK, Wendy, I'm shutting you off to take a look. I'll be back in touch."

Wendy's face faded as the program appeared. A collage of pictures of the ancient world whirled across the screen. The announcer's voice proclaimed, "Ancient mysteries are now being uncovered, revealing the wisdom of the past. In recent centuries we lost touch with the profound truths of our forefathers. Not so long ago, even *we* were considered to be gods."

"What?" Jimmy sat up in his chair. "I can't believe my ears."

A three-dimensional picture of a lion with a man's head leaped from the screen. "The people of antiquity lived without restraint. Complete freedom meant no moral inhibitions. Creativity and spontaneity were not squelched by laws and dogma. Wouldn't you like to recover the joys of primordial life?"

Ben hit the clicker but each channel was the same. "Wendy's right! Every station is controlled."

The announcer appeared on the screen dressed as an Egyptian priest in long, white filmy linens with a jeweled collar of red, yellow, and blue beads. From his waist dangled a gold belt with a center shield of multi-colored stones. "Look again on the colorful dress of the ancients. The time has come for us to recover the many-faceted values of our heritage. Each of these programs is presented to help you broaden your knowledge of the past. Do not be duped by those who want to repress the truth about our true heritage. Strike out *now* for a new and better tomorrow."

The picture faded to the sounds of powerful triumphant music.

Ben hit the clicker and Wendy reappeared. "You said something is also happening on the streets?"

"Yes, sir," the secretary answered. "Thousands of pamphlets are circulating throughout Jerusalem. The message is far more blatant than what was just on television." Wendy held up a pamphlet. "This material is similar to what appeared in Los Angeles but it's a much more pointed attack on Yeshua."

Ben drummed on the table with his fingertips. He shook his head and the white ponytail swung from side to side. "I see," he said slowly. "Our faith is directly under attack."

"There's no other way to describe what is happening,"

Wendy concluded. "We are being bombarded by an alternative religion."

"Just as I expected," Ben concluded. "We'll be back in touch shortly."

"But—," Wendy protested.

Ben clicked the phone off. The aroma of coffee filled the air.

"Let's go back to the television," Jimmy suggested. "I'd like to see if we can get any news reports from around the globe."

"Hey, the stations have returned to normal." Cindy set the tray of cups down. "Try the news channel."

"... No further explanation is now available on how the interruptions occurred," the announcer was saying. "However, worldwide communication is now restored. Authorities are investigating."

The scene changed to a view of Africa. "On other fronts a fast-breaking story reports an outbreak of a rare virus coming out of Africa and apparently breaking out in Los Angeles. The strain has been isolated and is much like the ancient AIDS epidemic, except it is moving faster and is proving to be more dangerous. No one in recent history has any memory of such a threat, and no cure exists. We are monitoring the situation and will report more results in the next hour."

"The story is out." Ben ran his hands nervously through his hair. "Everything I feared is now breaking loose."

The phone rang again. Ben sighed and pushed the button. Wendy's picture reappeared. "I'm sorry to interrupt again but I felt you should be aware of some news that is buzzing through the corridors of this building like a swarm of bees."

"What is it?" Ben sounded distant and professional.

"In addition to what happened in China some weeks ago, just moments ago the nations of Russia, France, Italy,

Egypt, Iran, Jordan, Syria, Iraq, and Ethiopia expelled their overseers and are pulling out of the world alliance of nations. No one has *ever* even intimated such an idea."

"Pulling out?" Ben's voice became almost a whisper.

"They are also calling on other nations to join them in rejecting the authority of Jerusalem," Wendy added. "Our people are very concerned and upset."

"They should be," Ben snapped. "These issues are serious. Thank you, Wendy. You did the right thing in calling me."

Ben stared at Jimmy and shook his head. "I think the real war is about to begin."

Cindy put her arm around Ben. "Don't worry, dear." She ran her hands through his hair and hugged him. "We've been here before and survived the onslaught. We can do it again."

The external security light began blinking. An intense disconcerting hum filled the house. Ben jumped up. "An intruder has gotten past the initial perimeters. That must mean someone has landed a shuttlecraft on the roof and has already gotten to the door."

"We may be under attack." Jimmy pushed back from the table. "We're not even prepared to defend ourselves."

"Hit the security system camera and see who's there," Cindy said.

Ben pressed the monitor button. A vague shape appeared.

"The guy's back is turned, and he's leaning on the door." Ben pressed his thick glasses near the monitor. "We can't see who it is."

"We have no choice but to protect ourselves," Ben answered. "Cindy, you take a mop handle from the closet and I'll get a skillet. Jimmy, use your cane. I don't know if we can do much, but at least we'll be ready for an attack."

Ben stood on one side of the door, watching Jimmy on

the other. "Hit the open button," he instructed Cindy. "As soon as the door slides open, we'll be ready to counter attack. Now!" He raised the skillet.

The door silently slid open. Isaiah Murphy nearly tumbled in. His eyes widened when he looked at his old friends, standing with mop handle, cane, and pan in hand. "You guys cleaning house?"

"Isaiah!" Cindy gasped. "What are you doing here?"

"Right now I can't remember."

Jimmy lowered the cane and shook his head. "Blue blazes, are we ever uptight. Come on in, Isaiah."

"You really know how to make a guy feel at home." Isaiah smiled mischievously.

Ben beckoned for the trio to follow him back to the kitchen table. "Things have gotten a little out of hand," he told Isaiah. "I suppose you know about the bombing."

"Frankly," Isaiah said, "I didn't let you know I was coming because I was concerned about security."

"You?" Ben frowned.

"I knew we had to talk face to face without any possible electronic eavesdropping. I've made some important discoveries that may have everything to do with the bombing."

"Sit down." Ben pointed to the chairs. "Whatever you have to tell us, I bet we can do you one better."

Isaiah stretched his long legs out under the table and began telling his friends about the strange movement of chemicals.

"Many years ago I worked with an Ethiopian named Hosni Gossos. I helped him solve some personal problems and we became close friends. In addition to working for the government, Hosni dabbled in politics. I flew to Addis Ababa to talk with him. Fortunately, Hosni thought I knew much more about the rebellion than I did. By playing it cool, I got him to admit that the Ethiopians were involved in an international intrigue."

Ben shook his head. "Excellent work, Isaiah."

"But I hit a brick wall and couldn't get Hosni to talk to me until the night of your television program. By providence, we had the TV on and saw your production. I was able to bear down on Hosni and he told me the rest of the story. Listen carefully."

Isaiah leaned forward and lowered his voice to nearly a whisper. "Right now a coalition of nations is uniting to attack Israel!" He looked deeply into his friends' eyes. "A war is brewing."

Each of the trio silently nodded.

Isaiah's forehead wrinkled. "You don't seem surprised."

"Keep rolling," Jimmy said.

Isaiah blinked. "Well . . . I . . . uh . . . got Hosni to fly with me to Russia and Egypt. Using his contacts, I was able to access warehouses and supply depots. Tons of sulphur and nitrates are now being shipped into these countries. Hosni introduced me as a colleague and I talked with soldiers in charge of making bombs and bullets. I learned names of conspirators and places where armaments are being manufactured and assembled. I know who the people are behind the bombing."

"Fits with the picture we have," Jimmy concluded. "We didn't know the source of the explosives, but we've got the big picture."

"Do we ever!" Ben shook his head.

Isaiah scratched his head. "Obviously I'm the one in the dark. Now, why don't you fill your old buddy in on *your* secrets?"

Cindy brought in a Bible and laid it on the table. Ben thumbed through the pages in the Book of Revelation. "Jimmy's always been the Bible scholar. I'll let him tell you the whole story." Ben pushed the twentieth chapter of Revelation in front of Isaiah.

"The answer is so obvious," Jimmy began. "I guess our first mistake was taking the Bible for granted and not reading it. If you don't keep up on the content, the message slips from your mind."

Isaiah looked down at the page. "I haven't looked at Revelation in maybe a century or more."

"Fortunately Sam Eisenberg has. We flew to Petra to study the Bible with him. He helped us carefully evaluate the whole chapter. Verses seven through nine tell the story. Read the passage."

Isaiah started reading at verse one: "Then I saw an angel coming down from heaven, having the key to the bottomless pit and a great chain in his hand. He laid hold of the dragon, that serpent of old, who is the Devil and Satan, and bound him for a thousand years; and he cast him into the bottomless pit, and shut him up, and set a seal on him, so that he should deceive the nations no more till the thousand years were finished. But after these things he must be released for a little while." Isaiah stopped. He rubbed his forehead and looked at his friends in bewilderment.

"On God's time clock a thousand years are up," Jimmy said. "We were here when the Evil One was chained, and we are still here when he is loosed."

Isaiah blinked and exhaled deeply.

"All these years we've been living out the promise in verse four," Cindy added. "Listen." Her small voice took on new authority. "And I saw thrones, and they sat on them, and judgement was committed to them. Then I saw the souls of those who had been beheaded for their witness to Jesus and for the word of God, who had not worshiped the beast or his image, and had not received his mark on their foreheads or their hands. And they lived and reigned with Christ for a thousand years. But the rest of the dead did not live again until the thousand years were finished. This is the first resurrection."

"This prophecy was fulfilled after the return of Yeshua when the Immortals came back to bring order to the world," Ben said. "The Immortals have already experienced the first resurrection."

"We *really* understand verse six," Cindy continued reading, "Blessed and holy is he who has part in the first resurrection. Over such the second death has no power, but they shall be priests of God and of Christ, and shall reign with Him a thousand years." Cindy smiled. "There's the good news. In this period King David and Paul, as well as Ruth, Jimmy's son, Jimmy's parents, and many others, governed the nations of the world."

"Certainly," Isaiah answered. "I understand about the Immortals."

"Here's the jackpot." Jimmy pointed to verse seven. "Now when the thousand years have expired, Satan will be released from his prison," Jimmy read slowly, "and will go out to deceive the nations which are in the four corners of the earth, Gog and Magog, to gather them together to battle, whose number is as the sand of the sea. They went up on the breadth of the earth and surrounded the camp of the saints and the beloved city." Jimmy stopped. "Got the picture, Isaiah?"

"So that's the meaning of what I saw in those warehouses in Russia and Egypt!"

"I'm afraid so," Ben said. "You've discovered the launch pad. The war is already on."

"But who would believe us?" Cindy mused. "Everything we've just said will sound crazy to most people."

"Cindy's right," Isaiah said. "We know the meaning of sin in Los Angeles but everyone has forgotten what Evil can do. We don't even have a point of reference."

Ben leaned back in his chair and stared at the blank TV screen. "At least we now see the common thread in the chaos we've uncovered. Satan is the source of illness and is behind the AIDS epidemic. Human lust and sin simply played into his hands."

"Exactly," Cindy agreed. "The rebellion of the nations and the attack on Yeshua are simply another dimension of Satan's plan. He is the author and father of all deceit and destruction."

Isaiah buried his head in his hands and slumped against the table. "What are we going to do?"

Ben looked at Jimmy. "That's the ultimate question!"

□ □ □

Zvilli Zemah was deeply tanned by the relentless June sunlight. Wearing the short-sleeved, casual shirt of the students, Zvilli was looking out of his small office in Hebrew University on Mt. Scopus when someone knocked on the door. "Come in," he called out without turning around.

"Dr. Zemah?" the gentle voice asked.

"Ah, Miss Zachary. I've been expecting you."

"I received your notice in my computer mail this morning." Rivka stood pensively in the doorway. The small woman's jet black hair was pulled back behind her head.

"Please sit down." Dr. Zemah pointed to a chair and leaned against the window. He had the tall, slender build of so many natives of the north. The striking appearance of his white hair against the sun-tanned complexion gave the professor an aura of great wisdom.

"Is there a problem with my work?" Rivka smiled apprehensively. Her large black eyes widened.

"Quite the contrary. You are clearly one of our very best students." Zemah picked up a file from the desk and opened it.

"Oh, good." Rivka settled back in the chair. The afternoon sun highlighted her dark, flawless skin, giving her a subtle glow. "I thought I had done something wrong."

"In fact, your excellent scores caused me to go back in your records to better understand your background. I was surprised to discover your family heritage is of both Jewish and Arab ancestry."

Rivka squirmed. "Well . . . uh . . . I don't exactly advertise the fact. You see, there have been some problems."

"Ah, but I do understand, dear. I would like to share a secret with you if you will keep my confidence."

"Of course." Rivka shrugged.

"I, too, have a similar background. My father was an Arab. In fact, I grew up in an Arab village. Because my mother was Jewish, I am considered to be a Jew. We are both aware that it is much better to present the Jewish side of our heritage here in Jerusalem." Zemah looked back out the window. "We are certainly surrounded by a *very* Jewish world."

"Yes," Rivka said slowly, "but I've never experienced any prejudice toward the Arabs. Actually my problem was with the—"

"You are young," Zemah's voice hardened. "In time you will come to see the problem clearly."

"Problem?" Rivka tilted her head slightly and frowned. "I'm sorry but I don't—"

"Oppression comes in many forms." Zemah cut her off. "My father was mistreated and slighted by my mother's people. Even from my earliest years I have seen the arrogance of the Jews."

Rivka rubbed her hands together nervously. "I guess I've been spared such an experience."

"You are fortunate," Zemah sounded bitter. "But I am glad for your friendship. I thought if you had been caught in the middle of the Isaac and Ishmael tug-of-war I might be of help."

"You are an excellent lecturer and teacher," Rivka said. "All the students admire you. I am flattered that you would take such a personal interest in me."

Zvilli smiled broadly. "Since you are now in my political science class on nationalism, I felt I could help you reflect on how the struggles of the Arab peoples have unfolded through the centuries."

"I would be grateful for any assistance you might offer, Dr. Zemah."

"Let me see if I can help you fully understand *our* problem." The professor walked around his small desk and sat in the chair next to Rivka. "Please, call me Zvilli."

CHAPTER 12

The Feinbergs' shuttlecraft flew swiftly from Jerusalem to Jordan, then swooped low over the wide clearing along the edge of Al-Khubtha Mountain and swept past the Urn Tomb on toward Petra. Isaiah kept his face pressed to the window.

"Sam will think we're nuts," Jimmy quipped. "He doesn't see us for decades and then the next day we're back again."

"I have a hunch Sam assumed we'd return fairly quickly after we digested the facts he gave us," Cindy answered.

Ben guided the craft close to the tops of the rugged rocky peaks and swung around to sail above the colonnaded street running away from Ad-Deir, the monastery. "He wasn't dismayed when I told him we were on our way," Ben added. "Sort of took the call rather casually."

Isaiah pointed out of the window as the imposing intrusions of red, gray, and black granite whizzed by. "Never seen any place quite like this," he muttered. "The valleys and mountains look like the desert and the Grand Canyon rolled into one."

The hot morning sun baked the sandy areas around the

foot of the mountains and sent long shadows across the steep canyons. The towering carved columns of pink granite rose majestically in front of the monastery, glistening in the dazzling sunlight.

"Here we are." Ben brought the shuttle down to the small landing strip in front of the monastery. "Safe and sound." Dust blew as the vehicle came to a halt.

Sam and Angie Eisenberg waved from the huge entranceway. The four friends hurried out of the shuttle and into Ad-Deir, quickly reassembling in the Eisenbergs' living room.

"Couldn't get enough of the old place?" Sam joked. "This pile of rocks does offer an ambiance of security when the rest of the world is falling apart."

"I'm impressed," Isaiah confessed. "And a little speechless. Your house feels like the Rock of Ages."

Angie offered cups of hot tea from a serving tray. "After centuries of peace and tranquility, no one is prepared for what's happened lately. It takes a little while to realize how startling Sam's insights are."

"You really think the Devil is unleashed?" Isaiah asked.

"Afraid so." Sam settled back in his large overstuffed chair. "What is now happening points to a new intrusion of Evil; sin has always created chaos, but those problems were generally ones of broken relationships or serious consequences for the individual. The avalanche of social disasters and the physical illnesses we're now discovering are an intrusion from the outside, an attack on the human race. The new spiritual deception of the masses is the work of that diabolical old deceiver himself."

"Indeed!" Isaiah rubbed his gray hair and shook his head. "Never thought I'd see the problem again."

"People always take God's goodness for granted," Sam added. "Self-centeredness and arrogance seem to be built-in flaws in the human character. Even with Yeshua in our midst, we slipped back into patterns of indifference. Our mind-set is a ready-made invitation for Satan's work."

"But why is the attack happening *now*?" Isaiah asked.

"The Scriptures don't tell us much," Sam continued, "except that a thousand-year period is about up."

"I've been thinking about some clues my father and Ruth gave us when they helped us escape from Los Angeles," Jimmy added. "The Immortals seemed to imply we were facing a test of some sort. Maybe God is taking us through one last time of sifting for the final perfecting of our character."

"Very insightful," Angie added. "What better way to purge the last vestige of self-centeredness from the faithful?"

"Big thought." Isaiah sighed. "Wish I could avoid the sifting."

"Don't we all?" Sam agreed. "Unfortunately, we don't recognize our problems except in retrospect."

"Well, another piece of the puzzle is coming together for me." Cindy sighed. "I can see at least one reason why Yeshua hasn't made any appearances lately. He's withdrawn to leave the leadership responsibility to people like us."

"Looks like you're right," Ben said. "The time has come for us to get busy. Sam, we need your help in putting some of the pieces of the last puzzle together. Isaiah made a frightening discovery that Egypt, Russia, and Ethiopia are manufacturing bombs and bullets in violation of the decree of the central government. We already know China has been belligerent. Just before we left Jerusalem, we also received the news that other governments are joining in open rebellion."

Sam folded his hands across his chest and nodded his head slowly. "The pattern makes sense. Prophecy was clear about the forces joining with the Antichrist a thousand years ago. However, Scripture indicates far more than a few nations will combine in the last rebellion and a final assault on Jerusalem."

"You mean . . . *many*?" Isaiah's eyes widened.

"I'm afraid so," Sam responded.

"But we just started a worldwide revival," Jimmy protested.

"The problem lies with the leaders of the nations," Sam countered. "Heads of state can manipulate citizens against their wishes."

"But why would Yeshua allow evil people to gain control?" Cindy asked.

"I'm not entirely sure." Sam peered off into space. "But God has never limited individual freedom. The ability to love demands the capacity to make bad choices. At one time every world leader could have been the source of great good. I'm sure Yeshua saw significant potential in the leaders of the rebelling nations. Obviously, Satan recognized the same capacity. Remember, Yeshua once chose a man named Judas."

"So, you think the entire world is going to swing behind a group of rebel governments," Cindy said.

Isaiah shivered. "We've got to find a way to warn the nations!"

"But who would listen to us?" Ben threw his hands up in the air. "Look at us? We're minor functionaries in the great scheme of things."

"I'm afraid that's the essence of our dilemma," Sam agreed. "People are likely to think our interpretation of the present state of affairs rather strange. We're likely to come off as a bunch of old kooks."

Ben got up and began pacing slowly. "Why not try an attack on the problem from a different direction? Try thinking about what the other side is likely to do. During the Great Tribulation the Bible gave us all kinds of clues of what to expect. The twenty-one judgments of the Book of Revelation were all listed in sequence. Once we started paying attention to the times and dates, we were in a position to anticipate what was coming next. Sam, can you help us make some intelligent guesses about timetables?"

Angie laughed. "Sam's been sitting around here for days working with his computer on that exact question. He thought no one would ever ask."

"Two dates immediately come to mind." Sam opened his Bible. "From biblical indications and as a result of everything that has happened in the past, I have a premonition that a confederation of nations will begin to move their armies this year around the seventeenth of Tammuz. The date is not far away. Of course, there's one time you can bank on to be the day of the final attack."

Jimmy stared at Ben and Cindy. He slowly turned to Sam. "The ninth of Av?" His voice dropped to a whisper.

Silence fell over the room. Sam slowly nodded his head.

Angie spoke first. "The Devil always had a propensity for that particular day. Just think of all the disasters visited on the Jewish people on Av 9 through the centuries!"

"The first Temple was destroyed on Av 9," Cindy observed.

"And the second one also," Jimmy added.

"Hitler formalized his plans to destroy Jews worldwide on Av 9 too," Ben said. "Satan is using evil rulers now just like he used Hitler and the Antichrist over a thousand years ago."

"Many major events of the Tribulation were connected to Av 9," Isaiah added.

"We could never forget the significance of that date."

"There you have it!" Sam slid forward to the edge of his chair. "I would suggest you get ready for a period of intense struggle beginning on the seventeenth of Tammuz and culminating on Av 9."

"We don't have much time left," Ben concluded. "We must move quickly."

"I think I ought to go back to Los Angeles," Isaiah said. "I can organize our old friends to be ready for the struggle."

"Maybe you should take a side trip and go through Ethiopia," Jimmy suggested. "Talk to your old friend Hosni Gossos and see what else you can find out about their war plans. We need some insight into how they will use weapons."

"H-m-m-m," Isaiah mused. "I might be able to do some first-class spying."

Ben covered his mouth with his hand and slowly rubbed his chin. "I don't know if we can make much of an impact but at least I can get my office staff organized to be ready for the onslaught."

Sam nodded. "Our heavenly Father never expects us to do more than we can. But we are examples that believers can accomplish more than they often dream possible."

"Why don't you come back to Jerusalem with us, Sam?" Cindy said. "You and Angie could help us organize the troops."

Sam shook his head. "Our work is out here where we can keep our minds and spirits clear. I think the heavenly Father wants us to intercede for you. Intercessors energize activists. We're the unseen power behind the scenes. You can count on us to pray continually for you."

"What a reassuring thought!" Ben offered his hand to his old friend. "We'll be calling on your counsel in the days ahead."

"We'll be here at work on our knees," Sam answered.

"Our time in the desert taught us the incredible power of prayer," Cindy added. "The heart of God is particularly attuned to pain. I think the most important place to start preparation for what lies ahead is through intercession.

Before we take one step into this battle, we must be saturated with prayer."

"Cindy's absolutely right," Sam agreed. "Once we've prayed, the heavenly Father has the most amazing ability to slip in the insights and discoveries we need. Prayer is always the right place to begin."

"Then let's get busy," Jimmy answered and slipped from his chair to the floor. The others silently knelt with him.

□ □ □

For the next hour the group prayed fervently for guidance. Finally, Ben opened his eyes and put his thick glasses back on. "I feel prayed up! I think I'm ready to go on."

"Stay close to the Father," Sam added, "and you'll be ready."

"Let's go!" Ben stood up forcefully. "We've got work to do." The group followed him out to the shuttlecraft and the foursome piled inside for the trip back to Jerusalem.

Jimmy waved from the window as Ben guided the craft up from the ground. Sam and Angie waved back as it slowly rose above the monastery and turned back toward Jerusalem.

"I'm extremely glad we came," Isaiah said. "My next step is to get in touch with Hosni Gossos. I must explore that connection to the fullest before I go back to Los Angeles."

"Wendy Kohn and Mrs. Netanyahu will probably think the desert has fried my brain," Ben concluded. "But they are the people I must start with if we're going to make a dent in the problem."

Cindy settled back into the seat. "Who knows where all of this is going to take us? I'm certainly apprehensive."

"I think I'll take an evasive course," Ben thought outloud. "I don't want to call any more attention than is necessary to our friends in Petra. I'll swing along the wilderness area bordering the Dead Sea and then shoot back to Jerusalem from another direction." The compact, shiny black shuttle glided quietly like a guided missile. Without wings, the anti-gravity capacity gave the craft total maneuverability, swinging and turning at the slightest touch of the controls. The bubble top gave the group a complete view of the area.

"Look!" Isaiah pointed out the window. "I've always wanted to see the desalination plant at work. I understand they siphon off the bromides and chlorides from the Dead Sea and use the remaining water for irrigation."

"The oranges grown here are as large as bowling balls," Jimmy said. "And the tomatoes are larger than grapefruits. The recycling process really works. Look around. The desert is truly blooming."

Suddenly the craft veered wildly to the left and dropped several hundred feet. Ben fought to lift the nose before they hit a rock peak. Isaiah bounced into Cindy, and Jimmy nearly sprawled on the floor.

"What's happening?" Cindy cried. "Make sure your seat belts are fastened tightly."

"I . . . I . . . just don't know." Ben kept pulling on the wheel. Red lights flashed on the guidance system. "This has never happened before. I can't seem to control anything."

The craft swung wildly out over the Dead Sea and then veered back straight into the rock cliffs. "Brace yourselves!" Jimmy yelled. "We're going to crash!"

Suddenly the craft shot straight up and sailed over a rough, broken valley. "The entire guidance system's gone crazy." Ben kept hitting buttons. "Nothing is responding."

The craft dropped into the grove between the walls of the valley and then maintained a height of a hundred feet above the ground. "Part of the time the altitude guidance is on," Ben called out. "Then it suddenly cuts out. I can't control our speed either."

Abruptly the craft pulled straight up toward the sun. In

seconds, it was several thousand feet above the wilderness before slowing down. Without warning the shuttle stalled. For a moment the small capsule hung in space before tipping backward and plunging toward the earth.

"Hit the anti-gravity system!" Jimmy cried. "That's our only chance!"

The pressure of the terrifying descent froze Ben's hand to the console. At the last possible moment his finger hit the button marked AG. The craft came to a terrifying halt just feet above the ground, shaking everything in it loose. The foursome jerked wildly, their seat belts cutting into their bodies as the shuttle skidded across desert rubble toward a boulder. The craft lifted slightly and then plowed into the ground, spraying sand and dirt in every direction. Silence and dust settled around the shattered shuttle.

□ □ □

For several seconds no one moved. Pieces of the broken windshield tumbled out. Broken metal clanked against rocks. Finally quiet settled over the winding valley. The silence of the barren desert became deafening.

"Cindy?" Ben finally called out feebly. "Are you OK?"

"I don't seem to have any pain. I'm alive . . . is about all I can say for sure."

"Isaiah?" Jimmy shook his friend. "Isaiah!"

Isaiah opened one eye. He slowly pushed his other eyelid open. "I'm afraid to look. What in the world happened?"

"Only the grace of God saved us," Jimmy concluded. "That's the only way we came out of that alive. I thought the force of the fall would devour us."

"I can't believe it." Ben fumbled to get his glasses back on while trying to unfasten his seat belt. "Never, never have I heard of one of these machines going crazy."

"The technology was perfected long ago." Jimmy tried to push away from his seat. "The automatic guidance system alone should have compensated for any maladjustment. There simply is no way for one of these things to go out of control."

"Obviously it can!" Cindy pushed hard on the door. "Now the locks won't open."

Ben threw all of his weight against the emergency lever and suddenly all the doors lifted up. The hot air of the desert immediately surged into the cabin. "Clearly the climate control was working." He climbed out the side. "We'll miss that small comfort in the desert."

Cindy stepped out on the barren hill. "My stomach really hurts, but I'm able to walk. My legs are unusually fine for an old lady." She looked up at the area towering above her. "Do we have any idea where we are?"

"We were over the Dead Sea before everything snapped. However, the craft was navigating up the ravines at a high rate of speed when we crashed, so we could have made up a lot of the distance between us and Jerusalem."

"Any idea what that means?" Isaiah looked around in bewilderment and rubbed his back.

"None," Ben answered. "At worst, we are miles off course. At best, we're only a short distance from Jerusalem."

"Anybody live out here?" Isaiah stared at the barren terrain.

"Centuries of advancement haven't changed the bedouins much," Jimmy answered. "They're still around—somewhere. But the chances of running into one is about the same as just happening to take the right gorge and ending up in Jerusalem in a few minutes. We're a long way from nowhere. Even the bedouins stay closer to the beaten paths."

"The only good thing is that we started back late enough in the day that nightfall will give us a reprieve of sorts from the heat of the sun," Ben added.

"Ever walk around out here when the cold sets in?" Jimmy pointed with his cane.

"That's the bad news," Ben answered and wiped the sweat from his forehead.

"I think we'd better start walking in the best direction the sun offers." Cindy pointed in a northeasterly arch. "People dehydrate in this weather very quickly."

Ben shook his head. "We didn't even bring any emergency supplies. We'd do better to stay with the craft in hopes someone would find us."

"But no one knows we took this trip," Jimmy added. "To make matters worse, our evasive action would probably have not been noted by telaport radar as anything more than a tourist trip. We've broken every rule in the book."

"The craft offers some shelter," Ben argued. "And it might be spotted from the air."

"We'd simply shrivel up and blow away if we waited inside that wreck," Cindy shook her head. "Maybe Jerusalem isn't so far away. I think it would be better to try to get out than sit here and roast."

"Cindy has a point," Jimmy added. "We might be closer to getting out of the wilderness than we know."

"I don't think so." Ben shook his head. "But I'll go with what the majority says. How many vote to walk?"

All hands went up.

"That settles the matter." Ben turned around and looked carefully. "I think we'd better walk up the side of this valley as best we can and see if we can get our bearings. At least that's a start."

A swirl of hot air kicked up the sand and stung the group with the sharp grit. "At our age we must keep our heads covered," Cindy worried. "But we don't have anything to use for shade."

"I'll rip out some of the seat covers." Isaiah pulled out a

pocket knife and returned to the craft. "I can cut off enough material to shade us."

Ben covered his eyes and looked up the steep embankment. "God help us," he muttered. "I don't see how we'll ever make it."

They locked arms with each other and started up the winding ravine. Within a few yards their stumbling made it clear they wouldn't be of much help to each other. Each fared better alone. Several times Cindy nearly fell. Near the top they grabbed at a few surviving scrubby bushes to pull themselves onto the ridge. However, once they reached level ground there was nothing before them except the endless winding cracks in the earth.

The deep valleys had been eroded by eons of spring rains interspersed between endless months of complete dryness before sparse cloudbursts returned for momentary seasonal visits. Lizards scurried away as the foursome trudged by but there was no other sign of life. No one spoke much to preserve all the moisture they could. Their throats quickly became uncomfortably dry. They clung to each other, fighting the sand and the treacherous terrain.

By walking the top, the foursome moved along the crest of other valleys but soon came to the end of the ridge and had to cut across another deep gorge to keep going. They were sweating profusely and draped their shuttle seat coverings low over their faces to ward off occasional sprays of sand.

After an hour of walking, Cindy slumped to the ground and held her stomach. The back of her jersey top was soaked with perspiration. "I don't think I can go on much longer," she mumbled to herself. "Maybe we should have stayed with the craft."

Back in Jerusalem, Rivka Zachary was finishing another private tutoring session with Dr. Zvilli Zemah in his office at the library. She smiled and turned nervously in her chair. "But, Dr. Zemah, the reign of Yeshua has brought nothing but good."

"Just make it Zvilli," he said for the third time that afternoon. "Rivka, you have ignored the Arab side of your nature. As long as you allow the Isaac portion of your heredity to dominate your mind, you can only see through eyes controlled by Jewish influences. You have no idea how much repression the people from the other side suffer."

Rivka shook her head. Her jet-black hair swung back and forth. "I'm sorry, Zvilli. My experience has been so different. Jews have always been good to me."

"You must realize compliance naturally brings reward. The central government continually panders to those who obey them, creating a type of conditioned reflex. We obey. We get rewarded. We feel good. We obey. So on and so forth, forever."

The raven-haired beauty crossed her arms over her chest. "I don't feel like an automaton. No one treats me badly or coerces me to do anything. I like following my leaders."

"That's because you've never released your desert impulses. You have a natural wildness in your soul, just waiting for expression. My social experiments during the last several years have opened my mind to see the larger truth: We have all been duped by the Jerusalem system. Rivka, you must throw off the shackles of mind and body to truly understand total fulfillment. Believe me." Zvilli's voice became low and intense.

"How can I be sure?" Rivka asked innocently.

"Because I've done it!" Zemah stared deep into her eyes. "I've cast aside the impositions of authority to enjoy unrestrained ecstasy. Listen to me!" He leaned forward and took her hand. "I can take you to a place of capacity and passion beyond your dreams. Give me your mind and I will open your eyes to see beyond even the confines of these mountains that surround Jerusalem."

Rivka tried to shake her head but his eyes had taken control of her thoughts. She swallowed hard. "Really?"

Zemah smiled. "Absolutely, my dear." He squeezed Rivka's hand; his hypnotic eyes held her captive.

CHAPTER 13

Maria Marchino, the president of Italy, had said little during the confederation strategy sessions. Although she had been the leader of Italy for four decades, it was not her nature to be demonstrative or intrusive. The Marchino technique was to listen silently in the background while carefully plotting her own course.

When Maria Marchino entered a room everyone observed. The tall, imposing head of state had been a fashion model in her youth. She had learned the secrets of presence and beauty well. The influence of that early period continued in her elaborate wardrobe, which defied the worldwide generally accepted code of dress. Whereas most leaders wore the usual knit jersey uniform, Maria's more exotic dresses and pantsuits called attention to her striking beauty. Clothes did the talking for Maria Marchino.

The head of state sat down at her desk and punched in the code for the state palace where Claudine Toulouse, the head of France, awaited her call. Just before hitting the last number, she paused to look at her government's crest on the wall in front of her.

When the Italian state reformed after the Great Tribulation, the nation avoided any indication of its role in the previously re-constituted Roman Empire of Damian Gianardo. The Antichrist had commandeered Rome as the final seat of power, leaving a historically embarrassing stigma on the city. The new emblem of government was a straightforward shield with the colors of the national flag decorating the quadrants of the crest. Maria never liked the plainness of the design. She preferred something more glorious.

Although no one wished to evoke that unfortunate image, the idea of a Holy Roman Empire had always captured Maria Marchino's imagination. Her earliest studies of the ancient world fascinated her with the role Rome once played on the world stage. The thought of re-creating a new worldwide empire held a secret fascination for Maria. In fact, her concealed ambition had been an important factor in propelling her into politics.

The president of Italy punched in the final digit and waited for the hologram phone to respond. Maria knew she was a striking beauty compared to the plain leader of France; she enjoyed the contrast. Maria kept her hair dyed black and lined her eyes with an iridescent gray to increase their piercing quality. In a few moments the form of Claudine Toulouse materialized in front of Maria's desk.

"Peace to you." Maria offered the usual diplomatic greeting. "How good to see you, my dear."

Claudine Toulouse bowed her head ceremoniously. "Peace to you, great leader of the Italians." The French head of state wore the usual jersey pullover. She was small and the brightness of her blonde hair had long been washed out with wide swaths of gray. "You are gracious to call," she said.

Maria reached for another button. "Let us lock privacy into our conversation for security's sake."

"Exactly," Toulouse responded and pushed a similar tab on her hologram system. "Some matters are best kept only for our ears."

"We've not talked since our private conversations in Egypt," Maria began. "I'm wondering how your reflections have gone."

"I believe your initial assessments were quite accurate." Claudine Toulouse settled back into a large blue velvet-covered gold-leaf chair. "If this restored world order comes to pass, Arab influence will dominate the rest of the nations, leaving us with second-class status. I see their aims demonstrated clearly in every word coming out of Atrash's mouth. Abu Sita is merely his shadow.

"My sister," the French head of state continued, "we must stand together. You are right. These particular Arabs still hold all women in an inferior position. They are not comfortable with our presence in planning sessions. I, too, noticed their avoidance of our responses to many of their comments."

"Then we are in one accord," Marchino concluded. "We must find our own way in the midst of this treachery."

"I still believe we can become free of the control of the central government in Jerusalem." Claudine folded her hands and tapped the edge of her chin. "I'm not sure what I make of this spirit guide talk of Atrash and Abu Sita's, but the government of Yeshua does seem to have lost control. The time appears to be ripe for us to strike out in our own direction."

Maria Marchino nodded her agreement. "Hard to tell whether old El Khader is a schizophrenic or epileptic." She laughed at her own joke. "At least he puts on quite a show. Who knows?"

"I was once a very religious person," Claudine said. "I would have been deeply offended by all this gibberish about other gods, but I suppose I've changed a great deal." She paused, raised her eyebrows, and shrugged. "Maybe the pressures of running a government, the worries, the distractions of everyday problems changed me."

"We change as we age," Maria congealed. "Just part of the nature of things."

"I am much more concerned with this manifesto Atrash sent." Claudine Toulouse held up a sheet of paper. "He really has a hate for the Jews. Such emotionalism and madness can confuse one's thinking."

Maria held up her own copy of the document and started to read. "The Restored World Order swears to conduct a holy war against Jerusalem and every and all Jews until victory is achieved." She looked up from the document. "This language must be changed or other world leaders will not respond. Atrash sounds like a racist fanatic. Listen to this, 'by command of the gods, we must fight and kill Jews wherever they are.'

"Claudine, I suggest we lodge a formal complaint."

"I agree. Listen to this." Claudine read further. "Only a jihad, a holy war waged as a religious duty, can cleanse the earth of the influence of subversive religion and free us of the oppressive hand of Yeshua." The French leader shrugged. "The government of Yeshua has been strict prior to this past year, but never oppressive. Everyone knows that. We simply intend now to develop our countries as we please—without yielding to anyone's intervention."

"I would suggest a larger picture to you, my sister." Maria stopped and studied the hologram image carefully, measuring her counterpart. "Should Jerusalem topple, we must be aware of the possibility of considerable instability for a long period of time. Atrash and Abu Sita probably have other plans for us."

Claudine Toulouse sat up and leaned forward. "What are you suggesting?"

"Is it not to our advantage to be prepared to reform and create our own alliance?"

The French leader stared. "Our own coalition?"

"I would humbly suggest the boys from Baghdad could turn on us as easily as they have on the central government. Where would we be then?"

Toulouse settled back in the gold chair, folded her hands once more, and resumed tapping her chin. "Exactly what are you suggesting?"

"Perhaps the time has come to develop our own contingency plans. Maybe we should be ready for our own counterattack at the end of this war."

"How?"

Maria Marchino laid Atrash's manifesto down and picked up another piece of paper. "I've been making a few notes. First, I would suggest we secretly stockpile every form of armament we can. We must develop a private stash known only to us. Second, as soon as the attack plans are formulated, we must outline a secret military response for counteraction as the battle unfolds. Third, we should conclude with a secret agreement to bind our nations together. Our accord can form the basis for negotiations with other governments to bring them into our sphere of influence once matters start to unravel with Atrash and Abu Sita."

Claudine stared straight ahead for what seemed like an indefinite period of time. Finally, she reached out and offered her hand. "My sister! You are a true descendant of the Caesars."

□ □ □

For a long time after Claudine terminated the call from Italy, the beautiful face of Maria burned in her mind like an image of personal failure. Claudine's plainness had been one of the reasons she had doggedly pursued politics rather than what she painfully referred to as a "normal life." She knew men only as formidable adversaries—never as passionate lovers. That had been fine with her until Khalil Hussein came to power in Jordan. Known as the "boy genius" of politics, Hussein's meteoric rise had been admired across the world, and Claudine had instantly been physically drawn to this much younger man. But he hadn't responded to her invitation at the conference.

"I want him," Claudine murmured aloud. "Whatever it takes . . ." the words trailed away.

She thought of the promises Abu Sita had pushed at every meeting. "Meditations and prayers to Marduk will bring you new power and authority over others," he had claimed.

Claudine closed her eyes and tried to let her mind shift into complete neutral. After ten minutes of struggling to clear her mind, Claudine started the chant. "Come, Lord Marduk, come spirits of the past, come spirits of the dead. Come to me." She repeated the phrase over and over, slipping further and further into a trancelike state. "I will serve you . . . serve you," she muttered.

Suddenly Claudine stopped. An intense feeling of lust and desire shot through her mind. She felt an insatiable desire for Khalil. Her body burned and her mouth was dry.

Claudine began breathing heavily. "What . . . what's happening to me?" she sputtered.

□ □ □

As the hot afternoon faded, Ziad Atrash stood at his command post in Cairo, carefully inspecting the new surveillance equipment being installed around the war room. Workmen busily connected wires and hooked up both television monitors and hologram devices.

"How soon until everything is complete?" he barked at a general.

"We expect most of the work to be finished by this time tomorrow," the aide advised.

"Tell them to hurry up," Atrash ordered. "Everything is taking far too long." The general saluted and began mingling with the technicians and shouting orders.

Ziad had chosen this particular bunker near the Red Sea because of the ancient defeat Egypt suffered there at the hands of Moses centuries earlier. He had every intention of reversing the disaster and named the outpost Rameses in honor of the pharaoh of the Exodus.

Atrash flipped on a portable telephone. "What is the status of the arrangement for international satellite transmission of the heads of state? I want the information now."

"Details are falling into place quickly," the aide answered briskly. "However, we have received one communique you will want to review immediately."

"What?" Atrash snapped.

"The leaders of Italy and France just sent in a response to your manifesto. I can place it on your television monitor, channel 3."

"Do it." Ziad turned on the screen in front of him and hit the correct channel. The message filled the screen.

To: President Ziad Atrash
From: Presidents Maria Marchino & Claudine Toulouse

After careful study we believe your manifesto states very clearly the objectives we have agreed upon for immediate military pursuit. As always you are clear and erudite.

Atrash laughed and pulled at his black moustache. "Of course, I am the master of all languages!" He continued to chuckle as he read further:

However, aspects of the manifesto may be misunderstood in some world capitals. Your attack on the Jews seems particularly vitriolic and racist. We suggest all language about divine direction be dropped. A simple call to liberation and freedom will be sufficient to enlist other nations in our campaign. We respectfully suggest immediate revision before release.

Ziad's eyes narrowed and his neck turned red. "How dare those old bags tell me what to say!" he shouted. "Who are they to even make comment on *my* manifesto?" Atrash shook his fist at the screen. "Their impertinence will not be tolerated!" He stormed out of the room and walked outside.

The sun was setting over the Red Sea and the heat of the day subsiding. *Unfortunately,* he thought, *I need those nations in the alliance. I have no choice but to respond positively to their arrogance. At the right time I will send those two sows sailing across the River of the Dead.* Atrash kicked at a pile of sand. *I will keep them off balance by treating them with more respect than they deserve.* He paced back toward the bunker. *Possibly, I should let Abu Sita respond and not even acknowledge the issue.* Atrash slammed the door behind him and stormed down the hall. *Whatever Abu Sita works out will be acceptable— if he has the brains to know what to say to them. Maybe I'd better do it myself.*

Atrash marched down the hall into the communications command post and flipped on a portable phone. "Return this message to Italy and France," he ordered the aide. "Your ideas and thoughts are always of the highest value to our cause. Please send your suggested revisions and adjustments. With highest regards, Supreme General Ziad Atrash. He clicked off the phone. "That will keep the old bags happy."

"Excellency," an aide carrying papers entered the room. "I made further inquiries about the international television hook-up. We have now reached agreement with the other leaders to apportion each head of state equal space on the screen during the announcement of the attack on the

Jerusalem government. However, without mentioning the fact, I have arranged for your picture to always appear first. Our people believe that projecting the images of the pyramids and the tombs of the kings behind you, we will create the preeminent image of ultimate authority."

"Excellent." Atrash smiled for the first time that afternoon. "Good planning. How is the training of our soldiers going?"

The general's demeanor changed. "Well, the men have no previous history of military training. Their skills are not good, but they are being pushed hard."

"What you mean is, they are behind schedule."

"We are now practicing twelve hours a day, Excellency."

"Don't let up," Ziad growled. "Time is of the essence."

□ □ □

The setting sun cast haunting and foreboding shadows over the wilderness chasms that wound seemingly nowhere. Cindy clung to Ben as they inched up the side of a gorge. Their white hair hung down in their eyes. Isaiah and Jimmy waited at the top.

"I'm drying out," Jimmy called down. "Thank goodness the sun is disappearing. We will preserve moisture and get some of our energy back."

"I don't know," Cindy answered from the side of the bank. "I'm not sure how much further I can go—even in the next few minutes—much less tomorrow."

Ben pulled her up to the top and dropped into the sand. "I'm almost spent." He sprawled out on the ridge.

Jimmy shielded his eyes and looked around. "We have a reprieve between now and sunset. But if we don't find some form of shelter, we may be even worse off when night comes."

"I hate to say it," Isaiah stood up and rubbed his sore legs, "but we need to keep tracking. The sun offers us a compass of sorts; in the dark we could end up just going around in circles."

"Isaiah's right," Jimmy said. "We'll help you." He offered his hand to Cindy.

Ben rolled over and tried to stand. His bulbous shape made getting to his feet difficult. "I know you're right. I just don't know if I can keep on."

"We must," Cindy urged. "We don't have any choice. Too much depends on us getting back." She struggled to her feet.

Jimmy cupped his hand over his eyes and studied the terrain. "Let's go for that high point. Maybe if we can get on top of the bluff we'll see something." He stuck his cane into the sand like a walking stick.

The group slowly trudged forward, pushing on across the jagged side of the valley. The winds began to pick up, making the trek even more difficult. Cindy hung on Ben's arm, her steps becoming more halting the closer they came to the top.

"I think we must stop," Ben called out. "Cindy and I will rest here. The two of you go on by yourselves. We'll catch up later."

Isaiah shook his head. "We must not get beyond visual contact. We'd never find each other again."

Jimmy kept walking but called over his shoulder. "Isaiah's right. We've got to stay together. I'll get up here on the ridge and see if I can find a better direction, but we must stay within shouting distance."

Isaiah dropped to his knees and watched the Feinbergs below him. He kept looking up to observe Jimmy's progress in reaching the plateau. Finally, his old friend disappeared over the top. The sun was quickly setting.

"I can't see Jimmy anymore," Ben called.

Isaiah nodded but he looked apprehensively toward the

bluff. Time was passing and nothing seemed to be happening. Ben finally helped Cindy up to where Isaiah was sitting.

"I'm worried about Jimmy," Ben said. "He should have returned by now."

"We're all exhausted," Cindy sighed. "Our strength is gone."

"He could have slipped and fallen into another canyon," Ben concluded. "We've got to get up there and find out."

Isaiah painfully pushed himself up to his feet. Ben and Cindy followed behind struggling to move forward. At the top of the bluff, Jimmy was nowhere in sight. A gale bore down, sweeping away the dirt like a giant wind-driven broom.

"J-i-m-m-y," Isaiah called out but no reply followed.

"God help us!" Cindy clung to Ben. "Jimmy's fallen off the edge somewhere."

"H-a-r-r-i-s-o-n," Ben yelled at the top of his lungs, "where are you?"

"He could be trapped at the bottom of one of these pits." Cindy pointed to the blackness filling the ravines. "He wouldn't be able to hear us. We'll never find him." She started to cry.

Suddenly from the direction of the setting sun, a voice answered. "Over here! I'm over here. Hurry up."

"Where?" Isaiah looked around. "I can't see you."

Cindy pointed toward a rise. "The sound had to come from just behind that incline."

"Jimmy?" Ben hollered. "Direct us to where you are."

"Over here" echoed across the canyon.

"Yes." Cindy pointed. "He's definitely just over the hill."

"Jimmy, you okay?" Isaiah tried again but got no response.

"I don't understand." Cindy struggled to walk faster. "You'd think he'd answer us."

"He didn't sound bad," Isaiah puffed. "In fact, his voice was rather strong."

With their last ounce of energy, the threesome cleared the final hill on the bluff. Straight ahead they could see the shape of an old building. A figure was lying on the ground at the doorway.

"There's Jimmy!" Isaiah pointed. "He's not moving!"

"Hurry!" Ben led the way. "We've got to help him." Ben limped more than ran but he beckoned the others to follow him.

"Jimmy!" he kept calling. "Can you hear us?"

"It's an old abandoned army outpost," Isaiah exclaimed. "Even the tin roof is intact. The arid climate preserved the place." He huffed as he trotted.

"Jimmy," Ben dropped beside the limp form, "are you OK?"

Jimmy groaned but didn't move.

"He must have passed out." Ben rolled his friend over. "Exhaustion finally got him."

Isaiah fell next to Jimmy. "Come on, partner. Don't check out on us now." He gently shook Jimmy's face.

The old man slowly opened his eyes. "Where am I?" he moaned.

"You're a hero!" Ben laughed in relief. "You saved us." He helped Jimmy sit up.

Cindy trudged up from behind. "Thank God he's alive!"

"What happened to me?" Jimmy kept blinking his eyes.

"You've found us a hotel for the night, old buddy," Isaiah answered. "Not bad accommodations, considering."

Cindy peered inside the dilapidated building. "The army must have used this as a reconnaissance post centuries ago." She stepped inside. "Look!" Cindy pointed at plastic containers still stacked along the wall. "Supplies are still here!"

"I thought it was a mirage," Jimmy mumbled. "The last thing I can remember is thinking I was going mad."

"You hit the jackpot," Isaiah exclaimed. "You pulled us out."

"Ben," Cindy called from inside the shack, "you won't believe this. There's still water in these containers! Smells stale but it still feels like heaven to me!"

"Praise God!" Ben proclaimed.

"I thought I was hearing voices." Jimmy's voice was still very weak. "I kept hearing someone calling, 'Over here.' That's why I kept going. I knew I was delirious, but the voice sounded so clear."

"We heard *you* calling," Isaiah said. "Sure saved us."

Jimmy looked puzzled. "I didn't call."

"I'm bringing some water out for Jimmy," Cindy called out. "It will help revive him."

"But we heard you directing us this way," Ben insisted.

"Couldn't have been." Jimmy shook his head. "My mouth has been almost too dry to speak!"

CHAPTER 14

The cold night and the unforgiving hard ground inside the desert hut were severe punishment to human body and soul. As the sun rose Cindy snuggled closer to Ben to try to keep warm. Jimmy curled in a tight ball against the back of the shed to preserve all the body heat possible.

Isaiah was the first to awake. For a long time he stared through a crack in the dilapidated building, looking out across the empty wilderness. Isaiah found it difficult to sit because of his excruciating back pain. He tried not to move.

Jimmy eventually stirred. He rolled over on his side, slowly curled his knees under him, and tried to push himself up. Only with great difficulty did he get to his feet. He quietly looked around at the rest of the sleepers.

When Ben stretched, Cindy woke up. "What time is it?" Cindy's voice was dry and raspy.

"About six in the morning," Jimmy answered.

Ben opened his eyes slowly and stared at the corrugated metal roof above him. "Where am I?" He fumbled around searching for his glasses.

Jimmy shuffled around. "I wish I knew the answer myself. Everything always looks the same out here."

"I don't think I can go on," Isaiah muttered. "My tired old body is simply too battered. I don't have it in me anymore."

"I agree," Cindy answered. "Yesterday I didn't realize what the strain against the seat belts did to me. But this morning my abdomen is so sore. I'm wracked with pain."

Ben reached for Cindy's hand. "We've got to get you medical attention. I should have insisted you stay with the shuttlecraft."

"No," she said softly. "We took the right course. The water saved us."

Jimmy peered out the door at the barren terrain. "Yesterday the wilderness seemed crossable. Today, the journey looks impossible. We're just too old and tired to make it."

"I'm starving," Isaiah rubbed his stomach. "We expended a lot of energy tramping around out there."

Jimmy slumped down close to the door. "Wouldn't it be ironic if this shelter became our final death trap?"

Ben kept looking at the roof. "Last night the tin saved us from the cold but I suspect in a few hours this metal building will become an oven."

"You're right," Cindy said. "Unless there's an unlikely breeze, we will be like chickens roasting in an oven."

"Won't take long," Isaiah said. "Probably in an hour the heat will really start to work on this place. Two hours and you could fry an egg on the roof."

Ben finally got to his feet. "Here we are in the midst of what might be the most important task of our lives and we're lost in the middle of nowhere." He ran his hands through his disarrayed hair. "Time is running out and we can't even find first base."

"I'm afraid we're not even in the ball park," Jimmy

answered. "I don't think any of us can live through another day like yesterday."

Cindy started to weep. "We're going to die out here. There's no hope." She buried her face in her hands. Her body shook as she wept.

Ben dropped to his knees by her side. "I'm sorry. I've run out of ideas. I just don't know what to do."

"We thought we were going to take on the world powers, the Evil One himself," Isaiah smirked. "We couldn't even fly home. That's just how effective *we* are!"

Jimmy threw a handful of sand toward the door and dropped to his knees. "We're a bunch of old 'has beens.' The truth is we're old fools who should have stayed out of the way of the traffic before we got run over by the cars."

No one answered. Defeat hung in the air like the desert heat.

"Hello?" a voice called from outside the building.

Jimmy jumped and toppled over.

"W-h-a-t!" Isaiah shouted.

"We've been found!" Ben exclaimed. "Thank God. A bedouin has found us."

"You have lost your way?" the voice answered.

"Who is it?" Jimmy rushed to the door.

"Don't you recognize me?" The handsome young man stepped into the doorway. "I thought by now you'd know my voice."

"Son!" Jimmy threw his arms around the Immortal. "My son, you're here."

"Didn't think I'd let you become pot roast for the vultures, did you, Dad?"

"Thank heavens you were watching over us." Ben hobbled forward. "We are fairly well spent."

"We had a wreck!" Cindy blurted out. "Crashed out there somewhere." Cindy pointed out the window.

"We thought we were goners." Jimmy hugged his son a second time. "We didn't think anyone could find us."

"Few people ever come this way," Jim Jr. explained. "You found an old security post left from the days before the Great Tribulation. You obviously need to get out of this place."

"The truth is," Jimmy agreed, "we're really spent and rather beat up. Cindy may have injuries."

Ben explained, "We need you to get us back to Jerusalem as quickly as possible. You see, our craft went berserk and . . ."

"I know. You must realize that these days nothing happens to you by chance or accident. You must be attuned with the ears of a fox."

"Not an accident?" Jimmy immediately queried. "Are you suggesting that the shuttle wreck was planned?"

"Your landing was cushioned by grace," Jim Jr. answered simply. "You might have plowed straight into the ground or you could have hit the final boulder head on. Remember?"

"You were there!" Cindy declared.

"The battle has already begun, my dear ones, but you have not fully appreciated the dimensions of the conflict. Do you think the Evil One is unaware of everything you've been doing? In the past month you have proclaimed the truth to billions and brought many back from the brink of destruction. Do you believe such heroics would go unnoted by your enemy? The war is on but you are treating the engagement like a slight tiff."

Ben's eyes widened and his lips parted before he spoke. "You had something to do with us surviving the bomb attack . . ."

Jimmy Jr. nodded his head. "For reasons you do not yet fully understand, our role in these latter days has become very limited. Yes, I saw the spy drop an electronic timing device into my father's pocket when he entered the Internal Affairs Building and I delayed the opening of the elevator door. But you must not assume further intervention after today. Each of you must fight the battle through your own integrity."

"What should we do?" Cindy asked.

"Have you forgotten the principles of spiritual warfare? Have you let every lesson from the past escape you?"

"Please, Jim," his father implored, "be more specific."

"Where is the *real* battleground?"

Cindy brightened. "In our hearts!"

"Exactly, child. You remember well. Fear and doubt are always the Enemy's initial weapons of war. Your lack of faith and courage are an invitation for attack. Once the door is open, the Devil will flog you with your own anxiety and hound you through your personal worries. The greatest threat has not been the dangers of the desert but your loss of confidence in the heavenly Father's ability to provide for you."

"What's the next step, Jim?"

"Your friend Sam instructed you well. Your journey must be bathed in prayer. You must continually seek the Holy Spirit's guidance. Whatever assistance I give is minor compared to the value of asking for the hand of God to guide you directly."

"Thank you, good friend," Cindy answered. "We've been fighting this war in our own strength."

"And none of you is big enough to spar with the Devil," the Immortal added. "Never forget that even in His crucifixion, Yeshua proved the weakness of God to be far more efficacious than the worst Evil could offer."

"So what should we do?" Isaiah asked.

"You are already on your knees," Jim Jr. observed. "Is not kneeling a posture of impotence? Can you think of a better place to begin to turn your weakness into strength?"

"Jim Junior," Cindy answered, "we shouldn't need you to remind us to pray. We won't make the same mistake again." She closed her eyes and bowed her head.

Ben began spontaneously, "O gracious Father, forgive us of our self-serving arrogance in trying to do everything in our own strength and not through your power . . ."

The group joined in the prayer and responded one by one. Conversational prayer moved back and forth in a gentle dialogue with the unseen Presence of life Himself. Finally, Ben closed with an "Amen."

"That was wonderful," Cindy stretched. "I already feel more energized. Jim . . . Jim Junior?"

"Where is that boy?" Jimmy jumped to his feet.

"He's gone!" Isaiah reached out into the empty space around him.

"But Jim Junior said he would get us out of here." Ben ran to the door. "Where'd he go?"

"He *said* we wouldn't be abandoned," Isaiah followed.

"Why would my boy come and then leave?" Jimmy asked.

"Look!" Cindy pointed through the door behind the shed. "There's a road! We have found a road out of this place."

"No," Ben said soberly. "We didn't find a road. God provided a way."

□ □ □

"Wendy," Ben spoke into his office portable phone, "I wanted you to know I'm back at my house now."

"Where have you been?" the secretary sounded irritated. "We've tried to locate you all over the world."

"I had to take a trip to sort things out."

"Let me call you on the hologram phone so we can speak more directly," Wendy Kohn answered.

Ben glanced around the room. Isaiah was slumped over

a chair sound asleep. Jimmy and Cindy sat next to him listening but they looked like they had been run over by an avalanche. "I don't think so." Ben glanced in the mirror. His white hair stuck out like a porcupine and dark circles lined his eyes. "It would take unnecessary time. Just tell me what's happening."

"You must have been on the other side of the pyramids not to have picked up on the fast-breaking news."

"Something of that order," Ben mumbled.

"Just after we last talked, the chairman of China, Fong, came on television and made a scathing attack on the central government. He declared Jerusalem had suppressed information on the outbreaks of an AIDS epidemic in Africa and America. Fong said this was only another sign of the impotence of our leadership. He called for a worldwide revolt against Yeshua."

"I see."

"Six hours later the president of the United States appeared on international television and confirmed Fong's discoveries about AIDS. Unlike AIDS in the twentieth century, this mutant develops full-blown AIDS in its victims shortly after they become HIV positive. He said the entire Los Angeles area was in an epidemic of the virus and Yeshua's leadership had failed his country." Wendy Kohn stopped and caught her breath. "I couldn't believe my ears. Apparently thousands of people are dying in the southern California region and people are rioting. The American president sounded frightened and off balance. He said he would no longer take directives from Jerusalem."

"Events are moving very fast." Ben was sober but not shaken.

"We've done everything possible to contact King David's office and the Immortals." She paused. "I hope you won't mind. We even used your name to ask for an audience directly with Yeshua."

"And nothing happened," Ben answered.

"Why . . . yes!" Wendy sputtered. "How did you know?"

"You will not be able to get any response from our leadership," Ben began speaking rapidly. "We are in a state of crisis and in a few hours the rest of the world will be plunged into addition turmoil."

"Are you serious?"

"Deadly," Ben shot back. "Listen to me carefully. Wendy, you are to immediately order maximum security around all offices. Yes, use my name to get action. You must be prepared for dangerous attacks and espionage. Anything is possible."

"Oh, my!" Wendy's voice faded.

"Things are going to get much, much worse before they get better but you are to show no signs of fear or panic. Be calm and stay in control until I arrive."

"Look," Wendy sounded apprehensive, "level with me. You obviously know more about what is going on than you're saying."

"Wendy, do you still have a Bible around?"

"Of course, but I haven't looked at it for a long time."

"I would suggest you start reading the Book of Revelation and praying a lot," Ben concluded. "You'd be surprised how much that will help. I'll be there as quickly as I can."

"I got the picture from just this side of the conversation," Jimmy said.

"My secretary was about to panic. I've got to get to the office immediately. Cindy, are you OK?"

"I'm tired but the short walk out of the wilderness to the road helped my stomach pains. Nothing a little rest and a couple of days won't cure. Who would have believed we were so close to the old highway?"

"You know, that old dump truck showed up very quickly after we got to the road," Jimmy observed. "In fact, I haven't seen one of those things around for years."

"I hate to wake Isaiah." Ben looked at his sleeping friend. "He may not be able to find out anything. On the other hand, I wouldn't have dreamed he could have made the other discoveries. Isaiah might come up with another breakthrough. Who wants to wake up the slumbering giant?"

Cindy laid her head on the table and closed her eyes.

"I was just leaving." Jimmy started toward the kitchen.

Ben shook his head. "You can wake up now, Cindy. I'll get Isaiah up before I leave."

Cindy opened one eye and smiled.

Ben took a quick look at the other numbers registered on his message recorder. Few people had access to the Feinbergs' private phone. He punched a separate button that deciphered each number, indicating the source. Most of the numbers were Wendy Kohn's repeated calls. A number near the end flashed an unexpected name. Ben looked a second time. The small display window read, "Rivka Zachary."

Ben hit the play button and the message began. "Dr. Feinberg, you may not remember me but I spoke to you some time ago when you lectured at Hebrew University. You said I might call if I needed your help." After a long pause, Rivka sounded like she was crying. "I have become very confused. I need your guidance badly. I know you are a very busy man. If you could ever spare a moment, I would be most grateful." The phone clicked off.

How strange, Ben thought. *I've got to get to the office.* He picked up a small electronic reminder and dictated her telephone number and name into the machine. *I'll call her as I fly down.*

"Good grief!" Ben spoke more to himself. "I don't have a shuttle anymore. My craft is a pile of junk out there in the wilderness. Esther Netanyahu will have to requisition me a new one immediately." He punched in her private phone number.

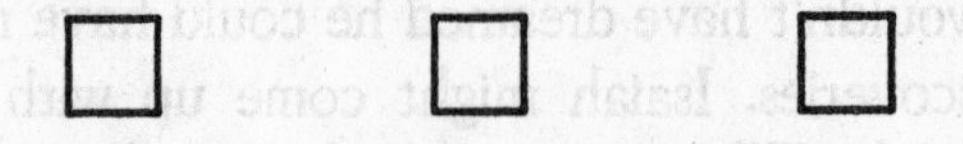

Rajah Abu Sita listened intently in his planning room under the palace in New Babylon as Ziad Atrash spoke in Arabic on the hologram phone. He nodded but said little. "So, there is no question of at least ten more countries joining our alliance?" he finally asked.

"None," the Egyptian leader confirmed. "The reports keep pouring into our central office in Cairo. Our religious propaganda is having an extraordinary result. We've touched a nerve and our campaign is working. Fong's declaration certainly had its affect."

"And the explosive devices?" Abu Sita asked.

"All of the attacking nations are fully armed now. The military campaign is virtually ready to begin. I don't expect any more television appearances from those two old fools who popped up the last go around."

"Your men perfected the sabotage mechanisms?" the Assyrian leader asked.

"I have been able to infiltrate the Jerusalem area with selected spies who know how to use electronic and explosive devices," Ziad boasted. "The central government is totally unprepared for our attacks. The attack will come so quickly every Jew in sight will be totally demoralized."

"What about those two old jerks?"

"Before long I expect to receive an international communique mourning one or both of their deaths in an unexplained shuttlecraft crash. Just more evidence of the central government falling apart."

"How'd you do it?"

"A timing device hooked to an altimeter. When the shuttle gets high enough for a crash to be fatal, the craft will become unmanageable. Clever, no?"

"Excellent." Abu Sita shook his head whimsically. "Strange thing happening here with El Khader. He's really gotten into these meditations and believes he's the voice of Marduk all the time."

"Hmmm," Atrash mused. "What do you mean?"

"It's almost like El Khader is being swallowed by these seances and is losing touch with everyday reality," Rajah explained. "Occasionally, he will order me around as if he has become the supreme power."

"Cut him off at the knees," Ziad scowled. "Don't put up with his nonsense."

"The strange thing is that what he says is profound half the time. He has developed an uncanny knowledge of the future. He seems to read minds. The staff and the guards are afraid of him."

"What do you make of it?" Atrash asked.

"I don't know. I just don't know."

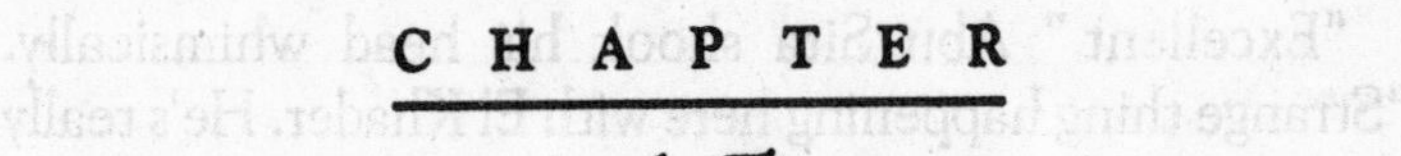

CHAPTER 15

Ben paced back and forth across his office, firing off instructions with the explosive staccato of a machine gun while Wendy Kohn and Esther Netanyahu listened intently. The women periodically scribbled notes on their electronic notepads.

"Dr. Harrison," Wendy interrupted, "people in the government offices are looking to you for leadership. Since we no longer have access to the Immortals, people see you as the only source of dependable guidance. We need to send your instructions to every office in the entire government complex."

"I suppose so," Ben mumbled to himself. "I don't want to be in such a prominent role but perhaps . . ."

"Absolutely," Esther Netanyahu insisted. "You are the first person to make any sense of this information."

"Let me stress," Ben repeated his earlier dictation, "we must be keenly aware that the enemy is quite capable of using destructive devices on us and our offices. We must be prepared for a concentrated attack on Jerusalem."

"I will send out memos under your signature," Wendy answered.

A gray-haired man burst into the office. "Please turn on your telescreen," he requested nervously. "Several important communiques are being received."

Ben quickly pushed the buttons on the command module on his desk. The screen lowered and messages began appearing.

> The United States, Mexico, Canada, and the Union of South Africa have declared, as of this day, their solidarity with the coalition identifying themselves as "The Restored Order" and are in the process of signing treaties of support and confederation. While military intentions have not been defined at this time, official statements imply defense agreements are imminent.

Ben shook his head. "Just what we anticipated. You can bet more bad news is on the way." He kept staring at the screen.

> Ziad Atrash, president and supreme general of the sovereign state of Egypt, has demanded the central government in Jerusalem cease and desist from further intervention in the affairs of his and other nations. If this demand is not met within the next twenty-four hours, President Atrash will declare war on Yeshua.

A flashing red light at the bottom of the screen signaled the need to switch to the special security channel. Ben hit the control module. A number of symbols marched across the screen. Ben pushed the clicker again and the symbols became Hebrew. He read aloud, "The source of all pirated television interruptions has now been identified. The nefarious religious programming is produced and channeled from the tourist site called New Babylon, located in Assyria. In addition, some input seems to be coming from Jerusalem." Ben stared at the screen.

"What!" Wendy's mouth dropped. "Here in Jerusalem?"

"We have a most cunning enemy," Ben answered. "Anything is possible when one is dealing with the father of all lies."

Wendy rubbed her forehead nervously. "I'm terrified."

"No!" Ben snapped. "You mustn't be afraid. The enemy feeds on fear like fish feed on plankton. Faith in God is the most important weapon we have in this battle."

"Yes, sir," Wendy answered sheepishly.

"Esther, I want you to draw up a list of the nations opposing our government. Go back a year and start forward, arranging the nations by date of confrontation. We will be in a position to get a hard, cold look at who is leading this parade."

"Immediately." The secretary scribbled on her pad.

"Until someone who really knows what he is doing comes along," Ben said, "we will make this office a command post for defense of the city. Please send that order out at once."

"Sir," the white-haired aide interrupted, "I hesitate to give you this message at a time like this but we keep getting repeated urgent requests from a student at Hebrew University to speak with you."

"Rivka?" Ben asked. "Rivka Zachary?"

"Why, yes, exactly."

"Thank you." Ben nodded. "I meant to call her earlier, but I've been swamped. Just leave the number."

The secretaries and aide quickly left to return to their posts. Ben settled behind his desk and stared at Rivka's number. *Urgent? How strange.*

☐ ☐ ☐

Rajah Abu Sita stood at the bottom of the steps in the Marduk Temple watching El Khader sway back and forth before the huge statue. The old man muttered sounds of ecstasy and threw handfuls of incense into the huge brass brazier at the top of the steps. Flames and great clouds of smoke shot up toward the ceiling. The sweet smell of frankincense saturated the air as the foglike clouds slowly drifted down the stairs.

"I want to talk to you," Rajah demanded. "Come down here at once!"

The secretary of state raised his bony arms over his head and waved them back and forth mechanically. Low, guttural moans of ecstasy spilled out of his mouth.

"I said," Abu Sita yelled, "stop and come down here!"

El Khader turned slowly and stared contemptuously at Rajah. The old man's bloodshot eyes were fiery red. His disarrayed hair stuck out in every direction. Drool ran down his matted beard. El Khader pointed at Rajah's face and screamed, "Be gone, fool!"

"How dare you address *me*, your lord and master, in those words! I am the ruler of Syria and Iraq!"

"I have but one master." The old man's voice crackled with disdain. "I serve none but my Lord Marduk!" He again shook his fist toward the ceiling.

"You're mad," Abu Sita shot back. "Psychotic."

"Would you call the divine voice of the gods crazy?" El Khader rubbed his hands together. "You, a puny, conniving little creature of the desert, accuse me, the divine expresser of the mystery of the ages?"

Abu Sita stared half terrified, half entranced. He started to take a step backward but checked himself. "Stop this nonsense at once!"

"Stop? *Stop?*" El Khader laughed like a maniac. "No one touched by the glory of Marduk can ever again settle for the mundane. I will no longer be the servant of the likes of you. I, El Khader, have been called by the gods to rule the universe." He threw his head back and laughed like a wild hyena.

"I'm going to call the guards." Rajah stepped back. "I will have you locked up."

El Khader slowly walked down the steps, pointing his finger straight in the face of the monarch. "None will touch me. My power is too great. Hear my prophecy!" He stopped on the bottom step and closed his eyes. "The armies shall gather from east and west like the vultures circling over corpses in the desert. Lightning will split the sky and blood will drip like the falling rain. As you battle over the bones of Yeshua's servants, I will again ascend to my rightful place on the throne of the heavens. None can stand in the way of omnipotent Evil!" The old man screamed aloud and ran out of the temple.

Rajah Abu Sita staggered backward and hurried after his mad secretary of state.

□ □ □

Isaiah Murphy's previous trip to Addis Ababa left him with a good working knowledge of the city. Once he cleared customs, Isaiah quickly left the airport and took a taxi shuttle into the heart of the city. He used his own portable phone to inform Hosni Gossos of his arrival. The Ethiopian sounded distant and evasive but agreed to meet him at a well-known downtown restaurant. Isaiah got out in front of the El Carbre.

For centuries the El Carbre had been an internationally known nightspot in the center of Addis Ababa. The restaurant's interior was decorated in African motifs, including stuffed lions and cheetahs. Famous people often conducted business there. The setting seemed an excellent place to make what would appear as casual contact. Thirty minutes later, Hosni arrived.

"Good to see you, old friend." Isaiah stood and offered his hand.

"Sorry, I can't say the same." Hosni quickly settled into the chair opposite Isaiah. "You shouldn't have come back."

Isaiah studied the black man across from him. Hosni looked tired and nervous. His gaze kept shifting across the room. "You look worried," Isaiah concluded.

"Are you sure you weren't followed?"

"Not a chance," Isaiah answered. "I came here straight from the airport. Tell me what's happened."

Gossos leaned across the table and whispered. "Don't you understand? The world is about to be plunged into war. The carefree attitude you see in this place is a facade. You've come to the center of the tornado."

"Look, Hosni. I need more specific information on what's ahead. We can't sit idly by and let mayhem be loosened on the world without doing our best to stop this avalanche of terror. You've got to help me."

"What exactly do you want?"

"Hosni, I need to know dates, times, places. When is the attack going to happen?" Isaiah cupped his hand over his mouth. "I need to have a more complete picture of the explosives being manufactured to get some sense of how this war might be fought."

"The last time you were here your presence was observed. Everyone is being watched. Directional microphones may even be picking up this conversation right now."

"What about your house? Wouldn't we be safe there?"

"Only if *you* weren't observed entering."

"Got any ideas?"

Gossos looked around the restaurant carefully. "In just a minute I will leave the entry card for my solar car on the table. It's parked just across the street, a big green eight-passenger job. Once inside, push 1 on the computer to lock you into the electrical guide wires under the street. Once you get moving, lie down in the seat. The automatic guidance system will drive you straight to my house and into the garage. Anyone seeing the vehicle enter the garage will just assume the car's been out on courier service. I'll get home another way."

"I'm putting you into jeopardy," Isaiah concluded. "We can call the whole thing off right now, and I'll go back to the telaport."

"Too late." Hosni shook his head. "Since you're here we might as well do everything possible to stop the madness breaking out around us." He slipped a small rectangular card onto the table. "I'm going to leave now. Give me ten minutes lead." He quickly got up and hurried toward the front door.

When the waiter returned, Isaiah explained that his friend had become ill. In light of the problem, Isaiah excused himself and left the astonished waiter staring.

The sleek solar-powered car was exactly where Gossos said it would be. Isaiah slipped the card in the slot on the side. The side of the vehicle raised straight up and Isaiah slipped inside. Because accidents were virtually impossible with both the internal guidance system and the traffic-controlled computerized response, the car's body was made of a very light alloy, allowing it to reach one hundred miles an hour in seconds. Isaiah slipped the card into the dashboard and the computer lights lit up. When he pushed the 1 button, the steering mechanism receded into the control panel and the side door dropped and locked into place as the silent engine effortlessly propelled the car forward. In a matter of seconds, the car swung into the express lane shooting through downtown at speeds between 80 and 90 miles per hour. He was soon traveling quickly through the suburbs. He slipped down into the seat and stretched out his long frame.

After several minutes, the solar car slowed down and began turning corners at more modest rates of speed.

Overhead, a mechanical voice advised the garage door was now open and the journey would be completed in twenty seconds. Before Isaiah could decide what to do, the car stopped as effortlessly and silently as it started. The garage door closed and the side door raised automatically.

"I'm never quite prepared for these automated gadgets," Isaiah said to himself as he got out of the car. "Just too confounding for an old codger like me."

"Come on in," Hosni called from an open door. "I just got here."

Isaiah followed his friend down the dim corridor into Gossos's living room.

"Sorry to be so blunt at the restaurant." Hosni pointed to a chair. "But I'm very concerned. People have gone stark raving nuts and you never know who is a government agent." He sat down across from Isaiah. "Everything is starting to feel like those ancient films of the Nazis taking over Berlin. Remember those old spy thrillers?

"I try to practice the faith I know I should have but I'm terrified most of the time. I don't think you realize how serious these matters are."

"Oh, I *s-u-r-e* do now." Isaiah rubbed his white curly hair. "Yes sir-e-e-e. I am a believer."

Hosni looked intensely into his friend's eyes. "We are just days away from the beginning of hostilities. As best I can tell, Tammuz 17 is the date troops start to march toward Jerusalem. Martial arts experts will be mixed in with armed soldiers. The final assault begins on Av 9."

"I see," Isaiah said slowly. "I'm not surprised."

"In the last few weeks, old manuals on how to make a wide assortment of bombs surfaced. I really fear what's ahead. The devices are primitive but effective."

"Give me some examples," Isaiah asked.

"Mercury fulminate crystals will explode by either shock or heat. They can be used by themselves or with other substances to cause explosions. Large quantities of nitric acid, sodium bicarbonate, and glycerine are being turned into nitroglycerine. Oxidizable materials are being treated with perchloric acid to make low-order explosives. Some of these materials will create sufficient shock waves to set off larger amounts of tri-nitro-toluene, TNT. Getting the picture?"

"Yes, rather clearly." Isaiah's eyes widened. "Anything else?"

"Anfos are being developed on a large scale basis," Gossos continued. "That's an old acronym for ammonium nitrate plus fuel oil solution. The whole thing has to be detonated but it makes quite a boom. Same result is possible by mixing potassium chlorate with Vaseline."

"I discovered the shipment of these chemicals weeks ago. That's how I got into the whole business." Isaiah scratched his head. "I didn't know that much about explosives then but I figured something big was coming down."

"Ever hear of nitrogen trichloride?" Gossos asked. "It's an oily yellow liquid that explodes when heated above 60 degrees celsius or ignited by a spark. Summer's a great time to use the stuff."

"I suppose they have developed delays and delay fuses?"

"Yes," Hosni said slowly, "but the plan is for straightforward assault tactics. There won't be many delays on any front."

"Is there anything else I should know?"

"One other thing would be very important . . ."

Suddenly the front door shattered. Splinters of wood flew in every direction. Three men broke into the room. Isaiah leaped to his feet, but the first man whirled around and smashed his shoe against the side of Isaiah's head. The black man flew backward, slamming into the wall and then bouncing face down onto the floor.

The other two intruders grabbed Hosni and slung him

against the opposite wall. The attackers pinned Gossos's head against the wall.

"You vile traitor!" the larger of the two thugs hissed in Gossos's ear. "Did you think you had tricked the government?" He brought his elbow down sharply into Hosni's solar plexus, doubling him in pain.

The second man pulled Hosni back up against the wall. "No longer will the likes of you be tolerated!" With one powerful blow he smashed the black man in the mouth, knocking him senseless.

Isaiah didn't move or open his eyes, but he could hear faintly.

"Sure the delay fuse is set right?" one of the men asked. A different voice answered, "This crazy thing is no different from the timer on a VCR." Another man grumbled, "Don't distract me." The first man insisted, "I still think we should have used a lightbulb bomb and turned all the lights out. They would have eventually destroyed themselves." The third man barked, "Shut up and hook these wires together. We've got four minutes before this house blows." The three men ran through the open door.

Isaiah tried to push himself up on his knees. He quickly saw the explosive device was locked in a box snapped shut as the assailants left. Hosni was slumped on the floor in a heap. As quickly as possible, Isaiah crawled to the side of his friend.

Gossos was totally unconscious. Isaiah pulled Hosni's arm over his shoulder but he could barely budge his friend. "I don't think I can get him out of here in time," he moaned.

Isaiah's stomach churned and his vision kept blurring. The blow to his head caused him to fade in and out. Inhaling as deeply as possible, he pulled Hosni behind him out of the living room. Precious seconds ticked away as he strained with everything left in him.

□ □ □

Ben quickly surveyed the list Esther Netanyahu just handed him. "I would conclude the Chinese are right at the front of this rebellion. The core of the coalition seems to be composed of Ethiopia, Iran, Jordan, Syria, Iraq, Egypt, and Russia. Looks like France and Italy are key players, too." Ben looked up at his secretary. "Who would you guess is the leader of the pack?"

"Egypt," Esther answered immediately. "From all of his statements, Ziad Atrash sounds like he's the mastermind."

"What do we *really* know of this man?"

"Anticipated your question." Esther smiled and pointed to the control module. "I have programmed in a great deal of information on the leader of the Egyptians."

"Excellent." Ben brought the screen up to full operation. Instantly biographical data detailing the educational and political development of the Egyptian president streamed before their eyes.

"You've got just about everything down to the size of his underwear," Ben noted. "Job well done."

"If I might be presumptuous," the secretary added, "I would suggest we scroll down to a special section on his psychological development."

"Oh?" Ben hit the clicker several times. "What have you learned?"

"Stop on page 62," Esther instructed.

Ben ran the report forward. He read with rapt interest.

Yeshua saw great promise for Ziad Atrash because of his unusual physical capacities and bright mind. However, the young man had to overcome the severe limitations of dyslexia. His early failures in school created a fiercely competitive personality and profoundly deep need to prove his worth by exceeding his contemporaries. One must be aware of the unpredictable aspects of Atrash's personality. He can be quite deceptive and deceitful when threatened.

"Could we be running for our lives because this guy couldn't get his act together?" Ben asked.

"Certainly looks like it, chief."

Ben read the rest of the report.

> Atrash was given the spiritual task of transforming his deceptive tendencies into spiritual integrity and honesty. However, he often lost interest in the demands of spiritual direction and retreated from the discipline of bringing his thought life captive to moral definition. One must always be aware that Atrash has large reservoirs of hostility. His anger can be explosive and destructive, making him treacherous when threatened. If he develops the necessary character traits to compensate for these problems, Ziad could make an exceptional national ruler.

"Says it all," Ben observed. "Not a pretty picture."

"Apparently, Atrash flunked the psychological exam. At least, we know something about what makes our enemy tick."

"Yes," Ben thought outloud. "We are faced with a very angry adversary who will stop at nothing to get his way. Obviously, a pawn of Satan's now."

□ □ □

Once Isaiah had pulled his friend into the garage, he was relieved to see the side of the car was still up. The computer card stuck out of the dash board.

If I can get Hosni in the vehicle, Isaiah thought, *maybe I can drop the doors and we'll have some protection against the blast.*

Isaiah pushed Gossos into the backseat and pulled himself into the driver's seat. He pushed the computer card deeply into the slot. The sides of the car dropped at once and the computer came on. Isaiah stared at the numbers without any idea what to hit.

"The 1 button got me here," he muttered. "Surely the 2 will take me somewhere else. What have I got to loose?"

He hit the switch. Instantly the garage door opened and the car went backward down the driveway into the street. The vehicle whirled around and started down the street.

"Thank you, Lord!" Ben said aloud.

Suddenly the car was rocked by a shock wave followed by a roaring boom. Isaiah hit the windshield and bounced back into the seat. The solar vehicle jerked to a stop for a moment and then started up again, speeding away. When Isaiah looked out the back window, he could see a nasty cloud of black smoke rising above the roof of Gossos's house.

"Where am I?" the voice in the back seat asked. "How did I get here?"

"It's a long story." Isaiah slumped. "The real question is where in the world are we going?"

The solar car swung wildly through the suburbs of Addis Ababa. Isaiah watched, trying to digest emotionally what had just transpired. Hosni sat up in the seat and held his swollen jaw.

"We'd best get you to the telaport and out of the country," Hosni finally said. "Our only hope is to put you on the next flight before they discover you're still alive."

"Who are *they*?"

"Government officials. No one else would have the explosives to blow up a house. You got a taste of what's coming to Jerusalem."

"You will have to go with me," Isaiah concluded. "They will be after you too."

"No." Hosni shook his head. "I belong in my own land. Who knows? I may yet prove to be of some help in the struggle ahead. I can hide out in the mountain country for the time being."

"I wish you'd go with me."

"Believe me, the offer is tempting. But I have family responsibilities here." Hosni looked around at the buildings flying past. "We're far enough away from the house to start back to the telaport. Punch in 6 and we'll be there in a few minutes."

The vehicle swung to the left and shifted into high, nearly flying at an oblique angle from the direction they had been going. "Hosni, you started to tell me one other important secret just as the assailants broke in. Remember?"

Gossos rubbed his jaw and blinked his eyes. "Nothing is coming back. My mind still feels like mush."

"Think hard."

The telaport loomed ahead. The solar car automatically turned toward the departure gates and slowed. Isaiah adjusted his clothes so they would not look so rumpled and prepared to leap out.

As the car pulled to a stop, Hosni reached for his friend's shoulder. "Now I remember. I don't know the details, but Jerusalem is vulnerable to sabotage from within. As hard as it is to believe, you have a traitor in your midst."

CHAPTER 16

On July 15, the nine leaders of the coalition against Israel assembled at the Red Sea command center outside of Cairo. The blistering sun was intolerable, the air was unbearably dry. The traditional dress of the past had been replaced by general's uniforms and military attire. Even Maria Marchino looked like a battle commander. Aides and assistants hurried in and out of the central conference room. Atrash's command center was fully operational with the satellite transmission capability completed.

President Ziad Atrash convened the meeting at noon to give all leaders ample time to arrive. Each of the heads of state gave brief reports of the readiness of their troops. The next item on the agenda was a survey of efforts to bring every possible nation into the political alliance.

"I have firm commitments from the United Kingdom and America," Maria Marchino reported. "New countries include Canada and Mexico. I have established direct connections with the Scandinavians including Norway and Sweden."

Fong rose to his feet. "We now have mutual defense

treaties with Japan, Korea, Indonesia, and India. Each country has agreed to commit troops in the event of unexpected counterattack."

"The African nations are firmly with us," Ali of Ethiopia reported. "Five new countries will stand behind us."

"Excellent!" Atrash shook his fist in the air. "The world is moving with us."

"You must appreciate," Marchino interjected, "that we have political commitments that do not necessarily reflect the consensus of the national populations. No one is sure exactly where the sentiments of the people are."

"When you've got the power and the control, plebiscites don't matter," Atrash snapped. "Bombs and bullets make the difference."

"We simply must be aware many people are still firmly committed to Yeshua," the Italian leader countered. "No one knows how significant the impact of their faith may be."

Ziad shrugged indifferently. "Come the night of Av 9, the world will be in the palm of our hands. That *fact* will change their minds."

Abu Sita rose to his feet. "We have divine assurance of victory. The gods have spoken in our midst."

Claudine Toulouse looked at Maria and rolled her eyes. Fong and Chardoff exchanged brief glances before turning their heads. The room became silent.

Abu Sita cleared his throat. "We continue to receive divine encouragement. In fact, Marduk has spoken of a great cosmic battle. . . ."

"Is it true your secretary of state is now completely insane?" the French leader broke in.

"El Khader . . . is . . . has been profoundly affected by his meditations," Rajah explained hesitantly. "The effect of such seances has occasionally been overpowering . . . but . . ."

"I hear he's gone stark raving nuts," Chardoff asserted bluntly.

"Unfortunately, he could not attend this meeting," Rajah spoke rapidly. "If he were here you would be reassured."

Leaders looked back and forward around the room but no one spoke.

"Let us move on to the review of our battle plan." Ziad beamed a laser pointer at the maps overhead. For the next five minutes, Atrash carefully detailed the attack plans, tracing the convergence of armies toward the Israeli border. The march of Chinese troops across Kazakhstan and Iran was complete. Soldiers were poised to link up with the Assyrians in their drive into Israel. Jordan and Iran were ready for a similar merger. Russian soldiers were massed for a quick sweep through Turkey into Assyria to join the Chinese. Atrash concluded, "Gentlemen, we are ready to begin the final overthrow of the central government."

Claudine Toulouse arose and pointed at the map of Europe. "You, *gentlemen*, will be glad to know that the joint command of Europe is poised for shuttle craft transport of troops leaving from Rome and Marseille simultaneously."

"Joint command?" Atrash interrupted. "We operate from one consolidated supreme command center in Cairo."

"With all due respect." Maria Marchino stood. "The European forces allied with us are organized under a subcommand to ensure absolute synchronization of timing."

"Such intervention is clumsy and unnecessary," the Egyptian barked. "*We* will maintain complete control from this base."

"Should our plans be intercepted," Marchino continued with cool detachment, "the European joint command will ensure continuity. No one knows for sure how the Immortals might intervene."

"No!" Ziad crossed his arms over his chest. "The battle

command must remain consolidated under my . . . er . . . our central control."

"Just a moment," Chardoff spoke out, "the women have a point. We should take every necessary precaution. I believe the Russians and Chinese must have a similar system as a secondary security check. We will operate as the Europeans do."

"No!" Atrash's voice rose even louder. "We must not fragment control or we expose ourselves to misunderstanding, inner divisions."

"I object!" Rajah Abu Sita waved a hand in the air. "We must stay with the basis on which the attack has already been defined."

"Why?" Claudine Toulouse shrugged. "Are you afraid of a better idea?"

"Women bother you?" Maria asked sardonically.

Atrash's bull neck turned deep red and the veins on his temple protruded. "Stop this distraction at once!" he bellowed.

"Don't try to intimidate me," Claudine snapped. "I'm not impressed by your macho charades."

"Women know *nothing* of war," Abu Sita hissed. "Shut up and listen to the experts."

"Experts?" Claudine laughed. "Not one of you chauvinists has even seen a battle much less fought in one. We know as much about warfare as any of you."

Suddenly the conference exploded in an uproar of cat calls and shouting. "Give her a broom to fight with," someone yelled. "I am in charge," Ziad bellowed back. "Arrogant chauvinist," a feminine voice hissed. Fong stomped his foot and asserted, "We will not be ignored." For ten minutes leaders screamed at each other like angry children.

"All right, all right," Atrash held up his hand in concession. "We can't go forward without total unity. I concede to the demands for an intermediate level command system." His face was red and he was trembling. "Abu Sita will now review the readiness of troops in his region." Ziad slid down in his chair, trying to regain composure.

The Assyrian leader carefully traced proposed battlefield lines and reviewed how the final march would begin. The rest of the afternoon was spent in fine tuning the strategy. Once consensus was achieved, the master plan was approved and the timetable for launching the invasion was complete. The coalition broke to prepare for supper.

Atrash pulled Rajah aside. "I don't like this sudden intervention of those two whining sows. During the first meetings, they said nothing!"

Abu Sita shrugged. "They're not smart enough to make much difference. Blow them off."

"I still don't like it."

"Who would listen to them once the war gets started?"

Ziad rubbed his chin. "Of course, we can always send them only the information we choose to release. Such a tactic would render their intermediate command useless."

Abu Sita leered cynically. "I knew you'd find a way to sack those old bags." He shifted to the other foot. "You did not mention the terrorist attack on the government buildings."

"Only the Ethiopians are aware of the broad guidelines of this plot. Even Ali doesn't know the details. You and I must have some secrets no one else knows, Rajah. The unexpected assures we stay in control. I don't trust these people."

At the same moment, the prime minister of Russia was slipping into Fong's room. The Chinese head of state pointed at the ceiling and shook his head. "Never know who is listening."

Alexi Chardoff knocked and winked. "We must discuss this 'new' intermediate command idea further."

"Everything is already in place." Fong's voice was flat, without emotion. "We could implement the approach immediately by using secondary means of communication."

"I would assume the other Asians will find this connection reassuring."

"Very," Fong answered.

Chardoff scribbled in Russian on his computer note pad, pushed the translation button, and the message appeared in Chinese. Fong read, "Once Jerusalem falls we will be in position to counter-attack the Arabs immediately."

"My friends are ready to move," Fong said solemnly.

Down the hall Claudine Toulouse quickly slipped past the guards at the end of the opposite corridor and hurried toward the suite at the far end. She didn't hesitate at the door but entered immediately.

Khalil Hussein was standing by the bar in the center of the room, wearing a bathrobe. For a moment he looked surprised when Claudine entered without knocking.

"I thought knocking would be too conspicuous." Claudine stood pensively by the closed door.

The king set the glass down and looked intensely at her. "Of course," he said. "Of course."

"Matters got a little tense today." Claudine took several steps forward. "I thought we might have a little talk about where we are."

"You want to talk politics?" Hussein let the robe slip open. He was only wearing a swimming suit underneath.

"Not really." Claudine stared at his hairy chest. Each time she meditated as Abu Sita instructed, the primitive urges became stronger. Suddenly, the power of raw lust surged through her veins. "I thought we might relax," Hussein suggested.

"I didn't bring a suit."

"Do you need one?" Hussein's question sounded innocuous, almost misleadingly innocent.

Claudine smiled but suddenly wasn't sure how to respond. Khalil was living up to his reputation for not committing himself. His face appeared quite passive. Claudine took a deep breath. "I want you." The words rushed out of her mouth.

"I'm not into sex," the king's voice was flat, emotionless. "Power is my game."

Claudine flinched and her face flushed. The words stung. She felt very old.

The king tossed the bathrobe aside. "Power is my aphrodisiac," the king continued. "Nothing turns me on like a touch of strength." He extended his hand. "That's why I find you so incredibly appealing. You feel like the most powerful woman I've ever known. I saw that capacity in you the first time we were in the same room."

Claudine swallowed hard and blinked, stunned.

"I see I've caught you off guard now." Khalil laughed uncharacteristically. "I love it when a woman is overwhelmed by me." He pulled her forward. "Particularly a powerful woman." Before Claudine could speak, the Jordanian king swept her into his arms and kissed her forcefully on the mouth. She knew the blood was rushing to her head and felt lightheaded. Claudine could barely breathe. The moment was beyond her wildest expectations.

Khalil let Claudine gently slip from his embrace, breathing on her face. "Now . . . who's in control?" He laughed.

□ □ □

Wendy Kohn buzzed Ben's office. "Dr. Feinberg, you have an urgent call from Isaiah Murphy. He says time is of the essence. Do you want to take it on your hologram phone?"

"Yes," Ben spoke into his wristwatch intercom phone.

"But we must lock in top security. I don't want this call monitored."

"Everything will be ready when you are." Wendy clicked off.

Ben immediately switched to the new hologram equipment. In moments Isaiah materialized in front of his desk. The third dimension image was so clear and sharp, Isaiah appeared to be present in the room. "Welcome back to Jerusalem," Ben joked.

"I must talk quickly," Isaiah sounded nervous. "We won't have much time."

"Where are you?" Ben's demeanor changed.

"I must not disclose my location," Isaiah spoke rapidly. "Suffice it to say I was identified in the Addis Ababa airport and had to flee before I got a flight out. I'm hiding out in the country."

"What can I do to help you?" Ben began reaching for computer and switch buttons.

"Record what I'm about to say. Jerusalem's government buildings are going to be bombed. The explosive materials are rather primitive but the detonating devices have all the electronic sophistication of today's technology. Watch out for anything unexpected that comes in large quantities."

"What should we do?"

"Expect the terrorists to attack sometime between Tammuz 17 and Av 9. They want to cripple you before the final assault on Av 9." Isaiah slowed down and spoke very deliberately. "Remember. Most of these bombs can be detonated either by heat or electric charge. The devices will not be particularly stable."

"We will be ready."

Isaiah's voice became more intense. "I don't know if you can protect yourselves. You have a traitor in your midst. I can't find out but some Jew will turn Judas. You won't have any way of knowing this person is lying."

"I am going to send a shuttle in to rescue you, Isaiah. You mustn't continue to be exposed to danger."

"Hosni's got to come out as well if I can locate him."

"Since I can't call you, contact me in exactly twenty-four hours and I'll have a plan ready."

"I'll do my best." Isaiah clicked off.

"Wendy," Ben yelled into his wristwatch phone, "get in here. Get Jimmy on the phone. He'll know about transportation. Get me a security person over here on the double."

"Of course, of course," the secretary answered. "Remember the appointment you made yesterday? Do you want me to reschedule the girl?"

"Rivka? I forgot about her." Ben thought for a moment. "No, don't send her away. I'll call Harrison myself and then talk to her."

For the next five minutes, Ben laid out plans for a special shuttle to deploy inside Ethiopia to pick up Isaiah. Jimmy agreed to find a pilot quickly to make the secret trip and took over the mission to rescue their friend. With that problem out of the way, Ben was ready to talk to Rivka Zachary.

The young woman hurried into his office. The black-haired beauty looked troubled and nervous. "Thank you for working me into your busy schedule, Dr. Feinberg." She awkwardly wrung her hands.

Ben pointed to a chair in front of his desk and sat down. He studied Rivka carefully. She was smaller than he remembered but certainly had the Zachary family eyes. "My assistants said you knew something about security problems," he came straight to the point.

"Y-e-s," Rivka pulled at her handkerchief. "I'm afraid . . ." her voice trailed away. "I've made a very big mistake." She began to cry.

"Please go on," Ben urged.

"Perhaps you remember Zvilli Zemah?" Rivka sniffed.

"No," Ben shook his head.

"When you lectured at the university, Zvilli heckled you."

"Oh yes," Ben nodded. "A rather arrogant student as I recall."

"He's both a student and a lecturer. Please understand." Rivka bit her lip. "I don't know how I ever got into this mess. I really have always been a good person."

Ben stared, trying to understand.

"You see . . . Zvilli was fascinating, very attractive. He is a very brilliant man, you know. I suppose I was just too immature."

"What are you suggesting, Rivka?"

"I was swept off my feet. He was so self-assured."

Ben crossed his arms over his chest and pulled at his beard. "Why are you telling me this story? Shouldn't you be talking with a religious counselor?"

"Oh, Dr. Feinberg. My family has always spoken so highly of you. I just knew I could trust you."

"You can."

"Then you must know what is being planned."

"Planned?"

"Because Zvilli and I became . . . involved . . . he was able to recruit me to be part of a plot to attack the government. Terrible things are underway." Rivka began to speak more rapidly, "People will be killed, property will be destroyed. I'm terrified that I am caught in the middle of the whole crazy thing."

Ben leaned forward, his eyes intense. "Tell me exactly what this Zvilli is up to."

"I'm not sure, but he seems to be an Arab agent in charge of sabotage in this city. He wants me to help him blow up buildings." Rivka began crying again.

Ben got up and walked around his desk. "I must ask you once more. Why are you telling me this information?"

"I can't go through with these terrible plans, no matter how I've come to feel about Zvilli. I don't want to hurt him, but I can't be part of destroying anyone else. I must stop this horrible plan."

"You want me to help you get away from him?"

"Well . . . no . . . I really want to keep him from doing something violent. And I don't want to be part of any diabolical scheme."

"You are willing to work with me and do what I tell you?"

"Yes, Dr. Feinberg. Yes, I'll do anything to make things right."

"Will you tell the date, time, and place of the first attack?"

"Of course," Rivka pleaded. "I will tell you everything you want to know."

Ben stared at her. *What a perfect way to set me up*, he thought. *She gets my sympathy and sucks me into this plot up to my eyeballs.* Ben bit his lip and looked carefully at her pleading eyes. *What a perfect traitor this descendent of Dr. Zachary makes. Like Judas, she can betray her friend with a kiss. They must think I am a complete fool.*

"The attack is set for tomorrow morning, Tammuz 17," Rivka began. "All I know is that the first bombing will occur in this building. Dr. Feinberg, you might be able to stop the disaster if you are here."

Ben put his hand on her shoulder. "Rivka, how do I know you are telling me the truth?"

☐ ☐ ☐

As the sun set over New Babylon, Rajah Abu Sita stood in the Temple of Marduk, watching his secretary of state performing rituals before the giant statue of the god. The Syrian king slowly walked up the steps to get closer to El Khader to observe him more closely. At the back of the Temple, guards lurked behind the pillars.

El Khader wore the ancient robes of the Babylonian priests with the domed hat perched above his white hair. He moved back and forth from the statue to the bronze brazier throwing handfuls of incense into the fire. The old man stopped periodically and lifted his hands above his head making unintelligible incantations. The huge sleeves of the robe fell down past his elbows.

Rajah stopped on the top step, only feet away from El Khader and watched carefully. For all of his complaints, Abu Sita had great affection for this strange man. He had been a family friend forever, one of the faces Rajah remembered from his childhood. In fact, El Khader had been an adviser to Rajah's father during the years he was king. Abu Sita could not allow harm to come to the old man.

El Khader lowered his hands and turned toward the head of state. His eyes were bloodshot and his vision unfocused. Even though he looked at Rajah, there was no recognition. The secretary of state kept on turning toward the brazier with slow, mechanical, zombie-like movements.

"El Khader," Rajah commanded sharply. "Speak to me."

Saying nothing, the secretary of state dropped more incense into the flaming brazier. The smoke bellowed up into his face, but El Khader did not flinch.

Abu Sita ran his hands nervously through his hair and crossed his arms over his chest. For several moments, he paced back and forth while the prayers continued. Finally he reached out and gently touched the old man's shoulder. "Please just speak to me," he said quietly.

El Khader turned slowly and blinked several times. "I must be about my work. My Lord commands I serve him day and night."

"I am your master, your king," Rajah spoke compassionately, "not this statue."

"No," the old man drawled, "not anymore. My thoughts

have been taken captive by him who is the Lord of the underworld."

"Please," Rajah begged, "you are not well. The strain of these meditations has overtaken you."

El Khader looked puzzled and nodded knowingly.

"I don't know what's happened, but this thing has gotten way out of control. Something has gone wrong."

"Do not doubt what you see. We have come to the greater truth."

"Please." Rajah held up his hands in supplication. "You must let me help you. You need rest, medication, treatment."

"Yes . . . I . . . do," El Khader spoke more coherently. "But all of that must come later. Now is the time for you, too, to worship the great Marduk. The final battle is about to begin, and our praise makes the lord of the dark world stronger. We must call the peoples of the world to adore our god as he goes forth tomorrow into this final battle in the heavenlies."

"No." Rajah shook his head. "You have been swallowed by this thing I've started. I want it stopped."

"Far too late." El Khader's voice seemed to come from some other place. "Far, far too late now."

"I will help you." The Syrian king took El Khader's arm and gently pulled him back from the statue.

The old man jerked away with extraordinary strength. "No!" El Khader's voice dropped to a threatening guttural sound. "I will help you! Beware! All is not as it appears. The spirits send you their warning. *You* are being betrayed."

"What?" Rajah's eyes widened.

"Our plans are in jeopardy!" For a moment the old man sounded coherent.

Abu Sita shook his head as if trying to clear his mind. "Please repeat what you said."

El Khader took a deep breath and opened his mouth. Suddenly his body convulsed. He swallowed hard and grabbed his chest. His eyes rolled back in their sockets; the color drained from his face. The old man slowly sank to the floor. Like the final spark in a burned-out ember turning to smoke, his life ebbed away.

CHAPTER 17

As the sun rose over the desert on the morning of Tammuz 17, Ziad Atrash moved into place at his Red Sea command post. During the night every system had been tested and retested for instant communication. Television monitors flashed images of troop convergence, recording every detail of the historic linkup.

Not far away at a reconstructed shrine erected before the pyramid of Cheops, priests of Osiris performed the ancient rites of the pharaohs. At Lexor in the Valley of the Kings, other priests had begun the same rituals, calling on the gods to arise and lead Egypt to the glory of the past.

The Russian and Chinese troops completed their double-time march across the Caucasus Mountains through Georgia and swept down into Azerbaijan. The combined armies were poised on the Iranian border at Zhdanovsk. Iran and Jordan were linking up with the Syrian army in the desert at Ar Rutbah. Near this town, Cyrus had defeated Belshazzar at Opis in 539 B.C., fulfilling the prophecy Daniel deciphered from the palace wall: *mene, mene, tekel, parsin.* Each army moved into place with precision.

The European television monitor flashed pictures of French troops loading at the Paris International Telaport. At the same time Italian troops marched across the runways toward large shuttles waiting for them to board.

Everything is unfolding according to plan, Ziad said to himself. *The rest of my scheme should be taking shape in just a few hours.*

□ □ □

At 9:30 A.M. Rivka Zachary left her apartment and walked through the back streets of Jerusalem. The rest of the city was relatively quiet as citizens observed the religious holiday.

The 17th of Tammuz had been a significant day of mourning throughout the history of Israel. Jews traditionally stayed in their homes and reflected on the past. Just as the prophet Zechariah predicted thousands of years earlier, the holy day was still observed in the millennial kingdom. Even though all days of fasting had become feasts during the reign of Yeshua, the occasion retained a grave and serious character. Moses broke the first tablets of the Law on this day because of the rebellion of the Israelites. In 587 B.C., the Babylonians broke through the walls of Jerusalem on this date. Twenty-one days later, they destroyed the Temple on Av 9. History repeated itself in A.D. 70. The Roman General Titus catapulted large stones into Jerusalem, killing many priests and stopping all temple sacrifices on the 17th of Tammuz. Again, twenty-one days later, on Av 9, the second temple was destroyed. The remembrance of the date could not but cause sober reflection.

At 10:00 A.M. Rivka Zachary arrived at a warehouse three blocks from Zvilli Zemah's apartment. Rivka shut the door quietly behind her and looked around the large room. A very dilapidated solar-powered van was parked in the center near the work area. Zemah was already at work, poring over a small box on a long mechanic's bench. Bottles of acid, strands of wire, and empty boxes littered the table.

"Ah, my love! You are here." Zemah laid down a wrench and opened his arms. "Come to me."

Rivka hurried across the cement floor and opened her arms. The white-haired man kissed her passionately.

"Today's the big day." Zvilli pulled her toward the table. "We are almost ready to leave as soon as the other men arrive."

"Other men?" Rivka jumped. "You never mentioned others."

"Didn't want you to have information that could put you in jeopardy." Zvilli pushed two small wires into place in the box and snapped the lid shut. "Three helpers are coming in from Egypt."

"Oh, no!" Rivka held her face with both hands. "I wanted to be just with you."

"Don't worry, darling. They don't know you either."

"Zvilli . . ." Rivka pulled on his arm. "This whole thing has gotten completely out of hand, we must—"

Zemah gripped her arm firmly. "We are fulfilling our destiny. Be who you are."

"We still have time to turn back."

"What?" Zvilli shook her slightly. "Don't say such a thing."

Suddenly the front door opened again and three large men hurried inside.

"You're here," Zvilli called out. "Good. Let's load. The battle is about to begin."

"In that thing?" One of the men pointed to the solar-powered van and grumbled, "Where'd you get that dinosaur?"

"We will use the engine to help detonate the Anfos mix in the back," Zemah explained. "Plus, the shape is just right. Your boss assured me this is how terrorists operated in the 'good ole days.' So few people will be out on the streets, the old crate won't make much difference today."

Rivka watched in bewilderment as the men silently went to work. They obviously knew exactly what to do.

After a couple of minutes Zvilli said firmly, "Get in the van and don't talk. I don't want anyone to be distracted. The time has come to act."

"But—" Rivka reached out, but the driver revved up the engine and the van drowned out her voice.

No one was on the streets as the rickety old van lumbered slowly toward the Knesset. The distance was short and the trip did not take long.

"Turn left," Zemah grunted to the Egyptian driver. "We're not far from the Knesset. Just keep a nice slow pace."

"Zvilli . . ." Rivka reached over the seat and put her hand on his shoulder. "I need to tell you—"

"Don't talk," Zemah snapped. His entire demeanor had changed during the trip from the warehouse. His eyes were cold and black.

"Circle around to the back and pull up in front of the Internal Affairs building," Zemah spoke rapidly. "We will park between it and the Knesset. When the van explodes, we can hit both buildings."

The driver pulled off the main thoroughfare and headed up the street between the two government office complexes. He slowed, pulled toward the empty curb, and shut the engine off.

Zemah turned around in his seat. "We're going to take care of some unfinished business for my friends before we set off the big firecracker in back. The last blast didn't accomplish what was intended and our leaders weren't happy. This time I will personally make certain we don't have any slip-ups. To make sure the Internal Affairs building is out of commission, we will wire it first before we explode the van."

"Okay. What's first?" the driver asked.

"Get those pyrotechnic bombs out," Zemah instructed. "I want all of us out of the van. We will plant bombs on several floors. We need to get these explosives in place quickly."

One of the Arabs opened the side panel of the van while another hooked wires from the engine to wires leading out of the piles of explosives in the back. Zemah and the third man quickly pulled out other crates and boxes of materials and set them on the sidewalk.

"The incline up to those steps is steep," Zemah noted. "Watch out for the stepped flower beds. We're going to have a hill and steps to climb, so hurry. Assemble the stuff up there on the plaza at the base of the steps into the building.

"I've *got* to talk to you," Rivka confronted Zvilli. "If anything that has happened between us is real and enduring, we must face the truth together."

"Stop it!" Zemah shook her violently. "I've waited my whole life for a moment like this. Now shut your mouth and get on with it." He forced a heavy box into her hands and slung a bag over his shoulder. "You should consider yourself lucky I even gave you the time of day." Zvilli pushed her ahead of him toward the steps of the Internal Affairs building. "You're too deep in this plot even to have the right to a second thought. Faster!" he shouted at her, hurrying forward.

"Why do you do this thing?" the voice came from the steps.

Zvilli looked up and to his astonishment, two white-haired men stood resolutely with their hands on their hips at the bottom of the steps. "Feinberg?" he gasped.

"You still have time to repent and change your course," Ben Feinberg answered.

"How . . . did you get here?" Zvilli sputtered. The three Egyptians ran to his side. "How did you find out?"

"The more important question is, what will *you* do now?" Jimmy Harrison asked.

"I tried to tell you." Rivka set the box on the ground and pushed it aside. "All of this is terribly, terribly wrong."

Zemah turned slowly, his eyes narrowing in anger. "You told them?"

"It was for our good, darling. We couldn't start a life together on such a wicked basis."

In one wild swing Zemah hit Rivka in the face, knocking her senseless into a flower bed. She rolled across the flowers and dropped down into the next terraced garden on the level below.

"Get them!" one of the Egyptians yelled.

"No!" Zemah dropped to one knee and whipped open the bag over his shoulder. He pulled out two bottles of yellow liquid and handed one to an Egyptian. "Perfect opportunity for us."

"What you do will be a judgment on your own head," Ben warned.

"Oh yeah?" Zvilli crept forward. "Ever hear of picric acid? Tri-nitro-pheno? TNP? A little sulfuric acid, a little nitric acid, and it's amazing what is possible." He raised his arm over his head. "Getting rid of you two creeps is a real bonus."

"Don't!" Ben held up his hand. His eyes filled the thick glasses to the rims, his ponytail swung back and forth. "Don't come any closer. I warn you."

"You warn me?" Zvilli laughed. He spoke out of the side of his mouth to the Egyptian, "Get close enough to throw the stuff and hit the ground."

"Stop where you are!" Jimmy shook his cane in the air.

"Now!" Zemah yelled and charged forward.

Suddenly the entire plaza was engulfed in a ball of fire, the attackers incinerated on the spot. The explosion sent the other two Egyptians rolling down the incline wrapped in flames. Clouds of black oily smoke shot up the front of the building. No one was left on the steps. Jimmy and Ben were gone.

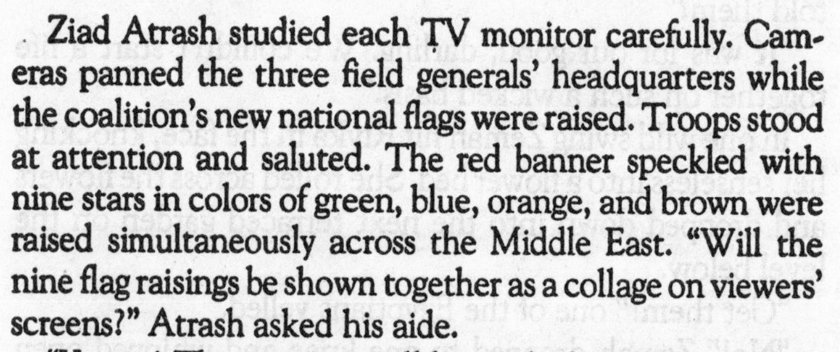

Ziad Atrash studied each TV monitor carefully. Cameras panned the three field generals' headquarters while the coalition's new national flags were raised. Troops stood at attention and saluted. The red banner speckled with nine stars in colors of green, blue, orange, and brown were raised simultaneously across the Middle East. "Will the nine flag raisings be shown together as a collage on viewers' screens?" Atrash asked his aide.

"Yes sir! The segment will be ready for insertion when we roll the footage of the nine leaders' declaration of war. We will intersperse these pictures while you read your intention of war."

"Excellent." Ziad smiled broadly. "Everything is on schedule." He looked to the monitor at the far end of the room; shuttles from Italy and France arrived and unloaded at the Damascus telaport. "The last piece in the puzzle is in place." He chuckled to himself. "The noose is about to be placed around the neck of Israel."

Another monitor flashed the prerecorded clip of Ziad's call for world rebellion. According to Atrash's instructions, he was in the most prominent position among the national leaders. Ziad listened carefully to his own speech. Pictures of the other eight conspirators clustered around his oversized image. "The time has come for the entire world to proclaim freedom from the tyranny of Jewish oppressors."

A wicked smile crossed the Egyptian leader's face. *The*

French and Italian broads didn't like the word 'tyranny.' Thought they overruled me! He snorted defiantly. *In the final days ahead, they will learn who is running the world!*

"Today our armies have joined in one single great effort on behalf of all humanity. We call on the nations of the world to link arms with us and join our armies." The Egyptian general's voice sounded fervent and inspiring. "For weeks satellite programming has given you religious instruction to set you free from fear of the Immortals. The gods are now with us! Have no fear of retribution for our efforts are undergirded by supernatural power."

"Everything is in place, pending your approval," the aide interjected.

"Yes," Ziad said slowly. "I am satisfied." He glanced at a special monitor at the far end of the room. "We will add one more piece of footage. I want the unexpected explosion in Jerusalem to come immediately after the pictures of the flag raisings."

"Explosion?" The aide glanced at his electronic notepad. "I don't have any indication—"

"Of course not," Ziad snapped. "The explosion was a state secret. I want to see the footage now."

"But sir . . ." The aide bit at his lip. "Nothing of that sort has come in from the satellites."

Ziad glanced at the clock. "Of course it has. The explosions were set to go off ten minutes ago. The agents know I will not tolerate any deviation from the plan."

"With all due respect." The aide took a step backward. "We do not show any TV transmission or seismographic data of a significant explosion."

Ziad stared at the screen. "Roll the tapes backward and restore zoom capacity. We should have clear pictures of the government buildings going up in smoke."

The aide quickly spoke into his wristwatch and commanded a reset to 11:00. The satellite pictures automatically enlarged, pinpointing three square blocks around the Knesset, but nothing unusual appeared.

"I don't understand." Ziad frowned and hit the table. "Rewind further!"

Just as the timer hit 10:45, a puff of smoke arose from the front of the Internal Affairs Building.

"Is that what you're looking for?" The aide spoke hesitantly. "That burst couldn't have been more than a small bomb. Doesn't look like any damage was done."

"Closer!" Atrash demanded. "Replay it slowly."

The images enlarged again. A van pulled to the curb. Small figures could be seen moving across the plaza. A fireball flashed and smoke obscured the area. When the cloud cleared, the van stood by itself.

Ziad cursed. "Those idiots have bungled everything! I wanted those pictures of destruction on the air! The world must see that revolution is already underway in Jerusalem itself!" He slung a chair across the room and into the wall. "I won't stand for incompetence!"

Aides snapped to attention. The Egyptian leader stormed around the room cursing. "How could they do this to *me*?!" He stared at the empty monitor.

"Uh . . . uh . . . sir," the aide squirmed. "An emergency call is waiting on the reserved security line from New Babylon."

Ziad glared. "Can't those idiots do anything right?" He snatched the receiver from the man's hand. "Hello."

Rajah Abu Sita cleared his throat nervously. "The bombing didn't happen. We've been monitoring from here. In fact, all contact with Zemah has been lost."

"I know," Ziad barked. "He was *your* friend. What happened?"

"Something went wrong."

"Obviously." Atrash sneered.

"I have other concerns," Rajah hesitated. "There . . . is . . . another problem."

"Can't it wait?"

"Uh . . . no. El Khader died last night during an incantation."

"*Died?*"

"It was bizarre, eerie . . . like something consumed him."

"What are you suggesting?"

"Just before he died," Rajah stopped and caught his breath, "he warned me we were being betrayed. And then he toppled over."

Ziad blinked rapidly and ran his hand through his hair. "Betrayed?" his voice lowered.

"I couldn't tell whether El Khader was giving me a message from the gods or if he had gone crazy."

"I don't understand," Ziad spoke slowly and deliberately.

"I had the feeling El Khader had seen some kind of vision. Listen, this business of contacting the spirits is more dangerous than we thought."

"The old frog just croaked, that's all."

"He was one of my best friends," Rajah warned.

"Of course, of course. Don't get excited."

"I've told you all that I know."

"Then pay attention to every detail you see anywhere," Ziad Atrash demanded. "Let me know if anything suspicious turns up. I've got to get back to the command post." He clicked off the receiver and returned to the monitors.

"Transmission of the international telecast is almost ready to begin," an aide advised.

Ziad cursed again. "I wanted those pictures of the Knesset in flames." He crossed his arms over his chest and shook his head. "Are all channels being monitored?"

"With the exception of the two intermediate command channels in Europe and Russia."

"Cut into them," Atrash demanded. "I want every international communique tapped and recorded."

The aide took a step back. "I'm sorry. We can't. Both transmissions are jammed with a code we can't break."

The Egyptian leader's glance darted back and forth. "When was this exception discovered?"

"Just this morning, excellency."

Atrash turned away and stared blankly at the bank of televisions. *What are they trying to pull? Was El Khader on to something?* He snapped his fingers and beckoned for the aide. "Record what you don't understand. Do everything necessary to intercept the messages on those two channels."

"At once." The aide bowed and hurried out of the room.

Atrash turned back to the two monitors of European and Asian troops assembling. He listened to the strange garbled sounds of the European leaders talking to each other. "Surely those two old bags couldn't be up to anything of much significance, but those Russians . . ."

In Rome, Maria Marchino listened carefully to the secret transmission as her field general reported the state of preparations. "Are all personnel unloaded and situated in Damascus?" she asked.

"Yes, Madam President," the general answered. "Our joint command center with the French has been consolidated and integrated. Everything is in place."

"Excellent. How is morale?"

The general hesitated. "Our troops will do as they are ordered. I am confident of my men."

"But their state of mind?"

"From their youth they were taught to obey the authorities as unto the Lord. We must believe that in some way we don't quite understand your directives are linked to the purposes of the Almighty."

"Well spoken, general. But you don't sound very convinced."

"Frankly . . ." He cleared his throat. "Many soldiers are confused. I have no way of knowing how many remain committed to the traditional faith. Of course, no one knows what could happen if the Immortals show up."

"Do not be afraid to speak freely, General," Maria spoke earnestly. "I want to know your mind on this matter."

After a long pause, the general answered. "What if we are wrong in our calculations? How do you rationalize what we are about to do?"

"If we are wrong," Maria said slowly, "we can take comfort in remembering the Immortals have always acted benevolently. We will plead for mercy and explain we were deceived by the Egyptian leaders. Does that answer bring you comfort?"

"Some."

"Then I offer you more assurance. When we reach a strategic place in the battle, you may be ordered to turn on the Egyptians. We will claim to have always been acting on behalf of Yeshua's government and be exonerated. If the Immortals don't appear and Atrash is right about these other gods, we can keep the Egyptians from becoming the supreme power."

"Amazing!" the field general gasped. "Brilliant."

"You will read the secret instructions to be opened following this phone call. The code is 666. At the right moment I will give you our alternative plan and tell you where to strike. The most important fact is not to trust the Egyptians."

"Your wish is my command!"

"My great and fearless general doesn't sound so intimidated now," Maria chided. "Let's get on with the war. We have no choice but to hit them with all the firepower we have."

"We're ready."

"And what happens if you receive orders that I have not confirmed?"

"I will ignore them."

Maria laughed. "Keep steady, old boy. You're about to make history. Ciao."

The general punched in the code necessary to open the courier's pouch lying on the table before him. He took out the large envelope marked Top Secret: Operation Scorpion, and tore open the top. The general dumped out a military map and several typed pages. On the map a semicircle was drawn from Damascus to Al Mawsil in northern Iraq back down to New Babylon over to Ar Rutbah and on to Amman, Jordan. The tip of the line at Damascus was sharpened like a stinger.

He read the instructions aloud. "Like the tail of a scorpion uncoiling, we will strike as our troops close the noose around Jerusalem. The final assault will come down from the north out of Damascus. Should any Jews escape, they will be driven south toward the Dead Sea and the desert.

"Due to distance, methodical placement of troops, and the time needed to solidify world opinion behind the coalition, we can anticipate the final assembling of troops will occur on the evening of Av 8. By this date a solid wall of soldiers will have formed to the east, west, and north of Jerusalem. The first violence will come like poison from the scorpion's tail."

The general traced the line carefully with his fingertip and looked at the day-by-day schedule for troop movements. He began reading again, "Should Immortals emerge and attempt to disrupt troop movement, do not hesitate or wait for command central authorization to use bombs. Even Immortals will not be able to withstand the explosion."

The general put the paper down and looked out the window at the troops going through their paces. He pursed his lips and scratched his head. "We certainly better hope somebody knows what he is talking about."

CHAPTER 18

Rivka Zachary slowly crawled out of the flower bed and onto the steep, sloping sidewalk. The stench of burning flesh hung in the air. She still felt woozy and her vision wasn't yet clear. A terrible ringing noise in her ears slowly subsided. With some difficulty, Rivka got to her feet and wiped the blood from her mouth.

She slowly looked around the plaza. Stains of black smoke covered the front of the building and windows were blown out. Not far away, lying in the shrubs, were the smoldering remains of two bodies. Near the van two other bodies were still burning.

"God help us." Rivka moaned and rubbed her eyes. "They killed Dr. Feinberg and his friend!" She ran toward the front stairs into the Internal Affairs Building. "Where are their bodies?" She hurried up the steps in despair. "I am responsible for their deaths," she sobbed.

"Not so, my child," a man's voice answered from behind the broken glass door at the top of the stairs.

Rivka froze in place.

Ben Feinberg and Jimmy Harrison stepped out of the glass door. "Do not fear, we are quite fine."

Rivka gasped and pointed but couldn't speak.

"I must apologize," Ben said as he walked down the steps. "I really wasn't sure if you were telling me the truth. I'm sorry I doubted you."

"But . . . I . . . was sure . . . the bomb got you."

"Actually, my distrust saved our lives," Ben explained. "Since I suspected a trap, Jimmy helped me make some unusual preparations for our visit from Zemah."

"But I saw you standing on the steps—" Rivka protested.

"No," Jimmy answered. "What you saw were carefully placed hologram images. Ben and I were inside talking to Zemah on the phone."

"Thank God," Rivka held her cheeks with both hands.

"In order to create the effect," Ben added, "we had to use the most powerful laser equipment available. It took an enormous amount of energy. The hologram was actually a very intense stream of hot light."

"Zvilli made a great mistake running at the images," Jimmy continued. "We warned him but he wouldn't stop. The heat from the lasers triggered his bombs. The rest of the story is scattered around the plaza."

Rivka slowly sank down on the steps and cried. "How could I ever have been so stupid? I jeopardized everyone . . . and I've been totally unfaithful. . . to God and myself."

Jimmy sat down beside the young woman and put his arm around her shoulder. "Rivka, your heart overwhelmed your head, but in the end you did the right thing. God is gracious to forgive and restore us when we confess and repent. In contrast, Zemah was destroyed by his own obstinacy.

"I really loved him," Rivka cried. "I would never, never have believed he could strike me."

"I am sorry." Jimmy patted her on the shoulder.

"I must do something to right the wrong I have done."

Rivka clung to him. "Surely, I can make some amends for the problems I have caused. Tell me what I can do."

"Hmmm . . . what an interesting thought." Ben sat down on the step on the other side of the young woman. "I think you could be of *significant* assistance if you are really serious."

"Oh, yes. Yes!"

"Rivka, you could go back to the university and spread the word about Zemah to the students. We are going to need their help in defending the city. Could you help organize a resistance movement?"

"We only have twenty days to get ready for a terrible assault," Ben added.

"I would do anything," Rivka assured. "Anything."

Jimmy leaned back on his cane and smiled. "We were just about your age at a very similar time in history. The place was Los Angeles and the attack of evil was coming at us full tilt. We were young but we made a tremendous difference. Maybe just such a moment has come again."

"Whatever you tell me, I will do," Rivka answered.

"Good!" Ben patted her on the back. "From now on, Rivka, we'll be a team just as we were with your ancestor, Dr. Zachary long ago in Bozrah and Petra during the Great Tribulation period."

□ □ □

Late that night Isaiah and Deborah Murphy sat glued to their television in their Los Angeles home, listening in silent dread to Egyptian President Atrash's declaration of war. Wearing a general's uniform bedecked with medals, the Egyptian's barrel chest looked massive.

"Arise, peoples of the globe!" the voice boomed over the television. "Join our righteous cause and strike out to realize your own destiny. Throw off the bonds of oppression now!"

Deborah reached for Isaiah's hand. "Thank God Jimmy was able to get you back home before the war began."

"Our armies are gathering today," Ziad hammered away. "Nations that stand with us now will reap the greatest rewards. Peoples of the world, demand your leaders lock arms with us." Pictures of flags rising over armies filled the screen. The exhilarating music of a military band blared in the background.

"What do you think?" Isaiah asked his wife.

"I'm terrified! We know all too well how people can be stampeded by political leaders into doing crazy, irresponsible things. The recent riots at the L.A. Courthouse are a sober reminder of how unstable this population is."

"You're right, Deborah. There is no way to predict public response. Much will depend on what the president of this country does."

"Want to make any predictions?"

Isaiah studied the television screen as he thought. Pictures of troops marching with weapons in hand flashed by. The faces of the nine leaders of the rebellion kept appearing on the screen. "The heart is deceitful and desperately wicked," he quoted aloud. "Who can know it?"

"So?"

"I think the odds are high the politicians will do whatever they think is expedient. So, get ready for a national call to join the war."

"We've got to get the old gang together and consider what we can do," Deborah concluded. She shook her finger at him. "This is no time to sit idly by and observe."

Isaiah scratched his head and rolled his eyes. "Didn't seem to me like I've been doing much sitting around lately."

□ □ □

As the day drew to a close in the Middle East, coalition leaders linked up in a satellite joint conference on the day's progress. The hologram images created an appearance of nine people sitting in a circle speaking to each other. Each wore a military uniform.

Ziad Atrash opened the meeting, calling for a report on the status of the army. Abu Sita responded with a detailed accounting of where all troops were located. "We are in place and have met our initial schedule," he concluded.

"Excellent," the Egyptian leader answered. "Do we have any pressing concerns?"

Ali of Ethiopia spoke up. "As has been reported, the joint forces of Ethiopia and Egypt will shortly be consolidated just outside of Elath on the Gulf of Aqaba. We are ready to march up the Jordanian side of Wadi al 'Arabah and on past the Dead Sea on our way to Jerusalem to complete the tail of the scorpion." He cleared his throat. "Nevertheless, many of our men are secretly afraid of what the Immortals may do."

The leaders solemnly looked at each other and turned to Atrash.

"No one has seen those creatures for months," the Egyptian said disdainfully. "We have received no interference. Why should we worry now?"

"What if it's a trap?" Fong asked.

"We are prepared to blast them with everything from fire bombs to dynamite," Ziad snapped. "Remember, *we* have the guns. No one remembers what incredible damage these devices can inflict."

"Still . . ." Fong's eyes narrowed even further. "We do not know where they are and why they've vanished."

Ziad turned to Rajah Abu Sita. "The time has come to share a communique received some time ago by El Khader from the gods."

"The urgency of war preparations delayed the report

until now," Abu Sita sounded nervous. He pulled a file from a briefcase at his feet and thumbed through several pages. "The god Marduk is preparing for a great heavenly battle. As we fight in the framework of earthly time, a war will begin in eternity. Our visible forces fight alongside the heavenly hosts of the gods. We can conclude the Immortals will be too busy with their own problems to deal with us."

"Where'd you get that non-s-e-n . . . stuff?" Chardoff grunted.

"During one of El Khader's midnight incantations," the Syrian king answered.

Khalil Hussein and Claudine Toulouse stared at each other but said nothing.

"Look," Atrash said harshly, "the time has come to decide where we stand. We are either with the gods or not.

"This whole crusade began because *I* discovered the power of Yeshua was not only waning but could be displaced by other gods. Now, are we polytheistic or not?" he scowled. "Decide!"

For several moments there was a long, awkward pause.

"We are already committed to the conflict," Fong spoke in emotionless tones that betrayed no hint of true feeling. "The issue is whether we are vulnerable to forces we do not fully understand."

"Only if we are divided," the Egyptian president shot back. He slowly looked around the circle. "Our only danger is division from within."

The leaders froze in place and no one spoke. Finally the Jordanian king said, "The day has been most successful. We have much to celebrate. The only significant question before us is how the rest of the world has perceived our actions."

"The reports will start coming in tomorrow," Atrash

answered quickly. "We are scheduled to reconvene at the same hour tomorrow afternoon. Is that agreeable?"

Heads nodded and the images faded from the hologram system.

Atrash immediately reconnected with the Syrian leader. "Rajah, I don't like the smell of any of this."

Rajah Abu Sita shook his head. "We have not been able to crack the code the Europeans and the Russians are using to contact their people. We have no alternative but to go through the leaders with our communiques."

Atrash sneered. "We have a blind spot and I don't like it. After we take Jerusalem and attack the Europeans, we have no way of knowing how they will respond without a line inside their communications. We must work harder to crack the code."

"We are," Rajah assured the Egyptian. "Don't worry. We'll have the answer by the time the counterattack begins."

"You better!" Atrash flipped the switch and the Syrian's image disappeared. Ziad sat for several minutes staring at the wall. Finally he rang for his first assistant to come in.

The aide walked briskly into the room. "At your service." The young general snapped to attention.

"I want a special monitor attached to all calls coming in and out of Abu Sita's headquarters. I want to know everything he says to anyone. Understood?"

The aide looked surprised. "You are speaking of the leader of Syria and Iraq?"

"Exactly! The order is top secret. But I want to know even when he snores."

"Of course." The aide frowned and hurried from the room.

Atrash cursed. "I control all of the world's communication systems and the only existing army, and yet I can't trust *one* of them."

□ □ □

"I'm glad Ben brought you to our house." Cindy scurried around her kitchen as she talked to Rivka. "I think it's time for us girls to have a chat." She stopped and looked out the window as the last light of day completely faded into total blackness. "Yes, the night is coming."

"I feel like such a fool." Rivka buried her face in her hands. "I have betrayed everything that was important in my life."

Cindy put her arm around the girl. "You trusted someone who deceived you. I know your pain is very deep."

"My ancestors would be so disappointed in me."

"The important thing is that you *did* wake up." Cindy gently pulled the young woman's head to her shoulder. "You tried to make things right, but no one could stop Zvilli."

"What's worse, I don't have the slightest idea what to do next." Rivka squeezed Cindy's hand. "How could anyone follow me?"

"Oh, quite to the contrary, Rivka. We don't have to reveal the secret of your sin to let people know you've been a very effective agent in uncovering the plot to destroy our government buildings. You have great credibility."

"Do you *really* think so?" Rivka dried her eyes.

"Absolutely."

"But what do I know about getting the students prepared to protect Jerusalem? I hate war and violence."

"All the better." Cindy beamed. "I am going to help you use your natural aversion to conflict as one of our most effective weapons of battle."

"I don't understand."

"I am going to teach you one of the greatest secrets Yeshua embodied during his earthly ministry three thousand years ago. Even Ben and Jimmy have forgotten the real secret of how to overcome both the world and our Enemy."

Rivka blinked several times. "I don't get it."

Cindy sat down opposite the raven-haired beauty. "I had almost forgotten that I had this little piece of jewelry." She reached around her neck and unfastened a tiny gold chain. "We haven't worn these emblems for centuries, but the time has come to once again proclaim the power of this symbol." Cindy slipped the chain away and put the gold piece in Rivka's palm. "We shall overcome by this sign."

Rivka looked down into her palm at a small gold crucifix.

CHAPTER 19

Ben stared through his thick glasses at the international communication screen in his office; dark circles ringed his eyes. Slumped down in his desk chair, Ben's large bulbous shape spilled over the leather chair. He read each line of the satellite report once again.

Jimmy sat on the other side of the desk with his hands perched on top of his cane. His head was tilted back with the resoluteness and confidence of a head of state. Jimmy's aquiline nose and sharp profile easily gave him the air of a person in complete control, regardless of the circumstances.

Wendy Kohn finally broke the silence. "The world is certainly in total turmoil but I can't see where there is any consensus among the nation's peoples about supporting the coalition of traitors.

"Your television appeal for renewed faith wasn't for naught!" Esther Netanyahu added.

"Things are up for grabs," Jimmy countered.

Ben shook his head and his white ponytail swished from side to side. "Ten days have passed since Tammuz 17 and only one thing is definite. The troops of the enemy are slowly but relentlessly circling us without any opposition."

Jimmy thumped his cane on the floor. "It doesn't make a lot of difference what people think! The national leaders are in control and no one is backing off."

"Afraid so," Wendy agreed.

"What is your wife up to with the students?" Esther Netanyahu asked.

"We've been so busy I haven't even had time to inquire," Ben said. "I know she and Rivka are working day and night to get students prepared and positioned before the final attack comes."

"Prior to the millennial kingdom, Av 9 had never been a good day for us Jews." Wendy looked down at the floor. "I can't but be apprehensive."

"The Immortals have left everything up to us. I guess we can take that sign as a vote of divine confidence."

"I've studied the Bible day and night," Jimmy added, "and I've come to the conclusion God is forcing the entire world to one last moment of decision. No assistance is going to be forthcoming. Everyone's faith is being tested and we're going to have to demonstrate what we're made of. So buckle up, ladies! It's time to get tough."

"Yes sir," Wendy said timidly. She stood up and the two secretaries left the room.

"I think we ought to see how Isaiah is faring about now." Ben began punching in Isaiah Murphy's personal code to locate him. "Let's see what too-tall Murphy thinks."

The picture cleared and for several moments only static lines crossed the screen. Slowly two shapes came into focus. Isaiah and Deborah were sitting in their living room in Los Angeles, dressed casually with their feet up on hassocks.

"Don't you guys ever knock?" Isaiah said. "I'm sitting here with my lovely wife enjoying the evening news and suddenly I get the Hardy boys from Jerusalem."

Ben laughed. "What a lucky man you are."

Deborah waved. "You can bet the James Bond of the Christian world is not sitting here *leisurely* enjoying himself. At least he's home and not somewhere over there about to get killed."

"How are things in L.A.?" Jimmy asked.

"Bad." Isaiah shook his head. "As you know our president has thrown his weight behind the coalition and is even proposing to send American troops to join the fight. People are completely confused."

"How many are standing with us?" Ben asked.

"I don't know," Isaiah answered. "I truly am not sure. We've become a lightning rod for opposition in this area. The old gang is hard at work trying to help people see through the smokescreen the Devil and his cohorts have created, but the government has turned on us, calling us unpatriotic."

"We are being attacked in the papers," Deborah added, "and on the news reports. I can't help but believe matters are going to get violent soon."

"How can we help?" Ben leaned forward in his chair.

"I think our job is to help *you*," Isaiah answered. "The problem is that television constantly encourages people to do whatever feels good. Unbridled freedom is the new message of the day. Lots of citizens are buying into it. Irresponsibility is rather intoxicating."

"I'll tell you what I think," Deborah broke in. "Here's what I think is going to—"

Suddenly the screen went dead. Ben feverishly began hitting buttons but nothing came up. Finally the earlier news report scrolled up on the screen. Ben grabbed a phone with a special line and tapped in his priority code. "What's going on in our transmission?" he barked.

The voice on the speaker phone answered, "We can't figure the problem out, sir. But it appears all worldwide communication has been commandeered. Every channel is jammed except the propaganda lines coming out of Egypt. We seem to be cut off from the world."

"See if you can get this corrected at once!" Ben ordered. "We mustn't lose touch with what is happening around the globe."

"We're doing everything we can but nothing is working. We'll not stop trying."

Ben lowered his voice. "Thank you." He hung up.

"We're cut off, aren't we?" Jimmy asked.

Ben slouched down further in his chair. "I'm afraid so. We have the best technology in the world. If our people can't fix the problem, it can't be done."

"They're closing in on us."

"Yes, Jimmy. They are."

□ □ □

Alexi Chardoff and Fong stood in their makeshift command post in the city of Al Mawsil. At one time the dusty little town was part of the Iraqi empire. During the ancient reign of Sennacherib, Al Mawsil was the king's sanctuary, but the royal city's demise was predicted by the prophet Nahum. The Medes and Persians fulfilled Nahum's prediction. Chardoff had chosen the city as a natural rendezvous point when the Chinese and Russian armies converged. The two men talked and watched the TV monitors of their troops moving out across the fertile countryside.

"Our men are cautiously reassured," Fong observed. "Each step forward further dispels their fear of the Immortals' intervention. By the time we get to the walls of Jerusalem, they'll be ready to charge."

Charoff nodded his head. "The Arabs don't seem to have even a hint of collusion on our part. I think they are almost more obsessed with getting rid of Toulouse and Marchino than taking the city. They have no idea we've read their intentions."

Fong's eyes narrowed. "Our loyal allies are nothing more than a traitorous pack." His voice betrayed no hint of emotion. "Their religious nonsense has left the world in total confusion. It will be up to us to pick up the pieces and restore order. By the time this war is over, people will again welcome a strong central government."

"Exactly!" Chardoff thumped the table.

Fong leaned back and crossed his arms over his chest. "I'll be honest. I got into this intrigue because I've never liked the Western world. I don't trust white and black people much, but I dislike Jews most of all. I'm here for a little revenge, pure and simple. But you, Alexi . . . what's your angle? You've never really told me."

Chardoff pushed his greasy hair out of his eyes. "About a hundred years ago, I started to think about what it all meant. Life just didn't add up for me anymore and I needed better answers than I had." Alexi gestured aimlessly in the air. "For a long time I wandered around trying to find a better way to understand the purpose of existence. One night I stumbled on to a completely different way of thinking about everything. I began to realize that the ultimate reality is *power*."

Fong stared for awhile and then nodded his head.

Chardoff grinned cynically. "I slowly began to see that the only significant truth about Yeshua and the rulers in Jerusalem was that they possessed the power. Take away their omnipotence and nothing is left."

"You don't believe in God?" Fong asked.

Chardoff shrugged. "God is only a symbol for what is ultimate. When you dig down to the center of everything, there is no personality hiding in there . . . only sheer force. My god is power."

"But what about the Immortals? Yeshua's miraculous abilities?"

The Russian leader laughed. "Superstition! Just as big a fraud as Abu Sita's garbage about this Marduk charade. The jerks call it prayer but they're doing nothing but talking to themselves."

Fong pursed his lips. "You're quite satisfied the Immortals won't show up?"

"Listen to me." Chardoff shook his finger in Fong's face. "When we have power, we are gods! The more we use power, the stronger we become! No, I don't know how these Immortals come and go but I am prepared to put a bullet in the brain of any who show up. One shot will level the playing field." Alexi shook his first in the air. "Exercise power and you are divine!"

Fong's eyes narrowed to bare slits. "I'm not sure I understand."

"Let me show you." Chardoff stood up and beckoned the Chinaman to follow him from the room. "Let me teach you what I've been practicing." He walked into the alley behind the building.

"You have a new insight?"

Chardoff pointed to three Arabs working at the end of the alley. "Let me demonstrate my new skill." The Russian pulled a pistol from beneath his uniform. "We found this little jewel in our stash. Gives one a wonderful sense of power. I've been practicing." He raised the pistol slowly and pointed it at the men. "Watch," he said coolly.

The explosion of Chardoff's first shot echoed off the buildings. One Arab tumbled forward on the ground. The other startled men looked up uncomprehendingly. Chardoff fired off two other shots in rapid order. The other two men crumpled to the ground.

"I've gotten quite good with this thing." Chardoff watched the thin trail of smoke rise from the barrel.

Fong stared, his mouth agape.

"Let's just say a Russian brought the first casualties of the war." He stuck the gun back inside his coat. "What a feeling! That's what power feels like." Chardoff grinned. "You ought to try it, Fong."

Fong stared in shock.

□ □ □

"We don't have much time to talk," Claudine Toulouse spoke quickly into the hologram speaker in her Damascus hotel. Even though Maria Marchino was on the other side of Damascus, she appeared to be standing in the French leader's large bedroom. A separate dining area opened to the side. "Everything is in place for a little midnight champagne supper," the French leader said. "Khalil will be here in minutes."

"You look ravishing, darling," Maria purred. "I really didn't know you had it in you."

"Rather different image for me." Claudine swirled her filmy gown around her waist. The unusually low-cut dress was made of red silk. Her hair was piled high on top of her head in a provocative twist. "I think Khalil will like what he sees."

"Just remember, I'm only blocks away if you need help." Maria laughed at her own little joke. "Are you sure Hussein knows nothing about our alliance?"

"Nothing. He thinks only of me and what we will have together."

"You have our agreement for him to sign?"

Claudine held up an official document. "Right here. At the right moment after he is . . . well . . . in a more passive mood I will put our accords before our little king of Jordan. Don't worry. We've got this one in the bag."

The Italian leader smiled. "Claudine, I have to admit you really surprised me with this ploy. Brilliant stroke on your part." Maria held up two other pieces of paper. "I have the agreements which Chardoff and Fong prepared. At the right time, we will be ready to offer them a separate peace with us. We will be able to move quickly and wrap up *our* new alliance."

"No time for further discussion," Claudine said. "Khalil will be here any minute."

"Ciao, darling." Maria waved. Her image faded.

Several minutes later an aide knocked on the door. "The king of Jordan is here, madam."

"Bring him up at once and begin serving the dinner."

Claudine took one final look in the mirror and carefully massaged her hair into place. She took a deep breath and hurried across the room. Just as she opened the door, the king appeared only feet away.

Before she could speak, the king of Jordan dropped to one knee and kissed her hand. "*Ma cherie,*" he cooed, "I am overwhelmed by your beauty." His light-colored suit gave his dark skin an intoxicating glow. The king's black eyes were mysterious and deep. His lips felt warm and gentle.

Claudine knew blood was rushing to her cheeks and she fought to keep a demure composure. "Come here, you handsome devil," she said impulsively and giggled. Claudine ran her hands through his dark black hair and then suddenly kissed him passionately on the mouth. "Oh, but you are good," she said and stepped back. Out of the corner of her eye, Claudine saw an aide bringing a cart with food. "Like a little something to take the edge off your hunger?" She beckoned Khalil into her room.

The aide quickly rolled the cart into the side room.

"Some hors d'oeuvres will whet your appetite. We can start with the soupe a l'aignon. I thought you would enjoy a special coq au vin prepared by my private cook from Paris. The chicken in wine sauce is exquisite. If that is not to your taste, I also have included boeuf bourguignonne." Claudine pointed to the elegant china on the table. "We have choix de legumes. I had the vegetables flown in tonight just for us." She led Khalil by the hand to the two chairs seated across the candlelit table. Claudine snapped her fingers at the aide. "Pour the Dom Perignon." The aide filled the crystal glasses then hurried out of the room.

The Jordanian king kissed her on the hand again. "Never have I met a woman as fascinating as you." He seated her at the table.

As they bantered, Claudine felt her usual facade of political professionalism melt like the candle wax. She found herself giggling like a school girl.

"A-a-a-h," Khalil sighed, "the wine sauce is superb. People just don't cook like this in our country."

Claudine studied his sparkling black eyes, while doodling with her food. He seemed to be the most handsome man she had ever seen.

"Your combination of style, taste, and magnificent strength is like an aphrodisiac to me," Khalil's voice was low and sultry. "My heart has become like the restless sea."

Claudine took a deep breath. Her pulse pounded and her hands trembled. "And we also have crêpes suzette. Perhaps, a little cognac to blend the taste? I also have crème de menthe should you desire."

"I crave the taste of *you.*" Hussein tossed the napkin aside and suddenly leaned over the table, kissing Claudine passionately. "You are what I desire." He pulled Claudine to her feet and kissed up and down her neck.

For a moment, Claudine felt so lightheaded she thought she might faint. The French woman clung to the Arab's coat for fear her knees would buckle. She felt him lift her off her feet and sweep her toward the bedroom. The silk bedspread soothed her skin and felt wondrously sensual.

When the dawn sunlight broke through the windows,

the first rays struck Claudine's face. She blinked several times, trying to remember where she was. Her hand fell across a hairy chest and she jumped. Only then did the night before come back into focus. She stared at the sleeping figure next to her.

Good grief! What have I done? I didn't even get the agreement signed. I let my emotions run away with me.

Hussein stirred and rolled over. "Ma cherie." He kissed her again. "We were made for each other."

"Indeed," Claudine purred. "We were meant to rule together, like Anthony and Cleopatra."

Hussein propped himself up on an elbow and laughed. "Shall we take over Egypt so I can give you the Sphinx?"

"Why not?" She ran her hand through his ruffled black hair. "Who knows what we might do if our armies merged?"

"Merged?"

"Look!" Claudine cuddled near the Arab. "I can get Maria Marchino to join us. Our three nations could tilt the balance of power and we could overwhelm Atrash's lock on control."

"The three of us?" Khalil frowned. "We don't need her. We're enough." Hussein grabbed the back of Claudine's neck and kissed her passionately again.

The warmth of Khalil's breath sent shivers up her spine. Her usual cold-hearted logic blurred and for the first time in years Claudine felt indecisive.

"You and I will be more than sufficient," Khalil insisted. "Just us . . . together . . . think about it!"

Claudine looked up into his all-engulfing eyes. Suddenly Khalil was all she wanted in the world. "Do you really think we . . . just us . . . could pull it off?"

Khalil lowered his face until the tips of their noses barely touched. "We can do anything." He kissed her so passionately Claudine could hardly breath.

Much later in the day the French leader finally got

around to calling her Italian counterpart. "Sorry for the delay," she began.

"Must have been some evening," Maria joked. "I thought maybe you had drowned in the champagne."

Claudine pursed her lips searching for the right words. "He turned out to be much more difficult than I thought," she said slowly. "He is actually quite . . . resistant . . . to political change."

"What do you mean?" The Italian leader frowned.

"He seems to like me . . . just . . . for my own sake." Claudine suddenly brightened. "Actually, the whole thing is turning out to be more of a romance than a political intrigue."

"The point was to get him into our coalition," Maria sounded impatient.

"It will take more time."

"We don't have much time left," Maria's voice raised. "Av 9 is just around the corner."

"Obviously," Claudine said defensively. "I'll be seeing Khalil later in the day. I will try to talk to him again."

"Just keep your mind on business," Marchino snapped. "I'll be back in touch." Her picture faded.

Claudine tossed her undone hair over her shoulder and looked pensively at a single rose in the bud vase in front of her. "Maybe there is something more significant than politics after all."

CHAPTER 20

Select student leaders filed into the large lecture hall at Hebrew University where only months before Ben had spoken to the students. The earlier atmosphere of casual indifference had been transformed into a new serious and sober intent. Cindy and Rivka watched the students closely.

"They are the key leaders?" Cindy asked

"We've checked all the files, records, and test results to identify people with real leadership capacity," Rivka answered quietly. "But I also know the outstanding students who naturally shape public opinion. They're all here."

The students sat respectfully. No one spoke.

Rivka walked to the microphone. "I'm sure by now everyone has read or heard my statement broadcast electronically through all the dormitories and across the campus. You know about the sedition and sabotage planned and executed by Dr. Zvilli Zemah. Dr. Zemah was a . . . special friend." Her voice faltered. "Of course, we are all disappointed." Rivka stopped and cleared her throat.

"You also know that in a very few days we are going to

be attacked by the first army assembled in virtually a thousand years," Rivka continued. "We have no choice but to help defend our city. You have been chosen to help organize our student body to face the fight."

The silence was broken as the students turned to each other and mumbled in consternation.

Rivka punched in buttons on the speaker's podium and the screen behind her filled with pictures of troops marching across the desert. "We have just learned our satellite communication with the world is now blocked and Jerusalem is virtually isolated."

The students became deathly quiet.

"Our only source of information on our enemy's armies is from shuttlecraft flying surveillance missions." Rivka pushed the enlargement button and the picture of a smashed vehicle appeared. "Tragically, the coalition troops have the ability to shoot us down. Two lives were lost in this crash."

The picture changed and a wide sweep of the desert appeared.

Rivka continued to explain. "Egyptian and Ethiopian forces are working their way up the Wadi al 'Arabah area across the Negev. These soldiers are quite accustomed to desert life, so they aren't bothered by this hottest time of summer. They are clearly preparing to stage an attack on Jerusalem from the south. The Jordanian army is quietly waiting in Amman for a quick dash at our city from the west. Are there questions?"

No one moved. The students stared at the scenes of men moving across the barren terrain of the wilderness.

Rivka changed the picture and the land became fertile and green. "Russian and Chinese armies," she continued, "are marching forward across the Euphrates River. As best as reconnaissance can tell, these two armies seem to be headed for a rendezvous with European forces that are waiting for them in the area around Damascus in Syria. Our experts believe they will converge on Jerusalem on Av 9." Rivka paused for emphasis. "They are the only people in the world with armaments that shoot and kill. In addition, we have reason to believe they will attack, first with troops trained in martial arts. We are virtually at their mercy."

Many students put their hands over their faces as if praying. Others looked stunned and immobile. Finally one young man stood up.

"Where are the Immortals, the protection of God Almighty?" the student implored. "We have always depended on Yeshua to lead and guide us. Where is He at this critical hour?"

Rivka turned to Cindy and raised her hands in consternation.

Cindy slowly stood and walked to the podium. Her wrinkled oriental skin and stark white hair made a striking contrast with Rivka's jet-black hair and olive complexion. Age had diminished Cindy's small size to a stature nearly that of a child. "I lived through the Great Tribulation," Cindy began. "Some days during this terrible time it seemed our heavenly Father had forgotten about us." She shook her head. "But we learned that sometimes God's seeming absence is the strategy He has chosen to actually be present with us. Though paradoxical, our God even uses emptiness."

Praying students opened their eyes and stared. The young man sat down.

Cindy continued, "At different times God expects different things of us. Now is a time of testing. All these years of divine intervention were meant to make us a mighty people for His service. Now, the time is come to see if we learned our lessons. The only significant question is, are you ready?"

Someone clapped. A student shouted, "Yes!" Another person clapped. Other students leaped to their feet and began clapping. "Yes!" rang through the air again and again. "We are ready!" one girl shouted over the uproar.

Cindy smiled and nodded again before motioning for the students to sit down. "I have a plan," she continued, "and we don't have much time left. If we organize well, we will be ready."

For the first time Rivka smiled. "My friends," she began, "Mrs. Feinberg and I have worked out a careful strategy for how you can help train other students. Each of you has been selected to be a centurion, in charge of a hundred other students. We will teach you what to do and in turn you will pass the instruction on to the others. Is this agreeable?"

Once more the students applauded enthusiastically.

"We are calling our plan 'Opposite Cheek.'" Cindy added. "I think you will be quite surprised." Cindy talked more rapidly as she explained the strategy.

Several hours later across town Jimmy Harrison was still sitting in Ben's office, studying the reports coming in from the shuttlecrafts. He pulled at the paunch beneath his chin and mumbled to himself.

"What do you think?" Ben asked.

"Because the Russians and Chinese have the greatest distance to go, I conclude once they are in place the attack will be set. No question but Av 9 is the day of destiny."

"You're worried."

Jim doubled his fists over the cap of his cane and rested his chin on top. "You have to meet force with force," he sighed. "And we sure don't have an ounce of capacity. It was one thing to trick Zemah with a hologram gimmick but stopping an army is another matter." He straightened up and bounced his cane off the floor. "Blue blazes! Do you think those students are of any value? I don't even know what Cindy's planning, but three times the number of that student body won't be any more than canon fodder for those guns. Nonsense!"

Ben's white ponytail swung from side to side. "You're right. I shudder every time I read Isaiah's report on this martial arts business he discovered in Ethiopia. Those desert apes will kick the living daylights out of our kids. All we're going to do is get people hurt and killed." Ben suddenly stood up and threw his hands up. "Look at us! We're a couple of old jokes without the slightest idea how to really defend this city or meet this crisis."

Jim shook his head despairingly. "I think we need to send a shuttle out to Petra to pick up our friends before they are surrounded by the army."

Ben shrugged. "Maybe they would be better off out there than in the city. I think the only objective of the coalition is to destroy Jerusalem."

"Perhaps, you're right." Jimmy stood up. "I wonder if they want to burn this place completely to the ground."

"They'll undoubtedly do everything possible to humiliate us. I think we can count on total destruction."

Suddenly the office door opened. Cindy and Rivka hurried in. "Things went tremendously well with the students." Cindy bubbled over with enthusiasm. "Operation Opposite Cheek is going to work!"

Jimmy and Ben looked at each other.

"We've got the right answer!" Rivka added.

"Wait, wait." Ben waved her away. "We've just been thinking how futile it would be to send hapless students into the midst of this battle. We can only get people killed and hurt. They don't have any weapons of war—"

"Oh, but they do!" Cindy shook both fists in the air. "We're not worried about those silly guns. Our battle is not with flesh and blood anyway."

Ben's eyebrows raised. "I beg your pardon?"

"Our approach is going to be nonviolent," Rivka interjected. "We are going to use the weapons of love."

"I'm teaching the students to turn the other cheek."

Ben turned to Jimmy and shook his head. "When she gets like this, there's no point in even talking. Let's go for a walk."

Jimmy nodded.

"Now just a minute!" Cindy protested. "I expect you to hear me out."

"Sure." Ben kept walking to the door. "Later."

"I want you to hear about Operation Opposite Cheek right *now*," Cindy insisted.

"I think we all need to give it a rest," Ben pulled Jimmy toward the door. "We've gone on overload." He gave a slight wave of the hand. "We'll be back later." He pushed Jimmy ahead of him out the door and closed it behind him.

"How dare you walk out on me, Ben Feinberg!" Cindy called after him.

"They've all gone nuts," Ben whispered to Jimmy. "Let's get some fresh air before it completely gets to us."

Jimmy and Ben walked up the street in front of the Knesset for a long time without saying anything. The hot sun of late summer wasn't pleasant but seemed appropriate to the mood of the moment. A new and disconcerting atmosphere of fear hovered over the city. People walking down the street didn't speak, preoccupied with their own fears. The two men trudged on without any sense of direction.

"We should have at least listened to Cindy," Jimmy finally said as he wiped his forehead.

"Yeah," Ben rolled his eyes. "Boy, will I catch it when I get home, but I just couldn't take it anymore. I feel too overwhelmed."

Jimmy shook his head. "I think we're in so far over our

heads that we are drowning. We need something to give us a completely different perspective."

"Like a little talk with Moses and Elijah," Ben added. "Boy, were they ever a tremendous help the last time Jerusalem was under the gun."

Jimmy stopped. "What an idea!"

"Idea?"

"Great idea, old man." Jimmy slapped Ben on the back. "As you suggested, let's go back to the old city. I haven't been there in ages. You know all the tourists flock there. Let's just go down and look at the great old stuff."

Ben shrugged and pulled his special taxi computer card from his pocket. He punched in several numbers. "It's too far to walk. I'll get us a ride."

In about thirty seconds an automated vehicle pulled up to the curb, the side door raised up, and the two men got in. "The old city," Ben spoke into a microphone in front of them. "Jaffa gate." Instantly the cab sped into the traffic. In a few minutes the car silently pulled up to the curb before the ancient entrance.

Jimmy got out, stretched his long legs, and looked around. To his right, he could see the Citadel and beyond the tower to the road to Bethlehem. He tapped his cane on the old cobblestone pavement, took a deep breath, and started toward the Street of the Chain.

"I'll never forget that awesome day when Moses and Elijah appeared on the Mount of Olives," Ben reminisced. "Wow, did they ever terrify the news media. Remember how they stopped President Gianardo out there on the Kidron Valley Road? Elijah told him the breaking of the Fourth Seal was at hand and a pale horse called Death would ride the skies by Passover. Happened, too. What a day!"

"And I remember what he said would happen by Tammuz 17 of that year," Jimmy added. "Just as he warned, one and a half billion people were slain." He turned at the corner and trudged down the narrow street between the tall limestone-and-granite buildings. "How could anyone forget those days?"

Ben rubbed his pudgy nose and readjusted his thick glasses in place on his bridge. "Someone said it somewhere, When people forget the lessons of history, they are doomed to repeat the mistakes of the past. What we've seen with our eyes, the mob treats like old fairy tales. But truth remains the truth."

"I can still see Moses and Elijah sitting there by the Western Wall." Jimmy stopped and smiled. "Way over there in Los Angeles we'd tune in that picture and just wait to see what would happen next."

"I came here with Sam Eisenberg in April of the year 2000," Ben said thoughtfully. "We had to sneak past the soldiers to get close enough to see the awesome sight. That afternoon Elijah prophesied that on the fifteenth of Nisan, God would bring vengeance on Babylon for her sins. On that exact day, the exodus of the Jews from Egypt began under Moses and that was the date when the last defenders of the Temple retreated to Masada and the Romans destroyed Jerusalem. I can still see Elijah pointing up the street to the Church of the Holy Sepulcher and proclaiming that on this very same day Yeshua died for the sins of the world."

Jimmy jerked at Ben's arm and pointed with his cane straight ahead. "That's a great idea!"

"What idea?"

"To go visit the Church of the Holy Sepulcher."

"I didn't say that." Ben rolled his eyes.

"Yes, you did!" Jimmy insisted. "I am always inspired to walk around inside that great dome and see where the empty tomb was and to climb up those steps to the top of Mount Calvary. That's just the lift we need!" Jimmy poked

Ben in the side. "I wonder if anything is still going on there."

"I just make the suggestions. I don't keep up on museum hours." Ben rolled his eyes again in mock consternation.

"Well, let's go find out." Jimmy hurried on.

The open-air vendors still plied their ancient trades along the narrow street. Tourist business had always made it lucrative to keep up the appearances of the ancient ways. Vegetable markets and spice shops operated next to little stores selling mementos of the old city. The smells of food and village life filled the two men's nostrils.

"I feel better just getting a whiff of this place," Ben said. He stopped and pointed. "Look! There's the gateway into the courtyard in front of the church. Let's go in."

The two old friends slipped through the entrance and found themselves in the place where Helena, the mother of Constantine, came 2,700 years earlier to restore the most precious site in Christendom. During the period of rebuilding after the Second Coming of Yeshua, the walls of the original church had been covered and reinforced by new stone facements but time had even turned these blocks of stone into artifacts. Nothing had changed the worn cobblestones covering the plaza leading into the door of the church.

"Feels like we have stepped into a time machine," Jimmy muttered. "Surely, we are standing on holy ground."

An old man in a black cassock pushed open the huge wooden door to the church and fastened it against the wall. The sound of music and chanting floated out on the evening breeze.

"Excuse me," Ben asked. "Are there *still* services going on in here after all these centuries?"

"Of course!" The man raised his white shaggy eyebrows in surprise at the question. "Every day."

"How interesting." Ben turned to Jimmy. "Let's see what is happening now."

"The Greek Orthodox are finishing afternoon prayers before the holy altar atop Calvary," the doorman answered. "Shortly, a Western rite service of Holy Communion will begin in the chapel in front of the empty tomb."

"I had no idea such worship continued until now." Ben beckoned his friend onward. "I suppose I've been so close to the government leaders I haven't thought much about these ancient customs."

Inside the church the high domed ceiling covered the remains of the past with sweeping arches and lingering shadows. The Stone of Unction, where by tradition the body of Christ was anointed for burial, was still a place washed by the tears and kisses of faithful mourners. The pitted rock was a reminder of the pain of death. Long ago the smell of incense saturated even the masonry between the stones, forever leaving a hint of the aroma of frankincense and myrrh. The pathways down steps and corridors were worn slick from millions of pilgrims walking the final steps of the Via Dolorosa.

Seemingly lost to the world but preserved in this place alone, a Latin chant began somewhere far off in a dark corridor and began coming closer. A priest singing and swinging incense appeared in a dark green chasuble, walking slowly at the end of a procession of other priests carrying candles behind a large cross.

"*Laudate, pueri,*" rang down the corridor. "*Laudate dominum.*"

"Let's follow them." Ben pulled at Jimmy's arm.

The procession wound its way into the chapel as the chanting continued. Clergy bowed to the altar and moved to their stations on the chancel. Ben and Jim slipped into a back pew and watched in rapt attention. Hymns were sung and Scripture read. A profound sense of awe and reverence settled over the two men.

The priests walked to the altar and began preparing the chalice for Communion. Altar assistants offered cruets of wine and water. The ancient rite of the Western Church continued as it had for nearly three millennia.

Ben leaned closer to Jimmy and whispered very quietly. "I had forgotten . . . just forgotten . . . that the real battle is never with flesh and blood. Cindy was right. I needed to be touched by transcendence. Worship is so important in restoring balance in the midst of the storm."

Jimmy nodded his head and both men slid from the pews to their knees.

The priest continued his prayers, finally lifting the chalice high in the air. He kneeled before the altar and then drank from the gold cup. The old man moved to the kneeling rail to await people coming forward.

Although such was not his regular custom, Ben felt an irresistible desire to receive the Holy Elements. He quickly slipped out of the pew, walked down the aisle, and dropped on the small pad before the wooden rail, polished to a soft glow from the touch of a million hands. Ben held out his palms for the bread and then waited for the priest to bring the chalice.

"*Deus noster refugium.*" The priest stopped before Ben. Then in excellent English said again, "God is our refuge and strength, a very present help in trouble." He offered the chalice.

Ben's memory supplied the next line of the Psalm: "Therefore we will not fear, even though the earth be removed, and though the mountains be carried into the midst of the sea. . . ."

For a brief moment their eyes met. Ben felt as if he were looking into the wisdom of the ages. In turn, he sensed the priest was reading the deepest need of his soul. He reached for the gold cup.

"The Blood of Christ, the cup of salvation . . . the body of our Lord Jesus Christ keep you in everlasting life," the priest again said in English and placed the chalice on Ben's lips.

Ben drank deeply and lowered his head onto the kneeling rail. The warmth of the wine burned as it settled in his stomach and then a profound sense of Presence arose within him and he felt overwhelmed. Where the fear and misgivings had been lodged in his soul, Ben discovered new joy. The moment of ecstasy was so wondrous, he feared he would cry out loud.

Just as he stood, a voice seemed to speak within his mind like a thought arising from beyond himself. "When you have done this to the least of these, you have done so unto me." Ben stood rigid, immovable. The message continued to race through his mind. "Your concern for the lost, the deceived, the wayward, is a concern for me. I have not only heard your prayers but read the sincerity and integrity of your heart. Rejoice my son; the dark night is almost finished."

Ben found his way back to the pew and dropped to his knees once more. As the final prayers were said, Ben wept. He was only slightly aware that the procession was preparing to leave the chapel. As the priest passed Ben's pew, the old man put his hand on Ben's shoulder and said simply, "*Non nobis, Domine.*" *Not to us, O Lord, but to your name give glory.* And then he was gone.

Ben stood up and shook his head signaling to Jimmy he didn't want to speak. Jimmy nodded back and the two old friends found their way out of the church.

Little was said on their way back to the Knesset office complex. Dusk was falling over Jerusalem and most of the staff had gone home by the time they got back to Ben's office. To their surprise, Cindy and Rivka were still there.

"Well, Mr. High and Mighty has come back," Cindy said to Rivka. "I'm sure he doesn't have time to listen to anything as mundane as what we've been doing with students all day."

"I'm sorry," Ben acknowledged. "I apologize for being so insensitive."

Cindy still had fire in her eyes. "Well, we've been just as busy," she snapped.

"I'm sure you have." Ben kept nodding his head. "We will try to do better."

Cindy looked away but winked at Rivka out of the corner of her eye.

Ben plopped down in his chair and ran his hand through his hair. "We've had quite an experience. I need to talk about it. I just seem to keep forgetting what this battle is really all about." Ben's head dropped down on his chest. He stared at the floor.

Cindy put her arms around her husband's shoulders and hugged him. "It's okay, dear. The truth is, you're doing a great job. Just tell me about it."

For the next several minutes Ben shared the trip to the old city and his experience of receiving Holy Communion. Rivka listened carefully. Jimmy kept nodding as Ben spoke.

"As I reflected on the meaning of the blood of Christ, I was reminded that our Lord's ultimate victory was won on a cross, the symbol of death and defeat." Ben stared out of his office window into the night. "In the darkest hour when everything seemed to be lost, the triumph of our God was actually closest at hand." Ben shook his finger in the air like a teacher instructing students. "But no human being caused the ultimate victory. Salvation is always God's gift acquired by nothing more or less than His decision of love. Everything is always in God's hands and His hands *alone*."

Jimmy looked up at the ceiling. For a moment his dignified profile gave him the regal look of a patriarch. "Ben was touched by the Holy Spirit today. We must remember that our God reigns, and we don't have to do anything more than be faithful servants. In the end, the victory isn't ours but His."

Cindy squeezed Ben's shoulder. "That's exactly what I wanted to tell you this afternoon. We are training the students to act on that very truth."

"Really?" Ben's eye's widened.

"Operation Opposite Cheek is simply applying Yeshua's teaching from the Sermon on the Mount." Rivka bubbled with enthusiasm as she talked. "What Yeshua did on the cross was actually the ultimate example of turning the other cheek. Yeshua showed us from the cross that the weakness of God is supremely more powerful than the power of men."

"How are you going to do *that?*" Ben asked.

Cindy looked thoughtful for several moments. "Don't forget," she began, "those foot soldiers of the coalition have been raised on the truth about our God and the reign of Yeshua. They are following orders from the generals, but no one knows what is truly in their hearts. Their lifetime of training is on our side."

Jimmy nodded in agreement. "But what does turning the other cheek have to do with the attack on our city?"

"Aggression begets aggression," Cindy continued. "Yeshua knows that an angry counterattack always escalates conflict. On the other hand, love calls forth love. It we refuse to fight and offer them compassion, we will appeal to the best in their hearts. I believe they will refuse to hurt us."

"The martial arts were meant for self-defense," Rivka added. "When we offer no resistance, these judo experts won't have anything to attack. Rather than a fight, we will offer our enemies the gift of love. The students will come out of the city bearing offerings of compassion to our enemies."

Ben stared at Jimmy. Finally he raised his hands as if to protest but dropped them on his desk. "This is the way of the cross," Ben concluded.

CHAPTER 21

Once the initial troop movements were completed, Ziad Atrash no longer needed his original command post in Egypt. Lack of opposition from the Immortals ended any worry about a retreat and confirmed his projections. By the dawn of Av 8, Ziad had moved his headquarters from the edge of the Red Sea to Masada. Rajah Abu Sita flew in from Syria to assume joint command.

TV screens lined the makeshift building and monitored every side of Jerusalem. Satellite dishes were scattered across the flat top of the ancient desert fortress. Pictures of the troops of the many nations were constantly flashing across other screens.

Even though the late summer heat scorched the Dead Sea basin, the air-conditioning barely kept the room comfortable. The Egyptian leader insisted on wearing a military uniform with medals. "We are poised for a quick flight into Jerusalem as soon as our troops take the Knesset," Atrash explained to Abu Sita. He traced lines across the electronic map in front of the men. "By being the first to take control inside the Knesset itself, we can send our images as supreme conquerors across the world."

Rajah wore the lightweight jersey uniform of soldiers on desert detail. He watched soberly. "Our secret plan to stop the Europeans will make our inability to crack their communications code superfluous. We will create so much confusion in their ranks no counterattack will be possible."

Atrash grinned and ground his huge fist in the palm of his hand. "In one stroke, those obstacles will be gone! But we must be sure the Russians and Chinese don't overreact."

"I have a shuttle prepared to fly to their headquarters once the attack begins," Abu Sita said. "Talking to them in person should alleviate any possible fears."

Atrash grunted and pushed another button on the electronic map. The picture shifted from the political center of Jerusalem to the perimeters around the city showing the placement of the troops. He pointed to the south and traced a line from the Valley of Hinnom up through the Valley of Kidron. "The Ethiopians are assembled on the far end of the Mount of Olives and our Egyptian troops are strung along the rest of the valley to allow us to take the Old City quickly. Your people are next to the Italians. The Jordanians are wedged between the Italians and the French. We've put our martial arts people in the fore of this effort. We want to preserve the Old City from damage, and their attack will ensure nothing will be destroyed."

Rajah said dryly. "I have our priests of Marduk just behind the lines, poised to rush into the Temple Mount and begin polytheistic worship the instant the Temple grounds are clear. Cameras will be ready to flash the pictures around the world."

"*That* sight ought to finish off any resistance from abroad." Atrash grinned. "We have the Europeans set to our immediate left around the tops of the hills to the east, and on the other side of them, the Jordanian army is in place. We will be able to turn our guns on the Italians and the French the moment the attack begins. All our firepower will be concentrated on *them*. In the chaos, they will have no idea how to respond. One quick blow should be enough."

"I will simply tell the Russians and Chinese the two women were preparing to attack them, and we have saved their troops from surprise assault," Abu Sita said.

"The rest of the allies will be ringed on the right side of the city, waiting for our signal to enter the city shooting at and bombing everything that moves. We won't worry about damage to the newer parts of the city." Atrash stepped back and defiantly crossed his arms over his chest. "What are the gods saying?"

The Syrian leader looked quite thoughtful. "Our priests worship before the altars of Marduk and Osiris day and night, constantly chanting and burning incense. We have commanded our soldiers to meditate every day using the prayers El Khader wrote." He paused and inhaled deeply. "Strange things happen the longer one immerses oneself in that atmosphere."

"Are you drunk yet?" Atrash chided.

Abu Sita shook his head. "I backed off after I saw what happened to El Khader. He definitely went crazy."

"He was crazy to begin with."

"You speak of my lifelong friend," Rajah snapped.

"No offense." Ziad tossed the comment aside. "Who knows what goes on inside anyone's head when you get a mixture of smoke and chants floating through the brain?"

"Something *more* goes on with people who sincerely pursue the gods," Rajah insisted. "They are touched by a power—a spiritual reality—that takes control of their minds. Something . . . a spirit . . . seems to attach itself."

"I have learned to use this power for my personal advantage." Ziad sneered. "All that counts is that we are the last people standing when everyone else is on the ground."

"You don't take any of this seriously, do you?"

Atrash laughed. "The bottom line is I am marching at the front of the army that will control the world in twenty-four hours."

"Listen!" Abu Sita pointed his finger in the Egyptian's face. "I watched my childhood mentor become consumed by whatever is on the other side of silence. I've spent enough time trying these meditations and prayers to know we have been playing with fire. You *better* pay attention to your own preaching!"

Atrash smiled. "Don't get so heated. I just don't let myself get hooked on superstition. Understand?"

"No." Rajah shook his head angrily. "You don't understand. We have called up something . . . someone . . . that has been dormant for a long time." He nervously ran his hands through his hair. "We're walking around with a lot more than dynamite in our hands. I warn you that we have a tiger by the tail."

"Listen!" Atrash poked him forcefully on the chest. "When you're talking to me, you've got a lion in your face. Now cut out the 'things-that-go-bump-in-the-night' speech and get ready to go to war."

"I'm sorry." Abu Sita shook his head. "Really sorry I ever went through this door." He turned toward the exit. "None of us will escape easily from this thing." He walked away.

"Have you gone nuts?" Atrash called after him. "Get a grip on yourself." Ziad watched the Syrian walk out across the top of the huge mesa. "Rajah's gotten as goofy as that quack he called a secretary of state."

In the Italian headquarters perched on the ridge along the back side of the Valley of Hinnom, Maria Marchino angrily kept punching in the code for contact with Claudine Toulouse. "Where is she?" Maria said aloud. "Time is running out." Just as she was about to give up, a signal light blinked. Maria hit the hologram button, but no image appeared.

"Claudine Toulouse," the voice said.

"Where in the name of the gods are you!" Maria barked. "And how come I'm only getting a voice signal? Where's your picture?"

"I can't talk right now."

"Can't talk!" Maria was indignant. "Don't you know we're about to go to war? What's happening with this agreement with the Syrians?" She pulled at the collar on her military uniform and mopped her forehead.

"We're talking right now. I need to call you later."

"Later! I've delivered the terms of agreement to the Chinese and the Russians. We've got to have the Jordanians. Cut out the champagne dinners and get business done."

"I said, *later.*" Claudine clicked the phone off.

The Italian leader stared at the silent speakerphone and kicked her chair.

Only five miles away, Claudine Toulouse flipped the silence switch to kill all incoming calls. "I've got to tell her something," she turned to Khalil Hussein. Her silk robe was tied loosely about her waist. She leaned against the bedroom wall, her bare leg propped up against a small end table.

The king laughed and abruptly pulled her close. "Tell her how good I am." He kissed her forcefully.

Claudine hung on to his neck and sighed. "I should tell Maria how wicked you are." She smiled and stepped back. "The truth is . . . what am I going to say? 'Sorry, the deal's off. I've got a better one.'" She whirled around like a dancer. "Too bad, Maria dear, but Khalil and I are sailing down the Nile to find Cleopatra's old throne. We worked out something on the side with the Russians and Chinese and I forgot to tell you."

Hussein shrugged. "Just keep telling her that I'm uncertain but I will offer no resistance to your previous plans. We mean Maria no harm. She just doesn't fit into what we have planned for the future." He began rubbing Claudine's neck. "I want you to spend the night with me. We can call Marchino in the morning with a good story."

"You make me feel so young," Claudine purred. "I keep forgetting how much difference there is in our ages."

"I prefer wines mellowed and seasoned with age. Claudine, you are a superb vintage."

The French leader breathed deeply. "I'll call her back later in the day and tell her something. Khalil, you are the consummate man. Are you sure Chardoff and Fong will sign with us?"

"How could you ever doubt me?" He kissed her again

□ □ □

Jimmy, Ben, Cindy, and Rivka sat in the command office in the Internal Affairs building, studying their wall screen filled with pictures of the armies positioned around Jerusalem. Each was dressed in the traditional jersey uniforms of government officials and even Rivka was newly outfitted to look like a government leader.

"We have a shuttlecraft flying as high as possible, beaming these pictures to us." Ben explained. "I pray they don't get shot. I think we've identified where all segments of the opposition are located. At this time, the top of the Mount of Olives is completely occupied by the Egyptians with the Ethiopians on one end and the Syrians on the other. Obviously, these troops will dash down the mountainside toward the Old City walls."

"What do you make of this tragedy?" Cindy asked Jimmy.

"I think they have two major objectives: take control of the Knesset building and occupy the Temple Mount. They want possession of the religious center of the city."

Ben nodded. "Jimmy's right. My guess is that they will send their martial arts people over the walls first. After they have taken the show places, their troops will start shooting."

"Then our students should line the walls of the Old City," Rivka observed.

"And that's where we need to be, too," Jimmy concluded. "If I'm going to go down, I want it to be in the same place where all the ancient sacrifices were made."

Ben nodded his head soberly. "I have asked all of our citizens to stay in their homes and pray. Resistance makes no sense. I have no idea what will follow, but if we must walk the way of the Cross, we have to be prepared to be slaughtered in the onslaught."

Cindy took her husband's hand. "The last time we faced such terror we were huddled together in an old farmhouse in California. On that dark night, God brought His light." She squeezed his fingers. "I am honored to stand with you again."

Ben took off his thick glasses and wiped his eyes. "Thank you, dear." He hugged her.

Jimmy pulled himself up to his full height. He brought his cane up under his arm and stood erect, like a general with a swagger stick. "I, too, am honored and humbled to march shoulder to shoulder with my friends. If we go down, we will do so together."

Ben reached out for Rivka's hand. "Your grandfather would be very proud of you, child. Never look back. Only forward. Our God is leading us to a victory we can't see. We trust it will come to pass."

Rivka bit her lip and nodded. "I will have our students in place tonight. We will sleep on the walls so as to be ready whenever the charge comes."

"The ancient pilgrims to Jerusalem once slept in the Church of the Holy Sepulcher to be close to the place of the crucifixion," Ben said. "I think I'd like to do the same. Would you all join me? I have nothing to offer but a stone mattress."

"Indeed!" Jimmy smiled for the first time.

Ben shook his old friend's hand. "I know that God has a plan in all of this confusion. I just don't know what it is."

"I wonder if Yeshua might intend to redeem everything after the city is totally destroyed," Cindy said pensively. "Maybe all of that dynamite and all of those bombs will be used to burn everything to the ground."

"We have to be prepared for the worst."

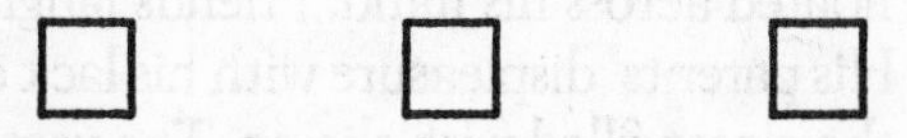

As the late summer sun sank behind the rugged terrain of the wilderness, Ziad Atrash and Rajah Abu Sita stood before the transmission camera to review the final plans for the attack the next morning with the other leaders. Atrash concluded, "Colleagues, we are poised for the ultimate victory. Nothing can stop us now. As the sun rises we will march to our destinies. The time of unified attack is precisely 7:00 A.M. We shall launch the assault while it is still cool. Good night and good luck." The leaders waved and their pictures faded.

"Everything is set," Rajah said resolutely.

Ziad reset the code and began again. "Brothers of the desert, you have just viewed the message heard by all coalition commanders and heads of state. Only you are receiving this final word of instruction. Your call to attack is one hour earlier, when no one is prepared. Six o'clock is the moment of decision for us. Do not issue assault orders until fifteen minutes before the strike. Surprise is of the utmost importance. Show no mercy. Are there any questions?"

No electronic response followed.

"Our final contact is complete. You will hear nothing more from us until after the assault is underway." Atrash saluted and turned off the cameras. Abu Sita had already left the command center.

Ziad walked slowly out of the center and across the hot sand until he came to the edge of the plateau. He looked out across the deep blue waters of the salty Dead Sea. The last light of day and the coming shadows of night painted a constantly changing panorama of beauty on the eroded crags and valleys that emptied into the barren basin.

"I don't need a god," Ziad spoke more to the wind than to himself. "I am enough."

Images floated across his mind. Friends laughing at him in school. His parents' displeasure with his lack of progress. Hiding in the closet filled with shame. The years of painful struggle to overcome the limitations of dyslexia. Each image left Ziad feeling diminished. He ground his teeth and clinched his fist.

"By the time the sun sets tomorrow evening, I will have made a mark all history will remember. No one will ever say again that I was insignificant!"

CHAPTER 22

The bedroom was totally dark. Dawn was starting to break but the curtains were still drawn. "Wake her up," the Jordanian king commanded his aides.

Two soldiers shook Claudine Toulouse several times before she opened her eyes. "Time to start the war?" she said drowsily.

"Afraid so." The king smiled sardonically.

Claudine sat up in bed and rubbed her eyes. "Who's in here?"

"Special soldiers selected to get things under way." Khalil Hussein punched a clicker and all the lights in the room went on. Behind the two soldiers were four other men standing with rifles in hand. "They have come to escort you."

Claudine pulled the sheet up and blinked uncomprehendingly. "I don't understand."

"I forgot to tell you a number of things yesterday." The king sat down on a silk padded chair in the center of the room. "We've made a number of changes in our original strategy."

"Get these men out of here," Claudine ordered, searching across the top of the bed for a robe. "I don't talk with subordinates around."

Khalil ignored her. "At first, we really had no idea that you and the Italian had some sort of plot going. It wasn't until you tried to pull me into your scheme that we really understood what was under way."

"What in the name of the gods is going on?" Claudine pushed her hair back out of her eyes. "I said, *get these men out of here!*"

Khalil laughed. "To think all this nonsense began because we just wanted to get two women out of the picture."

"We?" Claudine shook her head. "Stop talking in riddles."

"Oh, yes." The king settled back in the chair and crossed his arms over his chest. "I suppose I should tell you all the details. *We*, of course, is Atrash, Abu Sit , and myself."

Claudine swung her legs out of bed, pulling the sheet around her. She struggled to stand. "I . . . I . . . don't get any of this." She steadied herself against a night stand next to the bed.

"You offended Ziad one too many times. He sent me to simply distract you and make you vulnerable. We had no idea you were trying to work something out with the Russians and Chinese. How fortunate you confided everything to me."

"What?" Claudine's eyes widened in horror. She looked desperately around the room into the sea of stoic faces. "You . . . you . . ." She grabbed a rock statue from the bed stand and lunged forward. Before Claudine could raise the statue above her shoulders, the two soldiers grabbed the object and knocked her to the floor.

"You must understand," Khalil continued. "Arabs are brothers. I could never betray my kin over a silly little affair."

"No, no!" Claudine pounded on the floor. "No!"

Hussein looked at the clock on the far wall. "In two hours your friend Maria thinks the war will begin. In one hour we will begin our attack on *her*."

Claudine screamed a long, guttural cry and clenched her fists tightly. "N-o-o-o!"

"You will excuse me now." The king stood up. "Unfortunately, we have a war to attend to. Take her away."

The two soldiers jerked the French leader to her feet and shook her roughly. She tried to resist, but they held her tightly. "I thought you loved me!" she cried out.

"No," Khalil answered. "I said I found you very attractive. Your way of handling power was quite appealing. Lust, yes. Love, no."

"You betrayed me!" Claudine screamed at him.

"Oh no." Khalil smiled. "You betrayed yourself."

The soldiers pulled Claudine toward the door. "Where am I going?" she yelled over her shoulder.

"Someplace where you will be safe," the king answered.

Three soldiers with rifles fell in behind the aides dragging the French leader out. Her cries and protests could be heard far down the hallway. Only one aide stayed behind.

"I don't want her body ever found," Hussein said factually. "Stand her against the basement wall and shoot her on the spot. Bury the body underneath the stone floor in the basement. When it's done, I want you personally to shoot the five soldiers who observed everything." The king pointed his finger in the aide's face. "I don't want any eyewitnesses left!"

The aide saluted and turned on his heels.

"Khalil walked quickly down the stairs and across the courtyard in the center of the building. Once inside the command center he found a technician waiting for him.

"We have her recordings cued into the voice translator." The man began throwing switches. "Whatever you say into the transmitter will sound identical to the French woman's voice. We can transmit in French, Hebrew, or English."

"Go to English," the king commanded. "You also have her secret communique numbers in the system?"

"Yes, sir."

"Ok! Let's wake up the Italian sleeping beauty. Keep the hologram off."

Maria Marchino answered on the first beep. "Where are you?" she barked.

"I've got the agreement signed," Hussein said.

"Took you long enough, Claudine," Maria snapped.

"Forget the Jordanians. They are on our side now."

"Good. It was long overdue."

"What about the Russians and Chinese?"

"Once I tell them of Hussein's agreement, they will quickly align with us."

"I will not talk with you again, Maria, until after the attacks begin."

"At 7:00 A.M., we crush the Arabs. Ciao. See you inside the city." The Italian leader clicked off.

Hussein smiled. "Indeed! Perhaps, I won't ever see you again, my little pigeon." He turned to the technician. "Get me the Masada command post. I must speak with Ziad Atrash immediately."

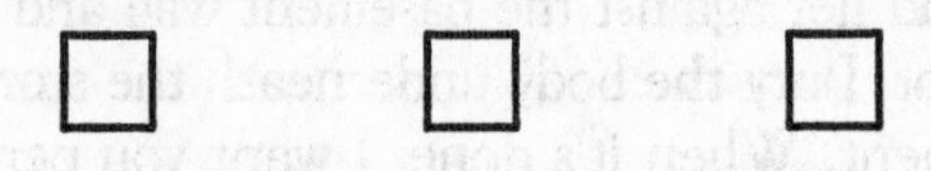

The sky over Jerusalem was already light by 5:30 A.M. Although the sun had not yet appeared, darkness was fading quickly. Av 9 had come once again to the Holy City.

Ben, Cindy, and Jimmy had already left the Church of the Holy Sepulcher and were walking slowly toward the Temple Mount and the Eastern Wall where some of the students were still sleeping.

"Are you scared?" Ben asked his wife.

"No." Cindy shook her head. "Every time I woke up, I

could hear people singing or praying somewhere in the church. I'm tired, but I feel wonderfully reassured."

Ben took his wife's hand. "At least we will have this opportunity to stand together one last time."

Jimmy walked unusually bent over, poking at the cobblestones with his cane. "I don't mind telling you that my back is killing me. If we're going to get slaughtered, I'm ready for it to come quickly."

"Little pessimistic there, James?" Ben asked. "You don't fool me. You are one tough old buzzard."

Jimmy's eyes were swollen and the paunch under his narrow chin shook. He ran his hands through his thin white hair. "I'm just way too old for this sort of adventure," he groused.

"You always were a bundle of cheer in the morning," Ben chided. He opened a wrought iron gate into the Temple area and let the other two pass by him. "Let's cut through the Court of the Gentiles and see how fast we can find Rivka."

"She said she'd be in the area by the Golden Gate." Cindy hung on Ben's arm. "You boys can walk a little slower, you know."

"Glorious summer morning," Ben observed. "A great day to face death if necessary."

"Over here!" someone called from the wall.

"Look!" Cindy pointed. "There's Rivka!"

"What's all this stuff?" Jim poked at crates scattered in front of the wall. "Looks like fruit."

Cindy answered, "When the attackers come, the students will go out of the gates with offerings of fruit, bread, and vegetables. We will welcome them as children of God."

"Sure hope you're right." Jimmy shook his head.

"Join us on the wall." Rivka kept waving.

Some students were still getting out of bedrolls. Several crews had already assembled in front of the wall to prepare coffee, juice, and bagels. Others were opening the crates and placing oranges, grapefruits, and strawberries in small baskets. They waved in respect as the trio passed.

Ben, Cindy, and Jimmy climbed the last stairs to the top of the wall where they could see out across the Kidron Valley. They saw the ancient path of the Palm Sunday procession down the Mount of Olives. The Basilica of the Agony and the Garden of Gethsemane were obvious at the bottom of the valley. Along the top of the mountain line to the east the coalition troops were obviously moving into place. Shuttles swooped over the ridge and troop carriers sped along the streets.

"I wouldn't think they would waste much time," Ben observed "There's no need for their men to wait to attack us."

"As soon as troops start coming up from the valley," Cindy pointed as she talked, "the students will start walking down the hill with gifts in hand. We will know quickly if our plan is going to work."

Jimmy drew himself up to his full height. "Ours will be the noblest of efforts, regardless."

"I left instructions with Mrs. Netanyahu at the office," Ben added. "Should we fail, there is a recorded statement for release declaring our allegiance to Yahweh to the end."

A formation of twenty coalition shuttles suddenly lifted off the top of the Mount of Olives. The v-shaped formation flew straight up and then silently nosedived toward the Old City.

"Here they come!" Ben yelled. "Get ready!"

The shuttles shot barely fifty feet over the heads of the students but kept flying straight across the city.

"I expected them to bomb us!" Ben pointed after the craft. "Must have been an initial reconnaissance."

The shuttles maintained formation until they reached the city limits and then broke into separate directions, flying directly over the coalition soldiers on the other side of the ridge. Each shuttlecraft again veered straight up into the sky before executing a barrel roll and diving straight toward the ground. Suddenly the ground shook as explosion followed explosion. The far ridge erupted in bursts of flame and bellows of smoke. Immediately, the echo of gunfire filled the valley. The crackle of hundreds of rifles sounded like strings of firecrackers going off in every direction.

"What's happening?" Jimmy shook Ben's arm. "What in the world are they doing?"

"I . . . I . . . just don't know. Looks like they are shooting at each other."

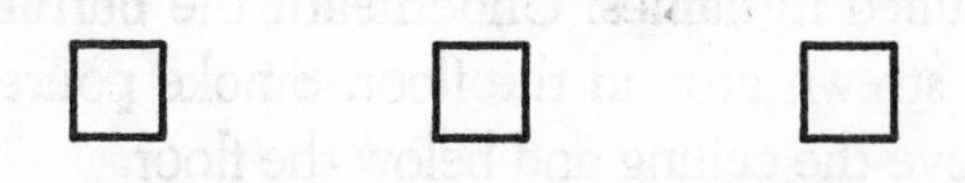

Ziad Atrash stood glued to his monitors, watching the bombing. Across the entire length of the European troop placements, bombs blew large holes in the soldiers' ranks. Bodies flew through the air like debris in a tornado. Buildings burst into flames and timbers scattered like toothpicks.

"Excellent!" Ziad pounded on the desk. "We are dead center on target." He turned to his command radio transmitter. "Give me a closeup of the Italian's command headquarters."

The picture zoomed into larger focus. The flat roof of the building was collapsed and fire poured out of the windows. Only the far end of the complex was still standing.

"Hit that command building again!" Ziad bellowed. "I don't want anything standing. Now!"

A shuttlecraft zoomed across the TV screen and dropped low over the damaged structure. The plane slowed to hover speed and then shot straight up. Immediately the top of the remaining building burst into flame.

"Excellent!" Ziad radioed the pilots. "Now get out of the

way so the infantry can move in." He turned to his other command system. "Troops of the New Order! Attack now. Kill everything in sight."

On the top of the ridge beyond the Hinnom Valley, the Egyptian troops charged. Beneath them in the valley, the Syrian troops began their advance forward. The two-pronged attack caught the Europeans off guard on both fronts. At that moment, the Jordanians stationed to the north turned their guns on the remaining flank of the Italians. Arab troops ran down alleys and up side streets, shooting like wild men at everything that moved.

The top of what remained of the Italian command post was engulfed in flames. Underneath the burning ceiling, men lay strewn around the floor. Smoke poured in from both above the ceiling and below the floor.

Maria Marchino tried to stand up but couldn't move the large table off her back. "Help!" she cried. "Somebody help me."

An aide struggled to his feet and hobbled across the room. He pushed with his last ounce of strength and the table slowly slid off her body. With a final sigh, the man rolled over on his side on the floor.

Maria tried to stand but her left leg wouldn't move. "What's happened?" She started to pull herself across the floor but could only move inches at a time, pushing herself forward by her elbows. The heat was increasing in intensity. "Somebody get me out!"

The sound of gunfire grew steadily louder. Men were hollering in the streets. The noise of chaos was nearly deafening.

Maria looked up at the scattered electronic receivers and broken screens. "I've got to find out what has happened."

Suddenly two men with rifles appeared in the door.

"That's her!" one soldier cried out. "We've found Marchino!"

"Get me out of here!" Maria cried.

Shots tore through the air. The Italian leader's body pulsated, jerking back and forth as the bullets blew her life away.

From his Masada compound, Atrash carefully studied the shuttlecraft's transmission. "It's safe to assume the European command is destroyed," he said to Abu Sita. "I think it's time for your trip to see Chardoff and Fong."

Rajah nodded. "I suppose so."

"For the time being, we won't let them know that Hussein knew about the attempts to bring their countries into the Europeans' camp. We only need them to sit still."

Rajah nodded his head and left the room without comment. His two-person shuttlecraft was ready in the center of Masada's landing strip. Within minutes, he was flying across the eroded wilderness to the west of the battle. Abu Sita's first pass went far north of Jerusalem across the fertile plain around Tel Aviv and then dropped low to glide into the area behind the lines held by the Russians and Chinese. Troops were running in every direction, obviously confused by the fighting to the west of their units.

The Syrian head of state landed on the street in front of the large hotel commandeered for the Russian and Chinese military command. He hurried out of the craft and into the hotel.

Coalition troops immediately recognized him and stood at attention as Abu Sita passed. "Take me to your leaders," he told a guard at the end of the first corridor.

Chardoff and Fong were standing at the window of the eighth floor, staring out at the fires burning on the other side of their eastern flank. They turned when Abu Sita entered but didn't seem surprised to see him.

Abu Sita began talking the moment he walked through

the door. "I came at once to alert you personally to what is happening. We discovered a most serious plot to defraud all of us. The Italian and French commanders intended to betray our alliance. We had no alternative but to protect you."

"Sit down." Chardoff pointed to a chair. Fong stood beside the Russian. "Tell us more."

Rajah nodded and dropped into the large chair. "For some time, we suspected an attempt to form a separate front in case the battle failed, but we soon found reason to believe the two women were plotting against all of us. We have maintained spies in the midst of their camp." He stopped and looked carefully at the impassive heads of state. "You do understand?"

Both men nodded but said nothing.

"We know that Toulouse is now dead and believe Marchino has met the same fate. We believe that we will have the rest of the quislings in line by the time we kick off our joint attack at 7:00 A.M. We should not experience any delays in our original projections."

"Such expert planning," Chardoff began. "But one would think you would have let your allies in on the details much earlier."

"We weren't quite sure of—"

"Of who all the players were," Fong interrupted. "Perhaps, you did not trust *us*."

"Oh! Nothing of the sort!" Abu Sita jumped from his chair. "We simply didn't want to create undue suspicion until we were sure of the facts."

"Or had us in a position to attack next," Chardoff added coldly.

"Next?" The Syrian's eyes widened. "Never!"

"Let me show you a little something that came in early this morning." Chardoff pointed to the screen on the opposite wall.

Maria Marchino's picture appeared. "Gentlemen, we have every reason to believe the Egyptians and Syrians will attack us first in the guise of assaulting the city. Once Europeans are out of the way, the Arabs will turn to your armies. Even Khalil Hussein has joined us out of concern for his future. Unless we have a mutual defense treaty, we will end up the slaves of Atrash. Jerusalem is no obstacle to world conquest for this Egyptian tyrant but we are. We must stand together or fall separately."

"No!" Abu Sita's mouth dropped. "It can't be! Hussein didn't mean that was his intention."

"Appears Miss Marchino was somewhat of a prophet," Chardoff said dryly.

"And even without the help of your god Marduk," Fong added.

"Don't jump to the wrong conclusions," Abu Sita said, gesturing frantically. "Her little speech is just part of their plot."

"Plot?" Chardoff turned to Fong. "Yes, but not the one you're trying to sell us, Rajah."

"Did you think us to be such fools that we wouldn't see through this little subterfuge of yours?" Fong's eyes narrowed. "However, we didn't expect you to come walking in here so easily. No, my friend, neither the Russians nor the Chinese have any intention of building bricks for you and your mad empire-building Egyptian despot."

"I tell you . . ." Rajah stopped and swallowed hard. "You've read all the signs wrong. Completely wrong."

"I liked you, Rajah." Chardoff unbuttoned his uniform. "You were so much more humane than that thick-headed bull. Unfortunately, the two of you were simply cut from the same cloth."

Chardoff drew his pistol from under his coat and pointed the gun straight at Rajah. His first shot struck the Syrian square in the forehead, knocking him over the back of the chair.

"The Arabs struck much earlier than we calculated." Chardoff put the gun back in his shoulder holster. "We have no choice but to hurl our men into the center of their lines. We must charge down the Hinnon Valley and wait until they finish with the Europeans."

"Undoubtedly, the Arabs will sustain casualties," Fong mused. "We will be able to take advantage of their losses as well as the fact they don't expect our attack."

"Our shuttles are loaded with explosives." Chardoff turned back to the window. "They've already spent their supply. We will soften them up with bombs before our men finish them off."

"Let us go instruct our commanders about the dash down the valley." Fong pointed to the door. "After you, Mr. Prime Minister.

The Russian laughed and the two men hurried out without looking back at Abu Sita's body.

At the other end of the military circle around Jerusalem, Ali of Ethiopia frantically watched his TV monitor's pictures of the battle raging on the other side of the city. He stared incongruously at the screen.

"What do you make of it, General Ali?" the aide asked. "Should we not call Ziad Atrash for information?"

"Something has gone completely wrong." Ali rubbed his chin with his long thin fingers. We must be careful not to get caught in the middle."

"Coalition troops appear to be fighting with each other."

"Yes," Ali said slowly, "or maybe . . . possibly . . . they are fighting against an enemy in their midst."

"I don't understand." The aide shook his head.

"What if the Immortals have finally reappeared?" Ali asked.

"We could never defeat them!" The soldier gasped.

"Exactly!" The Ethiopian leader exclaimed. "We have been lured into a trap set by the Immortals. They waited until we were massed in one place and then attacked. They are killing us!"

"We must contact Atrash for direction."

"No!" Ali barked. "Heavens no! We must not walk into the same trap!"

"What shall we do?" the officer begged.

Ali paced back and forth. "We must maintain radio silence, lest we be lured into a trap." He stopped and snapped his fingers. "We must make the Immortals believe we were always on their side."

"How?" The aide held up his hands in bewilderment.

"We must attack the Russians and Chinese . . . or anyone left standing! Order our soldiers to destroy all coalition flags and run up the colors of Yeshua's government. Tell our men we are on Yeshua's side and order the fighting to begin at once."

"Excellent!" The aide breathed deeply. "A brilliant stroke. We can still extricate ourselves."

"At once!" Ali ordered the solider out of his room.

Back on top of Masada, Ziad listened carefully to the communique that Marchino's body had been found. From the pictures he could tell his men were overwhelming her bewildered troops. The French were in total disarray as Hussein kept issuing confusing instructions over the voice translator.

"Much better than I thought," Ziad mumbled to himself. He pushed the buttons for special transmission to the field generals. "We are ahead of schedule. Send the martial arts people down the hill. I want to take the Temple compound as quickly as possible. Unlock the worldwide satellite transmission so these pictures can go through normal channels. There is no longer any need to block communication."

Ziad stepped back from the monitors. He rubbed the

back of his neck, realizing how tense he had been through the entire attack. "I need some fresh air," he said to his aides. "Don't bother me. I'm going to take a walk."

Who knows, he thought to himself, *by the time I get back this whole campaign could be over.*

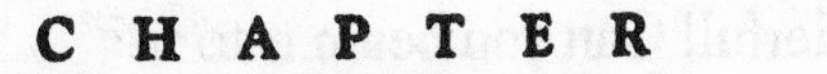

CHAPTER 23

Ben kept pointing up and down the valley. "I can't believe my eyes! Our enemies are killing each other! And look at how strange the sky is. Weird color everywhere!"

Explosions along the ridge sent large balls of fire up into the sky. Columns of smoke were turning the western sky black. The rapid staccato of gunfire continued unabated. Dark clouds of smoke drifted overhead.

"This scenario is just what happened to King Hezekiah," Jimmy shouted above the uproar. "We're sitting here watching the enemy kill themselves."

The students cheered and applauded. Rivka ran up and down the ramparts to encourage her troops. "We are winning," she shouted over and over. "Get ready for their attack."

Ben's wristwatch communicator abruptly buzzed. "Yes," he shouted into the receiver. "Who is it?"

Mrs. Netanyahu's familiar voice answered. "Ben, I didn't know whether to contact you under the circumstances, but I thought you'd want to know immediately. The international satellite system has started to work again. We have a message waiting from Isaiah Murphy."

"Wonderful! Can you beam it to us?"

"Hang on. I'll patch in the picture and audio."

Ben waved for Cindy and Jimmy to gather around. He shielded the small screen from the light and the prerecorded picture emerged. "We're back!" Isaiah's familiar face filled the small viewer. "We've tried everything to get through and couldn't. But we recorded this message and set our transmitters to send the communique as soon as the channels opened."

"Isaiah really is clever," Jimmy said. "Doesn't miss a lick."

Isaiah pointed to a map on the wall behind him. "We have organized resistance groups up and down the coast. Just wanted you to know that multitudes of people are remaining faithful. No matter what happens over there, the Believers aren't throwing in the towel. The president of this country can say anything he chooses but the majority is not with him."

"We aren't alone!" Jimmy shook his cane toward the sky.

"Just remember one little story," Isaiah continued. "A scorpion asked a frog to let him ride on his back across a river. The frog said, 'If I do, you'll sting me, and I'll die.' The scorpion assured the frog no such thing would happen as they would both drown. The frog let the scorpion on and started across the river. Halfway to the other side, the scorpion unleashed his venomous tail and stung the frog. 'Why?' the dying frog cried. 'Now, we will both die.' The scorpion shrugged. 'I am a scorpion and it is my nature to sting frogs. Sorry.'"

"I don't get it." Jimmy grunted.

"Remember that the Evil One is stuck on who he is," Isaiah continued. "He's clever but not shrewd enough to keep from outwitting himself. The Devil will not prevail." Isaiah waved and the picture faded.

The trio looked across the valley once more.

"Is not the scorpion stinging the frog?" Cindy asked.

Suddenly new cries filled the air. Men in black jersey uniforms charged across the creek at the bottom of the Kidron Valley and up toward the walls. A sea of black shapes swept across the field like locusts devouring everything in their path.

"Here they come!" Rivka called to the students. "Open the gates. Let us go forth in the name of our God!"

Cindy rushed down the steps. "I have to help my troops," she called over her shoulder.

"What do you think?" Ben asked Jimmy.

Jimmy peered over the edge. "They're not far away and coming fast. The hour of reckoning is at hand."

"Are we going to stand up here and watch?"

"You're right, Ben! We can't stay here. We have to join them."

"What?"

"No, I won't argue with you. Let's go." Jimmy started down the steps, testing each one with his cane.

Ben shook his head. "Here we go again." He hurried after his friend.

A few students pushed the Golden Gates wide open while others poured out along the front of the wall. Each person carried a basket of fruit or bread. The attackers were no more than a hundred yards away.

"Remember your instructions," Rivka called up and down the line. "Take what they give and give what they take." Rivka hurried to the center of the line of students to lead the group forward.

The soldiers stopped when the students walked slowly toward them. Students began waving as if greeting old friends. The attackers looked at each other uncomprehendingly. Some men assumed defensive positions, others began making slow circular motions with their hands. The students edged forward, offering their baskets of fruit and loaves of bread. The soldiers looked around for someone to give directions. They appeared confused.

"We are your friends," Rivka called out. "Our hands are extended in friendship. Are we not one people under Yeshua?"

Several attackers broke ranks and charged forward. A young man bore down on Rivka, stopping only a few feet in front of her. The soldier immediately spun around backward and swung his foot high over his shoulder. The man's foot caught Rivka across the side of her face. The basket of oranges spilled over the ground, as Rivka fell sideways and bounced on the hard rocks. The soldier settled back into a judo-defense stance. Both lines stopped and watched.

Rivka rolled on the ground writhing in pain. Immediately, another young woman stepped into her place and extended a loaf of bread. "We wish you no harm. Are we not your friends?" As the young woman took a step forward, the attacker backed away as if uncertain of what to do next.

Three other soldiers rushed at the defense line. Students opened their arms, offering no resistance, which gave the martial arts fighters an unprotected target shot. The soldiers made menacing jabs and slashes with their hands but the students smiled and didn't move. Suddenly an attacker lunged for the mid-section of one of the young men. When the boy doubled in pain, the solider struck him on the back of the neck with the side of his hand. The student crumbled to the ground. The judo fighter dropped back into a defensive stance ready for a counterattack. None came.

Soldiers kept looking around, trying to find someone to give them orders. Bombs were still exploding on the far ridges, but no one seemed to be in charge of directing military operations. The martial arts fighters looked like an isolated line of attackers.

Students began humming a popular hymn of the day. "Glor-or-ia, Glor-or-ia," their song continued, "Glory to the Lamb. For He is our peace." Others waved good-naturedly and kept smiling. "We are your brothers and sisters!" Some kids cried out, "We come armed only with love. We are one family of God." A voice called over the rest, "Come home to your people."

Cindy emerged from the ranks of the young people and stood near Rivka. Her snow-white hair and Oriental face made a sharp contrast with the black hair and dark complexions of most of the young people. She held both hands above her head as if petitioning in prayer. "Let's end all hostilities," Cindy called to the attackers. "Even now your leaders are in retreat. Don't be duped any longer."

"Blue blazes!" Ben gasped. "She's out there by herself. They'll strike her just like they did Rivka." Ben bolted forward, pushing his way through the students.

"You're right!" Jimmy shook his cane in the air. "We must protect her at all costs. Cindy's too old and frail to survive an attack."

The two men broke through the line of students and ran toward Cindy. "Don't you dare touch my wife!" Ben shook his fist in the air.

Two soldiers had cautiously crept toward Cindy. The men kept moving with their hands in front of them in slow circling movements. Cindy walked forward calling to the men to join her.

Ben rushed past Cindy and pointed his finger at the first soldier. "You wouldn't dare attack an old lady!" Jimmy was at his heels, swinging his cane through the air.

The soldier grabbed Ben's outstretched arm and swung the old man behind him. For a second Ben looked like he was flying a few feet above the ground. He landed with a hard, dull thud.

Jimmy swung his cane at the head of the second soldier.

With a simple pivot at the waist, the soldier used the cane to gain leverage, sending Jimmy head over heels in a somersault. Jimmy fell on his back in a clump of bushes.

Ben kept gasping for air. His face was white. He could barely breathe, his glasses smashed on the ground. Jimmy sprawled defenselessly staring at the sky, equally stunned. The soldiers dropped into their judo stance and started circling Cindy.

Cindy looked troubled but managed a smile. "You see," she addressed the soldiers, "my husband is only trying to protect me. He doesn't wish you harm. Can you gain anything by hurting old people?"

The soldiers took a step backward and glanced at Ben and Jimmy. Both men were barely able to move.

"We offer you nothing but love," Cindy continued. "We forgive you for any pain caused us."

"Hey, I know those men!" a soldier yelled. "They are the two leaders, the TV guys!"

"Take them into custody," the man in front of Cindy instructed. "Get them back to our command."

Cindy bit her lip but didn't move as Ben and Jimmy were dragged away. "Remember your training from the days of your youth," she shouted to them. "What did your parents teach you? Look into your hearts and recognize what is true." Cindy watched the coalition soldiers hustling Jimmy and Ben toward the creek. They were obviously calling someone for instructions. "Help us, Lord," she prayed aloud.

The students close to the soldiers inched onward and then dropped to the ground at the feet of their attackers. They pushed the fruit and bread forward. Only then did other students rush over to help Rivka. They carried her back to the city gate.

Finally a soldier bent down and picked up an apple. Another started to eat a peach. The men relaxed and gave up their judo stances. Conversations broke out and the atmosphere of tension eased.

Cindy kept looking up and down the line as the air of confrontation dissipated. She watched nervously as her husband and friend were dragged farther and farther away. By the time they reached the bottom of the valley, Jimmy and Ben were surrounded by many soldiers. Cindy kept her place, trying to smile and stay calm.

In a few minutes, it was clear Cindy and Rivka's strategy was working. The students and soldiers were about the same age. They looked into each other's faces and no longer saw an enemy. Students invited the attackers in to see the city. With no one to attack, the soldiers' sense of purpose was broken.

From the top of the Mount of Olives, a shuttlecraft flew up into the sky before swooping down into the valley and landing just at the edge of the creek. Cindy watched in horror as Jimmy and Ben were loaded into the craft. The plane lifted and sped down the valley, lifting up over the ridge of the mountains.

□ □ □

For the last twenty minutes, chaos had consumed the leaders in the Masada command center on the plateau high above the Dead Sea. Ziad Atrash lurched from monitor to monitor trying to grasp what was happening. He kept returning to the picture of the Ethiopian army marching under the banner of the Jerusalem government.

"I told you to get Ali on the intercom immediately!" Ziad bellowed at his aide.

The man gestured nervously. "They . . . just won't answer. Nothing gets a response."

"These idiots are attacking the Russians and the Chinese!" Atrash kept pointing at the TV screen. "What's that worthless flag doing up there?"

Another general dashed into the room. "Abu Sita can't be found anywhere. His staff has not heard from him since he landed in Jerusalem. His shuttlecraft is still there, but he's disappeared."

Atrash cursed violently. "Can't be! It just can't be. Get me Hussein on the phone."

Another monitor flashed pictures of Egyptian troops falling in the face of terrible explosions. Men were scattered about the streets and lying in heaps in the gutter.

"I can't believe my eyes!" Atrash screamed.

"We've just picked up a communique from the Ethiopian command that a statement is forthcoming." The aide hit buttons and the screens cleared. Ali's picture appeared.

"Peoples of the world," the Ethiopian spoke rapidly, "be aware that we are working with the Immortals to restore normalcy in Jerusalem."

"The *Immortals!*" Atrash grabbed the edge of the table.

"Obviously, our glorious leaders have returned and are now destroying your enemies. The Immortals have decimated the European armies and are now attacking the Arab coalition. We are offering support by assailing the flanks of these renegades. Order should be restored shortly. Rest assured, our efforts have always been with our glorious leader, Yeshua."

"The stupid fool has mistaken *our* attack as the work of the Immortals. That conniving idiot!" Atrash cursed again.

"What if he's right?" an aide asked.

"What do you mean?" Ziad screamed.

"Maybe the Immortals have led us into a trap." Color drained from the man's face as he spoke. "Maybe Ali is right."

Ziad glanced around the room. Every man in the command center was staring at the aide in shock, their eyes filled with consternation and misgiving. Atrash grabbed a rifle from the man at the door and swung the wooden butt into the face of the aide. The hapless man smashed into the wall and crumpled to the floor. With another staggering blow, Ziad cracked the unconscious man's head against the cement floor. He threw the gun back through the door.

"Anyone else got any other traitorous suggestions?" Atrash looked around the room. No one moved. "Let's get on with business. What's the current status of our troops?"

No one spoke.

Atrash pointed to the aide seated before the Egyptian monitor. "Speak up!" he demanded.

"We . . . lost . . . men . . . many men . . . hitting the Europeans. The Russians and Chinese are chewing up our troops." The aide inhaled and raised his arm slightly as if to protect his face. "Their bombs have ripped us to pieces."

"I've got to find Abu Sita." Atrash wrung his hands. "Where is he?"

No one answered. The only sounds in the room were the messages coming from the monitors.

"Get him out of here." Atrash pointed to the body of his aide. "The only squadron unaccounted for is our martial arts outfit. Get them on the line."

The soldier at the last monitor heaved a sigh of relief. "Good news!" He smiled broadly. "Our men have captured two of the opposition leaders—Harrison and Feinberg. They are being flown in here right now."

"A breakthrough!" Ziad shook both fists in the air. "Now, we will turn this thing around."

A general from the central screening area stepped forward. "Regardless of the cost to me, I must tell you some bad news. The Egyptian and Syrian armies are, for all practical purposes, destroyed." He stood at attention as if expecting a firing squad. "We knocked out the Europeans, but the Russians and Chinese prevailed. They are currently locked in mortal combat with the Jordanians."

Atrash ground his teeth and clenched his fist. "They will pay!" He could barely speak.

"I have just been able to get Hussein on the line," an aide interrupted.

"Khalil," Ziad spoke into the monitor, "are you all right?"

"No." The transmission was poor and without a picture. "The Ethiopians attacked me. They got inside our command center before we knew they had turned against us." Hussein's voice sounded weak. "We had a violent shootout . . . a bomb went off. Not much is left. The fighting is moving from house to house. They are eating us alive."

"Hang on," Atrash demanded. "Don't stop now! We still have a chance."

"For what?" Hussein choked. "I've been shot. The whole thing is going up in smoke." The receiver went silent.

Aides glanced at each other but said nothing. Atrash looked from man to man with hate and suspicion in his eyes. The men avoided eye contact.

"They're arriving!" the aide in charge of the martial arts platoon said confidently. "We have the enemy leaders in custody."

"Well!" Atrash ran his hands through his hair and pulled his uniform down tightly. "Let us greet our adversaries with all due hospitality." He stomped out of the building with his top aides following.

A strange cast covered the entire sky. Even though nothing could shield the unforgiving heat of the summer sun, the clouds grew dark and it looked as if a terrible storm was brewing. The craft came straight in from the north, breaking through a bank of red-lined thunderheads. The shuttle glided quietly to a halt on the runway in the center of the ancient fortress. The bubble top lifted and two soldiers in black uniforms got out. The men helped Jimmy and Ben down. Without his glasses, Ben had a hard time making out what was happening around him. Jimmy appeared equally helpless without his cane. For several moments they held to the side of the craft, trying to get their bearings.

"Bring them to me," Ziad commanded. "I want them over here by the ruins of Herod's palace."

The soldiers led the two men to the ancient terrazzo floor of what had once been a dining room for the infamous King Herod. The morning sun was now climbing high into the sky and the suffocating heat of summer was returning. Ben kept squinting and shielding his eyes, desperately trying to see.

"Latch them together to that column." Atrash pointed to the remnant of a granite support that once had held a massive roof. "I want them stretched tightly around the stone. Put them back to back and tie their hands together. If one falls, they'll both feel the pain!"

Jimmy and Ben's aged appearance contrasted strongly with the youthful martial arts experts who looked like mere boys. Ben gave no resistance but Jimmy jerked himself free from their grip and stood unusually erect against the stone support.

"Sir," a general spoke to Atrash. "Is there any value in harming these old men? Nothing can change what has happened."

Atrash's eyes widened and his face twisted in hate. He reached up toward the aide's throat. "You want to take their place?"

The young general hung his head and stepped back. He proceeded to tie Jimmy to the column.

Atrash cursed and began walking around the two helpless prisoners of war. Then he stepped back to take full measure of his captives. "As I live and breathe, the boys from Jerusalem. Yeshua's right hand men!" Ziad pulled a pistol from his waist and held the barrel inches from Ben's eyes. "Take a good look! I don't know whether to beat you to death or just shoot off an ear or a nose, a piece at a time."

Ziad stepped back and chuckled. "You perpetuated the legend of having lived through the so-called Great Tribulation, which, of course, none of us ever witnessed except on your doctored TV tapes. At the very least, history will record you didn't live longer than I did." Ziad put the gun back in his belt and started walking silently around the column.

An aide emerged from the door of the command center and called to the commander-in-chief. "I have the latest update from the martial arts unit. The news is not good."

Atrash looked annoyed but didn't reply. He kept walking.

Another general ran from the command center and walked onto the terrazzo floor. "Sir," he spoke forcefully, "the martial arts unit appears to have surrendered. Nothing is left of the attack."

Ziad appeared not to hear. He walked to a sign explaining the significance of the site and suddenly smashed it into splinters with his hand. With a swift kick, he knocked one of the support poles to the ground and picked up the long piece of wood.

"We could let you two old geezers just roast out in the sun." Ziad thumped the palm of his hand with the jagged stick. "Dehydration comes quickly in the month of Av. But you boys are hard to put away. I tried to blow you up in front of the Knesset and you escaped. I even sabotaged your shuttle and you walked away. My, my, you're an elusive pair!"

Ziad suddenly rammed the stick into Ben's stomach. Ben screamed and doubled forward. Atrash brought a counter blow to the side of his face and blood ran out of his mouth.

"The trouble is," Ziad continued to talk in a matter-of-fact tone, "I depended on others to do what I should have done myself. Big mistake!" Ziad stopped and whacked Jimmy across the nose. "I'm a generous man." He leaned into Jimmy's face. "Tell me the secret of how you do the appearing and disappearing act, and I'll let you live." Off in the distance a great bolt of lightning flashed across the purple sky.

"You are a fool!" Jimmy spit blood out of his mouth. "Even without divine intervention, we are more clever than you."

Atrash swung the heavy pole to smash Jimmy's chest and collarbone. Jimmy's shoulder sagged from the blow and his knees buckled pulling Ben even more tightly into the back of the column.

"You just don't seem to understand, Harrison! This information is your last bargaining chip. I need this technology to recover from what has happened today," Atrash barked in his face. "I still have guns and bombs in a world without armaments. I'm not through by any means. I have defense treaties with many other nations. Now talk!"

CHAPTER 24

The pain in Jimmy's shoulder and chest was excruciating. No matter how he moved, there was no escaping an additional burning rub when Ben's sagging body pulled the rope tighter on Jimmy's wrist. The increasingly hot sun was becoming unbearable. Burning sweat rolled down Jimmy's forehead and dripped into his eyes.

Each time Jimmy blinked to clear his eyes, Ziad was there. The Egyptian's eyes were wild and frantic. His red-blotched neck kept expanding like a puffing adder. The Egyptian general's hands shook but his rage was paradoxically controlled. Clearly he and Ben had become the focus of Atrash's frustration.

Jimmy's agony made it difficult to focus on what Atrash was saying. The despot's words rolled around in his head as if they were coming from across a great chasm or from a distant loud speaker. Jimmy blinked to clear his eyes. From high up on Masada, he could see far out across the Dead Sea basin. For a moment, the vast panorama seemed unexpectedly beautiful.

Atrash's hot breath on Jimmy's face was sour. Jimmy

tried to turn his head, fearing he was about to faint. He struggled to clear his mind. Only then did an image emerge. Jimmy remembered the inside of the Church of the Holy Sepulcher where they had slept the night before. During his first visit, Jimmy had not noticed the large icon of the crucified Christ, hanging in the Greek Orthodox section of the church. That night the picture had seemed to come to life and almost leap off the wall at him. Once more, Jimmy felt himself standing before the depiction of the crucifixion. The mental image seemed larger than life and three dimensional. As he looked the pain in his broken body diminished.

From somewhere deep within Jimmy an answer to Atrash spilled out. "I am not worthy to be crucified as was my Lord. But I would count it an honor to die at the hands of the likes of you."

Jimmy was surprised by his own words. Each syllable seemed to arise from a place that he had never known. An extraordinary sense of peace swept over him and pain wasn't important anymore.

Once again Ziad was shouting but the words didn't register. Jimmy's reprieve was so all-encompassing, little else mattered. His legs felt stronger and he could support himself better. Jimmy tried again to comprehend the words screamed in his face.

"After I crack your ribs, I'm going to crush your limbs before I break your head." Ziad's face was crimson and his eyes looked red. He raised the club above his head like an executioner preparing to deliver the final blow. "Say good-bye to this world, old man."

I must show absolutely no fear, Jimmy thought. *I will give God the glory regardless.* He forced a smile and tried to stand as erect as possible. *Let the final countenance on my face be a witness to my faith,* he prayed silently. *No man will be able to doubt where my trust and confidence were always placed.* He opened his eyes and looked at Ziad with total defiance.

The dictator rose on his toes to put the full force of his large body behind the terrible blow. His eyes widened, he ground his teeth. Suddenly a shot rang out. Ziad froze in place. His hate-filled look changed to surprise. A second shot rang out. The general's body sagged, the club rolled from his hand, and he grabbed his chest. Atrash turned slowly and a third shot exploded. He dropped to his knees and fell facedown on the terrazzo floor.

The general directly behind Atrash held a small smoking revolver. The rest of the military leaders stood silent, frozen in place.

Jimmy swallowed hard. *Am I dead? Hallucinating?* He blinked frantically trying to keep the sweat from blurring his vision. *I am finally losing it.*

"Untie them," the man with the gun said quietly. "The war is over." Only then did the soldiers move as if a magic spell had been broken.

When the bonds were cut, Ben tumbled forward. Jimmy began sliding toward the ground but a soldier held him up. The rest of the military gathered around the column.

"There is no atoning for our mistakes," the general with the gun said, dropping the weapon to the ground. "We must help you with your wounds."

"Help my friend," Jimmy said as he leaned on the stone column. "I'm worried about the blow to his head."

Immediately soldiers began attending to Ben.

"Your shoulder looks bad." The general pointed to Jimmy's sagging arm. "We must get you into a splint as quickly as possible."

"I need to get out of the sun," Jimmy answered. He held his arm against his chest.

"Let's get both of you inside," the solider answered.

"Help us carry him in," the general called to those around him and pointed at Ben. "Follow me."

"I want to look out over the Dead Sea just for a second," Jimmy answered. "A few moments ago, I didn't expect to be alive right now. I just need to get my bearings again. The sky has a strange cast." He pointed to the sun. Hues of violet and blue from strangely contorted clouds washed across the brilliant sunlight. Along the mountains the deep purple of a terrible approaching storm rolled over the jagged horizon line.

"We were raised to respect authority as unto the Lord," the young general continued. "No one knew quite what to do when the whole plot started to unfold. We had been taught to respect the chain of command between us and the government in Jerusalem." The general stopped and raised his eyebrows. "I know everything I say sounds like poor excuses, but I'm not trying to avoid responsibility. We are guilty of great error."

Jimmy only nodded his head. "Why don't you give me that piece of wood Atrash was swinging. It will make a good cane."

"Atrash was impossible to confront," another aide added. "The man simply overpowered all of us."

Again Jimmy nodded. "Boys, I'm not the one with whom you have to square things. The issue is between you and the Lord." Lightning crashed and crackled, and thunder rolled up from the far mountains. Violet clouds around the sun turned an ominous black.

"I suppose you want to get back to Jerusalem," the young general suggested as they walked to the edge of the cliff overlooking the Dead Sea. "We will fly you and your friend there as soon as you are ready."

Jimmy looked out over the broken terrain. "What a sight! Three thousand years ago the final remnant of Israel died right here . . . but the people survived. Today, the story was reversed. The enemy died on this ancient battle-field."

"Look at the clouds." The aide pointed at the sky. "They seem to be racing across the sky and yet there is almost no wind. The sun is disappearing behind those black thunder-heads."

A rumble began far off to the west. The ground trembled. Jimmy grabbed for the general's arm.

"Earthquake!" the young man shouted. "Hang on!"

The top of Masada shook with disconcerting vibrations. Soldiers tried to run for cover; others fell to the ground. The shuttlecraft waiting on the runway bumped up and down. The general lost his balance and fell backward. Jimmy grabbed a guardrail to keep from going over the edge.

The rumble became a frightening roar. Rocks broke loose and boulders tumbled down the steep banks of Masada, crushing the ground hundreds of feet below. Far across the valley avalanches of rocks and dirt slid down into the Dead Sea. Huge waves sloshed against the banks. The wavy surface bounced and swayed like water in a washtub.

Jimmy fell to his knees and clung to the metal pole for dear life. The roar was deafening. The ground shook harder and the few remaining buildings tumbled in. To the south, a terrible cracking sound pierced the morning sky. A whole canyon split open like a boulder breaking in two monstrous halves. The earth pulled apart, and in an awesome shift the entire base of Masada moved sideways. The movement crushed the ancient Roman causeway, built for Rome's final assault on the Jewish survivors. The huge, long mound split in a thousand pieces.

The soldier grabbed Jimmy's leg and pointed south. "That Valley runs up to Beersheba and on to the ocean. It's turning into the Grand Canyon! God help us!"

The crackling noise reached a deafening level, while the Dead Sea began to dry up. Like a sink emptying, the gigantic vortex of a whirlpool sent the salty ocean to the center of the earth.

"The bottom has fallen out of the world," Jimmy gasped. "The whole sea is disappearing!"

Suddenly, an all-engulfing cloud of steam exploded and sent huge boulders flying upward in every direction. Masada shook again as megaliths smashed into the top. Helpless soldiers cowered in trenches.

"The wrath of God has fallen on us for our evil deeds!" The general kept saying over and over. "Forgive us! Forgive us!"

Jimmy tried to peer into the bottomless lake that now looked like the center of a large volcano. As far down as he could see, there was nothing but black emptiness and boiling steam.

Another staggering, roaring sound rolled up the south end of the basin. The newly formed canyon split, then dropped again, as whole mountains spilled into the bottomless pit that had once been the Dead Sea. Farther to the west the rushing water grew louder and louder as if mountains were being washed away by a great tidal wave. Instantaneously, a torrent of water flooded through the valley and emptied into the vast hole. Behind the first onslaught came a tidal wave that looked at least a thousand feet high. The sea of water was so vast that it first filled the complete Dead Sea basin before dropping away as it poured into the gigantic hole.

Once again another eruption of steam sent dirt, rocks, and debris thousands of feet into the air. The first wave of boulders gave way to much smaller pieces of gravel raining down like hail. Bits of mud pelted Jimmy. He could see nothing but the mist covering everything like a heavy fog. Jimmy shielded his head but the stone pellets stung. The roar of a thousand oceans filled the air with the sound of terrifying power. Jimmy cowered next to the metal railing while the whole mountain swayed like a tree in the wind.

Jimmy stared again into the whirling abyss of water, steam, and smoke. A passage from the Book of Revelation came back to mind. "There shall be no sea." He thought to himself, *The Bible promises the new creation will have no oceans. Am I seeing the fulfillment of this promise? The oceans of the world emptying into the lowest point on the earth? Could it really be? But where else could such an endless amount of water come from?*

The terrible shaking and earthquakes subsided but the relentless flood only increased. Bellows of streams continued to shoot upward. Jimmy could no longer see anything inside the vast hole. He felt a tug on his coat. Jimmy turned and to his amazement found Ben groping across the ground.

"Ben! You're conscious!"

"What in tarnation is going on?" Ben shouted as loud as possible. "My glasses are gone! I can't see anything. What's happening?"

Jimmy locked his legs around the railing and reached out with his good arm. "Hang on to me."

"I can't see anything. When I regained consciousness, everything was covered by a cloud! What's going on?"

Jimmy hugged his old friend. "Unless I miss my guess, Yeshua is calling in all the cards. I think we're seeing the final wrap-up of history."

"Praise God!"

Slowly, the sound of rushing water receded and the clouds of steam diminished. A deep gurgling sound bubbled up from the vast hole in the earth. The smell of sulphur hung in the air. What had been the Dead Sea was now a vast gorge. Powerful sweeping winds roared down the empty valleys blowing the smoke and foglike clouds out to the south. The sky appeared blood red and the remaining clouds twinged with purple blackness. Streaks of light kept shooting overhead, leaving thin trails of smoke. Once again the two men could hear each other

"Look!" Ben pointed around the top of Masada. "Our captors are dead!"

Soldiers were piled in a heap as if trying to save themselves by massing together. Other men lay alone, covered with pieces of rock. The general who freed Jimmy and Ben was the only soldier left and was on his knees, thanking Yeshua for forgiveness.

"I still can't see anything very clearly without my glasses," Ben answered.

"There's not much going on now," Jimmy answered, "but I've got a feeling the fireworks are just about to start up there in the heavens."

"I wish I could see it."

"If what I think is happening," Jimmy said, "I've got a hunch you'll have a pretty fair idea of what's coming down."

"Describe what you're seeing."

Jimmy pointed to the clouds, then his finger dropped to the horizon line. "A great beam of light is splitting the sky now. Must be coming from some point far out in space."

As Jimmy watched, the dark clouds disappeared and a terrible calm settled, resembling the hush before a devastating storm. Streaks of fiery light began shooting across the sky like laser beams. Some of the luminous objects collided and exploded in a burst of red and blue energy.

"I can't believe it!" Jimmy began to shake Ben. "The sky is vibrating, just like an earthquake, but it's above us. Stars suddenly appear in broad daylight and then are gone. It makes me dizzy just watching."

"The sky is falling?"

"Some . . . thing . . . of . . . that order, I think."

Sprays of color filled the sky. The spectacle was like galaxies smashing together. The great beam of light slowly lowered until it cut straight across the earth. The light was like fire but the beam became, not flames, but dancing discharges of electric energy. The electronic fire devoured whatever it touched and surrounded every object with a golden glow. As pure energy popped and crackled, the electric discharges leaped from rock to tree to plant like a raging forest fire.

"What is it?" Ben pulled on Jimmy's arm.

"I don't know but everything is being transformed. And it's coming this way!"

The yellow light danced over the far edge of the barren wilderness. As it traveled down the sides of the stark terrain, even the ground changed. Sand turned into grass, dry ravines ran with streams. Plants appeared on the hillside and the scrubby little dwarf bushes filled with flowers. The desert bloomed.

"Ben, this thing is coming straight for *us*." The light split on both sides of what had been the Dead Sea, leaping past the gaping hole in the earth and sweeping over Masada. "Hang on!" Jimmy yelled. "Here it comes."

A staggering jolt of electricity shot through Jimmy's body as if he had stuck his finger in a light socket. His thoughts scrambled and every nerve in his body jumped. His muscles tingled and jerked in involuntary spasms. When his mind cleared, Jimmy was on the ground, on his knees. Perception returned slowly. Once again he could hear Ben's voice.

"Look!" Ben pointed across the top of the ancient fortress. "They're all gone! The dead soldiers have disappeared!"

Jimmy looked at Ben's outstretched finger. The skin was no longer wrinkled and blotched with liver spots. His hand was smooth and his skin glowed.

"Over there!" Ben jumped to his feet. "The mountains are covered with new trees!"

Jimmy looked into his friend's face. Every wrinkle was gone. His white hair had turned dark brown and Ben's cloudy eyes had cleared. He was once again a strapping two-hundred-pound young man.

"I can see!" Ben kept pointing toward the wilderness that had become a botanical garden. "I don't need glasses!"

Jimmy was speechless as he watched the miracle dancing before his eyes. In the twinkling of an eye, Ben was totally transformed.

Ben twirled around and froze in place. His mouth dropped. "J-i-m-m-y . . . unbelievable! . . . Is . . . that really you?"

For the first time, Jimmy looked at his own hands. They too were smooth, the fingers no longer crooked. His back wasn't stiff or bent. As he straightened up, Jimmy felt inches taller.

"You've become that six-foot-four blond Nordic weight-lifter that used to go with my sister!" Ben exclaimed.

Angels flying in formation shot across the sky and collided with the strange creatures of light, causing explosions of energy and smoke. One after another, disintegrating fire balls fell toward earth, streaking the Masada.

"We're going to get hit again!" Jimmy warned.

To his consternation, Jimmy watched the strange entities fly past him into the bottomless pit that had been the Dead Sea. Like a storm of meteors, thousands of the flaming substances descended over the edge and down to the boiling center of the earth.

"Demons!" Jimmy exclaimed. "Yeshua's angels are banishing evil spirits to hell forever!" He peered into the frightening hole. "I guess we now know where the Lake of Fire is."

Jimmy pointed to one last huge ball of light being surrounded and descended upon by a multitude of angels. "Satan is disguised as a messenger of light. I think our problems are just about completely and eternally over."

The ball of angry red light suddenly plunged toward the earth, zigging and zagging to avoid the ring of angels corralling its nebulous form. A hundred feet above Masada the glowing object stopped and hung in space.

"Look, Ben. The thing is changing form."

"It's becoming shaped like a . . . a . . . giant . . . human being."

"We always knew the devil could take on many disguises," Jimmy answered, "but I really had *no idea* how powerfully until now."

The light became a tangible form. A face of great beauty appeared. The giant red angel darted back and forward as if gesturing to the attacking angels to join him, but the perimeters of the angels circling him together forced him ever downward.

"These angels aren't buying it this time." Ben kept pointing at the multitude of flying hosts. "Can you believe your eyes?"

A swooping attack of angels with flaming swords sent the red angel tumbling backward nearly on top of Masada. When he swooped past Jimmy and Ben, the devil's countenance changed. His face contorted into pure hate and his eyes were filled with unrelenting rage.

Jimmy grabbed Ben's arm.

The angelic host made one final lunge with their flaming swords and the devil fell backward into the terrible pit. Jimmy and Ben peered into the vast crevasse. Wispy thin trails of smoke drifted upward. The world was filled with divine silence.

"I can't believe it's over," Ben said.

"Glory to God!" Jimmy shouted. "Yeshua has prevailed!"

"And so have you," a familiar voice answered from behind.

Jimmy spun around to find Ruth standing with her hands extended. "Never have I been as proud of you as in these days, my beloved. You have proven to be a man of God without measure." His former wife hugged him. "You have always been my heartbeat," the Immortal said.

Jimmy gasped and held Ruth tightly. Her hair felt like silk and her skin was wondrous to the touch. "I know there's supposed to be no tears in eternity," he choked back the words. "I am just so happy to see you I can't help myself."

"What a guy you proved to be, Dad."

To Ben's left Jim Jr. appeared. "Son! You wouldn't believe what we've been through."

"I've watched every minute of your battle, Dad. In fact, they had to restrain me a couple of times. Wow, did you ever prove to be a man of God!"

"Just did what we had to," Jimmy shrugged.

"Oh, no," another voice spoke from the other side "You were a hero."

Jimmy turned around and his mother and father stood beside Ruth. "A thousand years ago when I was a preacher back in Dallas, Texas, I prayed my son would be a great spiritual warrior." Reverend Harrison still spoke with a Southwestern drawl. "Never in my wildest dreams could I have guessed how those prayers would be fulfilled centuries later."

"The Immortals are back!" Ben said. "What a relief."

"Cindy's not here," Ben exclaimed. "She's still in Jerusalem."

"No, Ben." Cindy answered. "I'm with you, too." A tiny, dainty young woman with skin like porcelain held out her hands. All the wrinkles were gone. Her heart-shaped mouth was once again perfect. "We're all Immortals now."

"Cindy, you're gorgeous!" Ben laughed. "But how did you get here?"

"You've been so busy watching everything happen, you haven't gotten in touch with what this divine metamorphosis has done for you," Cindy explained. "Time and space no longer have any meaning. We are truly spiritual beings now. We can travel by thinking. Just imagine where you want to be and you're there!"

"*Really?*"

Jimmy held Ruth's hand. "How . . . how . . . do we relate?"

"With pure love," Ruth answered. "When we were married our relationships revolved around our needs. Now we relate to each other completely and totally through God's love. Nothing selfish will ever get in the way. We don't have exclusive and limiting bonds." Ruth pointed around her. "My parents, your parents, our ancestors, and our children comprise one great family of God."

"I'm just so glad to be able to see you when I want to," Jimmy answered, hugging his wife affectionately.

"And don't forget us," a bass voice rumbled. "You know we've been trying to get out of L.A. for years."

"Isaiah and Deborah!" Ben exclaimed. "You're here. The circle is complete."

Ben looked around at the desert that had become a paradise. He saw the sea of faces filling the top of Masada. His parents waved. His grandparents were there. Dr. Ann Woodbridge was waving. The old gang from California stood together. Joe and Jennifer McCoy, Erica and Joe Jr. were all part of the crowd. Everything Ben saw, heard, thought, and felt was in complete harmony.

A Concluding Postscript from Michael, Guardian Angel Compiler of the History of the Third Millennium

The many years I served as the Feinbergs' guarding angel were filled with great satisfaction. To be associated with human beings who played such a significant part in Yeshua's ultimate victory over the minions of the devil was a great honor. In the beginning they had no more idea of their purpose than they did of my existence and constant care. Standing behind the curtain of time, watching them make discoveries about the intentions and designs of God was especially fascinating.

Once eternity began I had the additional joy of being the Feinbergs' servant. We angels have always served humanity, anticipating our role as their attendants throughout the endless ages. Becoming the Feinbergs' liegeman compounded my joy.

As everyone knows, Yeshua returned with the hosts of heaven, the Immortals, and all the saints for the final wrap-up of all human history. I watched the Great White Throne and Him seated upon it appear above the earth in the center of space itself. The Father judged no one, but all judgment was given to the honor of the Son. The dead, great and small, stood before the throne and the awesome Book of Life was unlocked. The sea and Hades gave up their dead and each person was judged according to what he had done.

With a rod of iron the Messiah cleansed the earth of every vestige of sin and rebellion. The Devil and his legions were forever banished, having rejected the one-thousand-year opportunity to repent and worship God. They forever remain a sign to us of the terrible power of pride, rebellion, and sin to ruin God's good gifts. Death, itself, was finally cast into the abyss of destruction.

I saw the Holy City, the New Jerusalem, come down out of heaven prepared as a bride adorned for her husband. Totally different from the old Jerusalem, the new city was in every respect the center of the universe. During the millennial reign of Christ, the new city had hovered above the earth as the home of the Immortals from whence they went back and forth to the planet. Far up above, heaven was also renewed and completed with its many mansions accommodating the blessings of God.

Once the transforming fires spread over the world, the earth was perfected and balance completely established. With the end of sin, the Garden of Eden was restored in the midst of Jerusalem. The Tree of Life once again flourished. All creation blended together like a perfectly scored symphony.

The New Jerusalem descended from the sky in the awesome shape of a pyramid of twelve floors with twelve great gates and an angel by each entrance. Every gate was a pearl of awesome size. Over each gate was the name of one of the twelve tribes of Israel. Four gates were on the north, south, east, and west. The vast city was 1,400 miles in length, width, and height, making it the largest city on earth and open to all tribes and races. Pure streets of gold were of such purity the pavement appeared transparent.

The city of gold had walls of jasper as clear as glass. The first foundation was jasper, the second sapphire, the third chalcedony, the fourth emerald, the firth sardonyx, the sixth carnelian, the seventh chrysolite, the eight beryl, the ninth topaz, the tenth chrysoprase, the eleventh jacinth, and the twelfth amethyst. The blending brilliance of pure color revealed the indescribable beauty of God's grace in glory never seen before in creation. The redeemed were moved to complete ecstasy at the mere sight of such majesty.

In the very center of the New Jerusalem was the restored Temple of our God where He dwells forever. The light of the bright Morning Star, the Son of David, filled the city with a constant wondrous promise of tomorrows without beginning or end. The glory of the city sparkled with Light Eternal. From the Throne of God out through the center of the city flowed the sparkling River of Life.

Every living creature heard the supreme final summons. "The Spirit and the bride say, 'Come! Come! Whoever is thirsty, let him come; and whoever wishes, let them take the free gift of the water of life.'"